THE BRIGADIER
AND OTHER STORIES

THE WORKS

OF

IVÁN TURGÉNIEFF

TRANSLATED FROM THE RUSSIAN BY
ISABEL F. HAPGOOD

THE BRIGADIER
AND OTHER STORIES

ON THE EVE

Short Story Index Reprint Series

BOOKS FOR LIBRARIES PRESS
FREEPORT, NEW YORK

First Published 1904
Reprinted 1971

118459

INTERNATIONAL STANDARD BOOK NUMBER:
0-8369-4067-9

LIBRARY OF CONGRESS CATALOG CARD NUMBER:
71-178466

PRINTED IN THE UNITED STATES OF AMERICA
BY
NEW WORLD BOOK MANUFACTURING CO., INC.
HALLANDALE, FLORIDA 33009

891.709
tur

CONTENTS

THE BRIGADIER

(1867)

THE BRIGADIER [1]

I

READER, dost thou know those small manors of the gentry in which our great Russian Ukráïna abounded thirty years ago? Now they are rarely to be met with, and ten years hence the last of them will, probably, have vanished without a trace. A pond with a stream running through it, all overgrown with willow-bushes and reeds, the delight of scurrying ducks, which are now and then joined by a cautious " teal "; beyond the pond a garden with linden alleys, that beauty and honour of our Black Earth prairies, with beds weed-choked of " Spanish " strawberries, with dense thickets of gooseberry, currant, and raspberry bushes, amid which, in the languid hour of motionless midday heat, the gay-hued kerchief of a house-serf maiden will inevitably be gleaming, and her piercing voice will be ringing. There, also, is the little storehouse, on props,[2] a small greenhouse, a wretched vegetable-

---

[1] This military rank, between colonel and general, established by Peter the Great, was abolished by Paul I.—TRANSLATOR.

[2] Literally, on chickens' legs; like the favourite revolving hut of the Bába Yagá, or witch, in the national fairy-tales. — TRANSLATOR.

garden, with a flock of sparrows on the fence, and a squatting cat near the ruined well; farther on are gnarled apple-trees over tall grass, green below and grey above, spindling cherry-trees, and pear-trees, on which there is never any fruit; then flower-beds with flowers—poppies, peonies, heart's-ease,[1] spider-lilies, "maids in green" (wood-sorrel), bushes of Tatár honeysuckle, wild jasmine, lilacs, and acacia, with an incessant hum of bees and bumblebees in their thick, fragrant, sticky branches; and the narrow sashes, with a sloping, never-painted roof, with a small veranda from which the jug-shaped balusters have tumbled down, with a crooked mezzanine,[2] with a voiceless old dog in a hollow under the front steps. Behind the house is a spacious courtyard, with nettles, wormwood, and burdock in the corners, offices with sliding doors, with pigeons and daws on the perforated straw-thatched roofs, a small ice-house with a rusty weather-cock, two or three birch-trees with daws' nests in their bare upper branches; and yonder, beyond, is the highway, with little cushions of soft dust along the wheel-ruts, and the fields, and the long, wattled fences of the hemp plantations, and the grey little cots of the village, and the squawks of the geese from the distant overflowed meadows. . . . . Is all this known to thee, reader? In the

[1] In Russian, "pretty little eyes."—TRANSLATOR.

[2] A "mezzanine," in Russia, signifies a partial second storey, either in the middle, at the ends, or both.—TRANSLATOR.

house itself everything is a little awry,—everything is rather rickety,—but that matters not! It stands firm, and keeps one warm; the stoves are like elephants, the furniture is a motley collection of home manufacture; whitish paths, worn by trampling feet, run from the doors across the painted floors; in the anteroom are bullfinches and larks in tiny cages; in the corner of the dining-room is a huge English clock, in the form of a tower, with the inscription: " Strike—Silent." In the drawing-room are the portraits of the master and mistress, painted in oils, with an expression of surly fear on their brick-red faces, and sometimes, also, a warped old picture depicting either flowers and fruits, or some mythological subject; everywhere there is an odour of kvas, apples, varnish, and leather; flies buzz and drone close to the ceiling and on the windows, an audacious cockroach suddenly waggles his feelers from behind the frame of the mirror. . . Never mind! one can live, and even live far from badly, there.

II

IT was just such a manor that I chanced to visit, thirty years ago . . . . a thing of days long past —as you see. The tiny estate where the manor lay belonged to one of my comrades at the university. It had recently fallen to him, on the

THE BRIGADIER

death of a granduncle, a bachelor, and he himself did not live in it. . . . But a short distance thence extensive steppe marshes began, in which, during the period of the summer flight, there were a great many snipe. My comrade and I were both passionate sportsmen, and therefore we had agreed to set out—he from Moscow, I from my own little village—for his little house about St. Peter's day.[1] My friend was delayed in Moscow and was two days late; I did not wish to begin the hunt without him. . . . I was received by an old serving-man, by name Narkíz Semyónoff. He had been forewarned of my coming. This old servant did not, in the least, resemble "Savélitch" or "Caleb";[2] my comrade was wont to call him, in jest, "Marquis." There was something self-confident, even refined, about him; not without dignity did he look down upon us young folks; and for the other landed proprietors he cherished no special reverence. He expressed himself in careless terms about his former master, and simply despised his brethren—for their ignorance. He himself could read and write, expressed himself correctly and intelligently,—and did not drink liquor. He rarely went to church— so that he was called an "Old Believer."[3] In

[1] June 29 (July 12.)—TRANSLATOR.

[2] In the "Bride of Lammermoor." "Savélitch" is the typical faithful servitor, in Russian, to correspond.—TRANSLATOR.

[3] Literally, a schismatic; one of the sect which still clings to the clerical errors in the Scriptures and Church-service books that were corrected under the Patriarch Níkon, in the reign of Peter the Great's father.—TRANSLATOR.

6

personal appearance he was gaunt and tall, he had a long and comely pointed nose, and over-hanging brows which he was incessantly either contracting or elevating; he wore a roomy, clean coat, and boots to his knees, with the tops cut out in heart-shape.

III

ON the very day of my arrival Narkíz, after he had served my breakfast and cleared the table, halted at the door, gazed intently at me, and twitching his eyebrows, articulated:

"What are you going to do now, sir?"

"Why, really, I don't know. If Nikolái Petró-vitch had kept his word, and had arrived,—we would have gone hunting together."

"And did you really, sir, expect that he would come exactly at the time he had promised?"

"Of course I did."

"H'm."—Narkíz again looked at me, and shook his head, as though in compassion. "If you would like to amuse yourself with reading,"—he went on,—"the old master left some little books behind him; I will fetch them, if you wish; only, you will not read them, I am bound to suppose."

"Why?"

"They are empty little books; not written for the gentlemen of the present day."

"Hast thou read them?"

"I have not—I would not tell if I had. The Dream-book, for instance . . . what sort of a book is that? Well, there are others . . . only, you will not read them either."

" Why so? "

" They are religious books."

I maintained silence. . . Narkíz did the same.

" The principal thing that vexes me is,"—I began,—" is to sit at home in this weather."

" Stroll in the garden; or go to the grove. We have a grove behind the threshing-floor. Would not you like to go fishing? "

" But have you fish here? "

" We have; in the pond both gudgeons and perch are to be had. Now, of course, the best time is past: it is almost July. Well . . . you can try, nevertheless. . . . Do you command me to prepare the tackle? "

" Pray do."

" I will send a small boy with you . . . . to put on the worms. Or, I might go myself? "—Narkíz was evidently in doubt as to whether I could get along by myself.

" Pray come with me."

Narkíz grinned in silence, but to the full extent of his mouth, then suddenly lowered his brows and left the room.

IV

HALF an hour later, we set out on our fishing expedition. Narkíz had donned a remarkable sort of cap with ear-pieces, and had become more majestic than ever. He strode on ahead, with a stately, even pace; two fishing-rods rocked with measured sway on his shoulder; a dirty little bare-footed boy carried the water-can and a pot with worms after him.

"Yonder, near the dam, on a float, a shed has been built for comfort,"—Narkíz began to explain to me, then glanced ahead, and suddenly exclaimed:—"Ehe! why, our paupers are already there. . . . They've made a habit of it!"

I craned my head from behind him, and beheld on the float, in the shed of which he had spoken, two persons sitting with their backs toward us: they were catching fish with the utmost composure.

"Who are they?" I asked.

"Neighbours,"—replied Narkíz, with displeasure.—"They have nothing to eat at home, so they do us the favour to come here."

"But have they permission?"

"The former master permitted them . . . perhaps Nikolái Petróvitch here will give leave. . . . That long-legged one is a chanter out of a job: a thoroughly empty man; well, and the other, that fatter one, is a brigadier."

"What do you mean by a brigadier?"—I repeated in amazement. The clothing on the "Brigadier" was almost more dilapidated than the chanter's.

"But I tell you he is a brigadier. And he had

a good property.   But now, out of compassion, a
nook is provided for him, and he lives . . . . on
what the Lord sends.   But what are we to do?
They have taken possession of the best place. . . .
We must disturb our dear guests."

"No, Narkíz, please don't disturb them.   We'll
sit down yonder, to one side: they will not be in
our way.   I want to make acquaintance with the
Brigadier."

"As you like, sir.   Only, so far as making acquaintance is concerned . . . you must not count
on much satisfaction, sir; he has grown very dull
of understanding, and stupid in conversation . . . .
like a little baby.   'T is enough to say that he is in
his eighties."

"What is his name?"

"Vasíly Fómitch.   His surname is Guskóff."

"And the chanter's?"

"The chanter's, you say? . . . . His nickname
is 'The Cucumber.'   Everybody hereabouts calls
him that; but what his real name is, the Lord only
knows!   A foolish man!   A regular vagabond."

"Do they live together?"

"No, they don't; but the devil . . . you know
. . . has bound them with a cord."

V

WE drew near the dam. The Brigadier cast a glance at us . . . . and immediately riveted his eyes on his float. The Cucumber sprang to his feet, pulled out his rod, removed his threadbare priestly cap, passed a trembling hand over his harsh yellow hair, made a flourishing bow, and broke into a flabby laugh. His bloated face denoted the habitual drunkard; his little, screwed-up eyes blinked abjectly. He nudged his companion in the ribs, as though imparting to him a hint that they must take themselves off. . . . The Brigadier fidgeted on the bench.

" Sit still, I beg; don't disturb yourselves," I hastened to say.—" You are not at all in our way. We will place ourselves yonder; sit still."

The Cucumber wrapped his long, tattered crash kaftan about him, twitched his shoulders, his lips, his beard. . . . Our presence, evidently, embarrassed him . . . . and he would gladly have beaten a retreat, but the Brigadier had again become absorbed in the contemplation of his float. . . . . " The vagabond " coughed a couple of times, laid his cap on his knees, and tucking his bare legs up under him, modestly flung his line.

" Fish biting? "—asked Narkíz pompously, as he slowly unwound the reel.

" We've enticed five loach," replied the Cucum-

11

ber, in a hoarse, cracked voice;—"and he has caught a good-sized perch."

"Yes, a perch,"—the Brigadier repeated after him, in a squeaking voice.

VI

I BEGAN to watch intently—not him, but his reversed reflection in the pond. It presented itself to me as clearly as though in a mirror, somewhat darker, somewhat more silvery. The broad pond breathed coolness upon us; coolness exhaled also from the damp, steep shore; and it was all the more agreeable because overhead, in the golden-dark azure, high above the crests of the trees, the motionless sultry heat hung like a palpable burden. The water did not undulate about the dam; in the shadow which fell upon it from the wide-spreading bushes on the shore the water-flies, as they described their everlasting circles, gleamed out like tiny silver buttons; only now and then did a barely perceptible ripple emanate from the float, when a fish "toyed" with the worm. The fishing was poor; in the course of a whole hour we drew out two loach and one gudgeon. I could not have explained why the Brigadier aroused my curiosity: his rank could have no effect on me,—ruined noblemen were not accounted a rarity at that epoch,—and his personal appearance presented no remarkable features. Beneath the warm cap which covered the whole top of his head down to his eyebrows and his ears, there was visible a red, smooth-shaven round face, with a small nose, tiny lips, and small, light-grey eyes. That submissive, almost childish face expressed simplicity, and intellectual weakness, and a sort of helpless melancholy of long standing; there was something incapable, also, about his small, plump white hands, with their short fingers. . . . I was utterly unable to imagine how that poor old fellow could once have been a military man, have commanded, have filled an executive position—and that in the stern age of Katherine II, to boot! I gazed at him: sometimes he puffed out his cheeks, and panted softly, like a baby; sometimes he screwed up his eyes in an ailing way, with an effort, as all decrepit people do. Once he opened his eyes very wide and raised them. . . . They fixed themselves on me from out of their watery depths—and their mournful gaze seemed to be strangely touching and even significant.

VII

I TRIED to enter into conversation with the Brigadier. . . . But Narkíz had not misled me; the poor old man really had grown very feeble of understanding. He inquired my name, and after having interrogated me a couple of times, he reflected, and finally said: "Yes, I believe we did have a judge of that name. Cucumber, did we have a judge of that name—hey?"—"We did, we did, bátiushka,[1] Vasíly Fómitch, Your Highborn,"—answered the Cucumber, who, in general, treated him like a child.—"There really was one. But please give me your rod; the worms must be nibbled off.... Nibbled off they are."

"Are you acquainted with the Lómoff family?"—the Brigadier suddenly asked me, in a constrained voice.

"What Lómoff family do you mean?"

"What family?—Well, Feódor Ivánitch, Evstignyéi Ivánitch, Alexyéi Ivánitch, the Jew; well, and Feodúliya Ivánovna, the thief .... and besides them ...."

The Brigadier suddenly fell silent, and hung his head.

"He was very intimate with them,"—whispered Narkíz, bending toward me;—"it was through them, through that same Alexyéi Ivánitch, whom he called a Jew, and through one of Alexyéi Ivánitch's sisters, Agraféna Ivánovna, that he was deprived of his property, one may say."

"What's that thou art saying about Agraféna Ivánovna?"—suddenly exclaimed the Brigadier, and his head rose, his white eyebrows contracted in a frown.—"Just mind thine own business!

---

[1] Literally, dear little father: the genuine Russian way of addressing men of all ranks.—TRANSLATOR.

And what dost thou mean by calling her Agraféna?[1] Agrippína Ivánovna—that 's what . . . . she must be called."

" Come now, come, come, come now, bátiushka,"—stammered the Cucumber.

" Dost thou not know that Milónoff wrote verses about her? "—went on the old man, suddenly flying into fury, for which I was utterly unprepared. " ' 'T is not the wedding tapers that are kindled ' "—he began, in a singsong tone, pronouncing all the vowels through his nose, and the syllables " an " and " en " like those syllables in French,—and it was strange to hear this coherent speech from his lips;—" ' not torches ' . . . . No, that 's not right; this is it:

> "Not in the frail idol of corruption,
> Not in amaranth, not in porphyry,
> Do they so much delight . . . .
> One thing alone in them . . . . . .

That refers to us.—Hearest thou?

> "One thing alone in them is blameless,
> Pleasant, languid, longed-for:
> To cherish mutual fervor in their blood!

And thou call'st her Agraféna!"

Narkíz emitted a half-scornful, half-indifferent laugh.—" Ekh-ma,—what an idiot! "—he

[1] Agraféna (pronounced *Agrafáyna*) is the colloquial Russian form of Agrippína.—TRANSLATOR.

muttered to himself. But the Brigadier had already hung his head again, and the fishing-rod fell from his hands and slipped into the water.

VIII

"As I look at the matter, this affair of ours is no good,"—said the Cucumber;—"the fish, you see, don't bite at all. It has grown hot, and melancholy has overtaken our master.—Evidently—we ought to go home; it will be better so."—He cautiously drew from his pocket a tin flask with a small wooden stopper, uncorked it, shook out some snuff into the hollow of his hand,—and sniffed it up into both nostrils simultaneously. . . "Ekh, the dear snuff!"—he moaned, as he recovered;—"'t is as though a thrill began to play through one's teeth!—Come, my dear fellow, Vasíly Fómitch, please to get up—'t is time!"

The Brigadier rose from the bench.

"Do you live far from here?"—I asked the Cucumber.

"Why, he lives not far off . . . less than a verst."

"Will you permit me to go with you?"—I said, addressing the Brigadier. I did not wish to part from him.

He looked at me, and smiling with that peculiar, pompous, courteous, and somewhat affected smile, which always reminds me—however

it may strike others—of powder, strass buckles—
of the eighteenth century in general—he said with
old-fashioned faltering, that "he—would—be—
ve-ry hap-py " . . . . and immediately sat down
again. The cavalier of Katherine's day had
flashed forth in him for a moment—and vanished.

Narkíz was astounded at my intention; but I
paid no heed to the disapproving shaking of his
eared cap, and quitted the park in company with
the Brigadier, who was supported by the Cucumber.—The old man moved on quite briskly, as
though on wooden legs.

IX

WE walked along a barely-traced path, through
a grassy vale, between two groves of birch-trees.
The sun was blazing hot; orioles called to each
other in the verdant coppice, corn-crakes uttered
their rasping cry alongside the very path, blue butterflies flitted in swarms over the white and red
flowers of the low-growing clover; bees, as though
somnolent, got tangled up and buzzed languidly
among the motionless blades of grass. The Cucumber shook himself, grew animated. He was
afraid of Narkíz—he lived under his eye; I was a
stranger to him, a newcomer—with me he speedily felt at home.—"Here's our master, now,"—he
said repeatedly,—"he's a small eater, there's no
use talking about it! but how is he to have his fill

off of one perch? Perhaps you will contribute
something, Your Well-Born? Just round yonder turn in the road, in the little dram-shop, there
are capital fine wheaten rolls. And if you are
gracious, then I, great sinner that I am, will drink
a little glass of liquor, as the opportunity offers,
to your health—Many years, many days."[1]—I
gave him a twenty-kopék coin, and barely succeeded in withdrawing my hand, which he dashed
forward to kiss. He learned that I was a sports-
man, and set to talking about his having a good
friend, an officer, who possessed a min-din-den-
ger-off gun, with a brass barrel stock—" just
like a cannon! thou firest—and it seems as though
forgetfulness comes upon thee: the French left it
behind them! . . . . and his dog was simply a freak
of nature!"—how he himself had always had a
great passion for hunting, and the priest did n't
mind—he used to catch quail in his company—
but the ecclesiastical superintendent tyrannised
over them to the last degree. " And as for Narkíz Semyónitch,"—he said in a drawling tone,
—" if I 'm not an important man in this world,
in his opinion,—I 've got this much to say: he has
grown himself eyebrows equal to a woodcock's,
and fancies that thereby he has passed through
all the sciences."—At this point we reached the

---

[1] A partial quotation from the solemn proclamation in church, on
great occasions, of "Long Life" to the Imperial Family, and to
others, according to the circumstances.—TRANSLATOR.

dram-shop—an aged, isolated hut, without either back-yard or store-room; an emaciated dog lay curled up under the small window; a hen was scratching in the dust right in front of his nose. The Cucumber set the Brigadier down on the earthen bank which surrounded the house, and instantly whipped into the dram-shop. While he was buying rolls, and incidentally treating himself to a drink, I never took my eyes from the Brigadier, who, God knows why, seemed to be an enigma. "Something remarkable has certainly taken place in this man's life,"—I said to myself. But he did not seem to notice me at all; he sat, all crouched together, on the earthen bank, and turned about in his fingers a few clove-pinks which he had plucked in my friend's garden. The Cucumber made his appearance, at last, with a bundle of rolls in his hand; he presented himself all red and perspiring, with an expression of joyful surprise on his face, as though he had just seen something remarkably pleasant and unexpected. He immediately suggested that the Brigadier should eat a roll—and the latter did so. We continued our journey.

X

THANKS to the liquor he had drunk, the Cucumber was quite "set up," as the phrase goes. He undertook to compel the Brigadier, who continued to hasten onward, staggering as though he had wooden legs—" Why are you so sad, why do you hang your head, dear little father? Permit me to sing you a song. You 'll immediately receive every sort of satisfaction. . . . Please don't be surprised,"—he said, addressing me:— " my master is very greatly disposed to laughter, and my heavens! Yesterday I look, and behold, a peasant woman is washing a pair of breeches on the dam—and she happened to be a fat woman— and he is standing behind her, and fairly rooted to the spot with laughter, by heaven, he was! . . . Now, please to observe presently: do you know the song about the hare? You must n't mind if I am insignificant to look at; there lives a gypsy yonder in our town with a face like a regular snout—but when it comes to singing—death! you 'd just like to lie down and die."—He opened his moist red lips wide, and began to sing, lolling his head on one side, closing his eyes, and waggling his beard:

" The hare doth lie beneath a bush;
  The hunters ride in vain . . . .
      The hare lies on, he scarcely breathes—
      While he cocks his ear—
          Death he expects!

" How have I vexed ye, huntsmen?
  Or what harm have I done to you?
      Though I go among the cabbages,
      I eat but a leaf at a time—
      And that not in your gardens!
          No, sirs!"

20

THE BRIGADIER

The Cucumber constantly augmented his force.

" The hare bounded into the dark forest—
And showed the hunters his tail.
' Forgive me, ye hunters,
Look at my little tail,
I don't belong to you!' "

The Cucumber no longer sang. . . . He roared.

" The hunters rode until morn-ing . . . .
They followed the hare's tra-a-ail . . . .
They discussed it all among themselves
And each cursed the other:
' That hare's not ours!
Squint-eyes has deceived us! !' "

The Cucumber sang the first two lines of each verse in a drawling voice—the remaining three, on the contrary, he sang very fast, skipping in a foppish way the while, and shifting from foot to foot; and at the end of each couplet he "made a knee," that is to say, he kicked himself with his own heels. Shouting at the top of his voice: " Squint-eyes has deceived us!" he turned a somersault. . . His expectations were realised. The Brigadier suddenly broke out into a thin, tearful laugh, and laughed so heartily that he could not walk any farther, and squatted a little, impotently beating his hands against his knees. I glanced at his crimson, convulsively-distorted face, and felt very sorry for him—particularly at

21

that moment. Encouraged by his success, the Cucumber began a squatting and leaping dance, accompanied by incessant ejaculations of: "shildy —budyldy" and "natchiki-tchikaldy!". . . . At last, he banged his nose in the dust. . . . The Brigadier suddenly ceased to laugh, and hobbled onward.

XI

WE traversed about a quarter of a verst more.— A tiny hamlet made its appearance on the brink of a shallow ravine; on the other side, a "little wing" was visible, with a half-ruined roof, and a solitary chimney; in one of this wing's two rooms the Brigadier was lodged. The owner of the hamlet, who resided permanently in Petersburg, the wife of State Councillor Lómoff, had—as I afterward learned—allotted this corner to the Brigadier. She had given orders that a monthly stipend should be paid to him, and that there should be assigned to his service a fool who lived in a hamlet, one of the house-serfs, who, although she comprehended human speech but indifferently, yet was capable, in the opinion of the proprietress, of sweeping the floor and cooking cabbage-soup. On the threshold of the little wing, the Brigadier again turned to me with the same smile of the times of Katherine II as before: "Would not I do him the favour to enter his apartment?" We entered that apartment. Everything in it was filthy and poverty-stricken to the last degree, so filthy and so poverty-stricken that the Brigadier, probably perceiving, from the expression of my face, what impression his abode produced upon me, remarked, as he shrugged his shoulders and screwed up his eyes: *"Ce n'est pas . . . . œil-de-perdrix."* . . . Precisely what he meant by that was not quite clear to me. . . . When I addressed him in French, I received no reply in that language. Two articles in the Brigadier's abode particularly surprised me: in the first place, a large officer's cross of the Order of St. George [1] in a black frame, under glass, with an inscription in antiquated chirography: " Received by the Colonel of the Tchernígoff Derfelden regiment, Vasíly Guskóff, at the storming of Prague, in the year 1794 "; and in the second place, the half-length portrait, in oils, of a handsome black-eyed woman, with a long, dark-complexioned face, with her hair dressed high and powdered, with patches on her temples and chin, in a flowered farthingale, cut low in the neck, with blue trimmings, of the epoch of the eighties. The portrait was badly painted—but assuredly it was a very good likeness: something quite too vital and indubitable emanated from that face. It did not

---

[1] The most coveted of Russian military orders, which (like the Victoria Cross), must be won by remarkable personal bravery on the field of battle.—TRANSLATOR.

look at the spectator, it seemed to be averted from him, and it did not smile; an imperious, arrogant, irascible disposition was indicated in the arch of the thin nose, the regularly formed but thick lips, the eyebrows which almost met. No especial effort was required to imagine to one's self how that face was capable of suddenly blazing with passion or with wrath. Directly beneath the portrait, on a small pedestal, stood a half-withered nosegay of simple field-flowers, in a thick glass jar. The Brigadier approached the pedestal, thrust into the jar the pinks which he had brought, and turning to me, and raising his hand in the direction of the portrait, he said: "Agrippína Ivánovna Telyégin, born Lómoff." Narkíz's words recurred to my memory: I gazed with redoubled attention at the expressive and unamiable face of the woman for whose sake the Brigadier had lost all his property.

"You were present at the storming of Prague, I see, Mr. Brigadier,"—I began, pointing at the cross of St. George,—"and received this token of distinction, rare at any time, and much rarer then; you probably remember Suvároff?"

"Alexánder Vasílievitch, you mean?"—replied the Brigadier, after a brief silence, and seeming to collect his thoughts. "Of course I remember him. He was a lively little old man. You'd be standing there, so still you wouldn't dare to sneeze,—but he'd be running hither and thither" (the Brigadier roared with laughter).

"He drove into Warsaw with kazák horses; he himself was all covered with diamonds, but he says to the Poles: 'I have no watch, I forgot it in Peter; I have n't any, have n't any!' and they: '*Viva! viva!*'—The queer fellows! Hey! Cucumber! boy!"—he suddenly added, changing and elevating his voice (the buffoon-chanter had remained outside)—"where . . . are the rolls? And tell Grunka to fetch some kvas!"

"Immediately, dear little father,"—the Cucumber's voice made itself audible.

He handed to the Brigadier the bundle of rolls —and emerging from the wing, he went up to some dishevelled creature in tatters—it must have been that same fool Grunka—and, so far as I could make out through the dusty little window, he began to demand kvas from her—for several times he placed his hand like a funnel to his mouth, and flourished the other in our direction.

XII

AGAIN I tried to enter into conversation with the Brigadier; but he was evidently tired, dropped with a grunt on the stove-bench, and moaning: "*Oi, oi,* my poor bones, my poor bones,"—he untied his garters. I remember that I was astonished at the time that a man could wear garters; I did not take into consideration the fact that in former days everybody wore them. The Brigadier began to indulge in prolonged and open yawns, without taking his dimmed eyes from me, as very young children yawn. The poor old man apparently did not even thoroughly understand my questions. . . . And he had captured Prague! He, with naked sword, in the smoke, in the dust, at the head of Suvároff's soldiers, with the shot-riddled flag over his head, with mutilated corpses under his feet . . . . he . . . he! Was it not amazing?—But, nevertheless, I was impressed with the conviction that events still more remarkable had occurred in the life of the Brigadier. The Cucumber brought some white kvas, in an iron porringer; the Brigadier drank with avidity—his hands shook.—The Cucumber supported the bottom of the porringer. The old man carefully wiped his toothless mouth with both palms, and again riveting his eyes on me, he began to mumble and smack his lips. I understood the meaning of this, made my bow, and left the room.

"Now he will take a nap,"—remarked the Cucumber, as he followed me out.—"He has got very tired to-day—we went to the grave at daybreak."

"To whose grave?"

"Why, to pay reverence to Agraféna Ivánovna. . . . She is buried yonder, in our parish graveyard; it must be five versts from here. Vasíly Fómitch insists on going to it every week.

And he buried her, too, and erected a fence at his own cost."

"And did she die long ago?"

"Why—well-nigh . . . twenty years ago."

"Was she a friend of his?"

"She got every bit of property he had away from him . . . . good gracious! I myself did not know the lady, I admit,—but they say there were dealings between them . . . . we-ell now! —Sir,"—added the chanter hastily, seeing that I turned away,—" won't you have the kindness to contribute a farthing for a drink—otherwise, 't is time for me to go to the store-room and get under the coverlet."

I did not consider it necessary to interrogate the Cucumber, but gave him another twenty-kopék piece, and wended my way homeward.

XIII

At home I applied for information to Narkíz. He, as was to have been expected, demurred a little, assumed pompous airs, expressed his astonishment that such trifles could "anterest" me, and at last he narrated what he knew. What I heard was as follows:

Vasíly Fómitch Guskóff had made the acquaintance of Agraféna Ivánovna Telyégin in Moscow, soon after the Polish rebellion; her husband served under the Governor-General, and

THE BRIGADIER

Vasíly Fómitch was on furlough. He immediately fell in love with her, but did not resign from the service: he was a single man, forty years of age, with property. Her husband soon died. She was left a childless widow, in poverty, in debt. . . . Vasíly Fómitch heard of her situation, abandoned the service (he received the rank of brigadier on his retirement[1]) and hunted up his amiable widow, who was not more than five and twenty years old, paid all her debts, redeemed her estate. . . . From that time forth he never parted from her, and it ended in his taking up his residence with her. She, also, seemed to have fallen in love with him, but she would not marry him.—"The deceased was a stubborn person," remarked Narkíz at this point:—"she valued her own will more than anything else, I 'm told.—But as for making use of him,—she did that—'in all departments.'—And what money he had he brought to her, like 'an ant.'" But Agraféna Ivánovna's stubbornness sometimes assumed remarkable proportions: she was of untamable disposition, and harsh of hand. . . . One day she threw her page-boy down-stairs, and he took and broke two ribs and a leg. . . . Agraféna Ivánovna was frightened . . . . instantly gave orders that the page should be locked up in the lumber-room, and thenceforth did not leave the

[1] The rank of brigadier no longer exists in the Russian army.—TRANSLATOR.

28

house herself, and did not let any one else have the
key to the lumber-room, until the groaning there
had ceased. . . . They buried the page secretly.
. . . "And if this had happened under the Empress Katherine," added Narkíz in a whisper,
bending down to me,—"perhaps that would have
been the end of the matter; many such affairs remained hidden out of sight in those days. But as
it was . . . ." here Narkíz straightened himself
up, and raised his voice—"the upright Emperor
Alexander the Blessed was reigning then . . . .
well, and a suit was begun. . . . The judge came,
they exhumed the body . . . . marks of blows
were found . . . . there was the very devil to
pay. And what do you suppose? Vasíly Fómitch took it all on himself.—'I,' says he, 'was
the cause. I pushed him down, and then I locked
him up.'—Well, of course, all the judges, the
court clerks and police there . . . . immediately fell
upon him, and they stripped him, I can tell you,
until the last two-kopék bit flew out of his purse.
And the first he knew . . . . he was grabbed by
the scruff of the neck again. Down to the
very Frenchman,—that's the sort of Frenchman who came to us in Russia,—everybody
stripped him, then they abandoned him. Well,
but he had secured safety for Agraféna Ivánovna
—so he had; he had saved her, I'm bound to say.
Well, and afterward, until her death, he lived
with her,—and they say that she ill-treated him—

the Brigadier—horribly; she sent him on foot from Moscow to her estate, by heaven she did,— for quit-rent, that is. For her sake, for the sake of that same Agraféna Ivánovna, he fought a duel with an English lord, Hughes Hughes, with short-swords, and the English lord was forced to utter a compliment of excuse. And that 's the place where the Brigadier injured his leg. . . . Well, and now, of course, he does n't count as a man."

"But who was that Alexyéi Ivánitch, the Jew," —I inquired:—" through whom he was ruined?"

"The brother of Agraféna Ivánovna. He was a greedy soul, just like a Jew, it 's a fact. He lent his sister money on interest, and Vasíly Fómitch went security for it. And he paid, too . . . heavily!"

"And was Feodúliya Ivánovna a brigand? Who was she?"

"A sister—and clever, too—what 's called a . . a terror!"

XIV

"HERE 's a queer place to find a Werther," I thought on the following day, when I again betook myself to the dwelling of the Brigadier. I was very young at the time—and, perhaps precisely for that reason, I regarded it as my duty not to believe in the duration of love. All the same, I was struck and somewhat dumfounded at the tale I had heard, and I wanted frightfully to stir up the old man, and make him talk. " I will first allude to Suvároff again,"—thus I reasoned with myself,— "there must be at least a spark of his former fire concealed in him still; . . . and then, when he gets warmed up, I will turn the conversation on that . . . . what the deuce is her name? . . . Agraféna Ivánovna. A strange name for ' Charlotte ' !—Agraféna!"

I found Werther-Guskóff in the middle of a tiny kitchen-garden, a few paces from the house, near an old framework, overgrown with nettles, of a cottage which had never been completed. Over the mouldy upper beams of this framework frail young turkeys were running, uttering shrill cries and incessantly slipping and flapping their wings. Some sort of wretched garden-stuff grew in two or three beds. The Brigadier had just pulled a young carrot out of the ground, and drawing it through his armpit, " to clean it," he set to chewing its slender tail. . . . I bowed to him, and inquired about his health.

He evidently did not recognise me, and although he returned my salutation,—that is to say, touched his hand to his cap,—he did not stop chewing the carrot.

" You did not come to catch fish to-day? "—I began, in the hope of recalling my face to him by that question.

" To-day? "—he repeated, and became thoughtful . . . but the carrot, which he had thrust into his mouth, grew shorter and shorter.—"Why, it's the Cucumber who catches fish!—And I have permission also."

"Of course, of course, most respected Vasíly Fómitch . . . . I did not mean that. . . But don't you find it hot . . . dressed like that, out here in the sun?"

The Brigadier was wearing a thick, wadded dressing-gown.

"Hey? Hot?"—he repeated again, as though in surprise, and having finally swallowed his carrot, he cast an abstracted glance upward.

" Will you not come into my apartment? "— he said suddenly. Obviously, that phrase alone remained at the disposal of the poor old man.

We emerged from the vegetable-garden . . . but at this point I involuntarily stopped short. Between us and the wing stood a huge bull. With head lowered to the very earth, viciously rolling his eyes, he was snorting heavily and violently, and swiftly crooking one of his fore legs, was tossing on high the dust with his cloven hoof, lashing his flanks with his tail. Suddenly retreating a trifle, he shook his shaggy neck obdurately, and bellowed—not loudly, but lugubriously and menacingly. I must confess that I was daunted; but Vasíly Fómitch marched forward, and saying in a stern voice: " Go along with you, you clodhopper!" flourished his handkerchief. The bull retreated still farther, inclined his horns . . . and suddenly dashed aside, shaking his head to right and left.

"Well, he really did capture Prague,"—I thought.

We entered the house. The Brigadier removed his cap from his moist locks, exclaimed: "Fa!" . . . . sank down on the edge of a chair . . . and bowed his head.

"My real object in running in to see you, Vasíly Fómitch,"—I began my diplomatic attack,—"was that, as you have served under the command of the great Suvároff,—in general, have taken part in such momentous events,—it would be very interesting to me to learn the particulars."

The Brigadier fixed his eyes on me. . . . His face became strangely animated—I was already beginning to expect, if not a story, at least an encouraging, sympathetic word. . . .

"But, sir, I shall die soon,—I suppose,"—he said, in a low tone.

I was disconcerted.

"Why do you . . . . suppose that, Vasíly Fómitch?"—I articulated at last. The Brigadier suddenly began to fling his arms up and down,— exactly as babies do.

"Why, because, sir . . . . I . . . . perhaps you know . . . I frequently see Agrippína

Ivánovna—the kingdom of heaven be hers—in my sleep—and I can't possibly catch her; I'm always pursuing her—but I don't catch her. And last night—I saw her—she seemed to be standing in front of me, half turned away, and laughing. . . . I immediately ran to her—and caught her. . . . And she seemed to turn fully round, and say to me: 'Well, Vásinka, thou hast caught me.'"

"And what inference do you draw from that, Vasíly Fómitch?"

"Why, sir, this is what I infer: it must mean that we are to be together. Yes, and glory be to God, I tell you; glory be to the Lord God, to the Father, and to the Son, and to the Holy Spirit—" (the Brigadier began to chant) : "now, and ever, and unto ages of ages. Amen!"

The Brigadier began to cross himself. I could get nothing more out of him—so I went away.

XV

On the following day my friend arrived. . . . I mentioned the Brigadier, and my visits to him. . . . "Akh, yes! of course! I know his history,"—replied my friend;—"and I was well acquainted also with the wife of State Councillor Lómoff, through whose kindness he has found asylum here. But wait: it seems to me that I must have preserved here his letter to that same

State Councilloress; it was in virtue of that letter that she assigned him his nook."—My friend rummaged among his papers, and actually found the Brigadier's letter. Here it is, word for word, with the exception of the orthographical errors. The Brigadier, like all people of that epoch, confounded the letters "e" and "ye,"—wrote: "xkomu, shtop, sliudmi," [1] and so forth.—There is no necessity for preserving those errors: even without that, his letter bears the imprint of his time:

"DEAR MADAM! RAÍSA PÁVLOVNA! After the death of my friend, and your aunt, I had the happiness to write to you two letters, the first on the first of June, the second on July the sixth, of the year 1815—and she had died on the sixth of May of that same year; therein I was frank with you as to the sentiments of my heart and soul, which were oppressed with mortal grief, and described in full vista my bitter despair, deserving of compassion; both letters, despatched by royal post, were registered, and therefore I cannot doubt that they were perused by you. Through my frankness in them I had hoped to secure your beneficent attention to me; but your sentiments of compassion were diverted from me, the bitter sufferer! But being left, after the death of my only friend, Agrippína Ivánovna, in the most ruined and destitute condition, I placed my entire hope, according to her words, on your mercy; she, feeling already

[1] Instead of *k.komu, tchob. s.'liud'mi.* Moreover, there should be a character denoting hard pronunciation after *k, b,* and *s* (where I have placed a period), and a character denoting soft pronunciation where I have placed the apostrophe.—TRANSLATOR.

the end of her life, said to me, namely, in these, as it
were, funereal and for me ever-memorable words: ' My
friend, I am thy serpent, and the cause of all thy ad-
versity; I am conscious how much thou hast sacrificed
for me, and in requital I am leaving thee in a wretched
and, in truth, destitute condition; after I am dead,
do thou apply to Raísa Pávlovna '—that is, to you—
' and ask aid of her. Urge her! She has a feeling
heart, and I trust in her, that she will not leave thee an
orphan.'—Dear madam, accept in witness the almighty
Creator of the world, that these were her words, and
that I speak with her tongue; and therefore, relying
upon your beneficence, I have appealed to you first of all
with my open-hearted and frank letters; but receiving
no reply to them, after long-continued waiting, I had no
thought but that your beneficent heart had left me without attention! Such lack of benevolence toward me on
your part has reduced me to the depths of despair.
Where, and to whom, helpless I should appeal—I knew
not; my judgment was lost, my soul went astray,—at
last, to my utter ruin, it pleased Providence to chastise
me still further in the most cruel manner, and to turn
my thoughts to the deceased, to your aunt, Feodúliya
Ivánovna, born of one mother with Agrippína Ivánovna,
but not one with her in heart! Depicting to myself in
imagination the fact that for the last twenty years I
had been devoted to the whole house related to your house
of Lómoff—and especially to that Feodúliya Ivánovna
who never called Agrippína Ivánovna otherwise than
' my dear bosom-friend,' and me, ' the very respected and
zealous adherent of our family,'—depicting all this to
myself with abundant sighs and tears in the silence of

sorrowful watches of the night, I thought: Come, Brigadier! evidently, so it must be!—and on applying with letters to that same Feodúliya Ivánovna, I received an explicit assurance that she would share her last crumb with me! Being encouraged by this promise, I got together my poor remaining possessions, and went to Feodúliya Ivánovna! The presents I brought her, amounting to more than five hundred rubles, were accepted with remarkable satisfaction; and then the money which I had brought for my maintenance Feodúliya Ivánovna saw fit to take under her own charge, under the guise of keeping it safe for me, which, to please her, I did not oppose. But if you ask me: whence, and in virtue of what, I had such confidence,—to that, madam, there is but one answer: she was Agrippína Ivánovna's sister, and a scion of the Lómoff family! !—But alas! and akh! I was speedily deprived of all that money, and my hope which I had set upon Feodúliya Ivánovna—who wanted to share her last crumb with me—was idle and vain: on the contrary, she, Feodúliya Ivánovna, enriched herself with my goods. And, to wit, on the day of her angel, February the fifth, I presented her with green French material to the value of fifty rubles, at five rubles the arshín: [1] but I myself, of what had been promised, received: white piqué for a waistcoat, to the value of five rubles, and muslin for a neckcloth, which gifts were purchased in my presence, and, as is known to me, out of my own money—and that is all which I, through the benevolence toward me of Feodúliya Ivánovna, have enjoyed! That is ' the last

---

[1] The Russian measure corresponding to the yard·
twenty-eight inches.—TRANSLATOR.

crumb'! And I might also lay bare, in very truth, all Feodúliya Ivánovna's malevolent actions toward me—and also my expenditures, exceeding all measure, as for example, among other things, for confects and fruits, the which Feodúliya Ivánovna was extremely fond of eating;—but I hold my peace as to all this, in order that you should not ascribe such explanation about the dead woman in an evil sense; and moreover, since God hath summoned her to Himself for judgment—and everything which I suffered from her hath been exterminated from my heart,—so I have forgiven her long since, as a Christian should, and I pray to God that He should forgive her!!

"But dear madam, Raísa Pávlovna! Can it be that you will blame me for being a faithful and veritable friend of your family, and for having loved Agrippína Ivánovna so much and invincibly, for having sacrificed my life, my honour, and all my substance for her? I was entirely in her power, and therefore could not rule myself or my property—but she disposed, according to her will, both of me and of my property! It is known to you also, that through her deed with her people I suffer *innocently* a mortal insult—that affair, after her death, I carried to the Senate,[1] sixth department,—it has not yet been decided—by which I was made her accomplice, placed under surveillance, and am still condemned as a penal offender! In my profession, at my age, such dishonour is intolerable to me; and nothing is left for me, except to cheer my heart with this bitter thought, that, consequently, even after the death of Agrippína Ivánovna, I am suffering for her—and that

[1] The Senate, in Russia, is the Supreme Court of Appeal.—TRANSLATOR.

THE BRIGADIER

denotes traces of my unchangeable love and benevolent gratitude toward her!

" In my letters to you, to which I have alluded, I informed you of the funeral of Agrippína Ivánovna in all detail—and also what prayers were said for her; my love and friendship for her spared nothing in accordance with my means! For all this—and together with the requiem service on the fortieth day, and for reading the Psalter over her for six weeks—(over and above which, fifty rubles of mine disappeared, which I had given as deposit for the stone, as to which I informed you),—for all this I expended of my own money seven hundred and fifty rubles,—including a donation of one hundred and fifty rubles to the church!

"May thy benevolent soul take heed to the voice of one in despair and precipitated into a multitude of the most cruel torments! Thy compassion unto lovingkindness alone can restore life to the lost one! ! I, although I am alive—yet by the sufferings of my soul and heart, am dead; dead, when I recall what I have been, and what I am; I was a warrior, and served my country in all uprightness, and lived justly, as is indubitably befitting a true Russian, and a faithful subject,—and was rewarded with distinguished tokens,—and had an estate consonant to my birth and profession; but now, I bend my back like a hunchback for my daily bread and nourishment; and especially am I dead when I recall what a friend I have lost . . . . and what is life to me after that? But one cannot hasten his appointed limit, and the earth will not open, but rather does it turn to stone! And therefore I cry unto thee, benevolent soul, silence the public gossip, do not give thyself over to general condemnation, because in return for my unbounded devotion I have no shelter, cause wonder by thy mercy toward me, turn the tongue of the malevolent and envious to the praise of thy merits—and I make bold, with all submission, to add, comfort in the grave thy most precious aunt, the unforgettable Agrippína Ivánovna, who, for thine effectual aid, through my sinful prayers, will stretch out over thy head her hands in blessing, give rest in his declining days to a solitary old man, who had no reason to expect for himself such a fate! . . . And further, with the most profound respect, I have the happiness to call myself, dear madam—

Your most devoted servant

VASÍLY GUSKÓFF
Brigadier and chevalier.

XVI

A FEW years later I again visited my friend's hamlet. . . . Vasíly Fómitch had been dead a long time: he had passed away soon after my acquaintance with him. The Cucumber was still in good health. He guided me to the grave of Agraféna Ivánovna.—An iron fence enclosed a large slab with a detailed and elaborate epitaph to the deceased; and there, also, beside it, and, as it were, at her feet, was visible a small mound with a cross which had settled awry: the servant of God, Brigadier and Chevalier Vasíly Guskóff, rests beneath that little mound. . . . His dust has found refuge, at last, beside the dust of that being whom he had loved with such an unbounded, almost deathless love.

THE STORY OF
LIEUTENANT ERGÚNOFF

(1867)

THE STORY OF
LIEUTENANT ERGÚNOFF

I

THAT evening Kuzmá Vasílievitch Ergúnoff told us his whole story. He was in the habit of repeating it punctually once a month, and we listened to it, on each occasion, with fresh pleasure, although we knew it almost by heart, in all its details. These details had overgrown the original stem of the story, if one may so express himself, as mushrooms overgrow a felled tree-trunk. Being too well acquainted with the character of our comrade, we did not trouble ourselves to fill in his gaps and omissions. But since Kuzmá Vasílievitch is dead, and there will be no one to narrate his history any more, we have decided to bring it to general knowledge.

II

IT took place forty years ago, in the time of Kuzmá Vasílievitch's youth. He was wont to say of himself that he was then a dandy and a beauty, with a complexion like blood and milk, had red lips, curly hair, and the eyes of a falcon. We took him at his word, although nothing of the sort was visible in him. To our eyes, Kuzmá Vasílievitch presented himself as a man of very ordinary appearance, with a plain and rather somnolent face, a bulky and awkward body. But there is no denying the fact: the years disfigure beauty, no matter of what grade! The traces of dandyism were more plainly preserved in Kuzmá Vasílievitch. Into old age he wore tight trousers with straps, drew in his corpulent waist, had his hair cut very close behind and curled it on his brow, and tinted his moustache with Persian dye, which, however, had more of a crimson or even of a green cast than of black. Kuzmá Vasílievitch was, withal, a very worthy nobleman, although he was fond of " peeking " at his neighbours, in preference, that is to say, of taking a peep at their cards; but this he did not so much out of greed as by way of caution, for he did not like to lose his money to no purpose. But, away with anecdotes: let us proceed to the matter itself.

III

THIS affair took place in the spring, in the then new town of Nikoláeff, whither Kuzmá Vasílievitch had been officially despatched on government business. (He was a lieutenant in the navy.) His superiors had intrusted to him, as to a trustworthy and capable officer, the supervision over certain naval constructions, and from time to time, placed at his disposal very considerable sums of money, which he, for the greater safety, constantly wore in a leathern belt around his body. Kuzmá Vasílievitch really was distinguished for his prudence, and, in spite of his youthful years, bore himself in an exemplary manner. He sedulously avoided all indecorous acts, never touched cards, drank no wine, and even avoided society, so that his comrades—the peaceable ones—called him the pretty girl, and the roisterous ones, mommy's boy, and a sissy. Kuzmá Vasílievitch had one besetting sin: he cherished a hearty predilection for the fair sex; but even here he managed to repress his impulses, and permitted himself no faint-heartedness. He rose and went to bed early, he conscientiously discharged his duty, and his sole relaxation consisted in very long evening rambles in the outlying streets of Nikoláeff. He read no books, for he was afraid of a flow of blood to the head; every spring he drank a certain concoction for plethora. Having donned his uniform, and carefully dusted himself off with a whisk-broom, he took his way, with stately strides, along the fences of the fruit-orchards, halted frequently, admired the beauties of nature, plucked a flower as a memento, and felt a certain satisfaction. But he experienced particular pleasure only when he chanced to encounter a " little

Cupid,"—that is to say, a pretty burgher maiden, hastening homeward with her warm jacket[1] thrown across her shoulders, with a bundle in her bare hand, and a gaily-coloured kerchief on her head. Being, as he himself expressed it, of a susceptible disposition, but modest, Kuzmá Vasílievitch did not enter into conversation with the " little Cupid," but he smiled courteously at her, and gazed long and intently after her. . . . Then he would heave a deep sigh, wend his way homeward with the same stately gait, seat himself at the window, and dream for about half an hour, economically smoking strong plug tobacco from a large meerschaum pipe which had been presented to him by his godfather, a police officer of German extraction. Thus the days passed by, neither cheerfully nor tediously.

IV

ONE day, as he was returning to his quarters, just before dusk, through a narrow lane, Kuzmá Vasílievitch heard hasty footsteps behind him, and broken words mingled with sobs. He glanced round, and beheld a young girl of twenty years, with an extremely agreeable but utterly distracted face all distorted with weeping. A great and unforeseen grief seemed to have over-

[1] The short, wadded peasant-woman's jacket is called, literally, a " soul warmer."—TRANSLATOR.

taken her; she was running, and stumbling as she ran, talking to herself, moaning, gesticulating with her hands; her fair hair was dishevelled, and her kerchief (neither burnous nor mantilla was known at that epoch) had slipped from her shoulders and was hanging from one pin. The young girl was dressed like a gentlewoman, not like a woman of the burgher class.

Kuzmá Vasílievitch stepped aside; a feeling of compassion conquered in him the fear of " behaving in a faint-hearted manner," and when she came on a level with him he politely touched the visor of his shako, and inquired the cause of her tears.

" Because,"—he added, laying his hand on his dirk,—" as a military man I may be able to aid you."

The girl stopped, and, evidently, for the first instant, did not clearly comprehend what he wanted of her; but immediately afterward, as though delighted at the opportunity to express herself, she began to talk in Russian which was not quite pure:

" Good heavens, Mr. Officer! "—she began, and the tears descended like rain on her pretty cheeks,—" what does it mean! This is horri-bel, God knows what it is! We have been robbed of everything, gracious heavens! The cook has carried off everything, everything, everything—the silverware, the jew-el-box, and clothing . . . .

yes . . . . and even the clothing, and the stockings, and body-linen . . . . yes . . . and aunty's reticule, which had a twenty-five ruble bank-note in it in such a tiny case, and two plated spoons . . . and a cloak too, and everything. . . . And I tell all that to the police lieutenant . . . and the police lieutenant says: ' Get out, I don't believe it, I don't believe it. . . . I won't listen, I won't listen, you 're a bad lot yourself!'—I say: ' Goodness, the cloak . . . .' And he: ' I won't listen, that I won't!' He was so insulting, Mr. Officer! ' Get out,' says he, . . . ' get out!'— But where am I to go?"

The girl burst out sobbing convulsively, almost shrieking, and, utterly losing control of herself, leaned against Kuzmá Vasílievitch's sleeve. . . . He became agitated in his turn, and stood rooted to the spot, only repeating now and then: " Enough, that will do!" but he kept staring at the slender, incessantly quivering nape of the neck of the grief-stricken girl.

" If you will permit me, I will see you home," —he said at last, touching her shoulder lightly with his forefinger,—" for, you understand, this sort of thing won't do at all in the street. You shall explain to me your displeasure, and, of course, I will make every effort . . . . as an officer."

The girl half raised her head, and seemed, for the first time, to take a good look at the young man, who might have been said to be holding her in his arms. She was abashed, turned away, and, still sobbing, stepped a little to one side. Kuzmá Vasílievitch renewed his offer. The girl cast a sidelong glance at him through her hair, all wet with her tears, which fell over her face (at this point of his story Kuzmá Vasílievitch always assured us that that glance pierced him "like an awl," and one day he even tried to portray to us that marvellous glance), and placing her arm in the bended arm of the obliging lieutenant, she went off with him to her lodgings.

V

KUZMÁ VASÍLIEVITCH had had very little to do with women in the course of his life, and was, consequently, at a loss how to begin the conversation; but his companion chattered on very volubly, incessantly wiping away her welling tears. A few moments later, Kuzmá Vasílievitch learned that her name was Emilia Kárlovna, that she was a native of Riga, and had come to Nikoláeff to visit her aunt, who was from Riga also, that her papa had been in the military service, but had died " of lung trouble," that her aunt had had a Russian cook, very good and cheap, only without a passport,[1] and that that same cook, on that very

---

[1] An indication of untrustworthiness, which renders the person's service cheap, as an offset to the risk.—TRANSLATOR.

day, had robbed them and had fled, no one knew whither. It had been necessary to go to the police . . . *in die Polizei*. . . . But at this point the memory of the police officer, of the insult dealt her, surged up afresh . . . and again her sobs burst forth. Again did Kuzmá Vasílievitch endeavour to say something consoling. . . But the girl, all of whose impressions, evidently, came and went very rapidly, suddenly halted, and, extending her hand, said calmly:

" Here is our apartment! "

VI

THE apartment consisted of a miserable little house, which seemed to have grown into the ground, with four tiny windows on the street. The dark foliage of a geranium curtained them from within; in one of them burned a candle: night had already fallen. From the cottage itself, and almost on a level with it, stretched a board fence, with a barely discernible wicket-gate. The young girl approached it, and finding it locked, impatiently thumped with the iron ring of the rusty lock. Heavy footsteps became audible behind the fence, as though some one were walking, with a slovenly shuffle, in slippers trodden down at the heel, and a hoarse feminine voice made some inquiry in German, which Kuzmá Vasílievitch did not understand; he, like a genuine sailor, knew not a single tongue except Russian. The girl replied, also in German; the wicket was opened a mere crack, and, after admitting the girl, was instantly slammed in front of the very nose of Kuzmá Vasílievitch, who, nevertheless, succeeded in descrying, amid the semi-gloom of the summer twilight, the form of a fat old woman, in a red gown, with a dim lantern in her hand. Struck with surprise, Kuzmá Vasílievitch remained standing for some time motionless in the street; but at the thought that he, a military officer, had been so discourteously treated (Kuzmá Vasílievitch set great store on his vocation), he felt an excess of indignation, wheeled round abruptly to the left and started homeward. He had not gone ten paces when the wicket opened again and the young girl, who had already managed to have a whispered conversation with the old woman, made her appearance on the threshold and called loudly:—"Where are you going, Mr. Officer? Please come in!"

Kuzmá Vasílievitch hesitated a little, but turned back.

VII

His new acquaintance, whom we shall henceforth call Emilia, led him through a small, dark, damp storeroom, into a fairly large but low-ceiled and begrimed room, with a huge cupboard against the

118459

rear wall; an oilcloth divan; the peeling portraits
of a couple of bishops in their cowls, and of a
Turk in a turban, over the doors and between the
windows; with cardboard boxes and chests in the
corners; with mismatched chairs and a bow-legged
ombre-table, on which lay a man's cap by the
side of a half-drunk glass of kvas.[1] Kuzmá Vasílievitch was followed into the room by the old
woman in the red gown, whom he had noticed
at the gate, and who turned out to be an extremely
homely little Jewess, with morose, pig-like little
eyes, and a grey moustache on her bloated upper
lip. Emilia pointed her out to Kuzmá Vasílievitch and said:

"This is my aunt, Madame Fritsche."

Kuzmá Vasílievitch was somewhat surprised,
but he considered it his duty to introduce himself.
Madame Fritsche looked askance at him, made
him no reply, and asked her niece in Russian if
she would n't like some tea.

"Ah, yes, tea!"—chimed in Emilia.—"You
will drink tea, will you not, Mr. Officer? Yes,
aunty, give us tea! . . . . But why do you stand,
Mr. Officer? Be seated! Akh, how ceremonious
you are! With your permission, I will take off
my kerchief."

When Emilia spoke, she kept turning her head
incessantly from side to side and twitching her

---

[1] Small beer, made by pouring water on the crusts of sour rye
bread, or of rye meal, and allowing it to ferment. It is flavoured
with raisins, watermelon-juice, straw, and so forth.—TRANSLATOR.

little shoulders; birds do thus when they sit upon a lofty, bare bough and are illuminated on all sides by the sun.

Kuzmá Vasílievitch dropped into a chair, and imparting to his carriage the suitable dignity, namely, propping his hand on his dagger and riveting his eyes on the floor, he led the conversation to the robbery. But Emilia immediately interrupted him.

"Don't worry; that is of no account; aunty has just told me that the principal articles have been found." (Madame Fritsche mumbled something to herself and left the room.) "And it was n't at all necessary to go for the Polizei; but I never can have patience, I am so . . . . You don't understand German? . . . so hasty, *immer so rasch!* But I am no longer thinking of that . . . . *aber auch gar nicht!*"

Kuzmá Vasílievitch looked at Emilia. As a matter of fact, her face had assumed the most care-free expression. Everything was smiling in that pretty little face: the drooping, almost white eyelashes, the lips and the cheeks and the chin and the dimple in the chin, and even the very tip of the snub nose. She walked to the tiny mirror beside the cupboard, and humming through her teeth and narrowing her eyes, she began to adjust her hair. Kuzmá Vasílievitch watched her movements. . . . She pleased him very much.

VIII

" You will excuse me,"—she began again, as she twisted lightly to and fro in front of the mirror,— " for having . . . . brought you to my house in that manner. Perhaps you don't like it?"

" Oh, pray, don't say that! "

" I have already told you that I am so hasty. I act first and reflect afterward. And sometimes I don't reflect at all. . . . What is your name, Mr. Officer? May I inquire?"—she added, approaching him, and crossing her arms.

" My name is Ergúnoff, Kuzmá Vasílievitch."

" Ergú . . . . Akh, that 's no a nice name! That is to say, it is difficult for me. I shall call you Mr. Florestan. We had a Mr. Florestan in Riga. He sold splendid gros de Naples in the shop, and was a beauty. Quite equal to you. But how broad-shouldered you are! A regular dashing Russian! I love the Russians. . . . I 'm a Russian myself . . . . my papa was an officer. And my hands are whiter than yours! "—She raised them above her head, waved them through the air several times, in order to expel the blood from them, and immediately lowered them.— " Do you see? I wash them with Greek soap, ... with perfumes. . . . Smell. . . . Akh, but don't kiss them. . . . I did n't mean that. . . . . Where do you serve? "

"I serve in the 19th Black Sea naval battalion."

"Ah! You are a sailor! And do you get a big salary?"

"No . . . . not very, madam."

"You must be very brave. One can see that immediately by your eyes. What thick eyebrows you have! They say one must smear them with lard at night in order to make them grow. But why have you no moustache?"

"It is not allowed by the regulations."

"Akh! that's not nice! What's that you have —a dagger?"

"This is a dirk; the dirk is, so to speak, the attribute of sailors."

"Ah! A dirk! Is it sharp? May I look at it?"—She drew the blade from its sheath with an effort, biting her lips and screwing up her eyes, and laid her nose against it.—"Oh, how dull! So I can kill you on the spot."

She brandished the dirk at Kuzmá Vasílievitch. He feigned to be alarmed, and laughed. She laughed also.

"*Ihr habt pardon*—you are pardoned,"—she said, assuming a majestic attitude.—"Here, take your weapon! And how old are you?"—she suddenly inquired.

"Twenty-five."

"And I am nineteen! How ridiculous! Akh!"

And Emilia broke into such a ringing laugh

that she even threw herself backward a little.
Kuzmá Vasílievitch did not rise from his chair,
and stared more intently than ever at her rosy
face, quivering with laughter, and she pleased
him more and more.

Suddenly Emilia fell silent, and humming
through her teeth,—it was a habit she had,—again
approached the mirror.

" Do you know how to sing, Mr. Florestan? "

" Not at all, ma'am. I was n't taught, ma'am."

" And do you play on the guitar? No again?
But I can. I have a guitar with mother-of-pearl,
only the strings are broken. I must buy some.
Will you give me some money, Mr. Officer? I
will sing you a beautiful German romance."—She
sighed, and closed her eyes.—" Akh, such a beautiful song! But do you know how to dance?
Not that either? *Unmöglich!* I will teach you.
L'Ecossais and the kazák waltz. Tra-la-la, tra-
la-la, tra-la-la, la. . . . ." Emilia gave a couple
of skips.—" See what nice boots I have! From
Warsaw.[1] Oh, you and I will dance together, Mr.
Florestan! But what are you going to call me? "

Kuzmá Vasílievitch grinned, and flushed crimson to the ears.

" I shall call you, ' Loveliest Emilia!' "

" No! no! You must call me: *Mein Schätzchen,
mein Zuckerpüppchen!* Repeat that after me."

[1] Warsaw-made shoes were considered unusually good
at that epoch,—TRANSLATOR.

"With the greatest pleasure, but I 'm afraid it will be difficult for me. . . ."

"Never mind, never mind. Say, *Mein.* . . ."

"Ma—in. . . ."

"*Zucker.* . . ."

"Tzuk . . . . ker. . . ."

"*Püppchen! Püppchen! Püppchen!*"

"Piu . . . . piu . . . . I can't, ma'am. It turns out badly, somehow."

"No! You must. . . . You must! But do you know what that means? That 's the most agreeable word in German for young ladies. I 'll explain it to you later on. But now here comes aunty with the samovár for us. Bravo! bravo! Aunty, I 'm going to drink tea with cream. . . . Is there any cream?"

"*So schweige doch!*"—replied aunty.

IX

KUZMÁ VASÍLIEVITCH sat at Madame Fritsche's until midnight. Never had he spent so agreeable an evening since his arrival in Nikoláeff. Truth to tell, it occurred to him more than once that an officer and a nobleman ought not to be acquainted with the young native of Riga and her "anty," but Emilia was so pretty, she chattered away so amusingly, she cast upon him such caressing glances, that he disregarded his extraction, his profession, and resolved, for that once, to do as he pleased. One circumstance, only, troubled him, and left upon him a not altogether pleasant impression. Just as the conversation between him, Emilia, and Madame Fritsche reached its height, the door of the vestibule was opened a crack, and a masculine arm, in a dark cuff, with three tiny silver buttons, was quietly thrust in, and quietly deposited a tolerably large bundle on a chair beside the door. Both ladies immediately rushed to the chair, and began to inspect what had been brought. "These are not the same spoons!" cried Emilia; but her aunt nudged her with her elbow, and carried off the bundle without tying up the ends. It seemed to Kuzmá Vasílievitch that one of them was stained with something red, like blood. . . .

"What 's that?"—he asked Emilia.—"Have they returned to you some more of the stolen articles?"

"Yes,"—replied Emilia, with apparent reluctance,—"some more."

"Did that man-servant of yours hunt them up?"

"What man-servant? We have no man-servant."

"Some other man, then."

"No men come to our house."

"But, pardon me, pardon me. . . . I saw the cuff of a man's coat or hussar jacket. And, then, there 's that cap. . . ."

" Men never, never come,"—repeated Emilia, persistently. . . "What you saw . . . . You saw nothing! And that cap is mine."

" How so? "

" Why, just so. It 's useful in a masquerade. . . . . So, there now, it 's mine, *und Punctum!* "

" But who was it that brought you the bundle? "

Emilia made no reply, and pouting out her lips, she followed Madame Fritsche out of the room. Ten minutes later, she returned alone, without her aunt, and when Kuzmá Vasílievitch set to questioning her again, she stared at his forehead, said that it was shameful for a cavalier to be inquisitive (at these words, her face underwent a slight change, darkened, as it were), and taking from the ombre-table a pack of ancient cards, she asked him to tell her fortune, and that of the king of hearts.

Kuzmá Vasílievitch burst out laughing, took the cards, and all evil thoughts instantly leaped out of his head.

But they returned again, that very day. To wit: he had already emerged from the wicket upon the street, he had already taken leave of Emilia, for the last time he had shouted to her: *"Adieu, Zuckerpüppchen!"* when suddenly a man of low stature glided swiftly past him and, turning for an instant in his direction (night had long since closed in, but the moon shone quite brightly), displayed a gaunt, gipsy face, with thick black eyebrows and moustache, black eyes, and a hooked nose. This man instantly darted round the corner, but it seemed to Kuzmá Vasílievitch that he had recognised, not his face,—he had never beheld him before,—but the cuff of his sleeve: three silver buttons gleamed plainly in the moonlight. Troubled surprise stirred in the soul of the cautious lieutenant; when he reached home, he did not light his meerschaum pipe, according to his wont. Moreover, the unexpected acquaintance with the amiable Emilia, and the agreeable hours spent in her society, contributed to the agitated state of his feelings.

X

WHATEVER may have been the apprehensions of Kuzmá Vasílievitch, they were speedily dissipated, and left no trace behind them. He began to inquire quite frequently after the health of the two ladies from Riga. The susceptible lieutenant became intimate with Emilia. At first, he was ashamed of this intimacy, and concealed his visits; then he ceased to feel ashamed, and to affect concealment. It ended in his taking more pleasure in sitting with his new acquaintances than with any one else, not to mention his own not over-cheerful four walls. Even Madame Fritsche no longer aroused in him unpleasant sensations, although she treated him rudely and surlily, as before. Persons of small means, like Madame Fritsche, set particular value on the liberality of their visitors; but Kuzmá Vasílievitch was inclined to be parsimonious, and his gifts took the form, chiefly, of raisins, English walnuts, and ginger-bread cakes. . . . Only once did he, to use his own expression, "ruin himself," and present Emilia with a pink kerchief of genuine French material, rather light in quality; but she singed his gift in the candle that same day. He began to remonstrate with her; she tied the kerchief to the cat's tail; he waxed angry: she laughed in his face. Kuzmá Vasílievitch was compelled, at last, to confess to himself that he not only did not en-joy the respect of the ladies from Riga, but had not even earned their confidence. He was never admitted at once, without a preliminary scrutiny. Sometimes they made him wait, sometimes they sent him away without the least ceremony, and, when they wished to conceal something from him, they talked German in his presence. Emilia rendered him no account of her actions, and to his questions returned superficial replies, as though she had not rightly heard his words; and, chief of all, certain rooms in Madame Fritsche's house, which was quite spacious, although it ap-peared a hovel from the street, remained con-stantly closed against him. Nevertheless, Kuzmá Vasílievitch did not cease his visits, but, on the contrary, augmented them; he saw living people, all the same. His self-love was also satisfied by

the fact that Emilia continued to call him " Florestan," considered him a remarkable beauty, and
asserted that he had eyes like those of a bird of
paradise, " *wie die Augen eines Paradiesvogels!* "

XI

ONE day, in the very middle of the summer, at
noonday, Kuzmá Vasílievitch, after having
passed the entire morning in the sun, with the
contractors and labourers, dragged himself,
jaded, exhausted, to the wicket-gate of the too-
familiar little house. He knocked; he was admitted. He staggered into the so-called drawing-
room, and immediately threw himself down on the
divan. Emilia approached him, and wiped his
perspiring brow with her handkerchief.

" How tired he is, my darling! How hot he
is!"—said she, with compassion.—" Good heavens! he might have unfastened his collar. O
Lord! his throat is fairly throbbing."

" I 'm worn out, my dear friend,"—moaned
Kuzmá Vasílievitch.—" I 've been on my feet
since early morning, and in the very hottest of it,
to boot. Calamity! I wanted to go home. Those
beasts of contractors are there again! But it is
so cool here, with you. . . . I think I could get a
nap."

" Well, why not? Rest, my little chicken; no
one will disturb thee here. . . . ."

" But I 'm ashamed, somehow. . . . ."

" The i-dea! ashamed, forsooth! Sleep. And I 'll . . . . how is it you say it in your language? . . . I 'll sing thee a lullaby. '*Schlaf, mein Kindchen, schlafe!*' " she struck up.

" I 'd like a drink of water, first. . . . ."

" Here 's a glass of water for thee. Fresh! Like crystal! Wait, I 'll put a cushion under thy head. . . . And here, this is a protection from the flies."

She covered his face with a handkerchief.

" Thanks, my little cupid. . . . I 'll only just . . . doze a little. . . . ."

Kuzmá Vasílievitch closed his eyes, and immediately fell asleep.

" *Schlaf, mein Kindchen, schlafe!* "—sang Emilia, swaying from side to side, and laughing softly, both at her song, and at her movements.

" What a big baby I have! " she thought. " A boy."

XII

AN hour and a half later, the lieutenant awoke. It had seemed to him, in his dreams, that some one was touching him, bending over him, breathing on him. He groped about him, and pulled off the handkerchief. Emilia was kneeling, very close to him; the expression of her face struck him as strange. But she immediately sprang to her feet, walked off to the little window, and thrust something into her pocket.

Kuzmá Vasílievitch stretched himself.

" But how wildly I have been snoring! "—he said, yawning.—" Come hither, *maine ziusse freilen!* "

Emilia came to him. He raised himself alertly, thrust his hand into her pocket, and grasped a small pair of scissors.

" *Ach, Herr Je!* "—exclaimed Emilia, involuntarily.

" These . . . . these are scissors? "—muttered Kuzmá Vasílievitch.

" Why, yes, of course. What didst thou think they were . . . . pistols? Akh, what a ridiculous face thou hast! As crumpled as the pillow, and the hair on the back of thy head is all standing on end. . . And he 's not laughing. . . . Akh, akh, akh! And his eyes are swollen. . . . Akh! "

Emilia shrieked with laughter.

" Come, stop that,"—growled Kuzmá Vasílievitch, and rose from the couch.—" Have done with grinning without a cause. If thou canst not think of anything more sensible, I 'll just go away. . . I 'll go away,"—he repeated, perceiving that she did not stop.

Emilia relapsed into silence.

" Come, enough of that; stay; I won't do it again. . . Only, thou must smooth thy hair. . . . "

" No; it does n't matter. . . . Let me alone! I 'd better go,"—said Kuzmá Vasílievitch, and reached for his cap.

Emilia pouted.

" Fie, how ill-tempered! A regular Russian! All Russians are ill-tempered! So he 's going. Fie! He promised me five rubles yesterday, and to-day he gives me nothing, and is going off."

" I have no money with me,"—blurted out Kuzmá Vasílievitch, who was already at the door. —" Farewell! "

Emilia gazed after him, and shook her finger at him.

" He has no money! Listen, listen to what he says! Okh, what deceivers these Russians are! But just wait, you pug-dog! . . . Aunty, please come here; I 'll tell you something."

On the evening of that same day, Kuzmá Vasílievitch, as he was preparing for bed, and undressing, noticed that the seam on the upper edge of his leather belt was ripped for a distance of about two inches and a half. Being a particular man, he immediately got out needle and thread, threaded it, and himself sewed up the gap, but paid no further attention to this, apparently, insignificant circumstance.

XIII

KUZMÁ VASÍLIEVITCH devoted the whole of the
following day to his professional duties; he did
not leave the house, even after dinner—and until
nightfall, in the sweat of his brow, he scribbled,
and copied out neatly a report to his superiors,
ruthlessly confounding the letters *ye* and *e*,[1] and
placing an exclamation point after every " but,"
and a semicolon after every " however." On the
following morning, a bare-footed little Jew, in
a tattered smock, brought him a letter from
Emilia—the first letter Kuzmá Vasílievitch had
received from her.

" *Mein aller liebster* Florestan,"—she wrote to
him,—" is it possible that thou art so angry with
thy Zuckerpüppchen, that thou didst not come
yisterday? Please don't be angry, unless thou
wishest thy jolly Emilia to veep a very great
deel, and be sure to come to-dey, at 5 o'clock
in the evening." (The figure " 5 " was encircled by two wreaths.) — " I shall be very, very
glad. Thy amiable Emilia." Kuzmá Vasílievitch inwardly marvelled at the learning of his
" amiable " friend, gave the little Jew a couple
of kopéks, and bade him say, " Very well, I will
come."

[1] One of the most difficult points in spelling Russian correctly is
the proper use of these two letters, which differ more in appearance
and by grammatical rule than they do in sound.—TRANSLATOR.

XIV

Kuzmá Vasílievitch kept his word: before the
clock had struck five, he was standing in front of
Madame Fritsche's gate. But to his amazement,
he did not find Emilia at home; the mistress of
the house herself received him, and after having
made—oh, wonderful to relate—a preliminary
bob-courtesy, she informed him that unforeseen
circumstances had compelled Emilia to absent
herself, but that she would soon return, and
begged that he would wait for her. Madame Fritsche wore a clean white mob-cap; she smiled,
talked in an insinuating voice, and, obviously,
strove to impart a courteous expression to her
surly face, which, however, gained nothing
thereby, but, on the contrary, acquired a sort of
ominous aspect.

"Sit down, sir, sit down,"—she insisted, pushing forward an easy-chair,—"and we will entertain you, if you permit!"

Again Madame Fritsche made a ducking courtesy, quitted the room, and speedily returned
with a cup of chocolate on a small iron tray. The
chocolate seemed to be of dubious quality, but
Kuzmá Vasílievitch drank off the whole cupful
with pleasure, although he positively could not
comprehend what had impelled Madame Fritsche
to behave in that manner, and what all this meant.

Nevertheless, Emilia did not come, and he was beginning to lose patience, and to feel bored, when, suddenly, the sounds of a guitar became audible on the other side of the wall. First one chord resounded, then a second, a third, a fourth, —growing louder and louder and fuller. Kuzmá Vasílievitch was surprised: Emilia had a guitar, it is true, but it had only three strings: he was still preparing to buy the rest for her; moreover, Emilia was not at home. Who could it be? Again a chord rang out, and so resonantly, that it seemed to be in the very room. . . . Kuzmá Vasílievitch turned round, and almost shrieked aloud with terror. Before him, on the threshold of a low-browed door, which he had never observed hitherto,—the heavy cupboard had stood in front of it,—stood a being who was unknown to him: not exactly a child, nor yet an adult maiden. She was dressed in a little white frock with colored patterns, and red slippers with high heels; her thick black hair, caught up with a golden circlet, fell like a mantle from her little head over her slender body. From beneath its soft masses huge eyes gleamed with a dark glitter; bare, swarthy little arms, laden with bracelets and rings, held the guitar firmly. The face was hardly visible: it seemed so small and dark, only the lips glowed red, and the sharp, straight nose was clearly outlined. Kuzmá Vasílievitch stood for a long time as though rooted to the spot, and stared intently, without even once winking, at this strange being; and it gazed at him, and it also neither winked nor moved. At last he came to himself, and approached it, with tiny steps.

The dark little face began gradually to smile, the small white teeth suddenly gleamed forth, the little head was raised, and, faintly shaking its curls, displayed itself in all its clear-cut and delicate beauty. " What sort of a little demon is this? " thought Kuzmá Vasílievitch, and advancing still closer, he said in a low voice:

" Little figure! Hey, little figure! Who are you? "

" Hither, hither,"—said the " little figure," in a somewhat hoarse voice, with a slow, non-Russian pronunciation, and uncertain accentuation, retreating a couple of paces.

Kuzmá Vasílievitch followed it, crossed the threshold, and found himself in a tiny chamber, devoid of windows, the walls hung and the floor covered with thick rugs of camel's-hair. A powerful odour of musk fairly poured upon him. Two candles of yellow wax were burning on a small, round table in front of a low Turkish divan. In one corner stood a bed, with a cotton coverlet, and a long rosary of amber beads, with a red tassel at the end, hung near the pillow.

" But, pray, tell me who you are,"—repeated Kuzmá Vasílievitch.

" The sistér . . . the sistér of Emilia."

" You are her sister? And you live here? "

" Yes . . . . yes. . . ."

Kuzmá Vasílievitch attempted to touch the
" little figure." It recoiled.

" How comes it that she has never spoken to me
about you? "

" But it was not possíble . . . . not possíble. . ."

" So you are concealing yourself . . . . you
are in hiding? "

" Yes. . . ."

" Is there any cause for that? "

" There ees . . . . there ees."

" H'm! "—Again Kuzmá Vasílievitch tried to
touch the " little figure," again it recoiled.—
" That 's exactly why I have never noticed you.
I must confess that I never suspected your existence. And Madame Fritsche, that old woman,
—is she your aunt also? "

" Yes . . . my ont."

" H'm! You don't seem to understand Russian
very well. What is your name, if I may ask? "

" The Humming-bird."

" What? "

" The Humming-bird."

" The Humming-bird? Here 's a remarkable
name! I remember now that there are insects of
that sort in Africa."

XV

THE Humming-bird laughed, with a curt, strange laugh . . . as though bits of glass had clashed in her throat. She shook her head, rolled her eyes about, laid the guitar on the table, and stepping briskly to the door, shut it with one movement. She moved quickly and alertly, with a barely audible swift sound, like a hawk; her hair fell down her back lower than her knees.

" But why have you locked the door,"—asked Kuzmá Vasílievitch. The Humming-bird laid her finger on her lips.

" Emilia. . . . We don't want . . . . don't want her."

Kuzmá Vasílievitch smiled.

" Is it possible that you are jealous of her? "

The Humming-bird raised her eyebrows.

" Vat? "

" You are jealous . . . are angry,"—explained Kuzmá Vasílievitch.

" Oh, yes! "

" You don't say so! You do me great honour! . . . See here, how old are you? "

" Sevenyteen."

" Seventeen, you mean to say? "

" Yes."

Kuzmá Vasílievitch surveyed his fantastic companion with an attentive gaze.—" What a little beauty you are!"—said he, impressively.—"Wonderful! simply wonderful! What hair! What eyes! And eyebrows, what eyebrows! . . . . Phew!"

Again the Humming-bird laughed, and again she rolled about her magnificent eyes.

"Yes; I am a beauty! Sit down, and I will sit down . . . . beside you."

"Certainly, certainly. . . But, say what you will, how can you be a sister to Emilia? You do not resemble her in the least."

"No. . . I 'm her sister . . . . coujin. Here . . . take this . . . vlowér. Nice vlowér. It smells good."—She took from her girdle a spray of lilac, sniffed at it, bit off a petal, and gave him the whole spray.—"Would you like some preserves? Good . . . . from Constantinople . . . . sherbet."—The Humming-bird took from a small chest of drawers a gilded jar wrapped in a bit of scarlet silken material with steel spangles, a silver spoon, a small faceted crystal carafe of water, and a small glass of the same sort.— "Taste the sherbet, sir; it is very fine. I will sing to you. . . Shall I?"—She took up her guitar.

"And do you sing?"—asked Kuzmá Vasílievitch, as he put in his mouth a spoonful of really superb sherbet.

"Oh, yes!"—She threw back her hair, bent her head on one side, and struck a few chords, gazing diligently at the tips of her fingers and at the neck of the guitar. . . . Then suddenly she began to sing in a hoarse and agreeable, but guttural and, to the ear of Kuzmá Vasílievitch, somewhat wild voice, which was disproportionately strong for her size. " Akh, thou, my kitten! " he thought. She sang a mournful ditty, not in the least Russian in style, and in a language totally unknown to Kuzmá Vasílievitch. According to his assertion, the sounds: " kxa, gxa," recurred incessantly in the song, and toward the end she repeated in a drawl: " sintamar," or " sintzimar," or something in that style, propped her head on her hand, sighed, and dropped the guitar on her knees.—" Good? "—she asked.—" Do you want more? "

" With great pleasure,"—replied Kuzmá Vasílievitch.—" Only, why is your face always melancholy, as it were? You ought to try the sherbet."

"No . . . . do it yourself. And I 'll sing more. . . . This will be more merry."—She sang a second ditty, in the nature of a dance-song, in the same incomprehensible language. Again did Kuzmá Vasílievitch hear the same guttural sounds as before. Her swarthy little fingers fairly flew over the strings, " like little spiders." And this time she wound up by uttering a dashing shout: " Haida! " or " Hassa! " and thumped the table with her fist, her eyes flashing the while.

XVI

KUZMÁ VASÍLIEVITCH sat as though dazed. His head was reeling. All this was so unexpected. . . . . Yes, and that perfume, that singing. . . . candles by daylight . . . . sherbet flavoured with vanilla. . . . And there was the Humming-bird moving nearer and nearer to him, her hair was glittering and rustling, and heat was blazing from her, and that mournful face. . . . " A water-nymph!" thought Kuzmá Vasílievitch. Somehow, he felt uncomfortable.

" My little darling,"—said he,—" confess that you took it into your head to summon me to you to-day? "

" You are youthful, good-looking. . . I like that sort."

" Ah, you don't say so! But what will Emilia say? She wrote me a letter: she will be here directly."

" Don't you tell to her . . . . anyzing! Horrors! She 'll kill you! "

Kuzmá Vasílievitch burst out laughing.

" Is she really so wicked? "

The Humming-bird nodded her head gravely several times.

" And not to Madame Fritsche either. Ni! ni! ni! "—She tapped herself gently on the brow,— " Dost thou understand, Mr. Officer? "

Kuzmá Vasílievitch frowned.

" That means, it is a secret? "

" Yes . . . . yes."

" Well, all right. . . . I won't let drop the smallest word. Only, in return, thou must kiss me."

" No, later . . . . when thou art going away."

" That 's a pretty idea! "—Kuzmá Vasílievitch attempted to bend over her, but she slowly drew back and straightened up, like an adder which is trodden upon in the grass of the forest. Kuzmá Vasílievitch stared at her.—" What a creature thou art! " he uttered at last:—" how malicious! Well, I want nothing to do with thee! "

The Humming-bird reflected, and turned toward the lieutenant. . . . Suddenly, three dull, measured blows resounded somewhere in the house. The Humming-bird laughed, almost snorted.

" To-day—no, to-morrow—yes. Come to-morrow."

" At what hour? "

" At seven . . . in the evening."

" And what am I to do about Emilia? "

" Emilia . . . . no; she will not be here."

" Dost thou think so? Well, very good. Only, to-morrow thou wilt tell me . . . ."

" Vat? " (Every time the Humming-bird

asked a question, her face assumed an infantile expression.)

" Why thou hast hidden thyself from me for so long."

" Yes . . . . yes; to-morrow everything will be, the end will be."

" See here, I 'll bring thee a gift. . . ."

" No. . . I don't want it."

" Why not? I perceive that thou art fond of decking thyself."

" I don't want it. This . . . . this . . . this . . . ." and she pointed at her gown, her rings, her bracelets, at everything which surrounded her . . . . " all this is mine. Not a gift. I don't take."

" As thou wilt! And must I go now? "

" Oh, yes! "

Kuzmá Vasílievitch rose. The Humming-bird rose also.

" Farewell, thou toy! And when am I to have that kiss? "

The Humming-bird suddenly gave a light leap, and nimbly throwing both arms round the young lieutenant's neck, she did not kiss, but, as it were, pecked him on the lips. He attempted to kiss her in his turn, but she instantly sprang away, and stood behind the little couch.

" So it is for to-morrow, at seven o'clock? "— he said, not without confusion.

She nodded her head at him, and, taking a long

lock of her hair between the tips of two fingers, she bit it with her sharp little teeth.

Kuzmá Vasílievitch kissed his hand to her, left the room, and drew the door to behind him. He heard the Humming-bird immediately run to it. . . . The key clicked sharply in the lock.

XVII

THERE was no one in Madame Fritsche's drawing-room. Kuzmá Vasílievitch immediately wended his way to the anteroom. He did not wish to encounter Emilia. The mistress of the house met him on the front steps.

" Ah! you are going, Mr. Lieutenant,"—she said, with the same hypocritical and malicious grimace as before. . . . " Won't you wait for Emilia? "

Kuzmá Vasílievitch put on his cap.

" I must inform you, madam, that I can wait no longer. And perhaps I shall not come to-morrow, either. Pray tell her so."

" Very well, I 'll tell her. But surely, you have not grown bored, lieutenant? "

" No, ma'am; I 've not grown bored."

" Just so. I beg your pardon."

" Good-bye, ma'am."

Kuzmá Vasílievitch went home, and stretching himself out on his bed, he plunged into meditation. He was inexpressibly astonished. " What sort of a mystery is this!" he exclaimed more than once. And why had Emilia written to him? She had appointed a rendezvous, and then had not come? . . . He found her note, turned it about in his hands, smelled of it: it reeked of tobacco, and in one place he noticed a correction! it read, "I have wept," with the feminine termination, but it had first had the masculine termination. But what deduction could be drawn from that? And could it be possible that the mistress of the house knew nothing? And *she* . . . . Who was she? Yes, who was she. He could not get the bewitching Humming-bird, that "toy," that "little figure," out of his head, and with impatience he waited for the evening of the morrow, although, in secret, he almost feared that same "toy" and "little figure."

XVIII

On the following day, Kuzmá Vasílievitch went to the shops in the bazaar before dinner, and, after assiduous bargaining, purchased a tiny gold cross on a narrow velvet ribbon. "Although she declares," he meditated, "that she requires no gift, we know perfectly well how much such words mean; and, anyhow, if she really has so disinterested a nature, Emilia will not disdain it." Thus meditated the Don Juan of Nikoláeff, and that without even so much as suspecting what the real Don Juan was like, and how he lingers in the popular memory. At six o'clock in the evening, Kuzmá Vasílievitch shaved himself with care, and sending for a barber of his acquaintance, ordered him to pomade and curl well his crest of hair, which command the latter executed with particular zeal, using the government writing-paper for curl-papers, with no sparing hand; then Kuzmá Vasílievitch donned a brand-new uniform, took in his right hand a pair of new wash-leather gloves, and after spraying himself with lavender-water he left the house. On this occasion, Kuzmá Vasílievitch took a great deal more trouble over his personal appearance than when he had gone to appointments with the " Zuckerpüppchen," not because the Humming-bird pleased him more than did Emilia, but because there was something mysterious about the " toy," something which involuntarily aroused even what indolent imagination the young lieutenant possessed.

XIX

MADAME FRITSCHE received him as on the preceding day, and, as though in pursuance of a concerted agreement with him as to a conventional falsehood, again announced to him that Emilia had absented herself for a short time, and begged that he would wait. Kuzmá Vasílievitch bent his head, in token of assent, and seated himself on a chair. Again Madame Fritsche smiled, that is to say, she displayed her yellow teeth, and withdrew, without offering him any chocolate.

Kuzmá Vasílievitch immediately riveted his gaze on the mysterious door. It remained closed. He coughed loudly a couple of times, as though to give a sign of his presence. . . . The door did not stir. He held his breath, he listened. . . . Not the slightest sound or rustle could he hear; it was as though everything round about had died. Kuzmá Vasílievitch rose, approached the door on tiptoe,—and after having fumbled about it, in vain, with his fingers, he pressed his knee against it . . . to no effect. Then he bent down, and enunciated twice, in a forcible whisper. "Humming-bird, Humming-bird . . . Toy!"—No one replied. Kuzmá Vasílievitch drew himself up, adjusted his uniform—and, after standing for a while on one spot, he walked to the window with firmer footsteps, and began to drum on the panes. He was beginning to feel vexed, indignant; the honour of an officer was beginning to speak up within him. "What nonsense!" he thought at last,—"for whom do they take me? If this is the way they treat me, why, I 'll hammer with my fists! She 'll be forced to answer! The old woman will hear. . . . Well, what of that? I 'm not to blame!" He wheeled briskly round on his heels. . . The door stood half open.

80

XX

Kuzmá Vasílievitch instantly, and again on tiptoe, darted into the hidden chamber. On the divan, in a white gown, with a broad scarlet girdle, lay the Humming-bird, and covering the lower part of her face with a handkerchief, she was laughing noiselessly, but heartily. This time she had fastened up her hair; she had plaited it in two long, thick braids, and intertwined it with scarlet ribbons; the slippers she had worn on the preceding day, still adorned her tiny, crossed feet; but those feet were bare: to look at them, one might have thought that she had donned dark silken stockings. The divan stood in a different position from that of the day before; and on the table, upon a Chinese tray, was visible a pot-bellied, gay-coloured coffee-pot, beside a faceted sugar-bowl, and two small, sky-blue porcelain cups. There, also, lay the guitar, and a thin stream of dark-blue smoke curled upward from the top of a big, aromatic pastille.

Kuzmá Vasílievitch stepped up to the divan, and bent toward the Humming-bird; but before he could utter a word, she stretched out her hand, and without ceasing to laugh into her handkerchief, she plunged her tiny, hard fingers into his hair, and instantaneously rumpled up his well-arranged top-knot.—" What 's the meaning of this now?"—exclaimed Kuzmá Vasílievitch, not too well pleased with such unceremonious treatment.—" Akh, thou mischievous monkey!"

The Humming-bird removed the handkerchief from her face.

" It was n't nice so; it 's better thus."—She moved off to one end of the divan and tucked up her feet.—" Sit down . . . there."

Kuzmá Vasílievitch sat down where she bade him.

"But why dost thou go to a distance?"—he said, after a brief silence.—"Art thou afraid of me?"

The Humming-bird rolled herself up in a ball, and darted a sidelong glance at him.

" I 'm not afraid. . . . No."

" Thou must not be shy with me,"—continued Kuzmá Vasílievitch, in a hortatory tone.—" Of course, thou rememberest thy promise of yesterday, to kiss me?"

The Humming-bird clasped her knees with both arms, laid her head on them, and darted another glance at him.

" I remember."

" Exactly so. And thou must keep thy word."

" Yes . . . . I must."

" In that case . . . ." began Kuzmá Vasílievitch, and was on the point of moving toward her.

The Humming-bird freed her braids, which she

had clasped along with her knees, and with one of them smote him on the arm.

" More quiet, sir."

Kuzmá Vasílievitch was disconcerted.

" What eyes she has, the rogue,"—he muttered, as though to himself.—" But,"—he added, raising his voice, " in that case . . . why didst thou invite me? "

The Humming-bird stretched out her neck, like a bird. . . . She was listening. Kuzmá Vasílievitch became greatly agitated.

" Emilia? "—he articulated, interrogatively.

" No."

" Some one else? "

The Humming-bird shrugged her shoulders.

" But dost thou hear anything? "

" Nothing."—The Humming-bird threw back (and this with a bird-like movement) her small, hawk-like head, with its beautiful parting, and short whorls of curly tendrils at the nape, where the plaits began, and again curled herself up in a ball.—" Nothing."

" Nothing! Then now I 'm . . . ." Kuzmá Vasílievitch reached toward the Humming-bird, but instantly drew back his hand. A drop of blood made its appearance on his finger.—" What folly is this! "—he cried, shaking his finger.— " This is the result of your everlasting pins! But, devil take it, what sort of a pin is that,"—he added, glancing at the long, golden hair-pin which the Humming-bird was slowly thrusting into her girdle.—" That's a whole dagger, that's a sting. . . Yes, yes, that's thy sting, and thou art a wasp, that's what thou art, a wasp, dost understand? "

The Humming-bird was, apparently, greatly delighted by Kuzmá Vasílievitch's comparison. She burst into shrill laughter, and several times repeated:

" Yes, I sting. . . . I sting."

Kuzmá Vasílievitch looked at her, and thought: " See there, now, she's laughing, but her face is mournful. . . ."

" See here, what I'll show thee,"—he said aloud.

" Vat? "

" Why dost thou say 'vat'?[1] Art thou a Pole? "

" Naw."

" There you go now with 'naw'![2] Well, never mind! "—Kuzmá Vasílievitch drew forth his little offering, and dangled it in the air.—" Just look here. . . . A pretty little thing? "

The Humming-bird cast an indifferent glance at it.

" Ah! A cross! We don't wear."

" What? You don't wear a cross? Why, art thou a Jewess, pray? "

[1] In Russian: *tchto*. She pronounces it: *tzo*.—TRANSLATOR.
[2] In Russian: *nyét*. She pronounces it: *ni*.—TRANSLATOR.

" We don't wear,"—repeated the Humming-bird, and, suddenly starting up, she cast a look over her shoulder.—" Would you like? I will sing . . . ." she asked hastily.

Kuzmá Vasílievitch thrust the cross into the pocket of his uniform, and cast a glance behind him also. It seemed to him that he heard a faint crackling behind the wall. . .

" What 's that? "—he muttered.

" A mouse . . . a mouse,"—said the Humming-bird, hastily, and suddenly, quite unexpectedly to Kuzmá Vasílievitch, she encircled his head with her supple, smooth arms, and a swift kiss burned his cheek . . . as though a hot coal had been applied to it.

He clasped the Humming-bird in his embrace, but she slipped out like a snake—her body was not much bigger than that of a snake—and sprang to her feet.

" Wait,"—she whispered,—" we must drink coffee first. . . ."

" Enough! Who cares for coffee! That will do later."

" No, now. Now it is hot, later it is cold."—She seized the coffee-pot by the handle, and raising it on high, began to fill both cups. The coffee fell in a slender, as it were, twisted stream; the Humming-bird laid her head on her shoulder and watched it flow.—" There now, put in sugar . . . . drink . . . and I will! "

Kuzmá Vasílievitch tossed a bit of sugar into his cup, and drained it at a gulp. The coffee seemed to him very strong and bitter. The Humming-bird gazed at him with a smile, and with slightly inflated nostrils, over the edge of her cup. She slowly set it down on the table.

"Why dost not thou drink?"—asked Kuzmá Vasílievitch.

"I will . . . gradually . . . ." she replied.

Kuzmá Vasílievitch became ardent.

"Come, sit here beside me!"

"Directly."—She bent her head, and still without taking her eyes from Kuzmá Vasílievitch, grasped her guitar.—"Only, first I will sing."

"Yes, yes; only sit here."

"And I will dance. Dost thou wish?"

"Dost thou dance? Well, I'd like to see that. But canst not thou do that later?"

"No; now. . . . And I love thee very much."

"Thou lovest me? Look out . . . however, dance away, thou strange creature!"

XXI

THE Humming-bird stood on the further side of the table, and, after running her fingers over the strings of her guitar a few times, she struck up, —to the amazement of Kuzmá Vasílievitch, who was expecting a merry, lively air,—she struck up a slow, monotonous recitative, accompanying every separate sound, which seemed to be forced out with an effort, by a measured swaying of the whole body, to right and left. She did not smile, and she even contracted her brows, her high, arched, slender brows, between which stood forth sharply a blue mark, resembling an oriental letter, probably etched in with powder. She almost closed her eyes, but the pupils gleamed dimly from beneath the drooping lashes, and, as before, were riveted persistently on Kuzmá Vasílievitch. And he, also, could not wrest his gaze from those marvellous, menacing eyes, from that swarthy, gradually flushing face, from the half-opened and motionless lips, from the two black serpents, which swayed in measured rhythm on each side of the well-shaped head. The Humming-bird continued to rock to and fro, without moving from her place, and only her feet were brought into motion: she moved them slightly, raising now a toe, now a heel. Once, all of a sudden, she wheeled swiftly round, and emitted a piercing cry, brandishing her guitar high in the air. . . . Then she began her former monotonous dance, accompanying it with the same monotonous chanting. In the meantime, Kuzmá Vasílievitch sat very quietly on the divan, and continued to stare at the Humming-bird. He felt a strange, unusual sensation within him. He felt very light and free, even too light; it was as though he did not feel his body, as though he were dancing; but, at the same time, thrills were creeping over him, a sort of agreeable helplessness was diffused through his legs, and dreaminess tickled his eyelids and his lips. He no longer wished for anything, he no longer thought of anything, but he merely felt very much at his ease, as though some one were lulling him to sleep, " singing him a lullaby," as Emilia had expressed it, and he whispered to himself: " The toy!" At times, the face of the " toy " clouded over. . . . " Why is that? " Kuzmá Vasílievitch asked himself. " 'T is from the pastille,"—he reassured himself. . . . " It makes that sort of blue smoke." And again some one lulled him, and even narrated something nice in his ear. . . Only, for some reason or other, the sentences were never finished. But now, all at once, in the face of " the toy," the eyes opened, huge, of unprecedented size, regular bridge-arches. . . The guitar fell, and striking the floor, jingled somewhere far away in fairy-land. . . . Some very near and intimate friend of Kuzmá Vasílievitch's tenderly and closely embraced him from behind, and adjusted his neckerchief. Kuzmá Vasílievitch saw right before his very face, the hooked nose, thick moustache and piercing eyes of the stranger with the three-buttoned cuff . . . and, although the eyes were in the place of the moustache, and the moustache was in the place of the eyes, and the nose itself was upside down, still, Kuzmá Vasílievitch was not in the least surprised, but, on the contrary, thought that that was the way it ought to be; he was even preparing to say, "how are you, brother Grigóry," to that face, but changed his intention, and preferred . . . . preferred to set out immediately with the Humming-bird for Constantinople, for their approaching marriage, as she was a Turk, and the emperor had promoted him to be a real Turk.

XXII

By the way, there was a boat in front of him; he set his foot in it, and, although, through his awkwardness, he stumbled, and hurt himself rather badly, so that, for some time, he did not know where he was, still, he recovered himself, and seating himself in the boat, he floated off on that great stream, which, in the form of the River of Time, flows on the map on the wall of the Nikoláeff gymnasium, in Constantinople. With great pleasure did he glide along that river and observe a multitude of red grebes which kept incessantly coming to meet him; but they would not let him approach, and, diving, turned into round, rosy spots. And the Humming-bird was floating with him; but, in order to protect herself from the sultry heat, she had placed herself under the boat, and knocked on the bottom, from time to time. . . . Here, at last, was Constantinople.

The houses were in the shape of Tyrolean hats, as it is proper that houses should be; and the Turks have such large, stately faces; only, it is not well to look too long at them: they begin to writhe and make grimaces, and after that, they go all to pieces, like melted snow. And here is the palace, in which he is to dwell with the Humming-bird. . . . And everything in it is so capitally arranged! The walls embroidered with the general's pattern, epaulets everywhere, men blowing trumpets in the corners, and one can float into the drawing-room in the boat. Well, of course, there 's a portrait of Mahomet. . . . Only, the Humming-bird always runs on ahead through the rooms, and her braids of hair trail after her on the floor, and she positively will not turn round, and she grows smaller and smaller. . . . . And it is no longer the Humming-bird, but a little boy in a round jacket, and he is the child's tutor, and he must crawl after that boy into the sewer-pipe, and the pipe gets tighter and tighter, all the time, and now it is impossible for him to move any more . . . either forward or backward, and it is impossible to breathe, and something has crashed down on his back . . . and there is earth in his mouth. . . .

XXIII

KUZMÁ VASÍLIEVITCH opens his eyes. All around it is light, quiet . . . . there is an odour of vinegar, of mint. Over him, and at his sides, is something white; he looks more closely: it is the canopy of a bed. He tries to raise his head . . . and cannot; his hand . . . . he cannot do that, either. What does it mean? He drops his eyes. . . . There is a long body stretched out in front of him, and over that body there is a woollen coverlet, yellow, with a light-brown border. The body appears to belong to him, Kuzmá Vasílievitch. He tries to cry out . . . . no sound results. He tries again, he exerts all his strength. . . . A quavering moan resounds, and trembles beneath his nose. Heavy footsteps become audible, a sinewy hand draws aside the bed-curtains. A grey-haired invalid-soldier, in a patched military cloak, stands in front of him, and gazes at him. . . . . And he stares at the old soldier. A large pewter jug is put to Kuzmá Vasílievitch's lips. Kuzmá Vasílievitch eagerly quaffs the cold water. His tongue is limbered.—" Where am I ? " —The old soldier takes another survey of him, goes off, and returns with another man, in a dark uniform.—" Where am I ? "—repeats Kuzmá Vasílievitch.—" Well, now he will live,"—says the man in uniform.—" You are in the hospital,"

—he adds aloud,—"but please rest in quiet. It is injurious for you to talk." Kuzmá Vasílievitch is on the point of feeling surprised, but again falls into unconsciousness. . . .

On the following morning the doctor made his appearance. Kuzmá Vasílievitch had come to himself. The doctor congratulated him on his recovery, and gave orders that his head should be bandaged.

"What? My head? Why, have I . . . ."

"You must not talk, you must not worry,"—interrupted the doctor.—"And now lie quietly, and return thanks to the Almighty Creator. Where are the compresses, Poplyóvkin?"

"But where is the money . . . the government . . . ."

"Come! he has begun to rave again. . . More ice, Poplyóvkin!"

XXIV

ANOTHER week passed. Kuzmá Vasílievitch had improved to such a degree that the doctors found it possible to impart to him what had happened to him. This is what he learned.

On the sixteenth of June, at seven o'clock in the evening, he had visited Madame Fritsche's house for the last time; and on the seventeenth of June, about dinner-time, that is to say, nearly twenty-four hours later, a shepherd had found

him in the ravine, near the great Khersón highway, two versts from Nikoláeff, with a broken
head, and crimson splotches on his neck. His
uniform and waistcoat were unbuttoned, all his
pockets were turned inside out, his cap and dirk
were missing, so also was his leather belt with the
money. Judging from the trampled grass, from
the broad trail on the sand and clay, it was possible to draw the deduction that the unlucky lieutenant had been dragged to the bottom of the ravine, and only there had he been dealt that blow
on the head, not with an axe, but with a sword,—
probably with his own dirk. Along the entire
trail, beginning at the highway, not a drop of
blood was observable, but around his head stood
a perfect pool. There was no doubt of the fact
that his murderers had first drugged him, then
tried to strangle him, and, carrying him by night
out of the town, had dragged him to the ravine,
and there had dealt him the final blow. Kuzmá
Vasílievitch had not died, thanks solely to his
truly iron constitution.

He had come to his senses on the twenty-second
of July, that is to say, five whole weeks afterward.

XXV

Kuzmá Vasílievitch immediately reported to
his superior authorities the misfortune which had
overtaken him, set forth all the circumstances

of the affair verbally, and on paper, and communicated the address of Madame Fritsche. The
police rushed to the house indicated, but found
no one in it; the birds had already abandoned the
nest. They seized the owner of the house; but
got very little satisfaction from that owner, a
very aged and deaf petty burgher. He himself
resided in another ward, and knew only one thing.
Four months previously, he had rented his house
to a Jewess with a passport, in the name of
Schmul or Schmulke, which he had immediately
recorded at the police-station.—"Another Jewess joined her,"—so he deposed,—and she also
had a passport,—but what handicraft they exer-
cised he did not know; and whether they had other
lodgers was also a point on which he had heard
nothing and knew nothing; but the young fellow
who had lived in that house, in the capacity of
yard-porter or watchman, had gone either to
Odest or to Peter; [1] and the new porter had entered on his duties recently, on the first of July.
—Inquiries were made in the police-office and in
the neighbourhood. It appeared that Schmulke
and her companion, whose real name was Frederika Bengel, had left Nikoláeff about the twentieth of June, but whither they went, no one
knew. No one had seen the mysterious man with
the gipsy face, and three buttons on his cuff, or

[1] Common abbreviations of Odessa and
St. Petersburg.- -TRANSLATOR.

the dark-visaged young girl of foreign extraction, with the huge braids of hair. Kuzmá Vasílievitch himself paid a visit to the house which had proved so fatal for him, as soon as he was discharged from the hospital. In the tiny chamber, where he had chatted with the Humming-bird, and which was still redolent of musk, another door was found, also concealed; during his second visit, the divan had been moved against it, and through it, in all probability, the murderer had entered, and grasped him from behind. Kuzmá Vasílievitch entered a complaint, in proper form. The investigation began. Several numbered reports and writs flew in divers directions; in due time, seizure-papers and search-warrants followed . . . . but there the matter ended. The suspected persons had disappeared without leaving a trace,—and with them had disappeared the stolen government money, nineteen hundred and seventy rubles, and some kopéks, in bank-bills and gold. A sum far from insignificant in those days. Kuzmá Vasílievitch was ten whole years in repaying it, before he was admitted to the benefit of a most gracious imperial manifesto.

XXVI

In the early days, he himself was firmly convinced that Emilia, his crafty "Zuckerpüppchen," was responsible for the whole calamity; was the head of the conspiracy. He recalled how, on the very day of his last tryst with her, he had incautiously taken a nap on the divan, how, on waking, he had beheld her by his side, on her knees, and how disconcerted she had been, and how, in conclusion, on that very evening, he had discovered the slit in his belt, a slit which had, obviously, been made with her scissors.—" She saw,"—thought Kuzmá Vasílievitch; " she told the old devil and the two other devils, she decoyed me, by writing that letter to me . . . and they did me up. But who could have expected that from her! " He evoked before his mental vision the pretty, amiable face of Emilia, her bright little eyes. . . " Women! women! " he kept reiterating, as he gnashed his teeth. " Spawn of crocodiles! " But when he had definitively removed from the hospital to his own house, he learned one particular, which astounded and dumfounded him. On the very day when he was brought, half-dead, back to the town, a young girl, by all the tokens as like Emilia as one drop of water is like another, had rushed to his lodgings, all in tears, with dishevelled hair, and, after inquiring about him from his orderly, had flown to the hospital, like a madwoman. At the hospital, they told her that Kuzmá Vasílievitch must inevitably die, and she had immediately departed, wringing her hands, with an expression of despair on her face. It was plain that she had not foreseen, had not expected, murder. Or, perhaps, they had deceived her—had not given her her promised share? Repentance had suddenly taken possession of her. Nevertheless, she had afterward quitted Nikoláeff, in company with that repulsive old woman, who, most assuredly, knew everything. . . . Kuzmá Vasílievitch lost himself in conjectures, and thoroughly wore out his orderly, by making him incessantly describe afresh the personal appearance of the young girl who had run to his lodgings, and repeat her words.

XXVII

A WHOLE year and a half later, Kuzmá Vasílievitch received from Emilia—*alias* Frederika Bengel—a letter in the German language, which he immediately caused to be translated, and afterward repeatedly exhibited to us. It was variegated with orthographical errors and exclamation-points. On the envelope was the postmark: " Breslau." The following is as faithful a transtion of this letter as it is possible to make:

" My dear, unforgettable and incomparable Florestan ! Mr. Lieutenant Ergenhoff ! How many times I have felt impelled to write to you ! And always, to my regret, I have deferred it, although the thought, that you might regard me as an accomplice in that frightful crime, had always been for me a most murderous thought! Oh, my dear Mr. Lieutenant! Believe me, the day on which I learned, that you were alive and well, was the happiest day of my life! But I have no intention of wholly justifying myself! I will not lie! I really was the first one to discover your habit of carrying money on your stomach! (however, in our country, all butchers and traders do the same!) And I had the imprudence to say a little about it. I even said, in jest, that it would be a good thing to take a little of that money from you! But the old villain (Mr. Florestan, she *was not* my aunt) entered into a conspiracy with that godless monster Luigi, and his accomplice! I swear to you, by the grave of my mother, that to this day I do not know who those people were! All I do know is, that his name was Luigi, and that both of them came from Bucharest, and were, of a surety, great criminals, and were in hiding from the police, and had money and valuable things! Luigi was a frightful fellow (*ein schröckliches Subject*) to kill a fellow-man (*einen Mitmenschen*) who was nothing to him! He talked all languages,—and it was *he* who brought back the things from our cook that time! Don't ask how! He could do everything, everything, he was a frightful man! He assured the old woman, that he would only drug you a little, and then would lead you out and abandon you, and would say, that he knew nothing about it, and that you yourself were to blame . . . . you had tasted too much liquor somewhere or other! But the villain even then had in mind, that it would be better to kill you outright, in order that not even a single cock might crow about it! He wrote you that letter in my name, and the old woman got rid of me by cunning. I suspected nothing, and I was terribly afraid of Luigi. He said to me: " I 'll cut thy throat, I 'll cut it as I would a chicken's ! " And how horribly he twitched his moustache at these words! Besides, they led me off to a certain company. . . . I 'm very much ashamed, Mr. Lieutenant! And even now, I shed bitter tears at these thoughts! . . . . It seems to me . . . . akh! I was not born for such occupations! . . . . But it cannot be helped; and that 's the way it all came about! Then I was dreadfully scared, and had to go away, willy-nilly, because if the police had discovered us, what would have become of me then? That damned Luigi immediately absconded, as soon as he found out that you were still alive. But I speedily parted from all of them, and although I now am frequently without a morsel of bread, yet my soul is at peace! Perhaps you will ask me, why I came to Nikolaeff? But I cannot answer anything! I have taken an oath! I end with a request which is very, very important for me: please, when you think of your little friend Emilia, don't think of her as a black criminal! The eternal God sees my heart. I have a bad morality (*Ich habe eine schlechte Moralität*), and I am giddy, but I am not a criminal. And I shall always love you, and remember my incomparable Florestan, and I shall always wish you everything that is good on the earthly globe (*auf diesem Erdenrund*)! I do not know whether my letter will reach you, but if it does, write me a few lines, that I may see that you have received my letter! Thereby you will make happy your unchangeably devoted Emilia.

"P.S. Write to me under the letters F. E., *poste restante*, in Breslau, in Silesia.

"P.P.S. I have written to you in German; I could not otherwise have expressed my feelings; but do you write to me in Russian."

XXVIII

"WELL, and what did you do? Did you answer her?"—we were wont to ask Kuzmá Vasílievitch.

"I set out to, many a time. I set out to. But how was I to do it? I don't know German, and in Russian . . . . Who would have translated it to her? So I did n't write."

And every time, on finishing his story, Kuzmá Vasílievitch heaved a sigh, shook his head, and said: "That's what it is to be young!" And if among his hearers there chanced to be a novice, who was making acquaintance for the first time with his remarkable tale, he took his hand, laid it on his skull, and made him feel the scar of the wound. . . . The wound really had been terrible, and the scar extended from ear to ear.

A HAPLESS GIRL

(1868)

A HAPLESS GIRL

"YES, yes,"—began Piótr Gavrílovitch,— "those were distressing days . . . . and I would rather not recall them to my memory. . . . But I have made you a promise, so I must relate all. Listen."

I

I WAS living at the time (the winter of 1835), in Moscow, with my aunt, the sister of my deceased mother. I was eighteen years of age, and I had only just been promoted from the second to the third course of the " belles-lettres " faculty (that was what it was called in those days), in the Moscow University. My aunt was a quiet, gentle woman, a widow. She occupied a large wooden house on Ostozhónka Street, warm, extremely warm,—such as, I think, is nowhere to be found outside of Moscow,—and saw almost no one, sat from morning until night in the drawing-room with two companions, sipped

103

flower-tea,[1] laid out patience, and kept incessantly giving orders that the room should be fumigated. The companions would fly into the anteroom; a few minutes later, an old man-servant, in a livery coat, would bring in a brass basin, with a bunch of mint on a hot brick, and treading cautiously along the narrow carpet-walks, sprinkle the mint with vinegar. White steam surged around his wrinkled face, he frowned and turned his head away, and the canary-birds in the dining-room fairly cracked their throats with singing, excited by the hissing of the fumigation.

My aunt was very fond of me, and petted me, orphaned of both father and mother. She gave over the entresol to my sole use. My rooms were very elegantly furnished, not at all in student fashion. The bedroom was adorned with rose-coloured curtains, and a muslin canopy with blue pompons reared itself over the bed. Those pompons somewhat disconcerted me, I must confess: such " dainties " were bound, in my opinion, to lower me in the eyes of my comrades. Even without that, they called me " the institute girl ": I was utterly unable to force myself to smoke tobacco. I was not very studious—why should I conceal my offence?—especially at the beginning of my course. I went out a great deal. My aunt presented me with a roomy sledge, such as gen-

[1] Tea made from the flower-buds and surrounding small leaves at the tips of the sprays on the tea-bush most abounding in sap. Consequently, a very delicate, strong, and expensive tea.—TRANSLATOR.

erals use, with a bearskin laprobe, and a pair of well-fed Vyátka horses.[1] I rarely visited houses of the " gentry," but I was thoroughly at home at the theatre, and ate a tremendous quantity of cakes in the pastry-cooks' shops. Nevertheless, I permitted myself no indecorum, and behaved judiciously, *" en jeune homme de bonne maison."* Nothing could have induced me to pain my kind aunt; and, moreover, my blood flowed rather quietly in my veins.

II

FROM my early youth I had had a passion for chess. I had no comprehension of the theory, but I played far from badly. One day, in a café, I chanced to witness a prolonged chess-battle between two players, one of whom, a fair-haired young man of five-and-twenty, seemed to me a very strong player. The game ended in his favour. I proposed to him to engage in a contest with me. He consented . . . . and in the course of an hour, he beat me, jestingly, thrice in succession.

" You have aptitude for the game,"—he said, in a courteous voice, having probably observed how my self-conceit was suffering,—" but you

[1] Small, plump, spirited horses, generally yellow or sorrel, descended from the Livland cobs which Peter the Great sent to Vyátka. — TRANSLATOR.

do not know the openings. You must read the book of either Allgaier or Petróff."

" Do you think so? But where can I get such a book? "

" Come to my house; I will give it to you."

He mentioned his name, and told me where he lived. On the following day, I went to him; and a week later we had become almost inseparable.

III

THE name of my new acquaintance was Alexander Davídovitch Fústoff. He lived with his mother, a fairly wealthy woman, the widow of a State Councillor,[1] in a small detached house, in complete freedom, just as I did at my aunt's. He was in government service in the Ministry of the Imperial Court. Never before, in my life, had I met a more " sympathetic " young man. Everything about him was pleasing and attractive: his graceful figure, his walk, his voice, and, in particular, his small, delicate face, with its golden-blue eyes, its elegant little nose, which seemed to have been coquettishly modelled, with the perpetually amiable smile on its red lips, with its fair curls of soft hair above the somewhat narrow, but snow-white brow. Fústoff's disposition was characterized by its extreme evenness, and a certain agreeable, reserved affability; he never was gloomy, he was

1 A titular rank, in Peter the Great's Table of Ranks.—TRANSLATOR.

always pleased with everybody; on the other hand, he never went into raptures over anything. All superfluity, even in a good emotion, offended him: " That 's savage, savage," he was wont to say in such a case, with a slight shrug of his shoulders, and a slight narrowing of his golden eyes. And those eyes of Fústoff were wonderful! They constantly expressed sympathy, goodwill, and even devoted affection. It was not until later on that I noticed that the expression of his eyes depended solely upon their peculiar shape, and that it underwent no change even when he was eating soup or lighting a cigar. His punctiliousness became a proverb among us. His grandmother had been a German, it is true. Nature had endowed him with various talents. He was a capital dancer; he rode with foppish elegance, and was a superb swimmer; he did carpentry, turned on a lathe, pasted, did bookbinding, cut out silhouettes, drew bouquets of flowers in watercolors, or Napoleon in profile, in a blue uniform, played with feeling on the zither, knew a multitude of tricks at cards and so on, and had considerable knowledge of mechanics, physics, and chemistry, but all with limitations. Languages alone he could not conquer: he expressed himself very badly even in French. On the whole, he talked little, and in our student discussions he participated chiefly by the vivacious softness of his gaze and smile. There was no doubt whatever that Fústoff was liked by the fair sex, but he was not fond of dilating on that very important topic for young men; and he thoroughly deserved the nickname which his comrades had bestowed upon him, " the modest Don Juan." I did not admire Fústoff: there was nothing to admire in him; but I prized his good-will, although, as a matter of fact, it displayed itself solely herein, that he admitted me to his presence at all times. In my eyes, Fústoff was the happiest man on earth. His life flowed as smoothly as though oiled. His mother, brothers, sisters, aunts, uncles, all adored him; he dwelt with them on remarkably good terms, and enjoyed the reputation of being a model relative.

IV

One day I ran in to see him rather early, and did not find him in his study. He called to me from the adjoining room. Sounds of snorting and splashing were borne thence to my ears. Every morning Fústoff douched himself with cold water, and for a quarter of an hour afterward devoted himself to gymnastic exercises, in which he had attained to noteworthy proficiency. He did not tolerate superfluous anxiety over bodily health, but neither did he forget the indispensable. (" Do not forget yourself, do not get excited, work in moderation!" was his motto.) Fústoff had not yet made his appearance when the outside door of the room in which I was was thrown open, and there entered a man of fifty, in a uniform frock-coat, squat, thick-set, with eyes of a milky-whitish hue in a reddish-brown face, and a regular cap of curly grey hair. This man came to a standstill, looked at me, opened his huge mouth wide, and burst into a metallic horse-laugh, dealt himself a smart slap, with the palm of his hand, on his hip, and as he did so, kicked his leg high up in front.

"Iván Demyánitch?"—inquired my friend from behind the door.

"The very man,"—responded the newcomer. —"But what are you about? completing your toilet? That's right! That's right!" (The voice of the man named Iván Demyánitch had a metallic ring, just as his laugh had.) "I was all wound up to give that little scamp of a brother of yours a lesson; but he has caught cold, you know, and does nothing but sneeze. He isn't in working order. So I ran in here to you, for a bit, to get warmed up."

Again Iván Demyánitch gave vent to that strange guffaw, again he slapped himself resoundingly on the thigh, and pulling a checked handkerchief from his pocket, he blew his nose noisily, rolling his eyes savagely the while; and spitting into his handkerchief, he exclaimed at the top of his lungs: "Phe-e-ew!"

Fústoff entered the room, and giving a hand to each of us, asked us whether we were acquainted with each other.

" No, sir! "—thundered Iván Demyánitch, instantly,—" the veteran of the year '12 has not that honour! "

Fústoff first mentioned my name, then, pointing at " the veteran of the year '12," he said: " Iván Demyánitch Ratsch, instructor in—various subjects."

" Precisely, precisely, in various subjects,"—chimed in Mr. Ratsch. " When you come to think of it, what all have I not taught, what all am not I teaching now? Mathematics, and geography, and statistics, and Italian bookkeeping, ha-ha-ha-ha! and music! Do you doubt it, my dear sir? "—he suddenly attacked me.—" Ask Alexander Davíditch how I distinguish myself on the bassoon? What sort of a Bohemian, that is to say, a Czech, should I be otherwise? Yes, sir, I 'm a Czech, and my native place is ancient Prague! By the way, Alexander Davíditch, why have n't I seen you this long time past? We might have played a duet . . . . ha-ha! Really! "

" I was at your house day before yesterday, Iván Demyánitch,"—replied Fústoff.

" Why, I call that a long time ago, ha-ha! "

When Mr. Ratsch laughed, his white eyes rolled from side to side in a strange and uneasy way.

" I see, young man, that you are surprised at my behaviour,"—he again addressed himself to me.—" But that arises from the fact that you do not yet know my constitution. Do you make inquiries about me from our good Alexander Davíditch. What will he tell you? He will tell you that old Ratsch is a simpleton. Russian, if not by birth, at least in spirit, ha-ha! I was named in baptism Johann Dietrich, but my appellation is Iván Demyánoff! What I think, that I say; I wear my heart on my sleeve, as the saying is; I won't have anything to do with these diverse ceremonies! Damn them! Run in to see me some evening, you 'll see for yourself. My woman— my wife, that is to say—is simple also; she 'll stew and bake for us . . . . an awful lot! Am I telling the truth, Alexander Davíditch? "

Fústoff merely smiled, and I held my peace.

" Don't scorn the old man, do run in,"—went on Mr. Ratsch.—" But now . . . ." (He snatched a thick silver watch from his pocket, and held it up to his protruding right eye). " I suppose I had better take myself off. Another child is waiting for me. . . . The devil knows what I am teaching that one . . . mythology, I vow! And he lives so far away, the rogue! At the Red Gate! Never mind; I 'll trudge off there afoot, seeing your brother has made a miss of it; and, on the other hand, my fifteen kopéks for a drózhky will remain safely in my pocket! Ha-

ha! I beg to take my leave, my fine gentlemen; see you later! And as for you, young man, drop in to see me. . . . What 's that? . . . . We certainly must play a duet!"—shouted Mr. Ratsch from the anteroom, as he put on his galoshes with a bang, and his metallic laugh rang out for the last time.

V

"WHAT a strange man!"—I said to Fústoff, who had already succeeded in getting to work at his turning-lathe.—" Can it be possible that he is a foreigner? He speaks Russian so vigorously."

" He is a foreigner; only, he settled in Russia thirty years ago. Some prince or other brought him from abroad, in the capacity of secretary . . . . or, rather, one may assume, in that of valet, about the year eighteen hundred and two. But he really does express himself fluently in Russian."

" So boldly and daringly, with such tricks and twists of speech," I put in.

" Well, yes. Only, it 's very unnatural. They 're all like that, those Russianized Germans."

" But he is a Czech."

" I don't know; perhaps so. He talks German with his wife."

" But why does he boast of being a veteran of
the year '12? Did he really serve in the militia? "

"In the militia, indeed! During the conflagration he remained in Moscow, and lost
all his property. . . That 's all his service
amounts to."

" But why did he remain in Moscow? "

Fústoff did not cease his work at the lathe.

" The Lord knows. I have heard that he acted
as a spy for us; but that must be empty talk. But
that he received compensation from the government for his losses is a fact."

"He wears a uniform dress-coat. . . So he is
in the service? "

" Yes. He is an instructor in the cadet corps.
He is a Court Councillor."

" What is his wife like? "

" She 's a German of this town, the daughter
of a sausage-dealer . . . a butcher. . ."

" And do you go often to his house? "

" Yes."

" Well, is it jolly at their house? "

" Fairly jolly."

" And has he children? "

" Yes. By the German woman three, and by
his first wife a son and a daughter."

" And how old is the eldest daughter? "

" Twenty-five."

It seemed to me that Fústoff bent lower over
the lathe, and that the wheel began to revolve

more rapidly under the measured thrusts of his foot.

" Is she pretty? "

" That depends on one's taste. She has a striking face, and, altogether, she is a . . . . striking individual."

"Aha!" I thought. Fústoff continued his work with special zeal, and to my next question he replied only by a grunt.

" I must make her acquaintance! "—I decided, in my own mind.

VI

A few days later, Fústoff and I went to spend the evening with Mr. Ratsch. He lived in a wooden house with a large yard and garden, in Krivóy (Crooked) Lane, near the Pretchístenka [1] Boulevard. He came out into the ante-room to us, received us, and having greeted us with his peculiar chattering guffaw and din, he immediately led us into the drawing-room, where he introduced me to a fat lady in a tight-fitting camlet gown, Eleonora Kárpovna, his wife. Eleonora Kárpovna had, probably, in her early youth, been distinguished for what the French, heaven knows why, call " the beauty of the devil," that is to say, by freshness; but when I made her

---

[1] That is: All-pure; referring to the Virgin Mother. Religious nomenclature for streets is common in Russia.—Translator.

acquaintance, she involuntarily suggested to the vision a good piece of beef which the butcher had just laid out on a clean marble table. Not without intention have I employed the word "clean." Not only did the mistress of the house appear to be a model of cleanliness, but everything around her also,—everything in the house was fairly polished and shining; everything had been scrubbed, ironed, washed with soap; the samovár on the round table blazed like a conflagration; the curtains at the windows, and the napkins, were fairly curling with starch, as well as the frocks and chemisettes of Mr. Ratsch's four children, who sat there, sturdy, well-fed little creatures, bearing a great resemblance to their mother, with rough-hewn, strong faces, whorls of hair on their temples, and red, stubby fingers. All four had rather flat noses, thick, swollen-looking lips, and tiny, light-grey eyes.

"Here 's my guard!"—exclaimed Mr. Ratsch, laying his heavy hand, in turn, on the children's heads.—"Kólya, Ólya, Sáshka, and Máshka![1] This one is eight, this one is seven, this one is four, and this one full two years old! Ha-ha-ha! As you see, my wife and I are not idle! Ehe? Eleonora Kárpovna?"

"You are always saying that sort of thing,"—said Eleonora Kárpovna, and turned away.

---

[1] Constantine, Olga, Alexander (or Alexandra), and Mary (Molly).—TRANSLATOR.

" And she has given all her squalling brats such Russian names! "—went on Mr. Ratsch.—" The first you know, she 'll be having them baptised into the Greek faith! By heaven, she will! She 's a regular Slav; devil take me altogether, if there 's any German blood in her! Eleonora Kárpovna, are you a Slav? "

Eleonora Kárpovna waxed angry.

" I 'm a Court Councilloress, that 's what I am! And that 's as much as to say that I 'm a Russian lady, and everything that you are now going to say . . . . "

" That is, it 's simply awful the way she loves Russia! "—interrupted Iván Demyánitch.—" In the nature of an earthquake! "

" Well, and what of that? "—pursued Eleonora Kárpovna.—" And, of course, I love Russia because where else could I have obtained a title of nobility? And now my children are noble, too, are n't they? Kólya, *sitze ruhig mit den Füssen!* "

Ratsch waved his hand at her.

" Well, calm thyself, Tzarítza Sumbéka![1] And where 's the ' noble ' Viktórka? I think he 's prowling about at random, still! He 'll hit upon an inspector one of these days! He 'll get a thrashing! *Das ist ein Bummler, der Fiktor!* "

" *Dem Fiktor kann ich nicht kommandiren,*

---

[1] The legend of the lovely and unhappy Tatár Tzarítza is connected with " Sumbéka's Tower," in Kazán.—TRANSLATOR.

Iván Demyánitch. *Sie wissen wohl!*"—growled
Eleonora Kárpovna.

I glanced at Fústoff, as though desirous of
finding out from him definitively what made
him visit such people . . . . but, at that moment,
there entered the room a tall young girl in a black
gown, that eldest daughter of Mr. Ratsch, whom
Fústoff had mentioned. . . . I understood the
reason for my friend's frequent visits.

VII

I REMEMBER that somewhere Shakspeare speaks
of "a white dove amid a flock of black crows."
The young girl who entered produced upon me
a similar impression. There was too little in common between her and the world which surrounded
her. It seemed as though she herself were secretly perplexed and amazed at finding herself
there. All the members of Mr. Ratsch's family
looked like self-satisfied and good-natured robust
persons. *Her* beautiful face, which was, however,
already past its first bloom, bore the imprint of
dejection, pride, and sickliness. The others, obvious plebeians, bore themselves unconstrainedly,
even coarsely, if you like, but simply; mournful
trepidation exhaled from the whole of her indubitably aristocratic being. In her personal appearance there was no perceptible characteristic
of German descent; she resembled, rather, a na-

tive of the South. Her extremely thick black
hair, without a particle of lustre; her sunken eyes,
black also and dull, but beautiful; her low, protruding brow, her aquiline nose, the greenish
pallor of her smooth skin, a certain tragic line
about the thin lips and in the slightly hollow
cheeks, something harsh, and, at the same time,
helpless in her movements,—elegance without
grace . . . . in Italy, all this would not have
seemed unusual to me, but in Moscow, on the
Pretchístenka Boulevard, it simply astounded
me! I rose from my chair when she entered the
room; she flung at me a swift, uneven glance, and
lowering her black eyelashes, seated herself near
the window, " like Tatyána " (Púshkin's " Onyé-
gin " was then fresh in the minds of every one
of us). I glanced at Fústoff, but my friend was
standing with his back toward me, and accepting
a cup of tea from the plump hands of Eleonora
Kárpovna. I noticed, also, that the young girl
who had just entered had brought with her a
light current of physical cold. . . . " What sort
of a statue is that? " I thought to myself.

VIII

" Piótr Gravrílitch!"—thundered Mr. Ratsch,
addressing me,—" permit me to make you acquainted with my . . . . with my number one,
ha-ha-ha! with Susanna Ivánovna!"

A HAPLESS GIRL

I bowed in silence, and immediately said to myself: "There, her name does not match the others, either," but Susanna rose slightly, without smiling and without unclasping her tightly-clenched hands.

"And how about the duet,"—went on Iván Demyánitch,—"Alexander Davíditch? Hey? benefactor! You left your zither with us, and I have already taken the bassoon out of its case. Let 's tickle the ears of the honourable company." (Mr. Ratsch was fond of adorning his Russian; [1] he was incessantly breaking out into expressions like those wherewith all the ultra-popular poems of Prince Vyázemsky are variegated. I remember that one day Iván Demyánitch, carried away by his predilection for daring words with an energetic termination, began to assure me that his garden was full of limestone, fallen trees, and brushwood.[2])—"What say you? Is it a go?"—exclaimed Iván Demyánitch, perceiving that Fústoff did not turn round.—"Kólka, march to the study, fetch hither the stands! Ólya, haul along the zither! And be so good as to give us a candle for the music-stands, lovey-dovey!"—(Mr. Ratsch was spinning around the room like a top.)—"Piótr Gavrílitch, you love music, don't you? But

[1] In this case, he said "ushesa" (which is vulgar), instead of "ushi," ears. The author gives three other untranslatable specimens at this point.—Translator.

[2] Izvestnyák, khvorostník, and valézhnyak.—Translator.

119

if you don't, just engage in conversation; only,
look out and see that it 's with the soft pedal!
Ha-ha-ha! And where has that rogue Viktór
disappeared to? He might have listened also!
You 've spoiled him completely, Eleonora Kárpovna!"

Eleonora Kárpovna flared up thoroughly.

" *Aber, was kann ich denn,* Iván Demyánitch?"

"Well, all right, all right; don't nag! *Bleibe
ruhig, hast verstanden?* Alexander Davíditch!
Do me the favour!"

The children forthwith executed their father's
commands; the music-stands were set up, and the
music began. I have already mentioned that Fústoff played admirably on the zither, but that instrument always had the most depressing effect
on me. It has always seemed to me, and it seems
to me to this day, that in the zither there is confined the soul of a decrepit Jew-usurer, and that
it sings in nasal tones, and weeps over the player
who makes it give forth sounds. Neither could
Mr. Ratsch's playing afford me gratification;
added to which his suddenly empurpled face, with
its viciously-rolling white eyes, assumed an ominous expression: exactly as though he were preparing to murder some one with his bassoon, and
were swearing and threatening in advance as he
emitted one after another wonderfully hoarse,
coarse notes! I seated myself beside Susanna,

and, waiting for the first momentary pause, I asked her whether she also were fond of music, like her father.

She drew back as though I had struck her, and said abruptly:—" Who? "

" Your father,"—I repeated,—" Mr. Ratsch."

" Mr. Ratsch is not my father."

" Not your father! Pardon me. . . . I must have misunderstood. . . . But I remember that Alexander Davíditch . . . ."

Susanna gazed at me intently and shyly.

" You did not understand Mr. Fústoff. Mr. Ratsch is my stepfather."

I made no reply.

" And you are not fond of music? "—I began again.

Again Susanna shot a glance at me. Decidedly, there was something wild about her eyes. She, evidently, had not expected, and did not desire, a continuation of conversation.

" I did not tell you that,"—she slowly articulated.

" Tru-tu-tu-tu-tu-u-u . . . ." grumbled the bassoon, with sudden fury, as it executed the concluding fioritura. I turned round, saw Mr. Ratsch's red neck puffed out, like that of a boa-constrictor, beneath his protruding ears, and he seemed very repulsive to me.

" But, surely, you do not like that . . . . instrument,"—I said in a low tone.

"No . . . . I don't like it,"—she replied, as though she understood my covert innuendo.

"Just so!"—I thought, as though delighted at something.

"Susanna Ivánovna"—said Eleonora Kár-povna suddenly, in her German-Russian jargon —"is very fond of music, and plays beautifully herself on the piano, only, she will not play on the piano when she is much urged to play."

Susanna made no reply to Eleonora Kárpovna —she did not even look at her—and merely turned her eyes slightly, under their downcast lids, in her direction. From this movement alone —from the movement of her pupils—I was able to gather the nature of the sentiments which Susanna cherished toward the second spouse of her stepfather. . . . And again I rejoiced at something or other.

In the meantime the duet had come to an end. Fústoff rose, and approaching, with irresolute steps, the window near which Susanna and I were sitting, he asked her whether she had received from Lengold the music which the latter had promised to order from Petersburg.

"The potpourri from 'Robert le Diable,'"— he added, turning to me; "from that new opera about which every one is making such an uproar in this country just now."

"No, I have not received it,"—replied Susanna; and turning her face toward the window, she hastily whispered:—"Please, Alexander Davíditch, I beg of you, do not make me play to-day! I am not at all in the mood for it."

"What 's that? Meyerbeer's 'Robert le Diable!'"—roared Iván Demyánitch, approaching us.—"A capital thing, I 'll wager! He 's a Jew, and all Jews are born musicians, just as all Czechs are! Especially the Jews. Is n't that so, Susanna Ivánovna? Hey? Ha-ha-ha-ha!"

In Mr. Ratsch's last words, and even in his laugh, on this occasion, there was audible something different from his habitual jeering—there was audible a desire to wound. So, at least, it seemed to me, and in that sense did Susanna understand it. She involuntarily shuddered, flushed scarlet, and bit her lower lip. A brilliant point, resembling the glitter of a tear, flashed on her eyelashes, and hastily rising, she left the room.

"Where are you going, Susanna Ivánovna?"
—shouted Mr. Ratsch after her.

"You let her alone, Iván Demyánitch,"—interposed Eleonora Kárpovna.—"Wenn sie einmal so etwas im Kopfe hat . . . ."

"A nervous nature,"—remarked Ratsch, wheeling round on his heels, and he slapped himself on his thigh,—"the plexus solaris suffers. Oh! you need n't look at me like that, Piótr Gavrílitch! I have studied anatomy, ha-ha! And I can exercise the art of healing! Just ask Eleo-

nora Kárpovna here. . . . I treat all her indispo-
sitions! I have a method of my own."

" You always must have your joke, Iván
Demyánitch,"—replied the latter, with satisfaction, while Fústoff, laughing, and swaying pleas-
antly to and fro, gazed at the husband and wife.

" And why should n't I joke, *mein Mütter-
chen?* "—put in Iván Demyánitch.—" Life is
given to us to use, and chiefly for ornament, as
a certain well-known poet has said. Wipe thy
nose, Kólka, thou porcupine! "

IX

" THANKS to thee, I was placed in a very awkward position to-day,"—I said that same evening to Fústoff, as we were returning home together. — " Thou didst tell me that that . . . .
what 's her name? Susanna,—was Ratsch's
daughter, but she is his stepdaughter."

" Really! Did I tell thee that she was his
daughter? However . . . . what difference
does it make? "

" That Ratsch,"—I went on . . . . " akh, Alexander! how I do dislike him! Hast thou observed with what peculiar derision he expressed
himself to-day in her presence about Jews? Can
it be that she . . . is a Jewess? "

Fústoff was walking in front, swinging his

arms; it was cold; the snow crunched like salt under foot.

"Yes, I remember having heard something of that sort,"—he said at last. . . . . "Her mother was of Jewish extraction, I believe."

"So Mr. Ratsch married a widow for his first wife?"

"Probably."

"H'm! . . . . And that Viktór, who did not come to-day,—is his stepson?"

"No . . . he is his own son. But, as thou art aware, I do not meddle with other people's business, and do not like to ask questions. I am not curious."

I bit my tongue. Fústoff continued to hurry on ahead. As we approached the house, I overtook him, and looked into his face.

"Well,"—I asked,—"is Susanna really a fine musician?"

Fústoff frowned.

"She plays well on the piano,"—he muttered between his teeth.—"Only, she 's very shy, I warn you!"—he added, with a slight shrug of the shoulders. He seemed to be sorry that he had introduced me to her.

I relapsed into silence, and we parted.

X

ON the following morning I again betook myself to Fústoff's house. It had become a necessity for me to sit with him of a morning. He
received me affectionately, as usual; but of our
visit on the preceding evening—not a word! It
was as though he had filled his mouth with water.
I began to turn over the leaves of the last number
of *The Telescope.*

A new person entered the room. It turned out
to be that same son of Mr. Ratsch, Viktór, of
whose absence on the evening before his father
had complained.

He was a young fellow of eighteen years, already given to drink, and unhealthy; a button
was missing from his uniform overcoat, one of his
boots was burst, and he fairly reeked with tobacco.

" Good morning,"—he said, in a hoarse voice,
and with those peculiar twitches of the head and
shoulders which I have always observed in petted
and conceited young men.—" I thought of going
to the university, but landed at your house. My
chest is stuffed up, somehow. Give me a cigar."
—He walked the whole length of the room, languidly dragging his feet and without taking his
hands out of the pockets of his trousers, and flung
himself heavily on the couch.

" Have you caught a cold? "—asked Fústoff,

and introduced us to each other. We were both
students, but were in different faculties.

"No! . . . The idea! Last night, I admit . . . ." (here Mr. Ratsch, junior, smiled to
the full extent of his mouth, not unpleasantly,
but his teeth were bad) "we had a drinking-bout
—a hearty drinking-bout. Yes."—He lighted
his cigar, and cleared his throat.—"We were
giving Obikhódoff a send-off."

"And where is he going?"

"To the Caucasus, and he's taking his lady-
love along with him. You know, that black-eyed
girl with the freckles. The fool!"

"Your father was asking after you last night,"
—remarked Fústoff.

Viktór spat to one side.

"Yes; so I heard. You strayed into our camp
last night. Well, and what happened? Did you
make music?"

"As usual."

"And *she*. . . . She put on airs in the presence of the new visitor, I suppose?" (Here he
jerked his head in my direction.) "She would n't
play?"

"Of whom are you speaking?"—inquired
Fústoff.

"Why, of the most respected Susanna Ivánovna, of course!"

Viktór settled himself in a still more comfortable lounging position, raised his hand in a crook

above his head, inspected his palm, and emitted a dull snort.

I darted a glance at Fústoff. He merely shrugged his shoulders, as though desirous of giving me to understand that it was useless to interrogate such a lout.

XI

Viktór began to talk, as he stared at the ceiling, in a leisurely manner, through his nose, about the theatre, about a couple of actors of his acquaintance, about a certain Serafíma Serafímovna, who had " fooled " him, about the new professor, R., whom he designated as a beast,—because, " just imagine, what do you suppose the monster has devised? He calls the roll at the beginning of every lecture, and regards himself as a liberal, to boot! "— and, at last, turning his face and his whole body toward Fústoff, he said, in a half-complaining, half-jesting voice:

" I want to ask you something, Alexander Davíditch. . . . Can't you, somehow or other, bring my old man to reason? . . . You play duets with him, you see. . . He gives me five blue bank-bills[1] a month. . . . What does that amount to? ! It does n't pay for my tobacco. And he says, besides: 'Don't run in debt!' I 'd like to put him in my place, and see how he 'd

[1] The old blue bank-bill was for five rubles.—Translator.

manage! But, you see, I don't receive any pension. I 'm not like *some folks*" (Viktór pronounced this last word with a peculiar emphasis). "But he has a lot of cash, I know! There 's no use in singing poor Lazarus to me; you can't fool me! You 're just joking! And he has warmed his hands with bribes, too . . . . he 's a sly one!"

Fústoff looked askance at Viktór.

"I will mention it to your father, if you like," —he began. "Or, if you wish, I can . . . . in the meantime . . . lend you a small sum. . . ."

"No, what 's the use? It 's a great deal better to wheedle the old man. . . . However,"—added Viktór, scratching his nose with all five fingers, —"give me twenty-five rubles, if you can. . . . How much do I owe you, pray?"

"You have borrowed eighty-five rubles from me."

"Yes. . . Well, this will make one hundred and ten in all. I 'll give it to you in a lump."

Fústoff went into the next room, brought a twenty-five ruble bill, and handed it in silence to Viktór. The latter took it, yawned at the top of his lungs, without covering his mouth, grunted: "Thanks!" and writhing and stretching himself, he rose from the couch.

"Phew! but . . . . somehow, I 'm bored,"— he muttered. "I think I 'll go to *Italy*." He went toward the door.

Fústoff watched him. He seemed to be contending with himself.

"What pension was that to which you just alluded, Viktór Ivánitch?"—he asked at last.

Viktór halted on the threshold, and put on his cap.

"Why, don't you understand? Susanna Ivánovna's pension. . . . She receives it. 'T is a very curious anecdote, I assure you! I 'll tell you about it some day. Such doings, my dear fellow, such doings! But my old man, don't you forget my old man, please. He 's got a tough, German hide, of course, but with a Russian dressing, and so it can be pierced. Only, don't let Eleonorka, my stepmother, be present on that occasion! Papa is afraid of her; she intends everything for her own brats. Well, you 're a diplomat! Good-bye!"

"What trash that horrid little boy is, anyway!" —exclaimed Fústoff, as soon as the door slammed.

His face was blazing like fire, and he turned away from me. I did not attempt to question him, and soon went away.

XII

I SPENT the whole of that day in meditating about Fústoff, about Susanna, about her relatives; I dimly perceived something in the nature of a family drama. So far as I could judge, my friend was not indifferent to Susanna. But she? Did she love him? Why did she seem so unhappy? And, in general, what sort of a being was she? These questions recurred incessantly to my mind. An obscure but powerful instinct told me that it was not proper for me to apply to Fústoff to solve them. It ended in my setting off alone for Mr. Ratsch's house on the following day.

I suddenly felt very conscience-stricken and awkward as soon as I found myself in the tiny, dark anteroom. " She will not show herself, probably," flashed through my mind. " I shall have to sit with that disgusting veteran and his cook of a wife. . . . But even if she should show herself, what of that? She will not enter into conversation. . . She treated me far from amiably the other day. Why have I come? " While I was revolving all this in my mind, the page ran to announce me, and after two or three perplexed exclamations of: " Who is it? Who, sayest thou? " a heavy shuffling of slippers became audible in the adjoining room, and in the crack between the two leaves of the door, the face of Iván Demyánitch, a dishevelled and surly face, presented itself. It riveted its eyes on me, and did not immediately change its expression. . . . Evidently, Mr. Ratsch did not at once recognise me. But suddenly his cheeks grew round, his eyes narrowed, and from his mouth, as it opened, there

burst forth the exclamation, accompanied by a
guffaw:—" Ah, my dear fellow, my most respected! Is that you? Pray enter!"

I followed him the more unwillingly because it
seemed to me that that courteous, jovial Mr.
Ratsch was inwardly consigning me to the devil.
However, there was no escape. He conducted
me to the drawing-room, and what did I see? Susanna, seated in front of a table, with the income
and expenditure book. She cast a glance at me
with her gloomy eyes, and slightly gnawed the
nails on her left hand . . . it was a habit of hers,
I had observed—a habit peculiar to nervous people. There was no one in the room except herself.

" Here, sir,"—began Mr. Ratsch, and slapped
his thigh,—" see at what an occupation you have
caught Susanna Ivánovna and me: we are busy
with our accounts. My wife is not strong in
' arikhmetik,' and I am saving my eyes, I must
confess. I can't read without glasses, so what
would you have me do? Let the young people
toil, ha-ha! Order demands it. However, there's
no hurry about the matter. . . . Hurry, make
yourself ridiculous to catch fleas, ha-ha!"

Susanna closed the book, and rose to go.

" Stay; come, stay,"—said Mr. Ratsch.—
" Where 's the harm, if thou art not dressed
up?" . . . . (Susanna had on a very old gown,
almost fit for a child, with short sleeves.)—" Our

dear guest will not be exacting, and I 'd like to clear up only the last week but one. . . . You will permit? "—he turned to me.—" You and I are not on ceremonious terms, you know."

" Pray, do; do not disturb yourselves,"—I exclaimed.

" Just so, my most respected sir. You know the late Emperor, Alexéi Mikhaílovitch Románoff was wont to say: ' For business, time; for diversion, a minute!' And we will devote one minute to business . . . . ha-ha! What 's this thirty rubles, thirty kopéks? "—he added, in an undertone, turning his back on me.

" Viktór borrowed it from Eleonora Kárpovna; he said that you had given him permission,"—replied Susanna, likewise in an undertone.

" He said . . . he said . . . . I had given permission . . . ." growled Iván Demyánitch. " It strikes me that I was there on hand. They might have asked me. And to whom did these seventeen rubles go? "

" To the furniture-dealer."

" Yes . . . the furniture-dealer. . What was it for? "

" On account."

" On account. Show me! "—He snatched the book from Susanna, and placing astride his nose a pair of round-eyed, silver-mounted spectacles, he began to pass his finger over the lines.—" To the furniture-dealer . . . the furniture-dealer. . . . All you think of is to get money out of the house! You 're glad of it! . . . . *Wie die Croaten!* On account! However,"—he added in a loud voice, again turning his face toward me, and pulling off his spectacles,—" why should I do this, after all! I can attend to these dirty affairs later. Susanna Ivánovna, be so good as to carry off this bookkeeping to its proper place, and then please return to us, and enrapture the ears of this amiable visitor with your musical instrument; that is to say, by playing on the piano. . . . Hey?"

Susanna turned away her head.

" I should be very happy,"—I hastened to say; —" it would give me great pleasure to hear Susanna Ivánovna play. But I would not, on any account, incommode . . . ."

" Incommode, indeed! What do you mean? Come, now, Susanna Ivánovna, *eins, zwei, drei!*"

Susanna made no reply, and left the room.

XIII

I DID not expect that she would return; but she speedily made her appearance again: she had not even changed her gown; and, seating herself in the corner, she cast a couple of attentive glances at me. Whether it was that she instinctively recognised, in my behaviour to her, that involuntary respect which I could not even explain to myself,

which, more than curiosity, more even than sympathy, she aroused in me,—whether it was that
she was in a softened frame of mind on that day,
at all events, she suddenly went to the piano, and
irresolutely laying her hand on the keys, and
turning her head a little over her shoulder toward
me, she asked me what I would like to have her
play? Before I could answer, she seated herself,
got her music, hastily spread it out, and began
to play. I had loved music from my childhood;
but at that time, I still understood little about
it, was not much acquainted with the compositions
of the great masters, and had not Mr. Ratsch
growled out with some dissatisfaction: " Aha!
wieder dieser Beethoven! " I could not have
guessed what Susanna was playing. It was, as
I learned later on, the famous Sonata in F
Minor, opus 57. Susanna's playing surprised me
beyond description. I had not expected such
force, such fire, such dashing boldness. From the
very first bars of the impetuously-passionate alle-
gro at the beginning of the sonata, I felt that
stupor, that chill and sweet terror of rapture
which instantaneously makes its way into the soul
when beauty invades it with unexpected assault.
I did not move a single member until the very
end; I kept wanting, yet not daring, to sigh. I
happened to be sitting behind Susanna, and I
could not see her face; I only saw how her long,
dark hair leaped and smote her shoulders from

time to time, how impetuously her figure swayed,
and how her slender hands and bared elbows
moved swiftly and rather angularly. The final
echoes died away. I heaved a sigh, at last. Susanna continued to sit at the piano.

" *Ja, ja,*"—remarked Mr. Ratsch, who, however, had also listened attentively,—" *roman-
tische Musik!* That 's the fashion nowadays!
Only, why play in a slovenly way? Eh? With
a finger on two notes at once—why? Eh? That 's
just the trouble; we want to do everything as
quickly as possible, as quickly as possible. 'T is
more ardent so. Eh? Hot pancakes! "—he
quavered, like a pedlar.

Susanna turned slightly toward Mr. Ratsch.
I saw her face in profile. Her delicate eyebrows were elevated high above the drooping lids,
a blush spread unevenly over her cheek, her little
ear flushed scarlet under the lock of hair thrust
over it.

" I have heard all the very best virtuosi myself,"—pursued Mr. Ratsch, suddenly contracting his brows,—" and in comparison with the late
Field they are all . . . . phew! ciphers! zero! !
Das war ein Kerl! Und ein so reines Spiel! And
his compositions are the very finest! But all
these new ' *tlu-tu-tu,*' and ' *tra-ta-ta,*' are written
chiefly for scholars, I suppose. *Da braucht man
keine Delicatesse!* Bang away on the keys, at
random. . . There 's no harm done! Something

will come of it! *Janitscharen-Musik! Pkhe!*"
(Iván Demyánitch mopped his brow with his
handkerchief.) "However, I 'm not saying this
with reference to you, Susanna Ivánovna; you
have played well, and you must not take offence
at my remarks."

"Every one has his own taste,"—remarked
Susanna, in a quiet tone, and her lips quivered;
—"and you know that your remarks cannot of-
fend me, Iván Demyánitch!"

"Oh, of course! Only, you must not suppose,"
—said Mr. Ratsch, addressing me,—"pray, do
not suppose, my dear sir, that the same proceeds
from our superfluous kindness of heart, and, as
it were, meekness of spirit; but simply, Susanna
Ivánovna and I imagine that we are exalted so
high that, oh, my! Our cap is tumbling off behind, as they say in Russian, but no criticism can
reach us. Self-conceit, my dear sir, self-conceit!
We have smarted for it, yes, yes!"

Not without amazement did I listen to Mr.
Ratsch. Gall, poisonous gall, fairly seethed in
his every word. . . . And it had been long collecting! It choked him. He tried to wind up
his tirade with his customary laugh, and coughed
convulsively, hoarsely. Susanna uttered not the
smallest word of reply to him; she merely shook
her head, and raised her face,—yes, grasping her
elbows in both hands, she fixed her eyes straight
on him. In the depths of her motionless, widely-

opened eyes, with a dull, unquenchable fire, smouldered hatred of long standing. An uncanny feeling took possession of me.

"You belong to two different musical generations,"—I began, with forced ease, being desirous of letting it be understood, by that ease of manner, that I had observed nothing,—"and, therefore, it is not surprising that you do not agree in your views. . . . But Iván Demyánitch, you must permit me to take the side of . . . . the younger generation. I am a philistine, of course; but I must confess to you that nothing in the way of music has ever yet produced upon me such an impression as . . what Susanna Ivánovna has just played to us."

Ratsch suddenly pounced upon me.

"And why do you assume,"—he shouted, still purple in the face with coughing,—"that we wish to enlist you in our camp?" (He pronounced *Lager* in German fashion.) "We 're not in the slightest need of that, many thanks! Our wills are free! And as for the two generations, you 're right about that. It is difficult, very difficult, for us old people to live with you young folks! Our views do not agree on a single point: either as to art, or as to life, or even as to morals. Is n't that so, Susanna Ivánovna?"

Susanna emitted a scornful laugh.

"Especially, as you say, on the score of morals, our views do not and cannot agree,"—she replied;

and something menacing flitted athwart her brows, but her lips quivered slightly, as before.

"Of course, of course!"—chimed in Ratsch. —"I'm not a philosopher! I don't know how to stand ... in that way—loftily! I'm a plain man, a slave to prejudice, yes!"

Again Susanna laughed.

"It strikes me, Iván Demyánitch, that you have sometimes managed to place yourself above what are called prejudices."

"*Wie so?* That is to say, what do you mean? I don't understand you!"

"You don't understand? Are you so forgetful?"

Mr. Ratsch fairly lost his head.

"I .... I ...." he repeated.—"I ...."

"Yes, you, Mr. Ratsch."

A brief silence ensued.

"But, pray, pray,"—Mr. Ratsch began,— "how can you so audaciously ...."

Susanna, suddenly drawing herself up to her full height, with her elbows still clasped in her hands, gripping them as in a vice, and tapping them with her fingers, placed herself in front of Mr. Ratsch. She seemed to be challenging him to battle; she advanced upon him. Her face was transfigured; it became suddenly, in the twinkling of an eye, both remarkably beautiful and terrible; her full eyes began to glitter with a sort of merry and cold gleam—the gleam of steel;—

her lips, which had so recently been quivering, were compressed in one straight, implacably-stern line. Susanna was challenging Ratsch; but the latter, as the saying is, gazed on her, then suddenly relapsed into silence and dropped down like a sack, and drew his head down into his shoulders, and even tucked up his legs. The veteran of the year '12 had turned coward; there could be no doubt as to that.

Susanna slowly turned her eyes from him to me, as though summoning me to bear witness to her victory, and to the humiliation of the enemy, and laughing for the last time, she left the room.

The veteran remained motionless on his chair for some time; at last, as though he had just remembered the forgotten part he was playing, he started, rose, and clapping me on the shoulder, he burst out into his stentorian laugh.

" Come, now, just get out with you, ha-ha-ha! This is not the first decade that that young lady and I have lived together, I believe; but she never can understand when I am joking and when I am speaking seriously! Yes, and you, most respected sir, must have been surprised, I 'm sure. . . . Ha-ha-ha! The fact is, you don't know old Ratsch yet!"

" Yes . . I do know you now," I thought, not without some terror and loathing.

" You don't know the old man, you don't know him!"—he kept reiterating, as he escorted me to

the anteroom, patting himself on the belly. . . .
" I 'm a heavy, experienced man, ha-ha! But
I 'm good-natured—by heaven! I am."

I fled headlong from the steps into the street.
I wanted to get away from that good-natured
man as speedily as possible.

XIV

" THAT they hate each other is clear,"—I
thought, as I wended my way homeward.—" It
is also indubitable that he is a vile man, and that
she is a good young girl. But what has taken
place between them? What is the cause of this
continual irritation? What is the meaning of
these innuendoes? And how suddenly it blazed
up! Under what futile pretexts! "

On the following day, Fústoff and I were preparing to go to the theatre, to see Shtchépkin in
" Woe from Wit." [1] Permission had only just
been accorded to give Griboyédoff's comedy, after it had been preliminarily mutilated by the
censorship's excisions. We applauded Famúsoff
and Skalozúb a great deal. I do not remember
what actor played the part of Tchátzky; but I
do remember very well that he was inexpressibly
bad. First he made his appearance in a hussar
jacket and tasselled boots, then in a frock-coat

---

[1] Griboyedoff's famous comedy, whose scene is laid in Moscow, and
   still is played. It was completed in 1823.—TRANSLATOR.

of a hue fashionable at that time, " flamme de punch," and the coat fitted him as it would have fitted our old butler. I remember, also, that the ball in the third act excited our enthusiasm. Although, in all probability, no one ever executed such steps, it was the accepted thing at that epoch—and I believe that it is performed in the same way even at the present day. One of the guests leaped remarkably high, his wig fluttering in every direction the while, and the audience roared with laughter. As we emerged from the theatre, we ran across Viktór in the corridor.

" You were in the theatre! "—he exclaimed, flourishing his arms.—" How was it that I failed to see you? I am very glad that I have met you. You positively must sup with me. Come along. I 'll stand treat! "

Young Ratsch appeared to be in an excited, almost rapturous, state. His little eyes roved, he grinned, red spots broke out on his cheeks.

" Why this jollity? "—inquired Fústoff.

" Why? Here, then, would n't you like to see? "

Viktór led us a little aside, and pulling out of his trousers' pocket a whole package of the red and blue bank-bills of that day, waved them in the air.

Fústoff was astonished.

" Has your father grown generous? "

Viktór laughed aloud.

" A nice one you 've picked out for a generous
man! I should say so; hold your pocket tight!
. . . This morning, trusting to your mediation,
I asked him for money. And what answer do
you think the skinflint made? ' I 'll pay thy
debts,' says he, ' up to five-and-twenty rubles, inclusive!' Do you hear? 'inclusive!' No, my
dear sir, God has sent this to my orphanhood.
The chance befell."

" Been robbing some one?"—said Fústoff,
carelessly.

Viktór frowned.

" Well, then, I have! I won it, sir; I won it
from an officer, from a guardsman. He only
rolled in from Petersburg last night. And what
a concurrence of circumstances! It 's worth re-
lating . . . . only, it 's awkward here. Let 's go
to Yar's; it 's only two steps away. I 've said it
—I 'll stand treat!"

Perhaps we ought to have refused; but we
went without making any objection.

XV

At Yar's we were conducted into a private room,
supper was served, champagne was brought.
Viktór narrated to us, in full detail, how he had
met that officer of the guards in a certain pleasant
house, a very nice little fellow, and of good family, only without any sense in his head; how they

had struck up an acquaintance; how he, that is to say, the officer, had taken it into his head to suggest, as a joke, to him, Viktór, that they should play "fool" with old cards, for small stakes, trifles about equal to nuts, on condition that the officer was to play for the benefit of Wilhelmina, while Viktór was to play for his own luck; how afterward they got to betting.

"And I—I"—exclaimed Viktór, clapping his hands—"had six rubles altogether in my pocket. Imagine! And at first I lost everything. . . . What do you think of that for a position?! Only, at that point, thanks to I know not whose prayers, fortune began to smile. The other man began to get excited; he showed all his cards. . . . Behold! he just flung away seven hundred and fifty rubles at one swoop! He began to entreat me to play some more. Well, I 'm no fool; thinks I: no; one must n't misuse such bounty. I grabbed my cap and took myself off! So now I have n't got to make obeisance to the old man, and I can treat my comrades. . . Hey! waiter! another bottle! Gentlemen, clink glasses!"

We clinked glasses with Viktór, and continued to drink and laugh, although his story did not please us in the least, and his company afforded us little pleasure. He took to being affectionately demonstrative, to jesting; in a word, he laid himself out, and made himself more repulsive than ever. Viktór observed, at last, what sort of an impression he was producing on us, and hung his head; his speech grew more fragmentary, his glances more gloomy. He began to yawn, announced that he was sleepy, and after objurgating the restaurant servant, with his customary coarseness, for a badly-cleaned tchubúk, he suddenly, with a defiant expression on his distorted face, turned to Fústoff:

"See here now, Alexander Davíditch,"—said he,—"tell me, if you please, why it is that you despise me?"

"What do you mean?"—my friend could not immediately find an answer.

"Just what I say. . . . I feel and know very well that you do despise me, and that that gentleman there" (he indicated me with his finger) "does the same! And although you have distinguished yourselves by very lofty morality, you're just as much of a sinner as the rest of us. Even worse. Still water . . . . you know the proverb!"

Fústoff flushed crimson.

"What do you mean to intimate by that?"—he asked.

"Just this, that I'm not blind, as yet, and can see, capitally, everything that is going on under my nose; I see your capers with my sister. . . . And I don't object. In the first place, it's against my principles, and, in the second place, my sister, Susanna Ivánovna, herself has led a dissolute life. . . . . Only, why should I be scorned on that account?"

" You don't understand yourself what it is you are jabbering! You 're drunk,"—said Fústoff, taking down his coat from the wall.—" You certainly must have fleeced some fool or other, and now you 're inventing the devil knows what lies!"

Viktór continued to lie on the divan, and merely waggled his legs, which dangled over the arm.

" I did clean him out! But why did you drink the wine? It was bought with the money I won, you know. And there 's no need for my lying. I 'm not to blame, if Susanna Ivánovna, in her past life . . . ."

" Silence!"—Fústoff shouted at him.—" Hold your tongue . . . . or . . . . "

" Or what?"

" You 'll find out what. Let 's go, Piótr."

" Aha!"—pursued Viktór:—" our magnanimous knight takes to flight. Evidently, he does n't want to learn the truth! Evidently, it stings,—that truth!"

" Do come along, Piótr,"—repeated Fústoff, who had, at last, lost his wonted coolness and self-possession.—" Let 's leave this worthless little boy!"

" This little boy is n't afraid of you, do you hear?"—yelled Viktór after us.—" This little boy de-spi-ses you! Do you hear?"

A HAPLESS GIRL

Fústoff strode so rapidly along the street that it was with difficulty I kept pace with him. All at once he halted, and abruptly turned back.

"Whither art thou going?"—I asked.

"Why, I must find out what that stupid oaf . . . . He's likely, while drunk, to say God knows what. . . . Only, thou must not follow me. . . . We will see each other to-morrow. Farewell."

And hastily pressing my hand, Fústoff set off in the direction of Yar's restaurant.

I did not manage to see Fústoff on the following day, and on the day after that I learned, when I dropped in at his quarters, that he had gone out of town, to his uncle's in the suburbs of Moscow. I inquired whether he had left a note for me, but it appeared that there was no note. Then I asked the lackey whether he knew how long Alexander Davíditch intended to remain in the country.—"A couple of weeks, perhaps longer, I suppose,"—answered the lackey. By way of precaution, I took down Fústoff's precise address, and wended my way homeward, immersed in thought. This unexpected departure from Moscow, in winter, perplexed me to the last degree. My kind aunt remarked to me at dinner that I seemed constantly to be expecting something, and staring at my cabbage-patty[1] as

[1] Small patties filled with cabbage, rice, carrots, and so forth, also open patties with baked sour cream, are served with soup instead of bread.—TRANSLATOR.

though I had never seen such a thing before in my life.—"*Pierre, vous n'êtes pas amoureux?*" —she exclaimed at last, after having, as a preliminary precaution, sent her companions out of the room. But I reassured her:—no, I was not in love.

XVI

THREE days passed. I longed to go to the Ratsches'. I had a feeling that in their house I should find the solution to all that puzzled me, that I could not understand. . . . But I should be obliged to come in contact with the veteran again. . . . That thought deterred me. And behold, one tempestuous evening,—a February snow-storm was raging and howling out of doors, the dry snow was beating against the windows at intervals, like coarse sand hurled by a powerful hand,—I was sitting in my room and trying to read a book. My servant entered and announced, not without considerable mysteriousness, that a certain lady wished to see me. I was amazed. . . . Ladies were not in the habit of calling upon me, especially at that late hour; but I ordered him to show her in. The door opened, and with swift steps a woman entered enveloped in a thin, summer cloak and a yellow shawl. With an impetuous movement she flung off the shawl and cloak, all covered with snow, and I beheld before me Susanna. I was so astounded that I did not utter a word, and she walked to the window and, leaning her shoulders against the wall, stood motionless; only her breast heaved convulsively, and her eyes wandered, and the breath broke from her livid lips with a faint moan. I apprehended that no ordinary calamity had brought her to me. I understood, notwithstanding my giddiness and my youth, that the fate of a whole life had come to a crisis at that instant before me —a bitter and painful fate.

"Susanna Ivánovna,"—I began,—"how in the world . . . ."

She suddenly seized my hand in her ice-cold fingers, but her voice failed. She breathed spasmodically, and dropped her eyes. Heavy locks of her black hair fell over her face. . . . The snow-dust had not yet disappeared from them.

"Pray, calm yourself; be seated,"—I began again,—"yonder, on the divan. What has happened? Sit down, I entreat you."

"No,"—she said in a barely-audible tone, and dropped down on the window-sill.—"I 'm comfortable here. . . . Let me be. . . You could not have expected . . . . but if you only knew . . . . if I only could . . . . if . . . ."

She tried to control herself, but the tears burst from her eyes with shattering force—and sobs, impetuous, pitiful sobs, rang through the room. My heart contracted within me. I lost my head.

I had only seen Susanna a couple of times; I had divined that she did not find life easy; but I had regarded her as a proud girl with a firm character, and all of a sudden here were these uncontrollable, despairing tears. . . . Great heavens! Why, people weep in that way only in the presence of death!

I stood as though I were myself condemned to death.

" Forgive me,"—she said, at last, several times, almost viciously wiping one eye, then the other. —" I shall get over it presently. I came to you . . ."—She was still sobbing, but there were no tears now.—" I came . . . . You know, of course, that Alexander Davíditch has gone away? "

By this single question Susanna confessed everything, and, moreover, she looked at me as though she wanted to say: " Thou understandest, of course; thou wilt be merciful, wilt thou not? " The unhappy girl! It must have been that there was no other way open to her.

I did not know how to answer her. . . .

"He has gone away, he has gone away. . . He believed it!"—Susanna was saying meanwhile.—"He would not even ask me. He thought that I would not tell him the whole truth. He could think that of me? As though I had ever deceived him!"

She bit her under lip and, bending over a little,

she began to scratch with her finger-nail the ice-patterns which had formed on the pane. I hastily went into the adjoining room, and dismissing my servant, I immediately returned and lighted another candle. I did not know just why I did this. . . . I was extremely disturbed.

Susanna was sitting, as before, on the window-sill, and only then did I notice how lightly she was clad. A thin grey gown with white buttons and a broad leather belt—that was all. I approached her, but she paid no attention to me.

" He believed it . . . . he believed it,"—she whispered, swaying gently from side to side.— " He did not hesitate; he dealt me this last . . . . last blow! "—She suddenly turned toward me.— " Do you know his address? "

" Yes, Susanna Ivánovna. . . . I learned it from his people . . . at his house. He himself said nothing to me of his intention. I had not seen him for two days. I went to inquire, and he had already quitted Moscow."

" You do know his address? "—she repeated.— "Well, then, write to him that he has murdered me. You are a good man, I know. He did not talk to you about me, I am sure; but he did talk to me about you. Write . . . . akh, write to him to return as speedily as possible, if he wishes to find me still among the living! . . . But no! He will no longer find me! . . ."

Susanna's voice grew more and more hushed with every word, and she quieted down all over. But to me this composure seemed still more terrifying than her recent sobs.

" He believed him . . . ." she said again, and propped her chin on her clasped hands.

A sudden gust of wind beat against the window with a howl and a clatter of snow, a cold draught of air rushed through the room. . . . The flame of the candle flickered. . . . Susanna shuddered.

Once more I begged her to seat herself on the divan.

" No, no; let me be,"—she replied,—" I am comfortable here. Please."—She cowered against the frozen panes, as though she had found a nest for herself in the depths of the window.— " Please."

" But you are shivering, you are stiff with cold,"—I exclaimed.—" Look, your shoes are wet through."

" Let me alone . . . . please . . . ." she whispered, and closed her eyes.

I was seized with affright.

" Susanna Ivánovna! "—I almost shrieked.— " Come to your senses, I implore you! What ails you? Why this despair? Everything will be cleared up, you will see; there is some misunderstanding . . . . some unexpected occurrence. . . . You will see, he will soon return. I will

let him know; I will write to him this very day.
. . . But I will not repeat your words to him.
. . . How could I!"

"He will not find me,"—said Susanna, still in
the same quiet voice.—"Would I have come
hither, to a strange man, think you, if I had not
known that I should not remain alive? Akh, all
my last possessions have been swept away irrevocably! I did not want to die so, alone, in silence,
without having said to any one: 'I have lost
everything . . . and I am dying. . . Look!'"

Again she retreated into her chilly nook. . .
Never shall I forget that head; those immovable
eyes, with their deep and quenched gaze; that
dark, dishevelled hair against the pale panes of
the window; that grey, close-fitting gown, beneath whose every fold beat such young, ardent
life!

I involuntarily clasped my hands.

"You . . . you must die, Susanna Ivánovna!
You ought only to live. . . . You must live!"

She gazed at me. . . My words seemed to surprise her.

"Akh, you do not know,"—she began, and
quietly dropped both hands.—"I cannot live. I
have had to suffer too much—too, too much! I
have borne it. . . I hoped . . . but now . . .
when this also has fallen to ruin . . . . when . . . ."

She raised her eyes to the ceiling, and seemed
to meditate. The tragic line which I had pre-

viously noticed around her lips was now still more clearly defined; it had spread over the whole face. It seemed as though some pitiless finger had traced it irrevocably, had branded forever this doomed creature.

She persistently remained silent.

" Susanna Ivánovna,"—I said, in order, by some means, to break that terrible silence,—" he will return, I assure you! "

Again Susanna looked at me.

" What do you say? "—she articulated, with evident effort.

" He will return, Susanna Ivánovna; Alexander will return! "

" He will return? "—she repeated.—" But even if he should return, I cannot forgive him for this humiliation, this distrust. . . ."

She clutched at her head.

" My God! My God! What am I saying? And why am I here? What does it mean? What . . . what did I come to ask about? . . . and about whom? Akh, I am going mad! . . ."

Her eyes grew fixed.

" You wished to ask me to write to Alexander," —I hastened to prompt her.

She started.

" Yes, write . . . . write what you will. . . And here. . ." She hurriedly fumbled in her pocket, and drew forth a small note-book.—" I had begun to write this for him . . . before his

flight. . . . But, you see, he believed him . . . .
he believed him!"

I understood that she meant Viktór. Susanna
did not wish to mention him; she would not utter
his hated name.

"But, pray, Susanna Ivánovna,"—I began,—
"why do you assume that Alexander Davíditch
had an interview . . . . with that man?"

"Why? Why? But he himself came to me
and told me all about it, and boasted of it . . .
and laughed, just as his father does! Here, here,
take this,"—she went on, thrusting the note-book
into my hand;—"read it, send it to him, burn it,
do what you like, as you like. . . . But I cannot
die thus, without any one knowing. . . But now
my time is up. . . . I must go."

She rose from the window-sill. . . . I detained
her.

"Where are you going, Susanna Ivánovna,
for heaven's sake! Listen, what a blizzard! You
are so thinly clad. . . . And your house is not
near here. Allow me at least to send for a carriage, for a public cab. . . ."

"I don't want it; I want nothing,"—she said,
obdurately repelling me, and taking her cloak
and shawl.—"Don't detain me, for God's sake!
If you do . . . I will not be responsible for the
consequences! I feel an abyss, a dark abyss, beneath my feet. . . Don't come near me! Don't
touch me!"—With feverish haste she put on her

cloak, and threw the shawl around her. . . .
" Farewell. . . . Farewell. . . . Oh, my poor,
poor race, the race of eternal wanderers, a curse
lies on thee! But, you see, no one loved me; why
should he? . . ." She suddenly ceased speaking.
—" No, one man did love me,"—she said again,
wringing her hands,—" but death is everywhere
—inevitable death is everywhere! Now it is my
turn. . . Don't follow me,"—she cried in a
piercing voice.—" Don't come! Don't come! "

I stood rooted to the spot, and she rushed forth,
and a moment later I heard the heavy street-door
bang, and again the window-frames quivered under the shocks of the snow-storm.

I did not speedily recover myself. I had only
just begun to live, at that time. I had experienced neither passion nor grief, and had rarely
been a witness of the manner in which those powerful sentiments express themselves in others.
. . . . But the genuineness of that grief, of that
passion, impressed me strongly. Had it not been
for the note-book in my hands, I might have
thought that I had dreamed all this—so remarkable had the whole thing been, and so like a momentary thunder-storm had it passed off. I read
that note-book until midnight. It consisted of
several sheets of writing-paper, all scrawled over
in a large, but irregular chirography, almost without erasures. Not a single line ran straight, and
it seemed as though the tremulous quiver of the

hand which guided the pen could be felt in every one. The contents of the note-book were as follows (I have kept it until the present time):

XVII

MY STORY

I SHALL be twenty-eight years old this year. Here are my first recollections: I am living in the Government of Tambóff, in the house of a wealthy landed proprietor, Iván Matvyéevitch Koltovskóy, in his country-house, in a small room on the second story. With me lives my mother, a Jewess, the daughter of an artist, already deceased, who had been brought from abroad—a sickly woman with a remarkably beautiful face, as white as wax, and with such mournful eyes that, whenever she gazed long at me, I invariably felt, without even glancing at her, that sorrowful, sorrowful look, and began to weep, and ran to embrace her. Teachers come to me; I am taught music, and am called a young lady. I dine at the table of the house-master, together with my mother. Mr. Koltovskóy is a tall, stately man, with a majestic mien; he always smells of amber. I am deadly afraid of him, although he calls me Suzon, and allows me to kiss his thin, sinewy hand through his lace ruffles. With my mother he is exquisitely polite, but even with her he talks little: he will say two or three affectionate words to her, to which she immediately makes a hurried reply,—he will utter them, and then fall silent, and sit, gazing pompously around, and slowly toying with a pinch of Span-

ish snuff, in a round, gold snuff-box, with the monogram
of the Empress Katherine.

My ninth year has remained forever memorable to
me. . . . I then learned, through the maid-servants in
the maids' room, that Iván Matvyéevitch Koltovskóy was my father, and almost on that very same
day, my mother, at his command, married Mr. Ratsch,
who served him as a sort of manager. I could not in the
least understand how that was possible; I was perplexed,
I came near falling ill, my head gave way, my mind was
dazed. " Is it true, is it true, mamma,"—I asked her,—
" that that *scented bugbear* " (that was what I called
Iván Matvyéitch) " is my papa? " My mother was extremely frightened, and put her hand over my mouth.
. . . " Never speak of that to any one, hearest thou,
Susanna, hearest thou—not a word! " . . . she reiterated with a trembling voice, pressing my head closely
to her breast. . . . And I really never did mention it.
. . I understood my mother's command. . . . I understood that I must hold my peace, that my mother had
implored my pardon!

My unhappiness began at once. Mr. Ratsch did not
love my mother, and she did not love him. He had married her for the sake of money, and she had been obliged
to submit. Mr. Koltovskóy probably thought that, in
this way, everything had been arranged in the best possible manner—" *la position était régularisée.* " I remember, on the day before the wedding, my mother and I,
clasped in each other's arms, wept nearly the whole morning, bitterly, bitterly, and in silence. It was no wonder
that she held her peace. . . . What could she say to

me? But the fact that I did not question her proves merely that unhappy children acquire wisdom faster than the happy ones . . . . to their misfortune.

Mr. Koltovskóy continued to take an interest in my education, and even attached me more closely to his person. He did not converse with me . . . . but morning and evening, after flicking the snuff-dust from his lace shirt-frill with two fingers, with the same two fingers, as cold as ice, he tapped me on the cheek, and gave me some dark bonbons, which also had a scent of amber, and which I never ate. When I was twelve years old, I became his reader, " *sa petite lectrice.*" I read aloud to him the French works of the last century, the Memoirs of Saint-Simon, Mably, Raynal, Helvetius, Voltaire's Correspondence, the Encyclopedists, without understanding anything, of course, even when he, grinning and narrowing his eyes, ordered me: " *Relire ce dernier paragraphe, qui est bien remarquable!* " Iván Matvyéevitch was a thorough Frenchman. He had lived in Paris until the Revolution; he remembered Marie Antoinette; he had received an invitation to the Trianon from her; he had seen Mirabeau, too, who, according to his statement, wore very large buttons—" *exagéré en tout* " —and was, in general, a man of very bad style—" *en dépit de sa naissance.*" However, Iván Matvyéevitch rarely referred to that epoch; but twice or thrice in the course of the year he would declaim, addressing the one-eyed old *émigré* whom he supported, and whom he called, heaven knows why, " *M. le Commandeur,*"—he would declaim, with his leisurely, nasal voice, an impromptu, which he had once uttered at an evening party of the Duchesse de Polignac. I remember only the first two lines. . . . (The point was a comparison between the Russians and the French.)

> " *L'aigle se plait aux régions austères,*
> *Où le ramier ne saurait habiter* " . . . .

" *Digne de M. de Saint Aulaire!* "—M. le Commandeur was wont to exclaim, on every such occasion.

Iván Matvyéevitch seemed youthful until the day of his death: his cheeks were pink, his teeth white, his eyebrows thick and motionless, his eyes pleasant and expressive, his bright, black eyes, regular agate; he was not in the least capricious, and treated every one, even the servants, very courteously. . . . But great heavens! how painful it was for me to be with him, with what joy did I leave him every time, what evil thoughts agitated me in his presence! Akh, I was not to blame for them! . . . I was not to blame for what they made of me. . . .

After Mr. Ratsch's marriage, a small detached house, not far from the seigniorial manor, was assigned to him. I lived there with my mother. It was not cheerful for me there. A son was soon born to her, that same Viktór, whom I have a right to consider and to call my brother. After his birth, my mother's health, which had been weak before that, was never restored. At that period, Mr. Ratsch did not consider it necessary to display that joviality to which he is now given: he had a constantly surly aspect, and tried to acquire the reputation of a man with executive ability. To me he was harsh and rough. I felt satisfaction when I left Iván Matvyéevitch; but I also gladly quitted our cottage. . . . My

A HAPLESS GIRL

unhappy youth! Eternally floating from one shore to the other, and never wishing to make a landing on either! Sometimes I would run across the yard, in winter, in my cold little frock, run to the manor-house to Iván Matvyéevitch to read, and would seem to rejoice. . . . But when I arrived, and beheld those vast, gloomy rooms, that gay-coloured, upholstered furniture, that amiable and soulless old man in his silken *"douillette,"* open on the breast, in a white lace frill and white neckerchief, with cuffs falling over his fingers, with a *" soupçon "* of powder (that was the way his valet expressed it) on his hair, which was brushed back, my breath would be stopped by that stifling scent of amber, and my heart would sink. Iván Matvyéevitch generally sat in a capacious arm-chair; on the wall, over his head, hung a picture, depicting a young woman, with a clear and bold expression of countenance, dressed in a rich Jewish costume, and all covered with precious stones and pearls. . . I often looked at that picture, but only later on did I learn that it was the portrait of my mother, painted by her father, to the order of Iván Matvyéevitch. She had changed since then! He had managed to break her and humiliate her! "And she loved him! She loved that old man!" —I thought to myself. And yet, when I recalled certain glances of my mother, certain reticences and involuntary movements. . . . " Yes, yes, she loved him!" I repeated, with horror. Akh, God grant that no one may experience such sensations!

I read to Iván Matvyéevitch every day, sometimes for three or four hours in succession. . . . It was injurious to me to read so much and so loud, Our doctor was apprehensive for my chest, and even mentioned the matter one day to Iván Matvyéevitch. But the latter merely smiled (that is to say, he did not: he never smiled, but he puckered his lips to a point, and protruded them), and said to him: "*Vous ne savez pas ce qu'il y a de ressources dans cette jeunesse.*"—"But in former years, M. le Commandeur . . . . " the doctor ventured to remark. Again Iván Matvyéevitch smiled: "*Vous rêvez, mon cher,*"—he interrupted him:—"*le commandeur n'a plus de dents et il crache à chaque mot. J'aime les voix jeunes.*"

And I continued to read, although I coughed a great deal morning and night. . . .

Sometimes Iván Matvyéevitch made me play on the piano. But music had a somniferous effect on his nerves. His eyes immediately closed, his head gradually sank, and only from time to time did this become audible: "*C'est du Steibelt, n'est ce pas? Jouez moi du Steibelt!*" Iván Matvyéevitch regarded Steibelt as a great genius, who had managed to overcome in himself "*la grossière lourdeur des Allemandes,*" and had but one complaint to make against him: "*trop de fougue! trop d'imagination!*" . . . . But when Iván Matvyéevitch noticed that I had grown weary at the piano, he offered me "*du cachou de Bologne.*" Thus passed day after day.

And then one night—a night never to be forgotten!— a frightful calamity overtook me. My mother died almost suddenly. I had only just passed my fifteenth birthday. Oh, what a grief that was, in what a malignant whirlwind it swooped down upon me! How frightened I was at that first encounter with death! My poor mother! Our relations had been strange: we had loved each other passionately . . . passionately and hopelessly: we had both, as it were, preserved and hidden from ourselves our common secret, we had maintained persistent silence about it, although we knew, knew everything which went on in the depths of our hearts! Even about her past, her early past, my mother had not talked to me, and she had never complained in words, although her whole being was one dumb complaint! We had avoided all conversation which was in the least degree serious. Akh! I had kept on hoping that the hour would come when she would, at last, speak out, and I would speak out, and we should find relief. . . . But daily cares, an irresolute and timid disposition, illness, the presence of Mr. Ratsch, and, chief of all, that eternal question: "What's the use?" and that uncontrollable, uninterrupted flight of time, of life. . . . It all ended with a thunder-clap, and I was fated not to hear from my mother's lips not only those words which would have dispelled our secret, but even the ordinary words of farewell which precede death! All that remains in my memory is the exclamation of Mr. Ratsch: "Susanna Ivánovna, please come hither; your mother wishes to give you her blessing!" and then the pallid hand from beneath the heavy coverlet, the tortured breathing, the rolled-up eyes . . . Oh, enough, enough!

On the following day, and on the day of the funeral . . with what horror, with what indignation, with what painful curiosity did I gaze upon the face of my father . . . . yes, of my father. His letters had been found in her casket. It seemed to me that he had turned a little pale and had grown thin . . . . but no! Nothing stirred in that petrified soul! Exactly as of yore, he summoned me to his study, after the lapse of a week; in exactly the same voice did he request me to read: "*Si vous voulez bien, les observations sur l'histoire de France, de Mably, à la page 74 . . . là, où nous avons été interrompus.*" And he had not even ordered my mother's portrait to be removed! It is true that, on dismissing me, he called me to him, and giving me his hand to kiss a second time, he said: "*Suzanne, la mort de votre mère vous a privée de votre appui naturel; mais vous pourrez toujours compter sur ma protection,*" but immediately gave me a slight push on the shoulder with the other hand, and with his customary screwing-up of the lips, he added: "*Allez, mon enfant.*" I would have liked to scream at him: "Why, of course, you are my father!" but I said nothing, and left the room.

Early on the following morning, I went to the cemetery. The month of May was then in its full beauty of flowers and foliage, and I sat for a long time on the newly-made grave. I did not weep, I did not grieve; only one thing kept whirling through my brain: "Dost thou hear, mamma? He wants to show me his protection!" And it seemed to me that my mother would not be pained by the smile which involuntarily came to my lips.

I sometimes ask myself: What was it that made me so persistently desire, seek after—not a confession . . . . to what end! but at least one warm, paternal word from Iván Matvyéevitch? Was not I aware what sort of a man he was, and how little he resembled what I had imagined in my reveries a *father* to be? . . . But I was alone, so entirely alone on the earth! And then, that ever-importunate thought gave me no peace: "But she loved him? There was some reason for her loving him?"

Three years more passed. No change had taken place in our monotonous life, which was measured out and calculated beforehand. Viktór was growing up. I was nine years older than he, and would gladly have taken charge of him, but Mr. Ratsch was opposed to this. He provided for him a nurse, who was to keep strict watch over him, so that the child should not "get spoiled"; that is, I was not to be permitted to come near him. And Viktór himself was shy of me. One day, Mr. Ratsch came to my chamber in a perturbed, agitated, vicious mood. Already, on the preceding day, evil rumours concerning my stepfather had reached my ears: people asserted that he had been caught embezzling a considerable sum, and taking bribes from a merchant.

"You can help me,"—he began, drumming impatiently on the table with his fingers.—"Go, entreat Iván Matvyéevitch on my behalf."

"Entreat? On what ground?—what about?"

"Intercede for me. . . I'm not a stranger to you, you know. I am accused. . . Well, in a word, I may be left without a morsel of bread, and you also."

"But how can I go to him? How can I trouble him?"

"The idea! You have a *right* to trouble him!"

"What right, Iván Demyánitch?"

"Come, none of your pretending. He cannot refuse *you*, for many reasons. Is it possible that you don't understand me?"

He stared me audaciously in the eye, and I felt that my cheeks were fairly burning. Hatred, scorn arose within me on the instant—surged in a flood, drowned me.

" Yes, I understand you, Iván Demyánitch,"—I answered him at last. My voice seemed unrecognisable to me myself: " And I will not go to Iván Matvyéevitch, and I will not entreat him. If we are to be deprived of bread, so be it!"

Mr. Ratsch started, ground his teeth, clenched his fists.

" Well, never you mind, Tzarévna Melikitrísa!"—he whispered hoarsely.—" I'll pay you off for this!"

That very day, Iván Matvyéevitch summoned him to him, menaced him with his cane, that same cane which he had once received in exchange from the Duc de La Rochefoucauld, and shouted: " You are a scoundrel and a self-seeker! I'll put you on the outside!" (Iván Matvyéevitch was hardly able to speak Russian, and despised our " coarse jargon," " *ce jargon vulgaire et rude.*" Some one once said, in his presence: " That is a self-evident fact." Iván Matvyéevitch flew into a rage, and thereafter frequently cited this phrase as an example of the absurdity and clumsiness of the Russian language. " What's ' That is a self-evident fact'?" he was wont to inquire in *Russian*, emphasising every syllable. " And why not say simply: ' That is evident,' and why say: ' A self-evident fact'?")

Iván Matvyéevitch did not turn Mr. Ratsch out of doors, however; he did not even deprive him of his post. But my stepfather kept his word: he paid me off for *that*.

I began to observe a change in Iván Matvyéevitch. He began to grow melancholy and bored; his health gave way. His fresh, rosy face grew sallow and wrinkled; one of his front teeth dropped out. He ceased entirely

to go about, and put an end to the reception days, with
refreshment, which he had instituted for the peasants,
without the assistance of the clergy—"*sans le concours
du clergé.*" On such days, Iván Matvyéevitch, with a
rose in his buttonhole, had been wont to receive the peasants in the hall[1] or on the balcony, and, touching his
lips to a small silver-clasped glass of vodka, he had been
wont to make them a speech, in the following style:
" You are as satisfied with my deeds as I am satisfied
with your zeal: I am sincerely delighted at this. We
are all *brethren;* birth itself makes us equals: I drink
to your health!" He bowed to them, and the peasants
made him a reverence to the girdle, and not to the
ground, which was strictly prohibited. The entertain-
ment continued, as before, but Iván Matvyéevitch no
longer showed himself to his subjects. Sometimes he interrupted my reading with exclamations: "*La machine
se détraque! Cela se gâte!* " His very eyes, those brilliant, stony eyes, grew dim and appeared to diminish in
size: he fell into a doze more frequently than of yore,
and sighed heavily in his slumbers.

The only thing which underwent no change was his
treatment of me; there was merely a shade of chival-
rous courtesy added. He rose from his arm-chair, although with difficulty, every time I entered the room,
he escorted me to the door, supporting me with his hand
under my elbow, and instead of Suzon, he began to call
me, now, " *Ma chère demoiselle,*" again, " *Mon Anti-
gone.*" M. le Commandeur had died, a couple of years
after the death of my mother, and, apparently, his

---

[1] A large music-room, ball-room, winter play-room, general utility-
room in Russian houses.—TRANSLATOR.

death was a far deeper shock to Iván Matvyéevitch.
His contemporary had vanished: that is what disturbed
him. And nevertheless, M. le Commandeur's sole service
had consisted, of late, in his exclaiming: " *Bien joué,
mal réussi!* " every time that Iván Matvyéevitch, when
playing billiards with Mr. Ratsch, made a failure, or did
not pocket his ball. Also, when Iván Matvyéevitch addressed to him at table a question, in the nature, for example, of the following: " *N'est ce pas, M. le Commandeur, c'est Montesquieu qui a dit cela dans ses Lettres
Persanes?* " the latter, sometimes spilling a spoonful
of soup on his cuff, replied, with profundity of thought:
" *Ah, Monsieur de Montesquieu? Un grand écrivain,
monsieur, un grand écrivain!* " Only, one day, when
Iván Matvyéevitch said to him that " *les théophilan-
tropes ont eu pourtant du bon!* "—the old man cried
out, in an agitated voice: " *Monsieur de Kolontouskoi!* "
(in the course of five-and-twenty years, he had never
learned to pronounce his patron's name correctly)
" *Monsieur de Kolontouskoi! Leur fondateur, l'instiga-
teur de ce cette secte, ce La Reveillère Lepeaux, était un
bonnet rouge!* "—" *Non, non,*" said Iván Matvyéevitch,
grinning and taking a pinch of snuff:—" *des fleurs, des
jeunes vierges, le culte de la Nature . . . . ils ont eu du
bon, ils ont eu du bon!* " . . . . I always was surprised at
the extent of Iván Matvyéevitch's knowledge, and at the
uselessness of his knowledge, so far as he himself was
concerned.

Iván Matvyéevitch was evidently in a decline, but he
still made an effort to stand firm. One day, two or three
weeks before his death, he had a violent fit of dizziness
immediately after dinner. He reflected, said: " *C'est la
fin,*" and, when he had recovered and rested, he wrote a

A HAPLESS GIRL

letter to Petersburg, to his sole heir, a brother, with whom he had had no intercourse for twenty years. On hearing of Iván Matvyéevitch's illness, one of his neighbours came to call, a German, a Roman Catholic, formerly a renowned physician, who was living quietly in his little hamlet. He very rarely came to Iván Matvyéevitch's, but the latter always received him with special attention, and, in general, had a great respect for him. The old man advised Iván Matvyéevitch to send for the priest, but Iván Matvyéevitch replied that "*Ces messieurs et moi, nous n'avons rien à nous dire,*" and requested him to change the subject; but after his neighbour had departed, he gave orders to his valet in advance not to admit any one henceforth. Then he ordered me to be called to him.

I was frightened when I saw him: blue spots had made their appearance under his eyes, his face had grown long and wooden, his jaw hung loosely.—"*Vous voilà grande, Suzon,*" he said, pronouncing the consonants with difficulty, but still making an effort to smile (I was then nineteen years of age).—"*Vous allez peut-être bientôt rester seule. Soyez toujours sage et vertueuse. C'est la dernière recommandation d'un . . . .*" He coughed . . . . "*d'un vieillard qui vous veut du bien. Je vous ai recommandé à mon frère et je ne doute pas qu'il ne respecte mes volontés. . . .*" He coughed again, and anxiously felt of his chest.—"*Du reste, j'espère encore pouvoir faire quelque chose pour vous . . . . dans mon testament.*"

This last phrase cut me to the heart like a knife. Akh, this was too . . . . too scornfully insulting! Iván Matvyéevitch, in all probability, attributed to another feeling—a feeling of grief or of gratitude—

169

that which was expressed on my face, and, as though desirous of comforting me, he patted my shoulder, at the same time affectionately pushing me off, as usual, and said:—" *Voyons, mon enfant, du courage! nous sommes tous mortels. Et puis, il n'y a pas encore de danger. Ce n'est cu'une précaution que j'ai cru prendre. . . . Allez!* "

As on that other occasion, when he had summoned me to him, after my mother's death, I again felt like crying out to him: " But I am your daughter! I am your daughter! " " But," I said to myself, " in those words, in that cry of the heart, he will probably hear only a desire to claim my rights, rights to the inheritance, to his money. . . . Oh, not on any account! I will say nothing to this man, who never once has mentioned my mother's name in my presence, in whose eyes I am of so little importance that he has never even taken the trouble to find out whether I am aware of my parentage! But perhaps he suspected that, and knew it, and did not wish to kick up a row (his favourite expression, and the only Russian phrase he employed), did not wish to deprive himself of his good reader with the youthful voice! No! no! Let him remain as guilty toward his daughter as he was toward her mother! Let him carry both those crimes into the grave with him! I swear it, I swear it; never shall he hear from my mouth that word, which ought to ring with a sweet and sacred sound in the ears of all men! I will not say to him: ' Father! ' I will not forgive him on behalf of my mother and of myself! He does not need that forgiveness, or that appellation. . . . It cannot be, it cannot be, that he needs it! But there shall be no forgiveness for him—none, none! "

A HAPLESS GIRL

God knows whether I should have kept my oath, and whether my heart would not have relented—whether I might not have conquered my timidity, my shame, my pride . . . . but the selfsame thing happened in the case of Iván Matvyéevitch which had happened in my mother's. Death carried him off quite as unexpectedly; at night, also. The same Mr. Ratsch awakened me, and hastened with me to the manor-house, to Iván Matvyée-vitch's bedroom. . . . But I did not find even those last movements which precede death, which had stamped themselves in ineffaceable outlines upon my memory at my mother's bedside. On the lace-trimmed pillows lay a thin, dark-hued puppet with a pointed nose and dishevelled grey brows. . . . I shrieked with affright, with loathing, flew out of the room, and, at the door, ran into bearded men in long peasant coats, with red, festival girdles, and I no longer remember how I got into the open air. . . .

They related afterward that when the valet ran into the room, in answer to a violent ringing of the bell, he found Iván Matvyéevitch not in the bed, but a couple of paces from it. He was sitting, writhing, on the floor, it was said, and repeated twice in succession: " Who could have expected this!" And those, they said, were his last words. But that I cannot believe. Why should he have spoken Russian [1] at such a moment, and in such terms!

For two whole weeks we awaited the arrival of the new

---

[1] The purely and characteristically Russian proverb here employed means literally: "Here, grandmother, is St. George's Day!"—which contains a historical reference to the original binding of the serfs to the soil. It may also be rendered: "This is the end!"—TRANSLATOR.

master Semyón Matvyéevitch Koltovskóy. He sent orders that nothing was to be touched, nothing changed, no one's position altered until his personal inspection. All the doors, all the furniture, chests, tables—everything—were locked and sealed. All the people grew gloomy, and were on their guard. I suddenly became one of the principal persons in the house. I had been called " the young lady " before this; but now that word assumed a somewhat different sense, was uttered with peculiar emphasis. A whispering arose: " The old master died suddenly," it said, " and they did not have time to summon the priest to him, and he had not been to confession for a very long time; but it does n't take long to write a will, you know."

Mr. Ratsch also considered it advisable to alter his mode of action. He did not pretend to be good-natured and affectionate,—he knew that he could not deceive me, —but churlish meekness was depicted on his countenance: as much as to say, "You see, I submit." All fawned on me, tried to win my favour . . . and I did not know what to do, how to act, and was only astonished that these people did not understand that they were insulting me. At last Semyón Matvyéevitch arrived.

Semyón Matvyéevitch was ten years younger than Iván Matvyéevitch, and had travelled all his life along an entirely different road. He had been in the Government service in Petersburg, he occupied an important post. . . . He had been married, and had early become a widower; he had one son. In face, Semyón Matvyéevitch resembled his elder brother, but in stature he was shorter and thicker; he had a round bald head, the same brilliant black eyes as Iván Matvyéevitch, except that they were languishing, and thick, red lips. In contrast to his brother, whom, even after his death, he referred to as " the French philosopher," and sometimes simply as "the crank," Semyón Matvyéevitch almost always spoke Russian, loudly, volubly, and laughed incessantly, at which times he closed his eyes tightly and shook all over in an unpleasant way, as though he were shaking with ague. He set to work very sternly, entered into everything, demanded the fullest accounting from every one.

On the very first day of his arrival, he invited the priest, with his whole ecclesiastical staff, to come, and commanded him to celebrate a prayer-service with blessing of water, and sprinkle the water everywhere, in all the rooms in the house, even in the garrets, even in the cellars, in order, as he expressed it, " radically to expel the Voltairean and Jacobinian spirit." And during the first week several of Iván Matvyéevitch's favourites flew out of their places; one, even, was sent to a distance as a settler; others were subjected to bodily chastisement; and even the aged valet himself,—he was a Turk by birth, knew the French language, and had been given to Iván Matvyéevitch by the late Field-Marshal Kámensky,— that same valet received his freedom, it is true, but in company with it an order to take his departure within twenty-four hours, " in order that he might not be a temptation to others." Semyón Matvyéevitch proved to be a strict master; probably many regretted the deceased. "With the dear little father, with Iván Matvyéevitch," lamented one already completely decrepit old butler, "the sole anxiety we had was that clean linen should be provided, that the rooms should smell well, and that the voices of the servants should not be audible in the anteroom.—God forbid that! Otherwise there 'd be the very devil to pay! The late master never hurt a fly in all his life. Well, now, calamity! There 's nothing left but to die!" With equal swiftness did my position undergo a change—that is to say, the position into which I had fallen for a few days, and against my will. . . . Among Iván Matvyéevitch's papers no will was found, not a single line, written to my advantage. Every one suddenly fled from me. . . . I am not speaking of Mr. Ratsch, but all the rest were vexed with me, and tried to show me their vexation: just as though I had deceived them. One Sunday, after the Liturgy, which he always listened to inside the sanctuary,[1] Semyón Matvyéevitch summoned me to him. Until that day, I had seen him, caught glimpses of him, and he, apparently, had not noticed me. He received me in his study, standing by the window. He wore an undress-uniform coat, with the stars of two Orders. I halted near the door; my heart was beating violently with terror and another feeling, undefined as yet, but already oppressive.—" I wished to see you, young girl," —began Semyón Matvyéevitch, looking first at my feet, and then suddenly at my face,—that look fairly dealt me a blow:—" I wished to see you, in order to announce to you my decision, and my indubitable inclination to be of service to you." He raised his voice.—" Of course, you have no rights whatsoever, but as . . . . my brother's reader, you may always count upon my . . . upon

---

[1] Men are allowed, at the discretion of the clergy, to enter the sanctuary by a side door, and remain during the service. Women cannot go behind the ikonostásis (image-screen—chancel-rails), unless it be nuns, in their convent church.—TRANSLATOR.

my consideration. I am, ... of course, convinced of your good sense, and of your principles. Mr. Ratsch, your stepfather, has already received from me the requisite instructions. I must say, in addition, that your fortunate personal appearance serves me as a guarantee of your noble sentiments." Semyón Matvyéevitch suddenly burst into a shrill laugh, and I . . . . I did not take offence, but I felt sorry for myself . . . and on the instant realised that I was an orphan, bereft of both father and mother. Semyón Matvyéevitch advanced to the table with short, firm steps, took from a drawer a packet of bank-notes, and thrusting it into my hand, added:—
" Here is a small sum from me, by way of pin-money. I shall not forget you hereafter, either, my dear, and now, farewell, and be a sensible girl."

I took the packet mechanically—I would have taken anything he might have given me—and returning to my own chamber, I wept for a long time, as I sat on my bed. I did not notice that I had dropped the packet on the floor. Mr. Ratsch found it, and picked it up, and after asking me what I intended to do with it, kept it himself.

His lot had then undergone a significant change. After several interviews with Semyón Matvyéevitch, he became a great favourite with him, and soon received the post of manager-in-chief. From that time forth, that joviality, that everlasting guffaw, made its appearance in him: at first, he wished thereby to curry favour with his patron . . . . later on, it became a habit. From that time forth, he became a Russian patriot. Semyón Matvyéevitch was wedded to everything national; he called himself a real Russian, jeered at foreign clothing, which he wore, nevertheless; he banished to a distant

A HAPLESS GIRL

village the cook, to whom Iván Matvyéevitch had paid big wages,—banished him because he did not know how to prepare salt-cucumber soup with the necks of geese. From his post inside the sanctuary in church, Semyón Matvyéevitch joined his voice to the chanter's, and when the village maidens assembled for their choral dances, and to sing their ballads, he sang with them and stamped with them, and pinched their cheeks. . . . But he speedily went off to Petersburg, and left my stepfather practically the full master of the estate.

Bitter days began for me. . . . My sole consolation was music, and I devoted myself to it with all my soul. Luckily, Mr. Ratsch was extremely busy, but on every convenient opportunity, he made me feel his enmity; in accordance with his promise, he "paid me off" for my refusal. He harassed me; he made me copy his long and lying reports to Semyón Matvyéevitch, and correct his orthographical errors therein; I was forced to obey him unquestioningly, and obey him I did. He declared that he would tame me, that he would make me as pliable as silk. "Why have you such rebellious eyes?" he sometimes shouted at me at dinner, as he guzzled beer and thumped the table with his palm: "Perhaps you are thinking: 'I 'm as dumb as a sheep, so I 'm all right. . . . ' No! You will be pleased to look at me like a sheep also!"

My position became revolting, unendurable . . . my heart hardened. Something dangerous began to rise up within me more and more frequently; I spent the nights without sleep and without a light, thinking, thinking all the while, and a frightful resolve ripened in the outward darkness, the inward gloom. The arrival

176

of Semyón Matvyéevitch imparted another turn to my thoughts.

No one was expecting him: the autumn had long since set in. It appeared that he had retired from the service, on account of an unpleasantness: he had hoped to obtain the ribbon of St. Alexander Névsky—and he had received a snuff-box. Dissatisfied with the Government, which did not value his talent, with the society of Petersburg, which showed him small sympathy and did not share his wrath, he decided to settle down in the country, to devote himself to the management of his estate. He came alone. His son, Mikhaíl Semyónitch, arrived later on, for the holidays, about New Year's Day. My stepfather spent nearly all his time in Semyón Matvyéevitch's study: he was a greater favourite than ever. He left me in peace: he was in no mood to trouble himself about me then. . . .

Semyón Matvyéevitch had taken it into his head to set up a paper-mill. Mr. Ratsch knew nothing whatever about manufacturing affairs, and Semyón Matvyéevitch was aware that he knew nothing; but, on the other hand, my stepfather was " executive " (a favourite word at that time), " an Araktchéeff ! " [1] That was precisely what Semyón Matvyéevitch called him: " my Araktchéeff ! " " That 's enough for me," declared Semyón Matvyéevitch, " in conjunction with zeal; I 'll do the guiding myself." Nevertheless, in the midst of the innumerable cares connected with the mill, the estate, the

---

[1] A disinterested but harsh and reactionary administrator and favourite, in the reign of Alexander I, whose friendship he won, originally, through his devotion to the memory of the Emperor Paul I (Alexander's father), the instrument of whose tyranny he had been.—TRANSLATOR.

establishment of an office, and office routine, of new conditions and functions, Semyón Matvyéevitch managed to take notice of me. One evening I was summoned to the drawing-room, and made to play the piano: Semyón Matvyéevitch was still less fond of music than his dead brother had been, but he approved of me, and thanked me, and on the following day I was invited to the dinner-table. After dinner, Semyón Matvyéevitch chatted with me for quite a long time, interrogated me, sometimes laughed at my answers, although, as I recall them, there was nothing amusing about them, and stared so strangely at me . . . . I felt uncomfortable. I did not like his eyes; I did not like their frank expression, their brilliant gaze. . . . It always seemed to me as though that very frankness concealed something evil, that beneath that brilliant gleam his soul was dark down below. "You shall not be my reader," Semyón Matvyéevitch announced to me, at last, pluming himself and sprucing himself up, in a fastidious sort of way: "I'm not blind yet, thank God, and I can read for myself; but my coffee tastes more delicious from your hands, and it will give me pleasure to listen to your piano-playing." From that day forth, I went regularly to dine at the manor-house, and remained in the drawing-room until the evening, sometimes. I, also, like my stepfather, had been taken into favour; it was no joy to me. I must confess that Semyón Matvyéevitch did show me some respect; but I felt that there was something about the man which repelled, which frightened me. And that "something" was expressed not in words, but in his eyes, in those evil eyes, and in his laugh. He never talked with me about my father, about his brother, and it seemed to me that he avoided discussing him, not because he did not wish to arouse in me ambitious thoughts, or claims, but for another reason, which I was not able to enter into at the time, but which made me wonder and blush. . . . His son, Mikhaíl Semyónitch, arrived for the Christmas holidays.

Akh! I feel that I cannot continue as I have begun; these memories are too painful. Especially at this time is it impossible for me to narrate quietly. . . . And why should I dissimulate? I fell in love with Mikhaíl, and he fell in love with me.

How this came about, I will not relate either. I know that, from the very first evening, when he entered the drawing-room (I was sitting at the piano, and playing a sonata by Weber), when he entered, handsome and stately, in a velvet fur-lined coat of peasant fashion and felt boots, just as he was, straight from the cold air, and, shaking his frost-rimed sable cap, before he greeted his father, darted a swift glance at me and was amazed,—I know that, from that evening, I could not forget him, could not forget his kind, young face. He began to speak . . . . and his voice fairly adhered to my heart. . . . It was a manly and gentle voice, and such an honest, honest soul spoke in its every sound! Semyón Matvyéevitch rejoiced at his son's arrival, and embraced him, but immediately inquired:— "For a fortnight? hey? On leave? Hey?"—and sent me away. I sat for a long time at my window, and stared at the lights which flitted through the rooms of the manor-house. I watched them; I listened to the new, unfamiliar voice; I was interested in that lively turmoil, and something new, strange, and withal bright, darted through my soul. . . .

179

A HAPLESS GIRL

On the following day, before dinner, I had my first conversation with him. He ran in to see my stepfather on an errand for Semyón Matvyéevitch, and found me in our little drawing-room. I was on the point of retiring; he detained me. He was very vivacious and easy in all his movements and in his speech; he had not a trace of arrogance or insolence, of the scornful tone of the capital, nor of the military man, nor of the guardsman. . . . On the contrary, there was something caressing, almost shamefaced, about his very ease of manner, as though he were begging us to pardon him. The eyes of some people never laugh, even at moments of laughter; *his* lips almost never changed their fine mould, but his eyes smiled almost uninterruptedly. So we chatted about an hour . . . . what it was about, I do not remember; all I do remember is, that I looked him in the eye the whole time, and I felt so much at my ease with him! In the evening I played the piano. He was very fond of music; he sat in an arm-chair, and, resting his curly head on his hand, listened attentively. Not once did he praise me, but I understood that my playing pleased him, and I played with passion. Semyón Matvyéevitch, who was sitting by the side of his son, and looking over plans, suddenly frowned.—" Come, madam,"—said he, pluming himself and buttoning up his coat, as usual:—" that will do; what do you mean by rattling away there, like a canary-bird? It's enough to give one a headache. I don't believe you are exerting yourself in that way for old fellows like myself "—he added in an undertone, and again ordered me to begone.

Michel followed me with his eyes to the door, and rose from his chair.—" Whither away? whither away? "—

shouted Semyón Matvyéevitch, and suddenly burst out laughing, and then said something more. . . I could not catch his words; but Mr. Ratsch, who was present also, in a corner of the drawing-room (he was always " present," and on this occasion he had brought the plans), laughed obsequiously, and his laughter reached my ears. . . . The same thing, or almost the same thing, happened again on the following evening. . . . Semyón Matvyéevitch suddenly cooled off toward me, and laid me under a ban.

Four days later, I met Michel in the corridor which separated the manor-house into two parts. He took my hand, and led me into a room which adjoined the dining-room, and was called the portrait-room. I followed him, not without agitation, but with complete confidence. I think I would have gone to the end of the world with him then, although I did not, as yet, suspect what he had become to me. Akh, I had grown attached to him with all the passion, with all the despair of a young being who not only has no one to love, but who feels herself to be an unbidden and superfluous guest among strangers, among persons hostilely disposed toward her! . . .

Michel told me. . . And, strange to say! I gazed boldly and straight at him,—while he did not look at me, and flushed slightly,—he told me that he understood my position, and sympathised with me, and begged me to forgive his father. . . . " As for myself,"—he added, —" I entreat you always to trust me, and you must know that to me you are a sister, yes, a sister."—Here he pressed my hand warmly. I grew confused, and dropped my eyes in my turn; I seemed to have been expecting something else, some other word. Nevertheless, I began to thank him.—" No, please,"—he interrupted me,—" do not speak like that. . . . But remember: it is the duty of brothers to defend their sisters, and if you should stand in need of defence,—against any one whomsoever,—rely on me. I have not been here long, —but I already understand a great deal . . . . and, among other things, I have come to understand your stepfather."—Again he pressed my hand, and went away.

I learned, later on, that Michel had felt an aversion for Mr. Ratsch from their very first meeting. Mr. Ratsch had tried to win his good-will; but when he became convinced that his efforts were unavailing, he immediately took up a hostile attitude toward him, and not only did not conceal this from Semyón Matvyéevitch, but, on the contrary, tried to make a display of it, at the same time expressing regret that he had no luck with the young heir. Mr. Ratsch had made a thorough study of Semyón Matvyéevitch's character: his calculation proved to be correct. " That man's devotion to me is above suspicion, because when I am gone, he is ruined; my heir cannot endure him " . . . . this idea took firm root in the old man's mind. It is said that all people who hold power are readily caught by this bait, as they grow old—the bait of exclusive, personal devotion. . . .

Not without cause had Semyón Matvyéevitch called Mr. Ratsch " his Araktchéeff ". . . . He might have given him another name. " *Thou* never contradictest me," he was accustomed to say to him. He had begun to address him as " thou " almost from the very day of his arrival, and my stepfather gazed fondly at Semyón Matvyéevitch's lips, lolled his head on one side, like a helpless orphan, and laughed good-naturedly, as much as to say: "Here 's the whole of me; I 'm wholly yours" .... Akh! I feel my hand tremble, and my heart fairly thump against the edge of the table on which I am writing at this moment. ... It is terrible to me to recall those days, and my blood begins to boil. ... But I will tell all, to the very end .... to the very end.

Mr. Ratsch's manner toward me assumed a new tinge during the period of my brief exaltation to favour. He began to treat me with obsequiousness, to be respectfully familiar with me, exactly as though I had acquired wisdom and had become more intimate with him.—"You 've stopped making wry faces,"—he said to me one day, on his return from the manor-house to our wing.—"I approve! All those virtues, those sensibilities, those various airs and graces, in one word, are no business of ours, young lady, no business of paupers!"—But when I fell out of favour, and Michel no longer considered it necessary to hide either his scorn for him or his sympathy for me, Mr. Ratsch suddenly redoubled his harshness; he kept watching me constantly, as though I were capable of any sort of crime, and ought to have a tight hand kept over me.—"You just look out,"—he shouted, precipitating himself, without asking permission, into my room, in muddy boots, and with his cap on his head.— "I won't stand anything of the sort, you know! Don't you put on any airs with me! You can't impose on me, and I 'll humble your pride!"—And then, one morning, he announced to me that Semyón Matvyéevitch had issued an order that henceforth I was not to present myself at the dinner-table without a special invitation. ...

A HAPLESS GIRL

I know not how all this would have turned out, had not an event occurred which finally decided my fate. . . . Michel was passionately fond of horses. He took it into his head to break in a young trotter. The horse ran away, began to kick, and flung him out of the sledge. . . . He was brought home unconscious, with a dislocated arm, and his chest crushed. The old man was thoroughly frightened, and summoned the best doctors from the town. They helped Michel, but he was obliged to lie still for a month. He did not play cards; the doctors had forbidden him to talk; it was awkward to read, holding the book in one hand only. It ended in Semyón Matvyéevitch himself sending me to his son, in the capacity of reader, in memory of the olden days. Then began hours never to be forgotten! I went to Michel immediately after dinner, and sat at a small round table, by the half-veiled window. He lay in a small room off the drawing-room, against the rear wall, on a broad leather divan, in the " Empire " style, with a gilded bas-relief on the high, straight back; this bas-relief depicted a wedding procession of the ancients. Michel's pale, half-recumbent head immediately turned on the pillow, with the face toward me; he smiled with the whole of his bright face, tossed back his soft, damp hair, and said to me in a soft voice: " Good morning, my kind, my dear one! " I took my book—Walter Scott's romances were then at the height of their fame—and the reading of " Ivanhoe " has remained especially memorable to me. . . . How my voice involuntarily rang out and trembled, when I reproduced Rebecca's speeches! For Jewish blood flowed in my veins also, and did not my fate resemble her fate,—was not I nursing a beloved sick man, even as she did? Every time that I tore my eyes from the pages of the book and raised them to him, I met his eyes, with that same brilliant, quiet smile of the whole face. We talked very little; the door leading into the drawing-room was always open, and some one was always sitting there; but when silence reigned there, I stopped reading, I myself know not why, and dropped the book on my lap, and gazed immovably at Michel, and he gazed at me, and we were both happy, and somehow joyous, and ashamed, and at such times we told each other everything, everything, without a movement, and without words. Akh! Our hearts drew together, they advanced to meet each other, as subterranean rivulets flow together, unseen, unheard . . . . and inseparably.

"Do you know how to play chess or draughts?"— he asked me one day.

"I know how to play chess a little,"—I replied.

"Well, that 's capital. Order the board to be brought, and move up the table."

I seated myself beside the divan, but my heart fairly died within me, and I dared not look at Michel. . . . But from the window, clear across the room, how freely I had gazed at him!

I began to set out the chessmen. . . . My fingers trembled.

"I did n't do it . . . . for the sake of playing with you . . . " . . . said Michel, in a low tone, as he, also, set out the pieces,—"but in order that you might be nearer to me."

I made no reply, and without asking who should play first, I moved a pawn. . . . Michel did not respond to my play. . . . I glanced at him. With his head thrust slightly forward, all pale, with imploring eyes, he directed my attention to my hand.

Whether I understood him . . . . I do not remember, but something instantaneously, like a whirlwind, circled in my brain. . . . In confusion, hardly breathing, I grasped the queen, and moved her somewhere or other, clear across the board. Michel swiftly bent over, and capturing my fingers with his lips, and pressing them to the board, began to kiss them silently and eagerly. . . . I could not, I would not withdraw them; with the other hand, I covered my face, and tears, as I now recall the circumstances, cold but blissful . . . oh, what blissful tears! . . . . dropped one by one on the table. Akh, I knew, with all my heart, I felt then in whose power my hand was! I knew that he who held it was no boy, carried away by a momentary impulse, no Don Juan, no military Lovelace, but the noblest, the best of men . . . and he loved me!

" Oh, my Susanna! "—I heard Michel's whisper:— " I will never cause you to shed any other sort of tears. . . ."

He was mistaken. . . . He did.

But why should I linger over these memories . . . especially, especially now!

Michel and I vowed that we would belong to each other. He knew that Semyón Matvyéevitch would never allow him to marry me, and he did not hide this fact from me. I myself had no doubt on that point, and I rejoiced, not that Michel did not behave craftily: he *could not* behave craftily:—but because he did not attempt to deceive himself. I myself demanded nothing, and would have followed him whensoever and whither-

soever he would.—" Thou shalt be my wife,"—he repeated to me,—" I am not Ivanhoe; I know that happiness does not lie with Lady Rowena."—Michel soon
recovered. I could no longer go to him; but everything
was already settled between us. I surrendered myself
wholly to the future; I beheld nothing around me; I
seemed to be floating down a very beautiful, level but
rushing river, enveloped in a mist. And we were watched,
a guard was set on us. Now and then I noticed my stepfather's malicious eyes, heard his loathsome horse-laugh.
. . . But that laugh and the eyes also seemed to start
out from the mist, for a single instant. . . . I shuddered, but immediately forgot, and again surrendered
myself to that swift, beautiful river. . . .

On the eve of Michel's departure, which had been
agreed upon between us (he was to return secretly from
the road, and carry me away), I received from him,
through his confidential valet, a note, in which he appointed a meeting with me for half-past nine in the evening, in the summer billiard-room,—a large, low-ceiled
room, built on to the main body of the house on the garden side. He wrote me that he wished to have a final
talk with me, and definitively come to an understanding.
I had already met Michel twice in the billiard-room.
. . . I had a key to the outer door. As soon as the
clock struck half-past nine, I threw on a warm, short
jacket and made my way safely, over the crackling
snow, to the billiard-room. The moon, shrouded in
vapour, stood like a dull spot directly above the roof-tree,
and the wind was whistling shrilly round the corner of
the wall. A shiver ran over me, but I inserted the key in
the lock, notwithstanding. I entered the room, shut the

door behind me, turned round. . . . A dark figure separated itself from one of the partition-walls, advanced a couple of steps, halted. . . .

" Michel,"—I whispered.

" Michel, in accordance with my orders, is under lock and key, but it is I!"—replied a voice which fairly made my heart stop beating. . . .

Before me stood Semyón Matvyéevitch!

I tried to flee, but he seized me by the arm.

" Whither away? you good-for-nothing hussy!"—he hissed.—"If you know enough to keep trysts with young fools, just know enough to take the consequences!"

I turned deadly pale with terror, but still struggled to reach the door. . . . In vain! Semyón Matvyéevitch's fingers dug into me like iron hooks.

"Let me go, let me go!"—I implored, at last.

" You shall not stir from this spot, I tell you!"

Semyón Matvyéevitch made me sit down. In the semi-darkness, I could not scrutinise his face, for I had turned away from him; but I heard him breathing heavily, and gnashing his teeth. It was neither alarm nor despair that I felt, but a sort of irrational surprise. . . . A captured bird must sink down in just that way, in the claws of the hawk . . . . and the hand of Semyón Matvyéevitch, who still kept a firm hold of me, clutched me like a paw. . . .

" Aha!"—he repeated:—"aha! Just see there now . . . . to what . . . Come, stand up!"

I tried to rise, but he shook me with such violence that I almost screamed aloud with pain, and words of abuse, insults, threats, rained down in a torrent. . . .

" Michel, Michel, where art thou? Save me,"—I moaned.

Semyón Matvyéevitch shook me again. . . This time I did not restrain myself. . . . . I shrieked.

This, evidently, had some effect on him. He quieted down a little, released my arm, but remained where he was, a couple of paces from me, between me and the door.

Several minutes passed. . . . . I did not stir; he continued to breathe heavily as before.

" Sit still,"—he began, at last,—" and answer me. Prove to me that your morals are not yet thoroughly depraved, and that you are in a condition to listen to the voice of reason. I can pardon impulse; but rooted obstinacy—never! My son . . . . " Here he took breath.—" Mikhaílo Semyónitch promised to marry you? Is n't that true? Answer! Did he promise? Hey? "

Of course, I did not answer.

Semyón Matvyéevitch came near flaring up again.

" I accept your silence as a token of assent,"—he went on, after waiting a little.—" And so you thought you were going to be my daughter-in-law? Very fine! But, not to mention the fact that you are not a fourteen-year-old child, and ought to know that all young boobies are lavish of the most stupid promises, if only they may attain their ends,—not to mention that . . . is it possible that you could hope that I, I, a hereditary noble, Semyón Matvyéevitch Koltovskóy, would ever give my consent to such a marriage? Or did you intend to dispense with the parental blessing? . . . . You meant to elope, get married secretly, and then return, act a comedy, throw yourselves at my feet, in the hope that the old man would be touched. . . . Come, answer, damn you!"

I merely bowed my head. He might kill me, but make me speak . . . . that was not in his power.

He strode back and forth for a while.

"Here now, listen to me,"—he began in a calmer voice.—"You are not to imagine . . . I see that I must talk to you in a different way. Listen: I understand your position. You are frightened, distracted. . . . Recover yourself. At this moment, I must seem to you a monster—a tyrant. But do you enter into my position also: how could I help feeling indignant, saying unnecessary things? And nevertheless, I have already proved to you that I am not a monster, that I have a heart. Remember how I treated you after my arrival in the country, and afterward, until . . . . until quite recently . . . . until Mikhaíl Semyónitch's illness. I do not wish to boast of my good deeds, but it seems to me gratitude alone should have withheld you from the slippery path on which you have decided to tread! . . ."

Again Semyón Matvyéevitch stalked to and fro, and, coming to a halt, he lightly patted my arm, that same arm which was still aching from his violence, and on which, for a long time afterward, I bore blue marks. . . .

"The fact is . . . ." he began again—"we are hot-headed, hot-headed! We will not give ourselves the trouble to think, we will not consider wherein our profit lies, and where we should seek it. You ask me: Where is that profit? You need not go far. . . It is, perhaps, right under your hand. . . . Why, take myself, for instance. As a parent, as head of the house, I ought, of course, to be exacting. . . . That is my duty. But I am a man, at the same time, and you know it. Indis-

putably: I am a practical man, and, of course, I cannot
allow any nonsense; utterly incompatible hopes must, of
course, be banished from the mind, because, what's the
sense in them? I am not talking now of the immorality
of the deed itself. . . . All that you will, assuredly,
understand yourself, when you recover your senses. But
I will say, without boasting: I would not limit myself to
what I have already done for you; I have always been
ready—and I am still ready—to establish and consoli-
date your welfare, to provide for you in the fullest manner, because I know your value, I do justice to your
talents, to your mind, and, in short . . . ." (Here Semyón Matvyéevitch leaned slightly toward me) . . . .
" You have such eyes that I must confess . . . here I
am, an old man, but to behold them with perfect indifference . . . I understand . . . . is difficult, is very difficult."

These words sent a chill over me. I hardly believed
my ears. At the first moment it had seemed to me that
Semyón Matvyéevitch wanted to purchase my renuncia-
tion of Michel, to buy me off. . . . But those words!
My eyes had begun to grow used to the darkness, and
I could distinguish Semyón Matvyéevitch's face. It was
leering, that aged face, and he himself kept on walking
about, in short strides, shifting from foot to foot in
front of me. . . .

" Well, what do you say to it? "—he asked, at last,—
" does my proposal please you? "

" Your proposal? "—I repeated involuntarily . . .
" I have positively understood nothing."

Semyón Matvyéevitch laughed . . . . actually
laughed, with his shrill, repulsive laughter.

" Of course! "—he exclaimed:—" all of you, you

young wenches,"—he corrected himself:—"girls . . . .
girls . . . . all of you dream of but one thing: you
must always have young men! Youth is a good thing!
But are young men the only ones who know how to love?
. . . An old man's heart is sometimes more ardent, and
if the old man falls in love with any one,—his love is as
firm as a stone wall! It is eternal! It's quite a different
thing from those beardless dolts, whose heads are merely
filled with wind! Yes, yes; old men must not be despised! They can do a great deal! Only, one must
know how to deal with them! Yes . . . yes! And the
old men know how to caress, too, he-he-he! . . . ."
Again Semyón Matvyéevitch burst into a laugh.—
"Here now, permit me . . . your hand . . . on trial
. . . . only that . . . . by way of trial. . . ."

I sprang from my chair, and struck him in the breast
with all my might. He staggered back; he emitted some
sort of quavering, frightened sound; he almost fell. The
human language contains no words wherewith to express the degree to which he seemed to me disgusting
and insignificantly base. Every semblance of fear left
me.

"Go away, you despicable old man,"—burst from
my breast,—"go away, Mr. Koltovskóy, hereditary
nobleman! Your blood, the blood of the Koltovskóys,
flows in my veins also, and I curse the day and the hour
when it began to flow in my veins!"

"What? . . . . What's that thou art saying? . . .
What?"—stammered Semyón Matvyéevitch, panting.—
"Dost thou dare . . . at this moment, when I have
found thee . . . . when thou wert going to Míshka
. . . . hey? hey? hey?"

A HAPLESS GIRL

But I could no longer restrain myself. . . . Something ruthless, desperate, awoke within me.

"And you, you, the brother . . . . the brother of your brother, you have dared, you have presumed. . . . For whom did you take me? And can it be possible that you are so blind that you did not, long ago, observe the loathing with which you inspire me? . . . . You have dared to use the word ' proposal '! . . . Let me go at once, this very instant!"

I went toward the door.

"Ah, so that's it! that's how the land lies! Now she has had her say!"—squeaked Semyón Matvyéevitch, in a delirium of rage, but evidently unable to make up his mind to approach me. . . . "Just wait a bit! Mr. Ratsch, Iván Demyánitch! please come here!"

The door of the billiard-room, opposite to the one which I had entered, was thrown wide open, and my step-father made his appearance, a lighted candelabra in each hand. Illumined from both sides by the candles, his round, red face beamed with the triumph of satisfied revenge, of servile joy in his successful service. . . . Oh, those disgusting, white eyes! when shall I cease to behold them!

"Be so good as to take charge of this girl immediately,"—cried Semyón Matvyéevitch, addressing my stepfather, and pointing imperiously at me with his trembling hand.—"Be so good as to take her home, and place her under lock and key . . . . so that she . . . . cannot move a finger,—so that not even a fly can get to her! Until I give orders to the contrary! Nail up the window, if necessary! Thou shalt answer to me for her with thy head!"

A HAPLESS GIRL

Mr. Ratsch set the candelabra on the billiard-table, made a girdle-reverence to Semyón Matvyéevitch, and swaying slightly and smiling with malicious delight, walked toward me. That must be the way in which a cat approaches a mouse which has no way of escape. All my hardihood instantly deserted me. I knew that that man was capable of . . . . beating me. I trembled; yes; oh, disgrace! oh, shame! I trembled.

" Well, madam,"—said Mr. Ratsch:—" be so good, ma'am, as to come along, ma'am."

Without haste, he grasped my arm, above the elbow. . . . He understood that I would not resist. I myself moved forward, toward the door; at that moment, I was thinking of but one thing: to rid myself, as speedily as possible, of the presence of Semyón Matvyéevitch.

But the horrible old man sprang after us, and Ratsch stopped me, and turned me round to face his patron.

" Ah!"—screamed the latter, and shook his fist:— " ah! I am the brother . . . of my brother! The ties of blood? hey? And can one marry her cousin?[1] Can she? hey? . . . Take her away!"—he said to my step-father.—" And remember: keep a sharp watch! For the slightest communication with her,—death is too good a punishment. . . . Take her away!"

Mr. Ratsch conducted me to my room. As we passed through the yard he said nothing to me, but merely kept laughing to himself, without making a sound. He fastened the shutters, the doors, and then, as he was taking his departure for good, he made me a reverence to the girdle, as he had to Semyón Matvyéevitch, gave a snort-

[1] This is impossible in the Holy Catholic Church of the East:—TRANSLATOR.

ing guffaw, then burst into a roar of heavy, ecstatic laughter. "Good night to the Tzarévna Melikitrísa,"— he groaned in a stifling voice:—"she has not caught the Tzarévitch Mitrofán![1] What a pity! It was quite a bright idea in its way! Learn a lesson for the future: don't carry on correspondences! Ho-ho-ho! But how splendidly everything worked!"—he left the room, then suddenly thrust his head in at the door. "Well? I have n't *forgotten you*, have I? Hey? Have I kept my word? Ho-ho!" The key rattled in the lock. I heaved a sigh of relief. I had been afraid that he might tie my hands . . . . but they were my own,—they were free! I instantly tore a silk cord from my night-wrapper, made a noose, placed it on my neck, but immediately flung aside the cord. "I will not gratify you!" I said aloud. "And, as a matter of fact, what madness! Can I dispose of my life without Michel's knowledge,—my life, which I have given to him? No, my villain! No! You have n't won the game yet! He will save me, he will wrest me from this hell, he . . . . my Michel!"

But at this point I remembered that he was imprisoned, just as I was—and I flung myself face down on my bed, and sobbed . . . . and sobbed. . . . And the thought that my tormentor was possibly standing outside the door, and listening, and triumphing, was the only thing which made me swallow my tears. . . .

I am weary. I have been writing ever since morning, and now it is evening; if I once tear myself from this sheet of paper, I shall not be able to take up my pen again. . . . Let me get to the end quickly, as quickly

---

[1] Mitrofán is the name usually applied to a stupid young man. Hence, here, it means the Booby Prince. —TRANSLATOR.

as possible! And moreover, it is beyond my strength to pause over the horrors which followed that dreadful day!

Twenty-four hours later, I was transported in a covered sledge to an isolated cottage belonging to a house-serf; surrounded by peasant guards, I was kept locked up for six weeks! I was not alone for a single minute. . . . I afterward learned that my stepfather had set spies on me and on Michel from the very moment of the latter's arrival, and that he had bribed the servant who brought me the note from Michel; I also learned that a frightful, a shocking scene had taken place between him and his father, on the following morning. . . . His father had cursed him. Michel, on his side, had sworn that he would never again set foot in his father's house, and had gone off to Petersburg. But the blow dealt me by my stepfather rebounded on himself. Semyón Matvyéevitch announced to him that it was impossible for him to remain any longer in the country, or to manage the estate: evidently, clumsy zeal cannot be pardoned, and some one must be punished for the *scandal* which had occurred. However, Semyón Matvyéevitch lavishly rewarded Mr. Ratsch: he gave him the means wherewith to remove to Moscow, and settle there. Before our departure for Moscow, I was taken back to the wing, but, as before, I was kept under the strictest surveillance. The loss of the "warm" place, of which he had been deprived, "thanks to me," had still further augmented my stepfather's wrath against me.

"And whom did you think to surprise?"—he was wont to say, almost snorting with rage:—"really! The old man, of course, waxed angry, was over-hasty, and got into a scrape; now, of course, his self-love has suffered; it is impossible to repair the mischief now. You might have waited a day or two, and everything would have gone on as though it were oiled; you would n't be sitting now on a diet of dry food, and I would have remained as I was! That 's exactly the trouble: women's hair is long, but their wits are short! Well, it 's all right; I 'll get my due, and that precious pet " (he referred to Michel) " will not forget me."

Of course, I was compelled to bear all these insults in silence. And I never beheld Semyón Matvyéevitch again,—not even once. His parting from his son had shaken him also. Whether he felt repentance, or,—which is much more probable,—whether he wished forever to chain me to my home, to my family—to my family!—at all events, he assigned me a pension, which was to be paid into the hands of my stepfather, and doled out to me, until I married. . . . This humiliating alms, this pension, I am receiving up to the present day . . . . that is to say, Mr. Ratsch receives it for me. . . .

We removed to Moscow. I swear by the memory of my poor mother that I would not have remained two days, two hours, with my stepfather, after I got to town. . . . I would have gone away, no matter where . . . . to the police-station; I would have thrown myself at the feet of the Governor-General, of the senators; [1] I know not what I would have done, if, at the very moment of our departure from the country, my former maid had not succeeded in transmitting to me a letter from Michel. Oh, that letter! How many times have I re-read every line, how many times have I covered it with kisses! Michel implored me not to lose courage, to hope on, to be

[1] That is—the judges of the Supreme Court of Appeal.—TRANSLATOR.

assured of his unchangeable love; he vowed that he
would belong to no one but me, he called me his wife, he
drew a picture of our future, he besought one thing of
me: to have patience, to wait a little. . . . And I made
up my mind to wait, and to have patience. Akh, to
what would not I have assented, what would not I have
endured, if only I might fulfil his will! That letter became my sacred treasure, my guiding star, my anchor.
My stepfather would begin to upbraid me, to insult me,
and I would quietly lay my hand on my breast (I wore
Michel's letter sewed into an amulet), and merely smiled.
And the more Mr. Ratsch raged and swore, the happier
and sweeter was it for me. . . . At last, I saw by his
eyes that he was beginning to wonder whether I were
not going crazy. . . . After that first letter, another
arrived, still more filled with hope. . . . It spoke of a
speedy meeting.

Akh! instead of that meeting there came a morning.
. . . And I saw Mr. Ratsch enter my room,—and again
triumph, malicious triumph, was on his face,—and in
his hands was a sheet of *The Invalid,* and in it was announced the death of Mikhaíl Koltovskóy, Captain of
cavalry in the Guards. . . . Stricken from the muster-
roll.

What can I add? I remained alive, and continued to
live with Mr. Ratsch. He hated me as before, more than
before,—he had unveiled too thoroughly before me his
black soul: he could not forgive me for that. But it
made no difference to me. I had become, somehow, insensible; my own fate no longer interested me. To recall *him!* to recall *him!* I had no other occupation, no
other joy. My poor Michel had died with my name on

his lips. . . . This was communicated to me by a man who was devoted to him, who had come to the country with him. That same year, my stepfather married Eleonora Kárpovna. Semyón Matvyéevitch soon died, confirming and augmenting in his will the pension he had allotted to me. . . . In case of my death, it was to pass to Mr. Ratsch. . . .

One year, two years, three years passed . . . . six years, seven years elapsed. . . . Life lapsed, flowed on . . . and I merely watched it flow. Thus, in childhood, does one construct on the river-bank a little pond of sand, and erect a dam, and strive, in every way, to keep the water from leaking out, from breaking through. But lo, at last it breaks, and you cast aside all your cares, and it becomes amusing for you to watch all you have gathered together run away, to the last drop. . . .

Thus did I live, thus did I exist, until, at last, a new and unexpected ray of warmth and light . . . .

With this word the manuscript stopped short; the following pages had been torn away, and several lines, which completed the phrase, had been crossed out and smeared with ink.

XVIII

THE perusal of this note-book agitated me to such a degree, the impression produced by Susanna's visit was so great, that I could not get to sleep all night; and early in the morning I sent to Fústoff by special messenger, a letter in which

I adjured him to return to Moscow as speedily as possible, since his absence might produce the most painful results. I even gave him a hint of my interview with Susanna, of the note-book which she had left in my hands. After despatching the letter, I never left the house all day long, and meditated constantly on what must be taking place yonder, at the Ratsches'. I could not bring myself to go thither. But I could not fail to observe that my aunt was in a state of perpetual trepidation. She gave orders to disinfect the rooms almost every minute, and laid out the " Traveller " patience, famous for never coming out. The visit of an unknown lady, and late at night into the bargain, had not remained a secret from her. The yawning abyss on whose brink I was standing kept presenting itself to her imagination, and she kept sighing and moaning in an undertone, and uttering French sentiments which she had culled from a small manuscript book entitled: " Extraits de Lecture," and in the evening I found on my night-stand the works of De Gerandeau, opened at the chapter, " On the Perniciousness of Passion." This book had been brought into my room, of course, at the order of my aunt, by her oldest companion, who was called Amíshka in the house, in consequence of her resemblance to a tiny poodle of that name ("Ami "), and was an extremely sentimental and even romantic spinster of ripe age. The whole of the

following day passed in wearisome waiting for
Fústoff's arrival, for a letter from him, for news
from the Ratsch domicile . . . . although, why
should they send to me? Susanna would be more
likely to assume that I would call upon her. . . .
But, positively, I had not the courage to see her,
without having first discussed matters with Fústoff. I recalled all the expressions in my letter
to him. . . . Apparently, they were sufficiently
strong. At last, late at night, he made his appearance.

XIX

HE entered my room with his customary swift,
but unhurried step. His face seemed to me pale,
and while displaying traces of fatigue from his
journey, expressed perplexity, curiosity, dissatisfaction—feelings which, at ordinary times, were
little known to him. I rushed to meet him, embraced him, thanked him warmly for having
heeded me, and informing him, in a couple of
words, of my interview with Susanna, I handed
him her note-book. He walked off to the window,—that same window on which, two days previously, Susanna had sat,—and without saying a
word to me, he began to read. I immediately
withdrew into the opposite corner of the room,
and picked up a book to keep myself in counte-

nance. But I must confess that I gazed stealthily, all the while, over the edge of the cover at
Fústoff. At first he read with considerable composure, and with his left hand kept plucking
at the tiny hairs on his lip; then he dropped his
hand, bent forward, and made no further movement. His eyes fairly raced over the pages, and
his mouth opened a little. Then he finished the
note-book, turned it about in his hands, scrutinised it on all sides, meditated, and set to
reading again, and read it clear through for
the second time, from beginning to end.
Then he rose to his feet, thrust the book into
his pocket, and started for the door; but he
turned round, and stood still, in the middle of
the room.

" Well, what thinkest thou? "—I began, without waiting for him to speak.

" I am to blame toward her,"—articulated Fústoff, in a dull voice.—" I have behaved . . . .
thoughtlessly, unpardonably, savagely. I believed that . . . . Viktór."

"What!"—I cried:—"that same Viktór whom
thou despisest? But what could he have told
thee? "

Fústoff folded his arms, and stood with his side
toward me. He was ashamed; I saw that.

" Thou rememberest "—he said, not without an
effort—" that Viktór alluded to . . . . a pension. That unfortunate word rankled in me. It

is the cause of all. I began to question him. . . .
Well, and he . . . ."

" What did he do? "

" He told me that that old man . . . what 's
his name? . . . . Koltovskóy, had assigned this
pension to Susanna, because . . . . for the reason . . . . well, in short, by way of recompense."

I clasped my hands.

" And thou didst believe it? "

Fústoff bowed his head.

" Yes! I believed it. . . . He said, also, that
with the young man also . . . . In a word, my
step cannot be justified."

" And didst thou go away with the object of
breaking off everything? "

" Yes; that is the best means . . . . in such
cases. I have behaved barbarously, barbarously,"
—he repeated.

Both of us were silent. Each of us felt that
the other was ashamed; but I was relieved: I was
not ashamed for myself.

XX

" I 'd smash every bone in that Viktór's body
now,"—went on Fústoff, gritting his teeth,—" if
I did not recognise that I myself am to blame.
Now I understand why that whole affair was con-
cocted: when Susanna married, they would lose
her pension. . . . The villains! "

I took his hand.

"Alexander,"—I asked,—"hast thou been to see her?"

"No; I came straight from the road to thee. I will go to-morrow . . . . early to-morrow morning. Matters cannot be left in this state. Not on any account!"

"And dost thou . . . . love her, Alexander?"

Fústoff seemed to take offence.

"Of course I love her. I am greatly attached to her."

"She is a very fine, honest young girl!"—I exclaimed.

Fústoff stamped his foot impatiently.

"Why, what idea hast thou got into thy head? I was ready to marry her,—she has been baptised [1]—and I 'm ready to marry her now. I was already thinking of that, although she is older than I am."

That moment, it suddenly seemed to me as though a pallid female form were sitting on the window-sill, leaning forward on her arms. The candles had burned low; it was dark in the room. I shuddered, looked more intently, and, of course, saw nothing on the window-sill. But a queer sort of sensation, a mixture of terror, grief, pity, took possession of me.

---

[1] The marriage ceremony being exclusively religious in Russia, no marriage is possible between a member of the Orthodox Eastern Church and an unbaptised Jew or Jewess.—TRANSLATOR.

"Alexander!"—I began, with sudden impetuosity,—"I beg of thee, I entreat thee, go instantly to the Ratsches'; do not put it off until to-morrow! An inward voice tells me that thou must see Susanna to-day, without fail!"

Fústoff shrugged his shoulders.

"Why dost thou say that, pray? It's eleven o'clock now; probably everybody at their house is fast asleep by this time."

"Never mind. . . . Go, for God's sake! I have a premonition. . . . Please heed me! Go at once; take a cab. . . ."

"Come, what nonsense!"—returned Fústoff, coolly. "What's the use of my going now? I'll be there to-morrow morning, and everything will be cleared up."

"But, Alexander, remember, she said that she was going to die, that thou wouldst not find her. . . . And if thou couldst but have seen her face! Reflect, imagine to thyself how much it must have cost her to make up her mind . . . . to come to me. . . ."

"She has an extravagant brain,"—remarked Fústoff, who, evidently, had regained complete control of himself.—"All young girls are like that . . . . at the start. I repeat,—everything will be put straight to-morrow. Good-bye, for the present. I am tired, and thou art sleepy, also."

He picked up his cap, and left the room.

" But wilt thou promise to come hither immediately and tell me everything? "—I called after
him.

" Yes, I promise. . . . Good-bye! "

I went to bed, but there was an uneasy feeling
at my heart, and I was vexed with my friend.
It was late before I fell asleep, and I dreamed
that Susanna and I were roaming through some
damp, subterranean passages, climbing on steep,
narrow stairways, and descending ever deeper
and deeper, although we were bound, without
fail, to come forth above into the open air, and
all the time some one was incessantly calling to
us, monotonously and plaintively.

XXI

A HAND was laid on my shoulder and I was
shaken several times. . . . I opened my eyes, and
by the dim light of a solitary candle I beheld
Fústoff standing before me. He frightened me.
He was tottering on his legs; his face was yellow,
almost of the same colour as his hair; his lips
drooped; his dull eyes stared stupidly to one side.
What had become of his constantly-caressing and
affable glance? I had a cousin who had become
an idiot from epilepsy. . . . Fústoff resembled
him at that moment.

I hastily raised myself on my elbow.

"What's the matter? What ails thee? Good heavens!"

He made no reply.

"But what has happened, Fústoff? Do speak! Susanna? . . . ."

Fústoff gave a slight start.

"She . . . ." he began, in a hoarse voice, and relapsed into silence.

"What is the matter with her? Hast thou seen her?"

He riveted his gaze on me.

"She is no more."

"What dost thou mean by 'no more'?"

"She no longer exists. She is dead."

I sprang from my bed.

"What dost thou mean by 'dead'? Susanna? She is dead?"

Again Fústoff turned his eyes aside.

"Yes; she is dead; at midnight."

"He has gone crazy!"—flashed through my mind.

"At midnight! But what o'clock is it now?"

"Eight o'clock in the morning. They sent to tell me. She is to be buried to-morrow."

I seized his hand.

"Alexander, thou art not raving? Thou art in thy right mind?"

"I am in my right mind,"—he answered.— "As soon as I heard of it, I came to thee."

My heart was petrified with pain, as is always

the case at the conviction that an irretrievable calamity has happened.

"My God! My God! She is dead!" I repeated again and again.—"How is it possible? So suddenly! Or perhaps she killed herself?"

"I don't know,"—said Fústoff.—"I know nothing. I was told: 'At midnight she died. And she is to be buried to-morrow.'"

"At midnight!"—I thought. . . . "That means that she was still alive when I thought I saw her on the window-sill, when I implored him to hasten to her. . . ."

"She was still living last night, when thou didst urge me to go to Iván Demyánitch's,"—articulated Fústoff, as though he divined my thought.

"How little he knew her!" I meditated again. "How little either of us knew her! 'An extravagant head; all young girls are like that', he said. . . . And at that very moment, perhaps, she was raising to her lips . . . . Is it possible to love a person, and yet be so grossly mistaken about her?"

Fústoff stood motionless in front of my bed, with arms hanging by his side, like a criminal.

A HAPLESS GIRL

XXII

I DRESSED myself in haste.

"What dost thou mean to do now, Alexander?"—I asked.

He looked at me with surprise, as though amazed at the stupidity of my question. And, as a matter of fact, what was there to do?

"But thou canst not avoid going to their house,"—I began.—"Thou must find out how this came about; perhaps there is a crime concealed behind this. One is justified in expecting anything from those people. . . . The whole matter must be cleared up. Remember what is contained in her note-book: the pension ceases in case of her marriage, and *passes* to Ratsch in case of her death. In any case, thou must fulfil the last duty and pay thy respects to her ashes!"

I talked to Fústoff like a tutor, like an elder brother. In the midst of all this horror, grief, and amazement, a certain involuntary feeling of superiority over Fústoff suddenly revealed itself in me. . . . Whether it was that I beheld him crushed by the consciousness of his guilt, distracted, annihilated; whether it was that misfortune, when it overtakes a man, almost always lowers him, sends him down in the estimation of others—as much as to say, "So thou art a sorry creature, since thou hast not managed to extricate

thyself!"—the Lord only knows! At any rate,
Fústoff seemed to me almost a baby, and I was
sorry for him, and comprehended the indispensa-
bility of sternness. I stretched out my hand to
him, from above downward. Only woman's compassion does not proceed from above downward.

But Fústoff continued to stare at me dully and
wildly,—my authority, obviously, had no effect
on him,—and to my repetition of the question:
" Thou wilt go to them, of course?"—he replied:
" No, I will not go."

" Why not, pray? Is it possible that thou dost
not wish to find out for thyself, to inquire what
happened, and how? Perhaps she left a letter
. . . . some sort of document . . . . think of
that!"

Fústoff shook his head.

" I cannot go thither,"—he said.—" That is
why I came to thee, to beg thee . . . . in my
stead. . . . But I cannot . . . . I cannot. . . ."

Fústoff suddenly sat down at the table, covered his face with both hands, and began to sob
bitterly.

" Akh, akh,"—he reiterated through his tears,
—" akh, poor girl . . . . poor, wretched girl. . . .
I lo . . . . I loved her . . . . akh, akh!"

I stood beside him, and I must confess that
these indubitably sincere sobs aroused no sympathy in me. I was merely amazed that Fústoff
could weep in that way; and it seemed to me that

now I understood what a petty man he was, and how utterly different would have been my behaviour in his place. What is there to say of me, after that? Had Fústoff remained perfectly calm, I might, perhaps, have hated him; I might have conceived an aversion for him; but he would not have fallen in my estimation. . . . He would have retained his *prestige;* Don Juan would have remained Don Juan! Very late in life—and only after much experience—does a man learn, at the sight of actual sin or weakness on the part of a fellow-man, to sympathise with him and aid him, without secret personal delight in one's own virtue and strength, but, on the contrary, with all possible humility and comprehension of the naturalness, almost inevitability of the fault!

XXIII

I HAD ordered Fústoff off to the Ratsches' with great bravery and decision; but when I set out for their house at twelve o'clock (Fústoff would not consent, on any terms whatsoever, to go with me, and merely requested me to give him a detailed account of everything), when, from afar, as I turned the corner of the alley, I beheld before me their house with a yellowish spot produced by the death-candle in one of the windows, unspeakable terror oppressed my breathing; I would gladly have turned back. . . . But I conquered myself, and entered the anteroom. It smelled of incense and wax; the pink coffin-lid, edged with silver galloon, stood in one corner, propped against the wall. In one of the adjoining rooms, the dining-room, the monotonous mumble of a chanter boomed like a bumble-bee which had flown in.[1] The sleepy face of the maid-servant peeped forth from the drawing-room; saying, in an undertone: " Have you come to pay your respects? " she pointed at the door of the dining-room. I entered. The coffin stood with its head to the door. Susanna's black hair, beneath the white chaplet,[2] above the raised fringe of the pillow, first met my eye. I walked to the side of the coffin, crossed myself, made a reverence to the earth, and took a look. . . . O God! what a sorrowful aspect! The hapless girl! even death had not spared her, had not imparted

[1] When a member of the Catholic Church of the East dies, the Psalter is read over his remains, until the time comes to bury him—on the third day. This reading comforts the mourners, and inclines them to prayer. Inasmuch as the Psalter is designed chiefly in the light of prayers for the departed, it is interrupted by a commemoration of the dead, with special prayers, wherein the deceased is mentioned by name—the baptismal name only—which prayer is repeated after each of the appointed divisions of the Psalter.—TRANSLATOR.

[2] The chaplet is a strip of material whereon are depicted Christ, His Mother, and John the Baptist, together with the familiar hymn known as "The Thrice Holy." The idea of this is—that the dead Christian is adorned with the wreath of conquest, like a victorious athlete or warrior of the olden days. The figures printed on it signify that he hopes to receive the crown for his deeds only through the mercy of the Triune God, and the mediation of the Virgin Mother, and the Precursor of Christ, St. John.—TRANSLATOR.

to her—I will not say beauty—but even that composure, that gracious and touching composure,
which is so often met with in the features of the
dead. Susanna's small, dark, almost cinnamon-
hued face reminded one of the face of a saint in
very, very ancient holy images; and what an expression lay on that face! An expression as
though she had been on the point of giving vent
to a despairing shriek, and had died without uttering a sound . . . . even the fold between the
eyebrows had not been smoothed out, and her fingers were turned under her palms, and clenched.
I involuntarily averted my gaze; but, after waiting a little, I forced myself to look—to look long
and attentively at her. Compassion filled my
soul; and not alone compassion. "That young girl
died a violent death," I decided in my own mind;
" there is no doubt of it." While I was standing
and gazing at the dead woman, the chanter, who,
on my entrance, had begun to raise his voice, and
had uttered several intelligible sounds, began
again to buzz, and yawned a couple of times. I
made another reverence to the earth, and went
out into the anteroom. On the threshold of the
drawing-room, Mr. Ratsch was already waiting
for me, clad in a gay-coloured Bokhará dressing-
gown, and, beckoning to me with his hand, he
led me into his study; I had almost said, into his
lair. This study—gloomy, contracted, all-per-
meated with the sour odour of plug tobacco—

evoked in the mind a comparison with the dwelling of a wolf or a fox.

XXIV

"A RUPTURE! A rupture of those envelopes there
. . . . of the integument. . . You know, of the
envelopes!"—began Mr. Ratsch, as soon as he
had closed the door.—" Such a calamity! Even
yesterday evening nothing was noticeable, and all
of a sudden: r-r-r-rip! smash! broken in twain!
and that was the end! Why, it was exactly like:
'*Heute roth, morgen todt!*' In truth, it was to
have been expected; I always have expected it;
the regimental doctor in Tambóff, Galimbóvsky,
Vikénty Kazimírovitch . . . . Surely you have
heard of him . . . . an excellent practitioner, a
specialist!"

" This is the first time I have heard his name,"
—I remarked.

"Well, that does not matter. So he,"—went
on Mr. Ratsch, first in a quiet voice, and then
more and more loudly, and, to my astonishment,
with a marked German acccent,—" he had always
warned me: ' Hey! Iván Demyánitch! hey! my
friend, have a care! Your stepdaughter has an
organic defect of the heart—*hypertrophia cor-
dialis!* The least thing will cause a catastrophe!
She must avoid violent emotions most of all. . . .
She must act judiciously. . . .' But, good gra-

cious, how can you expect that of a young girl!
. . . . that she shall act judiciously? Ha . . .
ha . . . ha! . . ."

Mr. Ratsch came near emitting a guffaw, according to his old habit, but caught himself up
in time, and transformed the sound he had begun
into a cough.

Mr. Ratsch said that after all I knew about
him! . . . . However, I considered it my duty
to ask him: "Had a doctor been called in?"

Mr. Ratsch fairly bounded into the air at this.
—"Of course. . . Two were called in, but already everything was completely *abgemacht!*
And just imagine: both came into collision" (Mr.
Ratsch meant to say, "agreed" [1]) "that it was a
rupture!—a rupture of the heart! That's what
they cried out simultaneously. They suggested
an autopsy; but I, . . . you understand, did not
give my consent."

"And the funeral is to be to-morrow?"—I
asked.

"Yes, yes, to-morrow; to-morrow we shall
bury our darling! The body will be removed
from the house at precisely eleven o'clock A.M.
. . . . to the church of St. Nicholas on Chickens'
Legs,[2] . . . . you know? What strange names
our Russian churches have! Then, to her last

---

[1] *Stolkovális'* instead of *staknúlis'*.—TRANSLATOR.

[2] Many of the Moscow churches have quaint names, in popular
phraseology. This means "on supports."—TRANSLATOR.

resting-place, in damp Mother Earth! Will you favour us with your presence? We have not been acquainted long, but I venture to say that the amiability of your disposition, and the loftiness of your sentiments . . ."

I made haste to bow assent.

" Yes, yes, yes,"—sighed Mr. Ratsch,—"this . . . this is really, as the saying is, a flash of lightning from a clear sky! *Ein Blitz aus heiterem Himmel!*"

" And did Susanna Ivánovna say nothing before her death—did she leave nothing?"

" Nothing; absolutely nothing! Not the weeniest-tiniest bit! Not a single scrap of paper! Why, good gracious! when I was summoned to her, when I was roused out of my sleep—just imagine! she had already turned stiff! It was extremely painful for me; she has distressed us all greatly! Alexander Davíditch will, I suppose, also favour us with his presence, when he hears. . . . They say he is not in Moscow? . . . ."

" He did go away for a few days, it is true . . . ." I began.

" Viktór Ivánovitch complains that they are a long time in harnessing his sledge,"—interrupted the maid-servant, the same one whom I had seen in the anteroom. Her face, sleepy, as before, struck me, this time, by that expression of bold rudeness which makes its appearance in servants when they know that their masters are dependent upon them, and will not bring themselves to scold them, or to be exacting with them.

" I 'll come at once, at once,"—pattered Mr. Ratsch.—" Eleonora Kárpovna! Leonore! Lenchen! please come here! "

Something bustled clumsily outside the door, and at that same moment Viktór's imperious exclamation rang out: " Why don't they harness the horse? I can't plod along on foot to the police-station! "

" Immediately; I 'll be there immediately,"— stammered Iván Demyánitch again.—" Eleonora Kárpovna, please come here! "

" *Aber,* Iván Demyánitch,"—her voice became audible,—" *ich habe keine Toilette gemacht!* "

" *Macht nichts! Komm herein!* "

Eleonora Kárpovna entered, holding her kerchief to her bare shoulders with two fingers. She wore a loose morning wrapper, and she had not managed to comb her hair. Iván Demyánitch immediately sprang at her.

" Do you hear, Viktór demands his horse,"—he said hastily, pointing his finger first at the door, then at the window.—" Pray, take the proper measures as promptly as possible! *Der Kerl schreit so!* "

" *Der Viktór schreit immer,* Iván Demyánitch, *sie wissen wohl,*"—replied Eleonora Kárpovna. " And I myself have spoken to the coachman, only he had taken it into his head to give the horse oats. What a misfortune has suddenly happened,"—she added, addressing me:—" and who could have expected it of Susanna Ivánovna?"

" I have always expected it, always!"—shouted Ratsch, and raised his arms aloft, whereupon his Bokhará dressing-gown flew open in front, and disclosed extremely repulsive lower inexpressibles of chamois leather, with brass buckles at the waist.—" A rupture of the heart! A rupture of the envelopes! Hypertrophia!"

" Yes, of course,"—repeated Eleonora Kárpovna after him. . . . " Well, that 's it. Only, I 'm very, very sorry, I will say again. . . ." And her rough face became slightly contorted, her brows rose in triangles, and a tiny tear-drop trickled down her round cheek, which looked like that of a varnished doll. . . . " I 'm very sorry that such a young person, who should have lived and enjoyed everything . . . . everything. . . . And all of a sudden, such despair!"

" *Na! gut, gut . . . . geh, Alte!* "—interrupted Mr. Ratsch.

" *Geh' schon, geh' schon,* "—grumbled Eleonora Kárpovna, and left the room, still holding up her kerchief with her fingers, and shedding small tears.

And I followed her. In the anteroom stood Viktór, in a student's cloak with a beaver collar, and his military cap cocked over one ear. He hardly glanced at me over his shoulder, shook his collar, and did not bow, for which I mentally thanked him heartily.

I returned to Fústoff.

XXV

I found my friend sitting in one corner of his study, with bowed head, and arms folded on his breast. He was stupefied, and stared about him with the slow surprise of a man who has been sleeping very heavily, and has just been waked up. I told him about my visit to Ratsch, repeated to him the veteran's speeches, the speeches of his wife, the impression which they had both made on me, imparted to him my conviction that the unhappy girl had killed herself. . . . Fústoff listened to me without altering the expression of his face, and continued to gaze about him with the same amazement as before.

" Didst thou see her? "—he asked me, at last.

" Yes."

" In her coffin? "

Fústoff appeared to doubt that Susanna was really dead.

" Yes, in her coffin."

Fústoff darted a sidelong glance and dropped his eyes, and quietly rubbed his hands.

" Art thou cold? "—I asked.

" Yes, brother, I 'm cold,"—he replied falteringly, and nodded his head foolishly.

I began to demonstrate to him that Susanna had certainly poisoned herself, and, possibly, had been poisoned, and that things could not be left thus. . . .

Fústoff fixed his eyes on me.

" But what is there to do? "—he said slowly, and blinking broadly.—" It will be all the worse, you know . . . if they find out. They will not bury her. We must leave it . . . . thus."

This consideration—a very simple one, after all—had not occurred to me. My friend's practical good sense had not abandoned him.

" When . . . . is she to be buried? "—he went on.

" To-morrow."

" Shalt thou go? "

" Yes."

" To the house, or straight to the church? "

" Both to the house and to the church; and from there to the cemetery."

" And I shall not go. . . I cannot, I cannot,"—whispered Fústoff, and began to sob. He had begun to sob that morning at the selfsame words. I have noticed that this frequently happens with mourners; just as though certain words alone, generally insignificant words,—but precisely *those* words, and no others,—are endowed with the power of unsealing the fountain of tears

in a man, of shaking him, of awakening in him
a feeling of pity for others and for himself. . . .
I remember how a certain peasant-woman, when
telling me about the sudden death of her daughter during dinner, fairly deluged herself with
tears, and could not continue the story she had
begun, as soon as she uttered the following
phrase: " I says to her: ' Fekla? ' And she says
to me: ' Mámka, what hast thou done with the
salt . . . with the salt . . . . the sa-alt?'". . . . The
word " salt " overwhelmed her. But Fústoff's
tears did not affect me much, any more than they
had in the morning. I could not comprehend
how he could omit to ask me, whether Susanna
had not left something for him? Altogether,
their mutual love was a mystery to me; and it has
remained just as much of a mystery to me.

After weeping for about ten minutes, Fústoff
rose to his feet, lay down on the divan, turned
his face to the wall, and remained motionless. I
waited awhile, but, seeing that he did not stir, and
did not answer my questions, I made up my mind
to depart. I may be bringing a false accusation
against him, but I do believe he had fallen asleep.
However, even that would not have proved that
he felt no grief . . . . but only that his nature
was so constructed that it could not endure painful sensations for long at a time. . . . He had an
awfully well-balanced nature!

A HAPLESS GIRL

XXVI

On the following day, at precisely eleven o'clock, I was on the spot. A thin drizzle was sprinkling from the low-hanging sky, the cold was not great, a thaw was setting in, but keen, unpleasant draughts were abroad in the air. . . . It was the regular chilly weather which prevails during the Great Fast. I found Mr. Ratsch on the front steps of his house. Clad in a black frock-coat with weepers, with no hat on his head, he was bustling to and fro, flourishing his arms, slapping himself on the thighs, shouting now into the house, again into the street, in the direction of the hearse with its white catafalque, which was standing there, and two hired carriages, beside which four soldiers of the garrison, in mourning mantles over old military cloaks and mourning hats over their wrinkled eyes, were thoughtfully poking the poles of their unlighted torches [1] into the porous snow. The grey cap of hair fairly reared on end above Mr. Ratsch's red face, and his voice, that brazen voice, cracked with the strain.—" How about the fir-twigs? The fir-twigs! This way! The fir-branches! "—he roared.—" The coffin will be brought out directly! The fir! Strew the fir-twigs! Look lively! " [2] he shouted once more,

[1] The torches resemble street-lanterns.—Translator.

[2] The road to the church is strewn with twigs and branches of evergreen, symbolical of eternity.—Translator.

and rushed into the house. It appeared that, in spite of my punctuality, I was late. Mr. Ratsch had seen fit to hasten matters. The service was already over. The priests—one of whom wore a kamiláva,[1] while the other, a younger man, had carefully combed and oiled his hair—made their appearance, with their ecclesiastical staff, on the steps. The coffin, also, speedily appeared, borne by the coachman, two yard-porters, and the water-carrier.[2] Mr. Ratsch walked behind, holding the coffin-lid with the tips of his fingers, and repeating unintermittently: "Gently! gently!" After him waddled Eleonora Kárpovna, in a black gown, also with a weeper, surrounded by her entire family. Behind them all marched Viktór, in a new uniform, with his sword, and crape on the hilt. The bearers, grunting and quarrelling, placed the coffin on the hearse; the soldiers of the garrison lighted their torches, which immediately began to crackle and smoke; the wail of a stray beggar-woman resounded; the chanters intoned; the snowy drizzle suddenly increased, and swirled "like white flies"; Mr. Ratsch shouted: "God go with us! Drive on!"—and the procession started. In addition to

[1] A cap of purple velvet, shaped like a section of a cone, reversed, conferred on parish priests as a mark of distinction or reward.— TRANSLATOR.

[2] Until within a comparatively recent date, Moscow's water-supply was brought to the houses by one water-carrier (or more), from the public fountains, in barrels mounted on wheels, and drawn by man or horse-power.— TRANSLATOR.

A HAPLESS GIRL

Mr. Ratsch's family, five persons in all escorted the coffin. A retired, extremely shabby officer of Ways and Communications, with a faded Ribbon of St. Stanislaus on his neck, probably hired for the occasion, or something of that sort; the assistant district inspector of police, a tiny man with a humble face and greedy eyes; some old man or other, in a hooded camelot cloak; a remarkably obese fish-merchant, in a blue overcoat, who smelled of his wares,—and I. The absence of the female sex (for it was impossible to reckon as such two old aunts of Eleonora Kárpovna, the sausage-merchant's sisters, and another lop-sided spinster in blue spectacles on a blue nose), the absence of friends, male and female, surprised me at first; but on considering the matter, I perceived that Susanna, with her temperament and education, could not have had any friends in that sphere in which she lived. Quite a good many people had assembled in the church, more strangers than acquaintances, as was evident from the expression of their countenances. The funeral service did not last long. I was astonished to see Mr. Ratsch cross himself very assiduously, exactly like a member of the Orthodox Church, and all but join in with the chanters, with the notes only, however. But when, at last, the time came to say farewell, I bowed low to Susanna, but did not give her the last kiss. Mr. Ratsch, on the contrary, fulfilled that dreadful rite with great ease of manner. With a respectful inclination of the body, he invited to the coffin the gentleman with the Order of St. Stanislaus, as though he were giving him a treat, and grasping his children under the arms, he lifted them with a flourish, one after the other, to the corpse. Eleonora Kárpovna, on taking leave of Susanna, suddenly broke out crying so that she could be heard all over the church; but she soon quieted down, and kept inquiring, in an irritated whisper: " But where is my reticule? " Viktór held himself aloof, and by his whole bearing, apparently, wished to have it understood how alien he was to all such customs, and that he was merely fulfilling a duty imposed by decency. The person who displayed more sympathy than all the rest was the little old man in the hooded cloak, who had been a surveyor in the Government of Tambóff fifteen years before, and had not seen Ratsch since; he had not known Susanna at all, but had already contrived to drink a couple of glasses of liquor at the buffet. My aunt also had come to the church. By some means or other she had found out that the dead woman was no other than the lady who had paid me a visit, and she was indescribably agitated! She could not make up her mind to suspect me of an evil deed, but neither was she able to explain such a strange concatenation of circumstances. . . . She probably thought that Susanna had decided to commit suicide for my sake, and, donning her darkest garments, with a grieving heart, and in tears, she prayed on her knees for the repose of the soul of the newly-presented,[1] and placed a candle which cost a ruble in front of the holy image of the Consolation of Grief. . . . "Amíshka" had come with her, and prayed also; but she kept staring mostly at me; and being horrified. . . . That ancient spinster was, alas! not indifferent toward me! As my aunt passed out of the church, she distributed to the poor all the money in her pocket, to the amount of more than ten rubles.

The ceremony of bidding farewell came to an end at last. They prepared to cover the coffin. During the whole course of the service, I had not had the heart to look at the distorted face of the poor girl; but every time that my eyes had casually caught sight of it, it seemed to me that it wanted to say: "He has not come! He has not come!" They began to place the lid on the coffin. I could not contain myself: I darted a swift glance at the dead woman. "Why hast thou done this thing?" I asked involuntarily. . . . "He has not come!"—I seemed to hear, for the last time. . . .

The hammer beat upon the nails, and all was over.

[1] In ecclesiastical phraseology: "The newly-presented servant of God" means the dead person who has recently been summoned to God's presence. — TRANSLATOR.

A HAPLESS GIRL

XXVII

WE set out for the cemetery, following the coffin. There were forty of us, of varying quality; in reality, an idle throng. The wearisome procession lasted for more than an hour. The weather grew worse and worse. Viktór got into a carriage half-way there;[1] but Mr. Ratsch stepped out with spirit through the slushy snow, just as he must have stepped out through the snow when, after the fateful meeting with Semyón Matvyéevitch, he had triumphantly led to his home the young girl whom he had forever blighted. The " veteran's " hair, his eyebrows, were bordered with snowflakes; at times he panted and groaned, then valiantly inhaling his breath, he puffed out his strong, brown cheeks. Actually, one might have thought that he was laughing. " After my death, my pension is to pass to Iván Demyánitch,"—the words of Susanna's note-book again recurred to my memory. We reached the cemetery at last; we made our way to the freshly-dug grave. The last rite was speedily performed; every one was benumbed with cold, every one was in a hurry to get it over with. The coffin on its ropes slid into the yawn-

[1] It is customary for men to walk bareheaded behind the corpse from church to cemetery—and women sometimes do it also—as at the funerals of noted authors. The empty carriages follow to relieve the weary, if necessary, or in token of respect from persons who are not present.—TRANSLATOR.

ing pit; they began to throw earth upon it. At
this point, also, Mr. Ratsch displayed his vigor
of spirit; he hurled the clods of earth upon the lid
of the coffin so promptly and with such force, and
in so doing he thrust forward his foot and threw
back his torso in so dashing a manner . . . . he
could not have acted more energetically if it had
been a case of stoning his fiercest enemy to death.
Viktór, as before, held himself aloof; he kept
wrapping his cloak about him, and rubbing his
chin over the beaver of his collar. Mr. Ratsch's
other children zealously followed the example of
their father. It afforded them great pleasure to
fling sand and dirt, for which, however, they
cannot be blamed. A mound made its appearance in place of the pit; we were already preparing to disperse when, all of a sudden, Mr.
Ratsch, wheeling round in military fashion to
the left, and slapping himself on the thigh, announced to all of us, " Messrs. Men," that he invited us, and also " the respected clergy," to the
" feast of commemoration " which had been provided at a short distance from the cemetery, in
the principal hall of a very decent eating-house,
" through the efforts of the most amiable Sigismúnd Sigismúndovitch. . . ." As he uttered
these words, he pointed at the assistant district
police inspector, and added that, in spite of all
his grief, and his Lutheran faith, he, Iván
Demyánitch, as a true Russian, prized ancient

228

Russian customs above all things. "My spouse," he exclaimed,—"and the ladies who have been so good as to come with her, may go home, but we, Messrs. Men, will commemorate with a modest feast the shade of Thy deceased servant!" Mr. Ratsch's proposal was accepted with genuine feeling; "the respected clergy" interchanged expressive glances, and the officer of Ways and Communications slapped Iván Demyánitch on the shoulder and called him a patriot and the soul of society.

We wended our way in a horde to the eating-house. In the eating-house, in the middle of a long and broad but perfectly empty room on the second story stood two tables covered with bottles, viands, table utensils, and surrounded with chairs; the odour of the plaster united with the odour of vodka and fast-oil [1] struck one in the face, and oppressed the breath. The assistant police inspector, in his quality of manager, seated the clergy at the honourable end of the table, where the fasting viands were chiefly massed together; the other guests seated themselves after the clergy; the feast began. I would prefer not to employ so festive a word as feast; but no other word would suit the actual facts. At first, every-

[1] Butter (as well as cheese and eggs), being an animal product, is prohibited during the numerous fasts by the Eastern Catholic Church. In its stead nut-oils are used by the wealthy, and sunflower-seed oil by the less well-to-do, for culinary purposes.—TRANSLATOR.

thing proceeded very quietly, not without a shade of mournfulness. Mouths chewed, wine-glasses were emptied, but sighs were also audible, possibly the sighs of digestion, and, possibly, sighs of feeling. Death was alluded to, attention was directed to the brevity of human life, to the perishableness of earthly hopes. The officer of Ways and Communications narrated an anecdote,—a military anecdote, it is true, yet of an edifying nature; the priest in the purple velvet skull-cap encouraged him, and he himself contributed a curious instance from the life of holy John the Warrior; the other priest, with the capitally-dressed hair, although he paid attention chiefly to the food, nevertheless uttered something of an instructive character about the spotlessness of maidenhood. Gradually everything underwent a change. Faces grew red, voices began to be raised, laughter asserted its rights; abrupt exclamations began to resound, caressing epithets began to make themselves heard, such as: "my dear old chap," "my darling," and even "my pet" and "you dear piggy-wiggy"; in a word, all that sort of thing rained down of which the Russian soul is so lavish when it is, as the saying runs, "unbuttoned." When at last the corks of the Don-district champagne began to pop, things had grown decidedly uproarious; some one even crowed like a cock, and another guest proposed to chew up and swallow the wine-glass

from which he had just been drinking. Mr.
Ratsch, no longer scarlet but dark blue in hue,
suddenly rose from his seat; he had previously
been making a great deal of noise, but at this
point he begged permission to make a speech.
—"Talk away! Make your speech!"—roared
all. The old man in the old-fashioned hooded
cloak even shouted:—"Bravo!"—and clapped
his hands . . . . he was already sitting on the
floor, by the way. Mr. Ratsch raised his beaker
high above his head, and announced that he
intended in brief but "impressive" terms to
indicate the qualities of "that very lovely soul
which, having abandoned here its, so to speak,
earthly shell (*die irdische Hülle*), had soared to
heaven and had plunged" . . . Mr. Ratsch corrected himself: "and had got stuck in the
mire"[1] . . . He corrected himself again: "and
had plunged . . . ."

"Father Deacon! My most respected! My
dear!"—a suppressed, but persuasive whisper
became audible:—"They say you have a hell of
a voice; pray, strike up: 'We Live Amid the
Fields!'"

"Ssh! ssssshsssh!—Stop that! What do you
mean by it!"—flitted past the guests' ears.

" . . . . Has plunged the whole of her devoted
family,"—went on Mr. Ratsch, casting a severe
glance in the direction of the music-lover:—"has

---

[1] He said *pogryázla* instead of *pogruzíla*.—TRANSLATOR.

plunged the whole of her family in inconsolable sorrow!—Yes!"—exclaimed Iván Demyánitch, —" justly does the Russian proverb say: ' Fate persecutes, has no compassion, breaks . . . . ' "

" Stop! gentlemen! "—suddenly shouted a hoarse voice at the end of the table,—" my purse has just been stolen! . . . ."

" Akh, the rascal! "—squeaked another voice, shrilly, and bang! rang out a box on the ear.

Good heavens! What a scene followed! It was as though a wild beast which, up to that moment, had only now and then growled and made a movement at us had suddenly broken loose from his chain and had reared up on his hind legs, in all the terrible beauty of his dishevelled mane. Every one, to all appearances, had privately been expecting a " row " as the natural concomitant and conclusion of the feast, so all fairly flung themselves into the fray, and took a hand. . . . . Plates and glasses crashed, rolled, chairs were overturned, a piercing yell was raised, arms were flourished in the air, coat-tails fluttered, and a brawl began!

" Thrash him! Give him a good drubbing!" thundered my neighbour the fish-dealer, like one dazed, though up to that moment he had seemed the most peaceable man in the world. Truth to tell, he had silently emptied ten glasses of liquor. —" Thrash him! . . . . "

Who was to be thrashed, and for what he was

to be thrashed, he had no idea, but he howled frantically.

The assistant district police inspector, the officer of Ways and Communications, Mr. Ratsch himself, who, probably, had not in the least expected that so speedy an end would be put to his eloquence, tried to restore silence . . . . but their efforts proved fruitless. My neighbour the fish-dealer even attacked Mr. Ratsch.

" Thou hast killed the girl, thou dirty, thrice-damned German,"—he shouted at him, shaking his fists.—" Thou hast bribed the police, and now thou art blustering!"

At this point the waiters ran up. . . .

What happened after that I do not know. I caught up my cap as speedily as possible and took to my heels! All I remember is that something gave a tremendous crack; I also remember herring-bones in the hair of the old man in the hooded cloak, the priest's hat, which flew the whole length of the room, the pale face of Viktór, who was crouched in a corner, and some one's sandy beard, and some one's muscular hand. . . . These were the last impressions which I carried away from " the feast of commemoration," arranged by the most amiable Sigismúnd Sigis-múndovitch, in honour of poor Susanna.

After resting a little, I wended my way to Fústoff, and related to him everything of which I had been a witness in the course of that day.

He listened to me seated, without raising his head, and thrusting both hands under his leg, he said again: "Akh, my poor girl, my poor girl!" and again he lay down on the divan and turned his back to me.

A week later he had entirely recovered, and had begun to live as before. I asked him for Susanna's note-book, as a memento; he gave it to me, without making any difficulties over the matter.

XXVIII

SEVERAL years passed. My aunt died, and I had removed from Moscow to Petersburg. Fústoff, also, had betaken himself to Petersburg. He had entered the Ministry of Finance, but I met him rarely, and no longer saw anything in particular in him. He was an official like all other officials, and therein lies all there is to be said! If he is still alive, and has not married, he has, in all probability, undergone no change to the present day; he turns and glues and occupies himself with gymnastics, and devours his own heart, as of yore; and makes sketches of Napoleon in a blue uniform in the albums of his female friends. I happened to go to Moscow on business. In Moscow I learned, to my no small amazement, I must confess, that the affairs of my former acquaintance, Mr. Ratsch, had taken an unfavourable turn.

His wife, it is true, had presented him with twins, two boys, whom, as a "native Russian," he had had baptised Bryatchesláff and Vyatchesláff; but his house had burned down, he had been compelled to resign from the service, and, the most important item of all—his eldest son, Viktór, seemed a permanent resident of the debtors' prison. During my sojourn in Moscow, in one company, mention of Susanna was made in my presence, and in the most unfavourable, the most insulting manner! I endeavoured, in every possible way, to defend the memory of the hapless girl, to whom fate had denied even a merciful oblivion; but my arguments did not make much impression on my hearers. But I did shake one of them, a young student-poet. He sent me, on the following day, a poem which I have forgotten, but which terminated with the four following lines

> But even o'er the neglected grave
> The voice of scandal has not ceased . . . .
> It agitates the gentle ghost
> And sears the flowers upon its mound!

I perused these verses, and involuntarily fell into a reverie. Susanna's image rose up before me. Again I beheld that frost-covered window in my room; I recalled that evening, and the gusts of the snow-storm, and those words, those sobs. . . . . I began to meditate how Susanna's love for Fústoff could be explained, and why she had surrendered herself so hastily, so irresistibly to despair as soon as she perceived that she had been abandoned. Why had she been unwilling to wait, to hear the bitter truth from the lips of the beloved man himself, to write him a letter? How was it possible to hurl one's self headlong into the abyss in that manner?—Because she so passionately loved Fústoff, I shall be told; because she could not endure the slightest doubt as to his devotion, his respect toward her.—Perhaps so; and perhaps, also, because she did not love Fústoff so passionately; because she had not been mistaken in him, but had only placed her last hopes on him, and was unable to reconcile herself to the thought that even *that* man had turned away from her immediately, at the first word of the calumniator! Who shall say what killed her: wounded self-love, or the pain of an irretrievable position, or, in conclusion, the memory of that first, splendid, just being to whom, in the morning of her life, she had so joyously given herself, who had had such profound confidence in her, and had so respected her? Who knows? Perhaps at the very moment, when it seemed to me that over her dead lips hovered the cry: " He has not come! " her spirit was already rejoicing that she had gone away to him, to her Michel! Great are the mysteries of human life, and the most inaccessible of these mysteries is love. . . . But, nevertheless, even to the present day, whenever the image of Susanna rises up before me, I am unable to crush within me either pity for her, or reproach to Fate, and my lips involuntarily whisper: " The hapless girl! the hapless girl! "

A STRANGE STORY

(1869)

A STRANGE STORY

FIFTEEN years ago—[began Mr. X.], duties connected with the government service compelled me to pass several days in the governmental town of T . . . . I put up at a very decent sort of inn, built six months before my arrival by a Jewish tailor who had grown wealthy. They say that it did not thrive long, which is a very common occurrence in our country; but I found it still in full splendour; the new furniture detonated at night like pistols, the bed-linen, table-cloths and napkins smelled of soap, and an odour of varnish emanated from the painted floors; but this, in the opinion of the waiter, a very elegant although not quite clean individual, prevented the dissemination of insects. This waiter, a former valet to Prince G., was distinguished by his free and easy manner and his self-confidence; he went about constantly in a second-hand dress-suit and shoes down at the heel, carried a napkin under his arm and a quantity of pimples on his cheeks, and freely flourishing his sweaty hands, he gave utterance to brief but edifying remarks. He showed me some goodwill, as a man capable of appreciating his culture and knowledge of the world; but he surveyed his lot with somewhat disillusioned eyes.

" Everybody knows,"—he said to me one day, —" what my position is now. Take him by the tail and fling him out of doors! "—His name was Ardalión.

I was about to make several calls upon the officials of the town. That same Ardalión procured me a calash and a lackey, both equally rickety and shabby; but the lackey wore a livery, and the calash was adorned with a coat of arms. When I had finished all my official calls, I drove to a certain landed proprietor, an old acquaintance of my father's, who had long since settled down in the town of T . . . . I had not seen him for twenty years; he had contrived to marry and raise a good-sized family, had become a widower, and grown rich. He occupied himself with a government monopoly, that is to say, he lent the revenue-farmers money at a high rate of interest. . . . . " The risk . . . . is a noble act! " However, there was very little risk, either. In the course of our conversation, a young girl of seventeen, delicate and slender, entered the room with light but irresolute steps, as though on tiptoe.— " Here,"—said my acquaintance to me,—" this is my eldest daughter, Sophie. I bespeak your goodwill for her; she has taken the place of my dead wife: she keeps house, and looks after her brothers and sisters."—I bowed a second time to the young girl (in the meantime she had dropped in a chair), and thought to myself that she did not look much like a housewife or a governess. Her face was entirely that of a child, round, with small, pleasant, but immobile features, small blue eyes, beneath high, uneven brows, which, also, were immobile, and gazed attentively, almost in surprise, as though they had begun to notice something to which they were not accustomed; the plump little mouth, with its raised upper lip, not only did not smile, but apparently had not the habit of doing so at all; on her cheeks the rosy blood stood beneath the delicate skin in long, soft streaks, which did not increase or decrease. Fluffy fair hair hung in light clusters on both sides of her small head. Her breast rose and fell gently, and her arms were pressed tight to the narrow waist in an awkward, severe sort of way. Her sky-blue gown fell without folds—after the fashion of a child's—to her little feet. The general impression produced by this young girl was not precisely unhealthy, but enigmatic. I beheld before me not simply a shy, provincial young lady, but a being with a peculiar stamp, which was not clear to me. It did not attract me, neither did it repel me; I did not quite understand it, and merely felt that never yet had I happened to encounter a more sincere soul. Pity . . . . yes! Pity was what this young, serious, repressed life evoked in me—God knows why! " She is not of this earth," I thought, although in the expression of her face there was nothing " ideal," and although Mlle. Sophie had, evidently, merely presented herself for the purpose of playing the part of the housewife, to which her father had alluded.

HE began to talk about life in the town of T . . . . about the social pleasures and comforts which it afforded.—" We lead a quiet existence,"—he remarked:—" the Governor is a melancholy man; the Marshal of Nobility for the Government [1] is a bachelor. Day after to-morrow, however, there is to be a ball in the Assembly of the Nobility.[2] I advise you to go. We do not lack beauties here. And you will see all our *intelligéntziya,* too." [3]

My acquaintance, in his quality of a man who had once studied at the university, was fond of using learned expressions. He uttered them with irony, but with respect. Moreover, every one knows that the revenue-farming industry, in company with staidness, develops a certain profundity of thought in men.

" Permit me to ask whether you will be at the

[1] In the sense of a State in the United States.—TRANSLATOR.

[2] A club-house for the gentry—the nobility. The capitals and country towns are provided with them.—TRANSLATOR.

[3] Literally, the cultured class. But it sometimes has a special, restricted meaning in Russia, suggestive of untrustworthiness in politics, and so forth.—TRANSLATOR.

ball? "—I said, addressing my friend s daughter.
I wanted to hear the sound of her voice.

" Papa intends to go,"—she replied,—" and I
shall go with him."

Her voice proved to be gentle and slow, and
she pronounced every word as though she were
perplexed.

" In that case, permit me to invite you for the
first quadrille."—She bowed her head in token
of assent; but even then she did not smile.

I soon took my leave, and I remember that the
look of her eyes, intently fixed on me, seemed to
me so strange that I involuntarily glanced over
my shoulder to find out whether she saw any one
or anything behind my back.

RETURNING to the inn, I dined on the inevitable
" soupe Julienne," cutlets,[1] with peas, and hazel-
hens dried to blackness, then seated myself on the
divan, and gave myself over to meditation. The
subject of my musings was Sófya, that enigmatic daughter of my acquaintance; but as Ardalión cleared the table, he interpreted my
thoughtfulness after his own fashion: he ascribed
it to ennui.

" There are very few diversions in our town for

---

[1] Cutlets, in Russia, is the dignified appellation for boiled beef,
chopped and fried in cakes (something like Hamburger steak).
Fancy names are appended—often the name of a slashing military
hero, such as " Skobeleff cutlets." The difference lies in the season-
ing and the ingredients added to the boiled beef.—TRANSLATOR.

gentlemen who are temporary residents," he began, with his wonted free and easy condescension, at the same time continuing to slap the backs of the chairs with his dirty napkin: this slapping is, as every one knows, peculiar to well-trained servants only. . —" Very few! "—He paused, and the huge wall-clock, with a purple rose on its white face, seemed to be expressing confirmation of his words, by its monotonous and powerful ticking.—" Ve . . . . ry! Ve . . . . ry! " it rapped out.—" There are no concerts or theatres,"—went on Ardalión (he had travelled abroad with his master, and had almost been in Paris; he knew very well that only peasants say: " kiátr "),—" nor dances, for instance, nor evening receptions among the Messrs. Nobles; nothing of that sort exists."—(He paused for a moment, probably for the purpose of giving me a chance to take note of the exquisiteness of his style.) —" They do not even see each other often. Each one sits on his own stalk like some sort of a wooden doll. And the result is that visitors from out of town have nowhere—simply nowhere —to go."

Ardalión darted a sidelong glance at me.

" Unless it be . . . ." he pursued, halting between his words.—" In case you have a mind . . . ."

Again he darted a glance at me, and even grinned; but it must have been that he did not observe the proper inclination in me.

The elegant servant walked to the door, reflected, came back, and, after shifting from foot to foot, he bent down to my ear and said, with a playful smile:

" Would n't you like to see the dead? "

I STARED at him in amazement.

" Yes,"—he went on, still in a whisper;—" we have a man of that sort here. A plain petty burgher, and even illiterate, but he does astounding things. If, for example, you were to present yourself before him, and express a desire to behold any of your deceased acquaintances whomsoever, he will infallibly show him to you."

" In what way? `

" Why, that 's his secret. For, although he is an illiterate man,—to speak straight out, stupid, —yet he is very strong on divinity! The merchant class hold him in great reverence!"

" And is this known to every one in town? "

" Those who care about it know, sir; well, and, of course, he has an eye to danger from the police. Because, say what you will, these are prohibited affairs, and for the common people—a temptation; the common people—the rabble, that is to say, as is well known, would take to their fists at once! "

" Has he shown you any dead people? "—I asked Ardalión. I did not dare to address so cultured a mortal as " thou."

Ardalión nodded his head.—" Yes, sir, he has; he presented my parent as though he were alive."

I fixed my eyes on Ardalión. He was grinning, and playing with his napkin—and gazing condescendingly but firmly at me.

" Why, this is extremely curious,"—I exclaimed at last.—" Cannot I make the acquaintance of this petty burgher? "

" It 's impossible to do it directly, sir; but one must act through his mamma—a very staid old woman; she peddles wetted apples [1] on the bridge. If you command, I 'll ask her, sir."

" Pray, do."

Ardalión coughed behind his hand.—" And, of course, it is proper to hand a small gratuity, whatever you please, to her also, to the old woman. And I, on my part, will announce to her, sir, that she need not fear you, as you are a stranger, a gentleman—well, and, of course, you can understand that this is a secret, and that in no case will you get her into difficulties."

Ardalión took the tray in one hand and, gracefully wriggling both his figure and the tray, walked toward the door.

" So I can rely upon you? "—I called after him.

" Depend on me! "—rang out his self-confi-

---

[1] Apples, as well as the tiny Arctic cranberries, are wet down for winter use, the cranberries being eaten raw, with poultry, as well as the apples.—TRANSLATOR.

dent voice.—"I 'll have a talk with the old woman; and report the answer to you punctually."

I WILL not dilate upon the thoughts which were aroused in me by the remarkable fact imparted by Ardalión; but I am ready to admit that I awaited the promised answer with impatience. Late in the evening, Ardalión entered my room and expressed his vexation: he had not been able to find the old woman. Nevertheless, by way of encouragement, I handed him a three-ruble banknote. On the following morning, he made his appearance again in my room, with a joyful face: the old woman had consented to an interview with me.

"Hey! brat!"—shouted Ardalión into the corridor,—"artisan! come hither!"—There entered a child of six years, all smeared with soot, like a kitten, with closely-clipped hair, which even left the head bare in spots, in a tattered striped dressing-gown and enormous overshoes upon his bare feet.—"Here, thou art to conduct them [1] to the place thou knowest of,"—said Ardalión, addressing the "artisan," and pointing at me.—"And as for you, sir, when you arrive, inquire for Mastrídiya Kárpovna."

The lad emitted a hoarse sound, and we set out.

WE walked for quite a long time through the unpaved streets of the town of T . . . .; at last,

---

[1] Respectful for "him."—TRANSLATOR.

in one of them, about the most deserted and melancholy of them all, my guide came to a halt in front of a small, aged, two-story wooden house, and wiping his nose on his sleeve, he said:

" Here-a; turn to the right." I entered through a porch into the anteroom, and tapped on the right; the low-browed door screeched on its rusty hinges, and I beheld before me a fat old woman, in a short cinnamon-brown jacket, lined with hare-skin, with a bright-hued kerchief on her head.

" Mastrídiya Kárpovna? "—I asked.

" I 'm she herself,"—the old woman replied, in a squeaking voice.—" Pray, come in. Would n't you like a chair? "

The room into which the old woman ushered me was so crammed with all sorts of rubbish, rags, pillows, feather-beds, sacks, that it was almost an utter impossibility to turn round in it. The sunlight barely forced its way through two tiny, dust-covered windows; in one corner, behind a mass of boxes, piled one on top of another, some one or other was faintly groaning and wailing; perhaps it was a sick child, and, possibly, it was a puppy. I sat down on the chair, and the old woman planted herself squarely in front of me. Her face was yellow, half-transparent, like wax; her lips were sunken to such a degree that, amid the multitude of wrinkles, they seemed to be a transverse wrinkle; a tuft of white hair stuck out from beneath the head-kerchief, but the inflamed, grey little eyes gazed forth shrewdly and audaciously from beneath the jutting frontal bone; and a sharp-pointed little nose fairly stood out like an awl, and sniffed the air, as much as to say: " I 'm a knave! "—" Well! thou 'rt no fool of a woman! "—I said to myself; and, moreover, she exhaled an odour of liquor. I explained to her the cause of my visit, which, by the way, as I noticed, must have been already known to her. She listened to me, blinking her eyes rapidly, but merely protruding her nose in a still more acute point, as though she were preparing to peck with it.

" Just so, sir, just so, sir,"—she said at last;— " Ardalión Matvyéitch told us, sir, exactly so, sir; you require the art of my dear son, Vásinka. . . . Only, we are in doubt, my dear sir. . . ."

" Why? "—I interrupted.—" You may feel perfectly at ease so far as I am concerned. . . . I 'm not an informer."

" Okh, dear little father mine,"—put in the old woman hastily,—" why do you say that? Dare we think such a thing of your Well-Born? And what cause is there to tell tales of us? My son is not the sort of a person, dear little father, to consent to any suspicious affair . . . . or indulge himself with any sorcery. . . . God, and His Mother, the All-Holy Birth-Giver of God, forbid! " (Here the old woman crossed herself thrice.) " He 's the greatest faster and prayer in the government; the very greatest, dear little father mine, your Well-Born! I should think so! This is not the work of his hands. It is from above, my dear little dove; yes! "

" So you consent? "—I asked;—" when can I see your son? "

Again the old woman blinked her eyes, and shifted her handkerchief, which was rolled up in a ball, from one sleeve to the other, a couple of times.

" Okh, my good sir, my good sir, we are in doubt. . . ."

" Permit me, Mastrídiya Kárpovna, to hand you the following,"—I interrupted, and gave her a ten-ruble note.

The old woman immediately grasped it in her plump, hooked fingers, which were suggestive of the fleshy claws of an owl, thrust it hastily into her sleeve, pondered awhile, and, as though suddenly coming to a decision, she smote herself on the hips with both palms.

" Come hither this evening, between seven and eight,"—she said, not in her habitual, but in a more important and quieter voice;—" only, not to this room, but please to ascend to the second story; and thou wilt find a door on the left, and do thou open that door; and thou wilt enter, your Well-Born, into an empty chamber, and in that chamber, thou wilt see a chair. Seat thyself on that chair, and wait; and whatever thou mayest behold, thou must utter not a word, and must do nothing; and thou wilt please not to converse with my son, either, because he is still young and has epilepsy. He is very easily frightened; he quakes and quakes like a young chicken . . . . it's terrible!"

I looked at Mastrídiya.—"You say that he is young; but if he is your son . . . ."

"In spirit, dear little father; in spirit! I have a great many orphans!"—she added, nodding her head in the direction of the corner whence the plaintive whine proceeded.—"O-okh, O Lord my God, All-Holy Mother, the Birth-Giver of God! And you, dear little father mine, your Well-Born, before you come hither, please to reflect well whom of your deceased relatives or acquaintances,—the kingdom of heaven be theirs!—you are desirous of seeing. Sort over your dead, and whomsoever you select, hold that one well in mind, hold him until my little son comes!"

"And am not I to tell your son precisely whom. . . ."

"Naw, naw, dear little father, not a single word. He himself will discover in your thoughts what he requires. But do you hold your acquaintance tho-rough-ly in mind; and at dinner, drink some wine,—two or three glasses; wine never comes amiss."

The old woman broke into a laugh, licked her

lips, passed her hand across her mouth, and sighed.

" At half-past seven then? "—I asked, rising from my chair.

" At half-past seven, dear little father, your Well-Born; at half-past seven,"—replied Mastrídiya Kárpovna, soothingly.

I took leave of the old woman, and returned to the inn. I had not the slightest doubt that they were preparing to fool me, but how? that was what aroused my curiosity. I exchanged two or three words, no more, with Ardalión.—" Did she let you in? "—he asked me, contracting his brows, and when I replied in the affirmative, he exclaimed:—" A Minister of a woman! "—In accordance with the " Minister's " advice, I began to go over my dead friends in my mind. After somewhat prolonged hesitation, I fixed, at last, upon an old Frenchman, long since dead, who had once been my tutor. I chose him in particular, not because I felt any special affection for him; but his whole figure was so original that any imitation of it was absolutely impossible. He had a huge head, with fleecy white hair brushed back, thick black eyebrows, a hooked nose, and two large moles of a purplish hue, in the middle of his forehead; he wore a green frock-coat, with smooth, brass buttons, a striped waistcoat with a standing collar, a lace frill and wrist-ruffles. " If he shows me my old Dessert,"—I thought, " I shall be compelled to acknowledge that he is a sorcerer."

At dinner, according to the old woman's advice, I drank a bottle of claret of the very best quality, as Ardalión averred, but with a very strong flavour of burnt cork, and with a thick sediment of sandal-wood at the bottom of each glass.

PRECISELY at half-past seven I found myself in front of the house in which I had conferred with the respected Mastrídiya Kárpovna. All the window-shutters were closed, but the door was open. I entered the house, ascended the rickety staircase to the second story, and, briskly opening the door on the left, I found myself, as the old woman had foretold, in a perfectly empty, fairly spacious room; a tallow candle, placed on the window-sill, illuminated it faintly; against the wall, opposite the door, stood a chair with a wattled seat. I trimmed the candle, which had had time to burn down considerably, seated myself on the chair, and began to wait.

The first ten minutes passed rather quickly. In the room itself there was absolutely nothing which could attract my attention; but I lent an ear to every rustle, and gazed intently at the closed door. . . . My heart beat violently. The first ten minutes were succeeded by others; then half an hour, three quarters of an hour elapsed—and nothing even stirred around me! Several times I coughed, in order to let it be understood that I was present; I began to grow bored, and angry; to be fooled in *that* way had not entered into my calculations. I was already preparing to rise from my chair, and taking the candle from the window, to go down-stairs. . . . I glanced at it; again the wick had burned into the shape of a mushroom; but on turning my glance from the candle to the door, I involuntarily shuddered; leaning against the door itself, stood a man. He had entered so quickly and noiselessly that I had heard nothing.

HE wore a plain blue peasant overcoat; he was of medium height, and rather thick-set. With hands thrust behind his back, and drooping head, he riveted his eyes on me. By the dim light of the candle, I could not distinguish his features very clearly: I saw merely a shaggy mane of tangled hair falling over his brow, and large, slightly crooked lips, and whitish eyes. I was on the point of addressing him, but recalled Mastrídiya's directions, and bit my lips. The man who had entered continued to stare at me; and I likewise stared at him, and, strange to say! I felt, simultaneously, something akin to terror, and, as though by command, I began immediately to think of my old governor. *He* still stood at the door, and breathed heavily, as though he were climbing a hill, or lifting a burden, and his eyes seemed to open more widely, as though he were approaching me—and I began to feel uncomfortable under their persistent, oppressive, menacing gaze; at times those eyes blazed with malevolent inward fire; I had noticed the same sort of fire in the eyes of a greyhound, when it " sights " a hare, and, like the greyhound, *he* followed my gaze with *his* when I " made a spurt," that is to say, tried to turn my eyes aside.

THUS passed I know not how long a time; perhaps a minute; perhaps a quarter of an hour. He stared all the while at me. I, all the while, felt a certain awkwardness and terror, and thought steadily of my Frenchman. A couple of times I tried to say to myself: " What nonsense! What a farce! " I tried to smile, to shrug my shoulders. . . . . In vain! Every resolution instantaneously " congealed "—I can choose no better word . . . . within me. I was in the grip of some sort of stupor. All at once, I observed that he had left the door, and was standing a pace or two nearer me; then he almost hopped, with both feet at once, and came still nearer. . . . Then still nearer . . . . and nearer still; and his threatening eyes fairly bored themselves into the whole of my face, and his arms remained behind his back, and his broad chest breathed heavily. These hops appeared to me ridiculous, but dread fell upon me, also, and, something which I could not in the least understand, drowsiness suddenly began to descend upon me. My eyelids stuck together . . . . the shaggy figure, with whitish eyes, in the blue peasant coat, became double before me—and suddenly vanished altogether!—I started: again he stood between the door and me, but much nearer now. . . . Then again he vanished—as though a mist had descended upon him, again he reappeared . . . . again he vanished . . . . again he reappeared . . . . and always nearer, nearer . . . . his laboured, almost snoring breath already reached me. . . . Again the mist descended, and suddenly, from out of that mist, beginning with the white locks brushed back, the head of old Dessert began clearly to outline itself! Yes; there were his moles, his black eyebrows, his hooked nose! There was his green frock-coat with the brass buttons, and the striped waistcoat, and the lace frill. . . . I shrieked, I half-rose from my seat. . . . The old man had vanished, and in his stead I beheld the man in the blue coat. He walked, tottering, to the wall, leaned his head and both arms against it, and, panting like an over-fed horse, he said, in a hoarse voice: " Tea! " Mastrídiya rushed to him, from somewhere or other, and saying: " Vásinka, Vásinka,"—set herself anxiously to wipe away the perspiration, which was fairly streaming from his hair and face. I was about to approach her, but she exclaimed in so peremptory, so heart-rending a voice:—"Your Well-Born, merciful father, do not ruin him, go away, for Christ's sake!"—that I obeyed; and she turned again to her son—"Benefactor, dear little dove,"—she soothed him; "thou shalt have tea immediately, immediately. And do you, dear little father, drink tea at home!" she shouted after me.

On reaching home, I obeyed Mastrídiya, and ordered tea to be served; I felt weary—even weak. —"Well, how did it turn out, sir?"—Ardalión asked me:—"Have you been, sir? Have you seen anything, sir?"

"He really did show me something . . . . which, I must confess, I had not expected,"—I replied.

"He 's a man of great wisdom!"—remarked Ardalión, as he carried out the samovár. "He is gre-eatly reverenced by the merchant class!"

As I got into bed, and meditated upon what had happened to me, I imagined that, at last, I had got at the explanation of it. That man, undoubtedly, possessed remarkable magnetic power; acting, of course, in a manner incomprehensible to me, on my nerves, he had so clearly, so definitely evoked in me the image of the old man of whom I was thinking, that at last it had seemed to me as though I beheld him before my eyes.

A STRANGE STORY

. . . . Such "metastasi"—transferences of sensations—are known to science. Very good! but the power capable of producing such effects remained marvellous and mysterious, nevertheless. "Say what you will,"—I thought,—"I have seen with my own eyes my dead tutor."

On the following day the ball came off at the Assembly of the Nobility. Sophie's father ran in to see me, and reminded me of the invitation which I had given to his daughter. At ten o'clock that evening I was standing by her side in the middle of the hall, illuminated by a multitude of brass lamps, and was prepared to execute the simple steps of the French quadrille to the thunderous howls of the military band. A throng of people had assembled; the number of ladies was especially large, and very pretty they were. But the palm for superiority over them all would, infallibly, have been awarded to my lady, had it not been for the somewhat strange, even somewhat wild look of her eyes. I noticed that she very rarely winked; the indubitable expression of sincerity in her eyes did not redeem that which was unusual in them. But she was charmingly built, and moved gracefully, though shyly. When she waltzed, and bending her figure slightly backward, inclined her slender neck toward her right shoulder, as though desirous of avoiding her partner, nothing more touchingly-youthful and pure could be imagined. She was all in white, with a small turquoise cross on a narrow black ribbon.

I invited her for the mazurka, and tried to engage her in conversation. But she replied briefly and reluctantly, though she listened attentively, with the same expression of thoughtful surprise, which had struck me the first time I saw her. There was not a shadow of the coquetry usual at her age, with her personal appearance, and the absence of a smile, and those eyes, fixed unwaveringly and straight on the eyes of her interlocutor,—those eyes which, at the same time, seemed to be discerning something else, to be anxious over something else. . . . What a strange being! Not knowing, at last, how to entertain her, it occurred to me to relate to her my adventure of the preceding evening.

SHE listened to the end, with evident curiosity; but, quite contrary to my expectations, she was not surprised at my story, and merely asked me, whether *his* name were not Vasíly? I remembered that the old woman had called him " Vásinka " in my presence.—" Yes; his name is Vasíly,"—I replied;—" is it possible that you know him? "

" A pious man named Vasíly lives here,"—she said;—" I was wondering whether it was he? "

" Piety has nothing to do with the matter,"—

A STRANGE STORY

I remarked;—" it is simply the action of magnetism—a fact interesting to doctors and students of the natural sciences."

I undertook to set forth my views on that peculiar force which is called magnetism, on the possibility of subjecting the will of one man to the will of another, and so forth; but my explanations—which were somewhat obscure, to tell the truth—did not appear to make any impression on my companion. Sophie listened, dropping her clasped hands in her lap with her fan lying motionless in them; she did not play with it, she did not move her fingers at all, and I felt that all my words rebounded from her, as from a wall of stone. She understood them, but obviously she had steadfast convictions of her own, which were not to be uprooted.

" But do not you admit the existence of miracles? "—I exclaimed.

" Of course I do,"—she said calmly.—" And how is it possible not to admit that? Is it not said in the Gospels that he who has faith as one grain of mustard seed, can remove mountains from their places? One need only have the faith —and there will be miracles."

" Evidently, faith has become small in our day,"—I retorted:—" I don't seem to have heard of any miracles! "

" But they happen; you have seen for yourself. No; faith has not been exterminated in our day; but the beginning of faith . . . ."

" The fear of God is the beginning of wisdom,"
—I interposed.

" The beginning of faith,"—pursued Sophie,
not in the least disconcerted,—" is self-sacrifice
. . . . humiliation! "

" Even humiliation? "—I asked.

" Yes. Human pride, presumption, arrogance,—that is what must be thoroughly exterminated. You alluded, just now, to the will . . .
it, also, must be broken."

I surveyed with a glance the white figure of the
young girl, who was giving utterance to such
speeches. . . . " And this baby is not jesting,
either! " I thought. I glanced at our neighbours
in the mazurka; they, also, glanced at me, and it
struck me that my amazement was affording
them amusement; one of them even smiled sym-
pathetically at me, as much as to say: " Aha!
Well, have n't we a queer young lady? Everybody here knows what she is like."

" Have you tried to break your will? "—I said,
addressing myself once more to Sophie.

" Every one is bound to do that which seems
right to him,"—she replied, in a dogmatic sort of
tone.

" Permit me to ask you,"—I began, after a
brief silence,—" whether you believe in the possibility of calling up the dead? "

Sophie shook her head gently.

" There are no dead."

" Why not? "

" There are no dead souls; they are immortal, and can always reveal themselves whenever they like. . . . They are constantly around us."

" What? Do you assert, for instance, that a deathless soul may be hovering, at this moment, around yonder garrison major with the red nose? "

" Why not? The light of the sun illumines him and his nose,—and is not the sunlight, every sort of light, from God? And what does outward appearance matter? For the pure there is nothing impure! If one could only find a teacher! a preceptor! "

" But pardon me, pardon me,"—I interposed, not without malicious delight,—" you wish a preceptor . . . . but what is your confessor for? "

Sophie looked coldly at me.

" Apparently, you want to ridicule me. My father confessor tells me what I ought to do; but I want a preceptor who will show me himself, by example, how to sacrifice myself! "

She raised her eyes to the ceiling. With her childlike face, and that expression of imperturbable pensiveness, of secret, perpetual surprise, she reminded me of the pre-Raphaelite Madonnas. . . .

" I have read, somewhere or other,"—she went on, without turning toward me, and hardly moving her lips,—" that once a grandee gave orders that he was to be buried under the vestibule of the church, in order that all the people who came thither might tread on him, trample him under foot. . . . That is what one should do during one's lifetime. . . ."

" Boom! boom! tra-ra-rakh!"—thundered the kettle-drums from the gallery. . . . I confess that such a conversation at a ball appeared to me extremely eccentric; it involuntarily aroused in me thoughts . . . . of a nature diametrically the opposite of religious. I took advantage of my lady being invited out in one of the figures of the mazurka to relinquish our quasi-theological discussion.

A quarter of an hour later, I conducted Mlle. Sophie to her parent, and two days thereafter, I left the town of T . . . ; and the image of the young girl with the childlike face, and the impenetrable, as it were, stony soul, was quickly erased from my memory.

Two years elapsed, and again it so happened that that image rose up before me. To wit: I was chatting with a colleague in the service, who had just returned from a trip through southern Russia. He had spent some time in the town of T . . ., and communicated to me some news of the society there. . —" By the way!"—he exclaimed.—" Thou art well acquainted, I believe, with V. G. B.? "

" Of course I am."

" And dost thou know his daughter Sófya? "

" I have seen her a couple of times."

" Just imagine; she has eloped."

" What dost thou mean? "

" Why, just that. 'T is three months now, since she disappeared without leaving a trace. And the remarkable thing about it is that no one can say with whom she has eloped. Just imagine, there 's not a surmise, not the smallest suspicion! She has refused all suitors. And her conduct was as modest as possible. I 've no faith in those quiet women, those pious women! The scandal in the government is frightful! B. is in despair. . . . And what need was there for her to run away? Her father complied with her will in all things. The chief, the incredible point is, that all the Lovelaces of the government are on hand, every man of them."

" And she has not been found up to this time? "

" I tell thee there 's not a sign of her! There 's one wealthy bride less in the world, that 's the bad part of it."

This bit of news greatly amazed me. It was not, in the least, consistent with the memory which I had preserved of Sófya B. But all sorts of things come to pass!

IN the autumn of that same year, Fate again cast me, on government business, into the Government of S . . . ., which, as every one knows, ad-

joins the Government of T . . . . The weather was cold and rainy; the exhausted little nags from the posting-station dragged my tarantás through the dissolving black loam of the highway. I remember that one day was particularly unlucky: three times did we stick fast in the mud up to the hubs; my postilion kept abandoning one wheel, and crawling to the other with a hoot and a howl; but it was no easier than the first. In a word, toward evening, I was so fagged out that, on reaching the station, I decided to pass the night in the post-house. I was assigned to a room with a battered wooden couch, a sagging floor, and tattered paper on the walls; it reeked of small beer, bast-mats, onions, and even turpentine, and flies roosted in swarms everywhere; but I could shelter myself from the storm, at least; and it was wound up to rain, as the saying goes, for a stretch of twenty-four hours. I ordered the samovár to be brought, and seating myself on the couch, I surrendered myself to those cheerless thoughts inspired by the journey, which are so familiar to travellers in Russia. They were interrupted by a heavy knocking, which resounded throughout the cottage, from which my room was separated by a partition of boards. This knocking was accompanied by a spasmodic, sonorous jingling, like the clanking of chains, and a rough masculine voice suddenly yelled out—
" God bless all them that are in this house. Bless

them, O God! Bless them, O God! Amen, amen, disperse!"—repeated the voice, in an incoherent sort of way, and with a fierce prolongation of the last syllable of each word. . . . A vociferous sigh made itself heard, and a heavy body dropped down on the bench with the same clanking as before.

"Akulína! Servant of God, come hither!"—began the voice again;—"behold, how naked, how blest I am! . . . . Ha-ha-ha! Phew! O Lord, my God, O Lord, my God, O Lord, my God!"—boomed the voice, like a chanter in a church-choir,—"O Lord, my God, Sovereign Master of my life, look upon my ungodliness. . . . O-ho-ho-ho! Ha-ha! . . . . Phew! And grace be upon this house at the seventh hour!"

"Who is that?"—I asked the generous house-mistress, of the petty-burgher class, who entered my room with the samovár.

"Why, that, dear little father mine,"—she replied, in a hurried whisper,—"is a blessed fool, a man of God. He has made his appearance recently in our parts; and he is pleased to visit us. In what a storm! The water fairly runs off of him in streams, the dear man! And you just ought to see what chains he wears—they 're awful!" [1]

---

[1] These half-witted "men of God" frequently wear huge iron chains, weighing sixty pounds or more, on arms, legs, and body, by way of penance. They are greatly revered by the Russians, and often regarded as inspired.—TRANSLATOR.

A STRANGE STORY

"Bless, O God! Bless, O God!"—rang out the voice once more.—"Akulína! Hey, there, Akulína! Akulínushka—my friend! And where is our paradise? Our beautiful paradise? In the desert is our paradise . . . . paradise. . . And to this house, at the beginning of this age . . . . great joy . . . o . . . o . . . o . . ." The voice muttered something unintelligible, and suddenly, after a prolonged yawn, the hoarse laugh made itself heard again. That laugh burst forth, every time, as though involuntarily, and every time angry spitting was audible after it.

" Ekh-ma! Stepánitch is not here! so much the worse for us!"—said the mistress, as though to herself, halting at the door, with all the signs of the most profound attention.—"He will utter some saving word, and it will be beyond the understanding of a woman like me!"—She briskly left the room.

THERE was a crack in the partition; I put my eye to it. The pious idiot was sitting on a bench, with his back toward me. I could see only his shaggy head, as huge as a beer-kettle, and his broad, round-shouldered back covered with soaked patched rags. In front of him, on the earthen floor, knelt a puny woman in an old burgher's jerkin, also soaked, with a dark kerchief pulled down over her very eyes. She was trying to pull off the idiot's boots from his legs; her fingers

slipped over the muddy, slippery leather. The
hostess was standing beside her with arms crossed
on her bosom, and gazing devoutly at the " man
of God." He continued, as before, to grumble
out some unintelligible remarks or other.

At last, the woman in the jerkin succeeded in
pulling off a boot. She came near falling flat on
the ground, but recovered herself, and set to work
to unwind the idiot's foot-cloth. There was a
sore on the instep. . . . I turned away.

" Dost thou not command me to entertain thee
with tea, my dear man? "—the obsequious voice
of the hostess made itself heard.

" What art thou thinking of! "—returned the
fool.—" To coddle the sinful body. . . Okho-ho!
They shall break all his bones . . . . and she says
. . . . tea! Okh, okh, respected old woman,
Satan is strong within us! Upon him cometh
hunger, upon him cometh cold, upon him the windows of heaven are open, pouring rains and piercing, but he careth not, he liveth! Remember the
day of the Intercession of the Birth-Giver of
God! Then much shall happen unto thee, much
that is grievous! "

The hostess even uttered a faint exclamation of
amazement.

" Only, hearken thou to me! Give away everything, give thy head, give thy shirt! And they
will not ask thee, yet do thou give! For God
seeth! Doth it take long to scatter a roof? He,

the Merciful, hath given thee bread; well, set it in the oven! For He seeth all. He se-e-e-eth! Whose eye is it in the triangle? tell me . . . . whose?"[1]

The hostess crossed herself stealthily under her handkerchief.

"The ancient enemy, adamant! A . . . . da-. . . . mant! A . . . . da . . . . mant,"—repeated the fool several times in succession, gnashing his teeth.—"The ancient serpent. But God shall arise! Yea, God shall arise, and shall disperse His enemies! I will summon all the dead! I will march against His enemies. . . . Ha-ha-ha! Phew!"

"Have you any olive oil?"—articulated another, barely audible voice;—"give me some to put on the sore. . . . I have a clean rag."

Again I peeped through the crack; the woman in the jerkin was still fussing with the injured leg of the fool. . . . "Magdalen!"—I thought.

"Immediately, immediately, my dearest,"—said the hostess, and entering my room, she got a spoonful of oil from the shrine-lamp in front of the image.

"Who is that waiting on him?"—I asked.

"I don't know, dear little father, who she is. She, too, is working out her salvation, I think; she

[1] The fresco of the All-seeing Eye in the central cupola of a church.—TRANSLATOR.

271

is serving out her sin. Well, and he certainly is a holy man!"

"Akulínushka, my dear child, my beloved daughter,"—the fool kept reiterating the while, and suddenly fell to weeping.

The woman who was kneeling before him looked up at him. . . . My God, where had I seen those eyes?

The hostess approached her with the spoonful of oil. The woman finished her operation, and rising from the floor, asked whether there was not a clean garret and a little hay? . . . . "Vasíly Nikítitch likes to sleep on hay,"—she added.

"Why should n't there be? pray come,"—replied the hostess:—"Please, my dear man,"—she said, addressing the fool,—"dry thyself; rest."—The latter grunted, rose slowly from his bench—again his chains clanked—and, turning his face toward me, and seeking the holy pictures with his eyes, he began to cross himself with a huge, sweeping cross.

I immediately recognised him. He was that same petty burgher, Vasíly, who had, once upon a time, called up my dead tutor!

His features had changed very little; only, their expression had become more unusual, more terrible. . . . The lower part of his bloated face was overgrown with a dishevelled beard. Tattered, dirty, wild, he inspired me with even more loathing than terror. He ceased to cross himself, but his senseless gaze continued to rove over the corners, over the floor, as though he were expecting something. . . .

"Vasíly Nikítitch, please,"—said the woman in the jerkin, with a reverence. He suddenly tossed his head, and wheeled round, but his legs got entangled, he tottered. . . . His companion immediately flew to him, and supported him under the armpit. Judging from her voice, from her figure, she seemed to be still a young woman; it was almost impossible to see her face.

"Akulínushka, friend!"—said the fool once more, in an agitated sort of voice, and opening his mouth wide, and smiting himself on the breast with his clenched fist, he groaned, with a dull moan which welled up from the bottom of his soul. The two followed the hostess out of the room.

I lay down on my hard couch, and meditated for a long time on what I had seen. My magnetiser had become an idiot at last. This was where that power, which it was impossible not to recognise in him, had landed him!

On the following morning, I prepared to continue my journey. The rain was pouring down as on the preceding day, but I could tarry no longer. On the face of my servant, when he gave me my washing-materials, played a peculiar smile of suppressed derision. I understood that smile very well; it denoted that my servant had learned something unfavourable, or even discreditable about the gentry. He was, evidently, burning with impatience to communicate it to me.

" Well, what is it? "—I asked, at last.

" Did you see the blessed fool last night? "—said my servant, immediately.

" Yes; what next? "

" And did you see his companion, too, sir? "

" Yes, I saw her also."

" She 's a young lady, sir, of noble birth."

" What? "

" I 'm telling you the truth, sir. Some merchants from T. . . passed by to-day; they recognised her. They even mentioned her name, only I 've forgotten it, sir."

I was illuminated as by a flash of lightning.— " Is the fool still here, or has he already departed? "—I inquired.

" I think he has n't gone off yet. A while ago, he was sitting at the gate, and doing something so queer that I could n't understand it. He 's bursting with fat; for he finds that sort of thing profitable to himself."

My servant belonged to the same class of cultured house-servants as Ardalión.

" And is the young lady with him? "

" She is, sir; she 's on duty also."

A STRANGE STORY

I STEPPED out on the porch, and beheld the fool. He was sitting on the bench by the gate, and propping himself on it with both palms, was swaying his drooping head to right and left,— precisely like a wild beast in a cage. Thick locks of curly hair covered his eyes, and swirled from side to side, as did also his pendent lips. . . . A strange, almost inhuman muttering burst from them. His companion had just finished washing herself from the jug suspended on a long pole, and without having, as yet, thrown her kerchief over her head, was making her way back to the gate along a narrow board, which was laid over the dark puddles of the manure-yard. I cast a glance at that head, now uncovered on all sides, and involuntarily clasped my hands: before me stood Sófya B.!

She turned quickly round, and fixed on me her blue eyes, as immovable as ever. She had grown very thin, her skin had grown coarse, and had acquired the yellowish-red hue of sunburn, her nose had grown pointed, and her lips were more sharply outlined. She had not become homely; but to her former, pensively-surprised expression another—a resolute, almost audacious, concentratedly-ecstatic expression—had been added. Not a trace of childishness now remained in this face.

I went up to her.—" Sófya Vladímirovna! "—

I exclaimed,—" can it be possible that this is you?
In this garb . . . in this company . . . ."

She shuddered, gazed more intently than ever
at me, as though desirous of finding out who was
addressing her; and without answering me with a
single word, she fairly flew to her companion.

" Akulínushka,"—he faltered, with a heavy
sigh,—" our sins, our . . . ."

" Vasíly Nikítitch, let us go at once! Do you
hear, at once, at once,"—she said, pulling her kerchief down on her brow with one hand, and with
the other grasping the blessed fool under the elbow,—" come away, Vasíly Nikítitch. There is
danger here."

" I 'm coming, dear little mother, I 'm coming,"
—replied the fool, submissively; and bending his
whole body forward, he rose from the bench.—
" Here, only fasten the chain. . . ."

Again I approached Sófya and mentioned my
name, and began to implore her to listen to me,
to say one word to me. I directed her attention
to the rain, which poured down as from a bucket.
I begged her to spare her own health, the health
of her companion, I reminded her of her father.
. . . . But some malevolent, pitiless ecstasy had
taken possession of her. Without paying the
smallest heed to me, setting her teeth, and breathing in gasps, she spurred on, in an undertone,
with brief, imperious words, the bewildered fool,
put on his girdle, bound on his chains, clapped

on his hair a child's cloth cap with a broken visor, thrust his staff into his hand, flung over her own shoulders the beggar's wallet, and emerged with him from the gate into the street. . . . I had no right whatever to detain her, and it would have served no purpose in any case; and at my final, despairing appeal, she did not even turn round. Supporting the "man of God" by the arm, she strode briskly onward through the black mud of the street, and a few moments later, athwart the dim mist of the cloudy morning, athwart the close network of falling rain, the two figures glimmered before me for the last time—the figures of the fool and of Sófya. . . . They turned the corner of a projecting cottage, and vanished forever.

I RETURNED to my room. I was seized with doubt. I understood nothing. I did not understand how such a well-bred, young, wealthy girl could abandon everything and everybody, her father's house, her family, her friends, resign all the habits and the comforts of life, and for what purpose? For the purpose of following a half-demented vagrant, in order to become his servant? Not for a single moment was it possible to entertain the thought that the motive for such a decision was connected with the heart, nor even a perverted affection, love or passion. . . . One needed but to cast a single glance at the repulsive figure of the " man of God," in order instantly to banish such an idea from his head! No, Sophie had remained pure; and, as she had once said to me, for her there was nothing impure. I did not understand Sophie's step; but I did not condemn her, just as, later on, I have not condemned other young girls who have, also, sacrificed everything to what *they* regarded as right, in which *they* discerned their vocation. I could not help regretting that Sophie had chosen precisely *that* path; but neither was I able to refuse her admiration, even respect. Not without cause had she talked to me about self-sacrifice, about humiliation. . . . In *her* case, words were not divorced from deeds. She had sought a preceptor and a guide, and she had found him . . . . in whom, great heavens!

Yes, she had made people tread on her, trample her under foot. . . . Recently rumours have reached me that the family, at last, succeeded in hunting up the wandering sheep and bringing her home. But she did not live long at home, and died as a " silent woman," without having spoken to any one.

Peace to thy heart, poor, enigmatic being! Vasíly Nikítitch is, in all probability, pursuing his demented wanderings to this day; the iron health of such people is really astounding. Perhaps epilepsy has conquered him.

PÚNIN AND BABÚRIN

(1874)

PÚNIN AND BABÚRIN

PIÓTR PETRÓVITCH B'S STORY

I AM old and ailing now, and my most frequent thought is of death, which is drawing nearer with every passing day. I rarely think of the past, my spiritual gaze rarely is directed backward. Only at times, in winter, as I sit motionless before the blazing fire; or in summer, as I pace with quiet tread a shady alley, do I recall by-gone years, events, persons; but it is not on the riper period of my life and not on my youth that my thoughts dwell then. They carry me back either to my early childhood or to the days of my early boyhood. So it is now. I behold myself in the country, at the house of my stern, irascible grandmother—I am only twelve years old—and two faces rise up in my imagination. . . .

But I will tell my story in due order and sequence.

I

(1830)

THE old footman, Philíppitch, entered, as usual, on tiptoe, with his neckcloth tied in the form of a rosette, his lips tightly compressed, "in order that he might not infect the air with his breath," and his grey hair in a crest on the very middle of his forehead; he entered, bowed, and handed to my grandmother on an iron salver a large letter with an armorial seal. My grandmother put on her spectacles, and read the letter. . . .

"Is he there himself?" she inquired.

"What were you pleased to ask?" timidly said Philíppitch.

"Blockhead! Is the person who brought the letter—there?"

"Yes, he is. . . . He is sitting in the office."

My grandmother rattled her amber rosary. . . . "Order him to present himself. . . . And as for thee, sir," she said, addressing me,—"do thou sit quietly."

I did not stir in my corner on the tabouret assigned to me.

My grandmother kept a tight hand over me!

FIVE minutes later there entered the room a man of five-and-thirty, black-haired, swarthy-skinned, with a high-cheek-boned, pock-marked face, a hooked nose and thick eyebrows, from beneath which small grey eyes peered forth calmly and sadly. The colour of those eyes, and their expression, did not correspond with the Oriental cast of the rest of his visage. The entering man was clad in a sedate, long-tailed coat. He halted close to the door and bowed—with his head only.

"Thy family name is Babúrin?" inquired my grandmother, and immediately added to herself: "*Il a l'air d'un Arménien.*"

"Just so, ma'am," replied the man, in a dull, even tone. At my grandmother's first word, "thy," his brow had quivered slightly. He surely could not have expected that she would address him as "you."

"Thou art a Russian? An orthodox?"[1]

"Yes, ma'am."

Grandmamma removed her spectacles and surveyed Babúrin with a deliberate stare from head to foot. He did not lower his eyes, and merely clasped his hands behind his back. The thing which really interested me most was his beard; it was very smoothly shaved, but such blue cheeks and chin I had never seen in all my life!

"Yákoff Petróvitch," began grandmamma, "recommends thee highly in his letter as a sober and industrious man; but why hast thou left him?"

"He requires another quality of person in his domestic management, madame."

"Another . . . . quality? I don't understand that."—Again my grandmother rattled her ro-

---

[1] That is, a member of the Holy Catholic Church of the East.—TRANSLATOR.

sary.—" Yákoff Petróvitch writes me that thou hast two peculiarities. What are they?"

Babúrin shrugged his shoulders slightly.

" I do not know what he is pleased to call peculiarities. Unless it is that I . . . permit no corporeal punishment."

Grandmamma was astonished.—" Is it possible that Yákoff Petróvitch wished to flog thee?"

Babúrin's face crimsoned to his very hair.

" You have misunderstood me, madame. I make it a rule never to employ bodily chastisement . . . . on the peasants."

Grandmamma was more amazed than before, and even uplifted her hands.

" Ah!" she articulated at last, and inclining her head a little on one side, she again surveyed Babúrin intently.—" That is thy rule? Well, that is a matter of entire indifference to me; I am not inviting thee to be my manager, but as a scribe in the office. What is thy handwriting like?"

" I write well, ma'am, without orthographical errors."

" I care nothing about that. The chief thing for me is that it shall be distinct, and without those new capitals with tails, which I do not like. —And what is thy other peculiarity?"

Babúrin fidgeted about, coughed. . . .

" Perhaps . . . the noble landed proprietor was pleased to intimate that I am not alone."

" Art thou married?"

" No, not at all, ma'am . . . . but . . . ."

Grandmamma frowned.

" There lives with me a person . . . . of the masculine sex . . . a comrade, a poor man, from whom I have not been parted . . . going on ten years now."

" Is he a relative of thine? "

" No, ma'am, not a relative, a comrade. No inconvenience to the establishment can arise from him," Babúrin hastened to add, as though forestalling an objection.—" He lives on my victuals, he is lodged in the same room with me; he is bound rather to prove of advantage, since he is perfect in reading and writing I may say without flattery, and is of exemplary morality."

Grandmamma heard Babúrin out, mowing with her lips, and screwing up her eyes the while.

" He lives at thy expense? "

" Yes, ma'am."

" Thou supportest him out of kindness? "

" Out of justice . . . since it is the duty of one poor man to aid another poor man."

" Really! That 's the first I have heard of it! Up to this time I have always supposed that that was, rather, the duty of the wealthy."

" That is an occupation for the wealthy, if I may make bold to say so . . . but for fellows like me . . . ."

" Well, enough, enough, enough, very good," interrupted grandmamma, and after reflecting a while she said through her nose—which was always a bad sign:—" And how old is thy pensioner? "

" The same age as myself, ma'am."

"Thy age?—I supposed that he was thy pupil."

" Not at all, ma'am; he is my comrade—and, moreover . . ."

" Enough," interrupted my grandmother for the second time. " Evidently, thou art a philanthropist. Yákoff Petróvitch is right; in thy vocation that is a great peculiarity. But now let us discuss business. I will explain to thee what thy duties will be. And as for the wages . . . *Que faîtes vous ici?*" suddenly added grandmamma, turning toward me her yellow, wizened face.—" *Allez étudier votre devoir de mythologie.*"

I sprang up, approached and kissed my grandmother's hand and went off,—not to study mythology, but simply into the park.

THE park on grandmamma's estate was very ancient and very large, and ended on one side in a pond with a river flowing through it, in which not only carp and gudgeons but even barbels were to be found, the famous barbels which have now disappeared almost everywhere. At the head of this pond was a dense growth of vines; higher up, on both sides of the declivity, ran close-set bushes of hazel, elder, honeysuckle, and black-thorn, overgrown below with juniper and lovage. Only here and there among the bushes stood out tiny glades with emerald-green, silky, delicate grass, amid which, amusingly diversifying it with their pink, lilac and straw-coloured caps, peeped out extremely squat mushrooms, while the golden spheres of the buttercups[1] blazed in brilliant spots. There, in spring, nightingales sang, thrushes whistled, cuckoos called; there, even in the sultry heats of summer, it was cool, and I was fond of slinking off to this thicket and the coppice, where I had my favourite, hidden little nooks, known—at least so I imagined—to myself alone.

On emerging from my grandmother's boudoir I betook myself straight to one of those nocks which I had named " Switzerland." But what was my amazement when, before reaching " Switzerland," I saw athwart the close network of half-withered twigs and green branches that some one besides myself had discovered it. Some long, very long figure in a yellow frieze peasant coat and a tall cap of the merchant pattern, was standing on my most beloved spot! I crept up nearer and scrutinised the face, which was entirely unknown to me, and also very long, soft, with small, reddish eyes, and an extremely ridiculous nose; elongated like a vegetable pod, it depended over

[1] Unpoetically called " chicken-blindness " in Russian. They are double, and as large and fragrant as yellow roses.—TRANSLATOR.

the plump lips; and those lips, now and then quivering and pursing themselves up, were emitting a shrill whistle, while the long fingers of the bony hands, placed close together on a level with its breast, were briskly revolving in a circle. From time to time the movement of the hands relaxed, the lips ceased to whistle and quiver, the head was bowed forward as though listening. I moved up still nearer, and stared still more attentively. . . . The stranger was holding in each hand a small, flat disc, resembling those with which canary-birds are teased and made to sing. A twig crackled under my foot; the stranger started, fixed his purblind little eyes on the grove, and was on the point of darting away . . . but stumbled over a tree, uttered a groan, and came to a halt.

I emerged upon the glade. The stranger smiled.

" Good morning," I said.

" Good morning, little master! "

It displeased me that he should call me " little master." What familiarity! " What are you doing here? " I asked him sternly.

" Why, as you see," he replied, without ceasing to smile,—" I am challenging the little birds to sing."—He pointed to his little discs.—" The chaffinches are answering capitally! The warbling of the feathered fowl must delight you without fail, owing to the youthfulness of your years!

Be so good as to listen; I will begin to twitter, and they will immediately follow me—how agreeable!"

He began to rub his discs together. In fact, a chaffinch did respond from a neighbouring mountain ash. The stranger burst into a noiseless laugh and winked at me.

That laugh and that wink,—every one of the stranger's movements,—his weak, lisping voice, his bow legs, his gaunt hands, his very cap, his long peasant-coat—everything about him breathed forth good-nature, and something innocent and diverting.

" Have you been here long? " I asked.

" I came to-day."

" But you are not the person of whom . . . ."

" Mr. Babúrin was speaking to your grandmamma? The very man, the very man."

" Your comrade's name is Babúrin, but what is yours? "

" Mine is Púnin. Púnin is my surname; Púnin. He is Babúrin, I am Púnin."—Again he made his discs buzz.—" Listen, listen to the chaffinch. . . . How he is warbling! "

I suddenly took a " frightful " liking for this queer fellow. Like almost all small boys I was either timid or pompous with strangers, but I felt as though I had always been acquainted with this man.

" Please to come with me," I said to him. " I

know a still better place than this; there is a bench there; we can sit down and the dam is visible thence."

"Certainly, let us go," replied my new friend in a singsong voice. I let him go in front. He waddled as he walked, shuffling his feet, and throwing his head back. I noticed that a small tassel was dangling at the back of his coat, near the collar.—"What 's that hanging to you?" I asked.

"Where?" he retorted with a question, and felt of his collar with his hand.—"Ah! That little tassel? Let it alone! It was sewn on for ornament, you know. Don't meddle with it."

I led him to the bench and sat down; he placed himself beside me.—"It is fine here!" he said, and heaved a deep, deep sigh.—"Okh, very fine indeed! You have a most excellent park! Okh, okh-ho!"

I darted a sidelong glance at him.—"What a queer cap you have," I involuntarily exclaimed. —"Come, let me see it!"

"Certainly, little master, certainly."—He took off his cap. I was on the point of putting out my hand to take it, when I raised my eyes—and fairly burst out laughing in his face. Púnin was completely bald; not a single hair was to be seen on his conical skull, which was covered with soft, white skin.

He passed his hand over it and began to laugh

PÚNIN AND BABÚRIN

also. When he laughed he caught his breath as though he were sobbing, opened his mouth wide and shut his eyes, and over his forehead, from above downward, ran wrinkles in three rows, like waves.—"Well?"—he said at last.—"It 's a regular egg, is n't it?"

"A regular, regular egg!" I chimed in, rapturously.—"And have you been like that long?"

"Yes; but what hair I had!—A golden fleece, like that for which the Argonauts traversed the abysses of the sea."

Although I was only twelve years old, yet, thanks to my mythological studies I knew who the Argonauts were; I was all the more surprised to hear that word on the lips of a man who was clothed almost in rags.

"You have studied mythology, I suppose?" I inquired, turning about in my hands the cap which proved to be wadded, with a peeled fur rim and a pasteboard visor.

"I have studied that branch, dear little master, my dear one; there has been sufficient of everything in my life! But now restore to me my cover that I may defend my nakedness therewith."

He pulled his cap down over his eyes, and twisting his whitish brows awry he asked me who I was, and who my parents were.

"I am the grandson of the landed proprietress

here," I replied. " I am the only one she has. Papa and mamma are dead."

Púnin crossed himself.—" May the kingdom of heaven be theirs! That means that you are an orphan; well, and the heir also. The noble blood is immediately perceptible; it fairly dances in your little eyes, and sparkles . . . . sh . . . . sh . . . . sh . . . . sh . . . ." He represented with his fingers how the blood sparkles.—" Well, and do you know, Your Well-Born, whether my comrade came to terms with your good grandmamma, —whether he has received the place which was promised to him? "

" That I do not know."

Púnin grunted.—" Ekh! If we could only establish ourselves here! if only for the time being! Otherwise one roams and roams, no asylum is to be found, the anxieties of life are unceasing, the soul gets thoroughly tortured . . . ."

" Say,"—I interrupted him:—" do you belong to the ecclesiastical profession? "

Púnin turned toward me and screwed up his eyes.—" And what may be the cause of that question, my amiable child? "

" Why, you talk as—as they read in church."

" That is, I use Slavonic expressions? [1] But that should not surprise you. Supposing such

---

[1] The services of the Church are always in the Old Church Slavonic, and an ecclesiastical turn of phrase is as easily detected as liturgical language would be in English.—TRANSLATOR.

expressions are not always suitable in ordinary conversation, yet as soon as your soul begins to soar, then the lofty style immediately makes its appearance. Surely, your teacher —your instructor in Russian literature—teaches you that? Does not he explain that to you?"

"No; he does n't explain," I replied. "When we live in the country I have no teacher. In Moscow I have a great many teachers.

"And do you deign to live long in the country?"

"A couple of months; grandmamma says that I get spoiled in the country. I have a governess with me here."

"A French woman?"

"Yes."

Púnin scratched behind his ear.—"That is to say, a mamzell?"

"Yes; she is called Mlle. Friquet."—It suddenly seemed to me disgraceful that I, a lad of twelve, should have not a governor but a governess, exactly like small girls!—"But I don't obey her," I added scornfully.—"What do I care for her!"

Púnin shook his head.—"Okh, these little nobles! What a fancy you have taken to foreign women! You have declined what is Russian and inclined to what is foreign, have turned to the dwellers in other lands. . . ."

"What 's that? Are you talking poetry?" I inquired.[1]

"What do you think of it? I can always get off as much of that sort of thing as I like; for it comes natural to me. . . ."

But at that moment a strong, sharp whistle rang out in the park behind us. My interlocutor rose briskly from the bench.—"Good-bye, little master, that 's my comrade calling me, seeking me. . . . What will he say to me? Good-bye, be not wroth. . . ."

He dived into the bushes and disappeared, while I remained sitting on the bench. I felt perplexity and some other decidedly agreeable sensation. . . Never before had I met and talked with such a man. Gradually I became engrossed in meditation, but remembered my mythology and trudged homeward.

AT home I learned that my grandmother had come to terms with Babúrin. He had been assigned to a small room in the servants' cottage, at the end of the courtyard. He immediately settled down in it with his comrade.

On the following morning, after I had drunk tea, and without asking permission of Mlle. Friquet, I betook myself to the servants' cottage.

---

[1] Púnin here indulges in a sort of singsong rhyme which is in high favour with old nurses and people of that class. "Ot rossíiskavo vui otklonílisya, na tchuzhóe preklonílisya, k inozémtzam obratílisya.—TRANSLATOR.

PÚNIN AND BABÚRIN

I wanted to have another chat with my eccentric fellow of the day before. Without knocking at the door—that custom was not in use with us— I walked straight into the room. I found in it not the man of whom I was in search, not Púnin, but his protector, Babúrin the philanthropist. He was standing in front of the window, without his outer garment, with his legs straddled far apart, and was carefully wiping his head and neck with a long towel.

"What do you want?" he said, without lowering his hands, but contracting his brows.

"Is n't Púnin at home?" I asked, in the easiest sort of way, and without removing my cap.

"Mr. Púnin, Nikándr Vavílitch, really is not at home at the present moment," replied Babúrin, without haste. "But permit me to remark, young man—is it polite to enter another person's chamber thus, without asking leave?"

"I! . . . 'Young man!' . . . How dared he?! . . ." I flared up with wrath.

"It must be that you do not know me," I articulated, no longer in a free and easy manner, but haughtily;—"I am the grandson of the gentlewoman who owns this estate."

"That 's all one to me," retorted Babúrin, again setting to work with his towel. "Even if you are the proprietress's grandson, you have no right to enter another person's room."

"What do you mean by another person's

room? What are you talking about? I am at home—everywhere—here."

" No, pardon me, it is I who am at home here; because this room has been assigned to me, according to agreement,—for my labours."

"Don't try to teach me, if you please," I interrupted him. " I know better than you do that . . . ."

" You need teaching," he interrupted me in his turn, " for you are now at an age when . . . . I know my duties, but I also know my rights very well, and if you continue to talk to me in that manner I shall be obliged to request you to leave the room. . . ."

It is impossible to say how our wrangle would have ended had not Púnin entered the room at that moment, scuffling his feet and swaying to and fro. He probably guessed from the expression of our faces that something unpleasant had occurred between us, and immediately turned to me with the most amiable evidences of delight.

" Ah, little master! Little master! " he exclaimed, flourishing his hands loosely, and breaking out into his noiseless laugh. " My dear! He has come to visit me! he has come, the dear fellow! " (" What 's this? " I thought; " is it possible that he is addressing me as ' thou '? ") " Well, come, come along with me into the park. I have found something there. . . . What 's the use of sitting in a stuffy room? Come on! "

PÚNIN AND BABÚRIN

I followed Púnin, but considered it necessary to turn round on the threshold and hurl a challenging glance at Babúrin, as much as to say: " I 'm not afraid of thee! "

He answered me in kind, and even snorted into his towel—probably for the purpose of giving me thoroughly to understand to what a degree he despised me!

" How insolent your friend is! " I said to Púnin, as soon as the door closed behind me.

Púnin instantly turned his bloated face toward me in alarm.

" About whom are you expressing yourself in that manner? " he inquired, with eyes starting from his head.

" Why, about him, of course . . . about—what 's his name? . . . about that . . . . Babúrin."

" About Paramón Semyónitch? "

" Well, yes; about that . . . . blackamoor."

" Eh . . . . eh . . . . eh . . . . ! " said Púnin, with caressing reproach.—" How can you talk like that, little master, little master!—Paramón Semyónitch is a most worthy man, of the strictest principles, quite exceptionally so!—Well, of course, he will not allow any one to insult him, because he knows his worth. The man is possessed of great stores of information, and this is not the sort of place he ought to occupy! One must treat him politely, my dear young friend,

297

for he . . . ." here Púnin bent down to my very
ear—" is a republican! "

I stared at Púnin with widely opened eyes. I
had not in the least expected this. From Kaidá-
noff's text-book, and from other historical works,
I had gathered that there had existed, once upon
a time, in antiquity, republicans, both Greeks and
Romans, and, for some reason or other, I had
even imagined to myself that they all wore hel-
mets, carried circular shields in their hands, and
had big, bare legs; but that republicans were actually to be found at the present time, in the
Government of ***—this upset all my concep-
tions, mixed them up utterly!

" Yes, my dear, yes! Paramón Semyónitch is
a republican," repeated Púnin. " So now you
know beforehand how you must express yourself concerning such a man!—But now let us go
to the garden. Just imagine what I have found
there! A cuckoo's egg in the nest of a redstart!
Marvellous! "

I went off into the garden with Púnin; but
I kept mentally reiterating: " A republican! a
re-pub-li-can! "

" That 's exactly the reason," I decided at last,
" why he has such a blue beard! "

My relations to these two individuals, Púnin and
Babúrin, were definitively settled from that day
forth. Babúrin evoked in me a feeling of hos-

tility, with which, however, there speedily came to be mingled something akin to respect. And how afraid of him I was! I never ceased to fear him, even when the original sharp severity in his treatment of me vanished. It is unnecessary to state that I was not afraid of Púnin; I did not even respect him; I regarded him—to speak without circumlocution—in the light of a jester; but I loved him with all my soul! To spend whole hours in his society, to be alone with him, to listen to his stories became for me a genuine delight. Grandmamma was very much displeased at this " *intimité* " with a " common " man—a man " *du commun* "; but as soon as I succeeded in tearing myself free, I immediately ran off to my dear, diverting, strange friend. Our meetings became particularly frequent after the retirement of Mlle. Friquet, whom my grandmother sent back to Moscow, to punish her for having taken it into her head to complain to a passing staff-captain in the army of the boredom which reigned in our house. And Púnin, on his side, was not annoyed by prolonged conversations with a twelve-year-old boy; he seemed himself to seek them. How many of his stories did I listen to, as I sat in the perfumed shade with him, on the dry, smooth grass, under a canopy of silvery poplars, or in the reeds by the pond, on the coarse, damp sand of the shelving shore, out of which protruded gnarled roots, strangely interlaced, like huge black veins, like snakes, like emigrants from a subterranean realm! Púnin narrated to me, in detail, the story of his life, all his lucky and unlucky adventures, with which I always heartily sympathised. His father had been a deacon;—"he was a splendid man—but, when intoxicated, stern to the point of insensibility."

Púnin himself had studied in a seminary.[1] But being unable to endure the " floggings," and feeling within him no inclination for the ecclesiastical calling, he had become a layman, in consequence whereof he had passed through all sorts of trials, and had finally become a vagabond.—" And had I not fallen in with my benefactor, Paramón Semyónitch," Púnin generally added (he never alluded to Babúrin in any other way), " I should have been bemired in the whirlpool of poverty, indecency, and vice! " Púnin was fond of magniloquent expressions—and if not addicted to lying, he certainly was strongly addicted to inventing yarns, and to exaggeration. He was amazed at everything, and went into raptures over everything. . . And I, in imitation of him, also took to exaggerating and going into raptures.

" Why, what a demon thou hast become—cross

---

[1] An ecclesiastical school. The students are not bound to enter the priesthood, as the education provided fits boys for ordinary life also.—TRANSLATOR.

thyself—what ails thee?" my old nurse used to say to me.

Púnin's stories interested me extremely; but even more than his stories did I love the readings which he conducted in my company. It is impossible for me to convey an idea of the feeling which I experienced when, seizing a convenient moment, he would suddenly make his appearance before me like a fabulous hermit, or a good sprite, with a heavy book under his arm, and stealthily beckoning with his long crooked finger, and winking mysteriously, he would point with his hand, his eyebrows, his shoulders, his whole body, to the depths and recesses of the park, whither no one could force his way in search of us, and where it was impossible to find us! And now we have contrived to escape unobserved; now we have safely attained one of our secret nooks; now we are sitting side by side, and the book is being slowly opened, emitting in the process a piercing odour of mustiness and age which was then indescribably agreeable to me! With what trepidation, with what agitation of dumb anticipation did I gaze at Púnin's face, at his lips—at those lips from which presently would pour forth sweet speech! At last the first sounds of the reading ring out! Everything round about vanishes . . . no, it does not vanish, but becomes distant, is enveloped in a haze, leaving behind it only the impression of something friendly and protecting!

—Those trees, those green leaves, those tall blades of grass shield, conceal us from all the rest of the world; no one knows where we are, what we are doing;—but with us is poesy; we permeate ourselves with it, we satiate ourselves with it; a great, a weighty, a mysterious matter is in progress with us. . . .

Púnin stuck chiefly to verses; he was ready to lay down his life for them! He did not read, he shouted them out solemnly, in a flood, smoothly, through his nose, like a man intoxicated, like a madman, like a pythoness. And here is another trick of his; at first he would hum a verse over softly, in an undertone, as though muttering; then he would thunder out the same verse, in a fair version, and suddenly springing to his feet, he would uplift his hands in a half-prayerful, half-imperious way. . . In this manner did he and I go through not only Lomonósoff, Sumarókoff, and Kantemír (the older the verses were, the more to Púnin's taste were they)—but even " The Rossiad " of Kheraskóff![1] And, truth to tell, that same " Rossiad " particularly enraptured me. There, among other things, there comes into play a certain masculine Tatár woman, a giantess-heroine; I have forgotten her very name now; but at that time my hands and feet used to turn cold at the mere mention of it! —" Yes,"—Púnin was wont to say, nodding his head significantly, " Kheraskóff will give no

[1] Michaíl Matvyéevitch Kheraskóff, 1733–1801.—TRANSLATOR.

quarter. Some times he will set forth a wretched little verse—will simply forget himself. . . . But just hold on! . . . Thou art desirous of catching him, but just see where he has got to already! and he trumpets, trumpets like big cymbals! That was the reason his name was given to him! in a word: Kherrraskóff!!" Púnin found fault with Lomonósoff for having too simple and free a style, and toward Derzhávin he bore himself in almost hostile wise, saying that he was more of a loyal courtier than a poet.

In our house not only did no one pay any attention to literature, to poetry, but verses, especially Russian verses, were regarded as something entirely indecorous and insipid; my grandmother did not even call them verses, but " kantas "; [1] every composer of kantas was, in her opinion, either a bitter drunkard or an utter fool. Reared in such notions I was infallibly bound, either to turn away from Púnin with disgust—he was, moreover, so dirty and slovenly that he offended my well-bred instincts—or, carried away and conquered by him, to follow his example, to become infected with his rage for poetry. . . . And this last is precisely what happened. I also began to read verses or, as grandmamma expressed it, to chant kantas. . . . I even tried to compose something myself, namely, the description of a

---

[1] A *kanta* is a laudatory poem of the made-to-order sort indulged in by Court poets—like some of Derzhávin's efforts, for example.—TRANSLATOR.

hand-organ, in which the two following lines occurred:

> Now the thick crank revolves
> And begins to clatter its teeth. . . .[1]

Púnin approved, in this description, a certain imitation of sounds, but condemned the subject as low, and unworthy of lyrical jingle.

Alas! all these efforts and emotions and raptures, our isolated readings, our life together, our poetry—all came to an end at one blow. Like a clap of thunder a catastrophe suddenly crashed down upon our heads.

My grandmother was fond of cleanliness and order in everything, precisely like the executive generals of the present day, and our garden had to be képt in cleanliness and order also. Consequently, from time to time the landless, untaxable peasants, and supernumerary or disgraced house-servants were " rounded up " and made to clean the paths, to rake the vegetable-beds, and to sift and loosen up the earth of the flower-plots. So one day, at the very height of just this sort of rounding-up, grandmamma wended her way to the garden and took me with her. Everywhere—among the trees, over the glades—white, red, or blue shirts were flitting; everywhere there was audible the grinding and whining of scrap-

[1] In the Russian it reads: Vot vertítsya tólsty val—I zubtzámi zashtchelkál.—TRANSLATOR.

ing shovels, the dull thud of clods of earth against the slanting sieves. As she passed the labourers, my grandmother, with her eagle eye, immediately noticed that one of them was less diligent than the rest, and appeared to doff his cap reluctantly. He was a fellow still very young, with sodden visage and dull, sunken eyes. His nankeen kaftan, all tattered and patched, hardly held together on his narrow shoulders.

" Who is that? " inquired my grandmother of Philíppitch, who was tiptoeing after her.

" You . . . of whom . . . do you deign . . . ." Philíppitch began to stammer.

" Oh, fool! I 'm talking about that fellow who glared at me like a wolf. Yonder he stands—he is not working."

" That man, ma'am! Yes, ma'am . . . tha . . . tha . . . tha . . . at is Ermíl, son of the late Pável Afanásieff."

This Pável Afanásieff had been, ten years previous to this time, majordomo in my grandmother's house and had enjoyed her especial favour; but, having suddenly fallen into disfavour, he as suddenly had been converted into a herdsman, and not stopping at herdsman he had descended still further, headlong, had found himself at last in the fowl-hut of a distant village, on an allowance of thirty-six pounds of flour a month, and had died of paralysis, leaving behind him a son in abject poverty.

" Aha! " ejaculated grandmamma; " the apple has not fallen far from the tree,[1] apparently. Well, we shall have to take measures about that fellow. I don't want any people around who gaze askance at me."

Grandmamma returned home—and took measures. Three hours later Ermíl, all " equipped," was led under the window of her boudoir. The unhappy lad was being sent away to Siberia for colonisation. Beyond the fence, a few paces distant from him, a wretched little peasant-cart, laden with his poor effects, was visible. That was the way things went in those days!—Ermíl stood capless, with drooping head, bare-footed, his boots bound with a rope slung behind his back; his face, turned toward the mistress's manor-house, expressed neither despair nor grief, nor even surprise; a stupid grin had congealed on his colourless lips. His eyes, dry and contracted, stared intently at the ground. His presence was announced to my grandmother. She rose from the divan, walked to the window of her boudoir, faintly rustling her silken gown, and putting up to her eyes a double gold-mounted lorgnette, she stared at the new exile. There were four persons in the boudoir besides herself at the moment: the butler, Babúrin, the page in waiting, and I.

Grandmamma moved her head downward from above. . . .

---

[1] That is, he is a chip of the old block.—Translator.

" Madame," suddenly rang out a hoarse, almost choking voice. I glanced round. Babúrin's face had flushed crimson . . . . a black crimson; beneath his frowning eyebrows small, bright, sharp points had made their appearance. . . . There was no doubt about it; it was he, that Babúrin, who had uttered the word " madame! "

Grandmamma also glanced round, and transferred her lorgnette from Ermíl to Babúrin.

" Who was it . . . . speaking? " she articulated, slowly . . . . through her nose. Babúrin stepped forward a little.

" Madame," he began again, " it was I . . who made so bold.—I thought . . . . I venture to inform you that you have no cause for acting as . . . . as you have just been pleased to act."

" Meaning? " said my grandmother, in the same voice as before, and without removing her lorgnette.

" I have the honour . . . ." went on Babúrin, enunciating every word distinctly, although with evident effort,—" I will explain to you about that lad who is being transported for colonisation . . . . without any fault on his part. Such measures, I venture to affirm, lead only to dissatisfaction . . . . and to other consequences—which, God forbid!—and are nothing else than excesses of the power conferred upon Messrs. the Landed Proprietors."

" Thou . . . . where hast thou studied? " inquired grandmamma, after a brief pause, and lowering her lorgnette.

Babúrin was astonished.—"What were you pleased to ask, ma'am?" he mumbled.

"I ask thee where thou has studied?—Thou makest use of such hard words."

"I . . . . my education . . . ." Babúrin was beginning.

Grandmamma shrugged her shoulders disdainfully.—"So my arrangements do not please thee," she interrupted. That is not of the slightest consequence to me; I can dispose of my subjects as I see fit, and I am not answerable to any one for them; only I am not accustomed to have people argue in my presence, and meddle with what does not concern them; I need no philanthropic plebeians. I lived thus before I knew thee, and I shall continue thus to live after thy time also. I have no further use for thee: thou art discharged.—Nikolái Antónoff," said my grandmother, addressing the butler,—"pay this man his wages; let him be gone from here before dinner-time! Dost hear me? Don't enrage me. And the other . . . . the fool-parasite is to be sent away with him.—What more is Ermílka waiting for?" she added, glancing out of the window again.—"I have looked him over. Well, what else remains?"

Grandmamma waved her handkerchief in the direction of the window, as though chasing away an importunate fly. Then she seated herself in an arm-chair and, turning toward us, she said grimly: "Leave the room all you men!"

We all withdrew—all, with the exception of the page on duty, to whom my grandmother's words did not apply, because he was not a "man."

My grandmother's order was punctually executed. Before dinner Babúrin and my friend Púnin had left the place. I will not undertake to depict my woe, my sincere, downright childish despair. It was so violent that it even smothered that sentiment of awe-stricken amazement with which the bold sally of Babúrin the republican had inspired me. After the conversation with my grandmother he had immediately betaken himself to his own room and begun to pack up. He did not vouchsafe me a word or a glance, although I hovered around him all the while, that is to say, in reality, around Púnin. The latter lost his head completely, and he also said nothing; but, on the other hand, he kept casting incessant glances at me, and tears stood in his eyes . . . . always the selfsame tears: they did not overflow, and they did not dry up. He did not dare to condemn his "benefactor":—Paramón Semyónitch could not err in anything,—but he was very languid and sad.

Púnin and I tried to read, by way of farewell,

309

something from " The Rossiad." We even locked ourselves up in a lumber-room for that purpose—the garden was not to be thought of— but we both broke down over the very first line, and I began to bawl like a calf, in spite of my twelve years and my claims to be grown up. When Babúrin had already taken his seat in the tarantás he turned to me, at last, and softening somewhat the habitual sternness of his visage, he said: " 'T is a lesson to you, young sir; remember to-day's doings, and when you grow up try to put an end to such injustice. You have a kind heart, your character is as yet unspoiled. . . . Look out, have a care; 't is impossible to go on like this! " Through the tears which streamed in abundance down my nose, my lips, and my chin, I stammered that I would . . . . would remember, that I promised . . . I would do . . . . without fail . . . . without fail. . . .

But at this point, Púnin, who had exchanged a dozen embraces with me already (my cheeks were burning from contact with his unshaven beard, and I was thoroughly permeated with his odour), —at this point, Púnin was seized with a sudden transport. He sprang up on the seat of the tar- antás, elevated his arms on high and began in a thunderous voice (where did he get it from? !) to declaim the paraphrase of a psalm of David by Derzhávin, who was a poet for this occasion, not a courtier!

PÚNIN AND BABÚRIN

"Almighty God hath risen and will judge
    God's earthly in their throng! . . .
    How long, saith He, how long shall ye
    Be spared, ye evil and unjust?
    It is your duty to uphold the laws. . . ."

"Sit down!" said Babúrin to him.
Púnin sat down, but continued:

"Your duty to preserve the innocent from want,
    To furnish shelter to th' unfortunate,
    And from the powerful to protect the weak. . . ."

At the word "powerful" Púnin pointed his
finger at the manor-house, and then poked it into
the back of the coachman on the box:

"And from their shackles to release the poor!
    They do not heed! They see and do not know. . . ."

Nikolái Antónoff, who had run thither from
the manor-house, began to shout to the driver at
the top of his lungs: "Drive on, blockhead!
Drive on; delay not!" and the tarantás rolled off.
But from afar there still was audible:

"Arise, O God, O upright God! . . .
    Come, judge, chastise the wicked—
    And reign alone King on the earth!"

"What a clown!" remarked Nikolái Antónoff.
"He was n't flogged enough in his youth," de-

clared the deacon, making his appearance on the
porch. He had come to inquire at what hour the
lady wished to have the All-night Vigil celebrated.[1]

LEARNING on that same day that Ermíl was still
in the village and would not be transported to the
town until early on the following morning, for
the fulfilment of the customary legal formalities,
which, having as their object the repression of
the landed proprietors' arbitrariness, served
merely as the source of extra revenues for the superior powers,—on that same day I sought him
out, and in default of any money of my own, I
handed him a parcel, in which I had tied up two
pocket handkerchiefs, a pair of patched shoes, a
comb, an old night-shirt, and a perfectly new silk
cravat. Ermíl, whom I had to awaken—he was
lying in the back yard, beside the cart, on an arm-
ful of straw—Ermíl accepted my gift with considerable indifference, and even not without some
hesitation, then immediately tucked his head into
the straw and fell asleep again. I went away
from him somewhat disenchanted. I had imagined that he would be surprised and delighted
at my visit, and would descry therein a pledge of

[1] This service can be celebrated in an unconsecrated building,
and the devout (or the indolent, as was probably the case here)
often have it in their own houses. It generally consists of Vespers and Matins, or Vespers and Compline, and is obligatory (in
church) before the morning Liturgy.—TRANSLATOR.

my future magnanimous intentions—and instead of that . . . .

" Those people—say what you will—are unfeeling," I thought to myself, on my way back to the house.

My grandmother, who, for some reason or other, had left me in peace throughout that whole day so memorable to me, surveyed me with suspicion, when I began to bid her good night after supper.

" Your eyes are red," she remarked to me, in French,—"and you smell like a peasant's cottage. I shall not enter into an analysis of your feelings and your occupations—I should not like to be compelled to punish you—but I hope that you will discard all your follies and will again behave yourself as is befitting a well-born boy. However, we shall soon return to Moscow, and I will engage a governor for you, as I see that a man's hand is required to keep you in order. You may go."

As a matter of fact, we did speedily return to Moscow.

II

(1837)

SEVEN years passed. We were still living in Moscow, but I was already a student in the second course, and the authority of my grandmother, who had perceptibly grown decrepit during the last few years, did not weigh heavily upon me. Among all my comrades I had struck up a peculiarly intimate friendship with a certain Tárkhoff, a jolly, good-natured young fellow. Our habits, our tastes coincided. Tárkhoff was a great lover of poetry, and wrote little verses himself; and the seeds sown in me by Púnin had not gone to waste. As is proper between intimate young friends, we had no secrets from each other. But for several days past I had begun to notice a certain animation and agitation in Tárkhoff. . . He took to disappearing for hours together—and I did not know where he had gone to, which never had been the case before. I was already preparing to demand a full confession from him, in the name of friendship. . . . He forestalled me.

One day I was sitting in his room. . . "Pétya," he suddenly began, flushing gaily and looking me straight in the face,—" I must introduce thee to my Muse."

"To thy Muse! How strangely thou expressest thyself! Just like a classic!" (Romanticism was then at its height, in the year 1837.) "Dost thou mean to say that I have not been acquainted with her—with thy Muse—this long time? Hast thou written a new poem?"

"Thou dost not understand me," returned Tárkhoff, still continuing to smile and blush.—"I will introduce thee to a living muse."

"Ah! So that's it! But why is she thine?"

"Why, because . . . . Here, wait a bit, I think she is coming hither."

The light tap of brisk heels made itself heard—the door flew wide open—and on the threshold there appeared a young girl of eighteen, in a gay-coloured gown of cotton print, with a black cloth mantle on her shoulders, a black straw hat on her fair, somewhat ruffled hair. On catching sight of me she took fright and grew abashed, and re-coiled . . . . but Tárkhoff immediately sprang forward to meet her.

"Please, please come in, Múza Pávlovna; this is my most intimate friend, a very fine man, and mild, very mild, indeed. . . There is no need for you to fear him. Pétya," he said, addressing me,—"I recommend to thee my Muse—Múza Pávlovna Vinográdoff, my very good acquaintance."

I bowed.

"Didst thou say . . . . Múza?" I began. . . .

Tárkhoff burst out laughing.—"And art thou not aware that there exists such a name among the saints? Neither did I know it, my dear fellow, until I met this nice young lady. Múza! what a charming name! And it suits her so well!"

I made a second obeisance to my friend's pretty acquaintance. She left the door, advanced a couple of paces, and stood still. She was ex-

tremely pretty, but I could not agree with Tárkhoff, and even said to myself: " Well, she a Muse,
forsooth! "

THE features of her round, rosy face were small
and delicate; a breath of fresh, vivacious youth
emanated from the whole of her graceful, minia-
ture figure; but a Muse, the incarnation of a
Muse, I at that time—and not I alone, but all of
us young fellows—pictured to ourselves as something entirely different! First of all, a Muse
must, without fail, be black-haired and pale. A
scornfully-haughty expression, a caustic smile, an
inspired gaze—and that mysterious, demoniacal,
fatal " something "—those were points without
which we were unable to imagine a Muse, the
Muse of Byron, who reigned supreme over men's
minds. Nothing of that sort was to be discerned
in the face of the young girl who had entered.
Had I been a little older at the time, and more
experienced, I should, in all probability, have
paid more attention to her eyes, which were small,
deep-set, with slightly swollen lids, but black as
agate, brilliant and vivacious,—which is rare with
blondes. I should not have discovered poetical
tendencies in their gaze, which was evasive, as it
were, but signs of a passionate soul—passionate
to the point of self-forgetfulness. . . . But I
was very young then.

I offered my hand to Múza Pávlovna,—she
had not given me hers,—but she took no notice of

my movement. She seated herself on a chair which Tárkhoff moved forward, but did not remove her hat and mantilla.

She was, evidently, ill at ease; my presence embarrassed her. She breathed unevenly and with long breaths, as though she were inflating her lungs.

"I have run in to see you for just a minute, Vladímir Nikoláitch," she began. Her voice was very low and from the chest; in her scarlet, almost childish mouth it seemed rather strange,—"but our madame positively refused to give me leave of absence for more than half an hour. You were not feeling well the day before yesterday . . . . so I thought . . . ."

She faltered, and bowed her head. Her dark eyes overshadowed by thick, low-hanging brows, darted hither and thither inexorably. Precisely such dark, brisk, and glittering beetles are to be found, in a hot summer, among the blades of withered grass.

"How sweet of you, Múza, Múzotchka!" exclaimed Tárkoff. "But sit a while, sit just a little while. . . . Here, now, we will prepare the samovár."

"Akh, no, Vladímir Nikoláitch! How can you think of such a thing! I must go away this very second."

"Do rest, just a wee bit. You are all out of breath. . . You are tired."

"I am not tired. That is not the reason I

am . . . . Only, see here . . . give me another book; I have read this one through."—She drew from her pocket a grey, battered little volume of a Moscow publication.

" Certainly, certainly. Well, and what about it? Did you like it,—' Roslávleff '? " added Tárkhoff, turning to me.

" Yes. Only ' Yúry Miloslávsky ' seems to me much better. Our madame is very strict on the score of books. She says they interfere with our work. So, according to her ideas . . ."

" But assuredly, ' Yúry Miloslávsky ' is not to be compared to Púshkin's ' Gipsies '? " interposed Tárkhoff, with a smile.

" I should think not! ' The Gipsies ' . . . ." she drawled, with pauses between her words. " Akh, yes, and here 's another thing, Vladímir Nikoláitch; don't come to-morrow . . . . you know where . . . ."

" Why not? "

" You must n't."

" But why not? "

The young girl shrugged her shoulders, and suddenly rose from her chair with an abrupt movement, exactly as though some one had given her a push.

" Whither away, Múza, Múzotchka," cried Tárkhoff, plaintively. " Sit a while longer! "

" No, no, I can't."—She stepped briskly to the door, and grasped the handle. . . .

" Well, you will take a book at least? "

" Some other time."

Tárkhoff made a rush for the girl, but the latter instantly bounced out of the door. He came near banging his nose against the door.—" What a girl! A regular lizard! " said he, not without vexation, and then fell into thought.

I remained with Tárkhoff. I must find out the meaning of this. Tárkhoff made no mystery of it. He told me that that young girl was of the petty burgher class, a seamstress; that he had seen her for the first time three weeks previously, in a man-tua-maker's shop whither he had gone to order a hat, at the request of his sister, who lived in the provinces; that he had fallen in love with her at first sight, and had succeeded in entering into conversation with her on the following day, on the street; that she appeared to be not indifferent to him.

" Only thou art not to think, please," he added, with fervour,—" thou art not to imagine anything evil about her. Up to the present time, at least, nothing has taken place between us of that sort. . . ."

" Nothing bad," I interposed. " I do not doubt it; neither have I any doubt that thou sincerely regrettest it, my dear friend! Have patience—all will turn out well."

" I hope so! "—said Tárkhoff, with a laugh, although through his teeth. . . . " I 'll tell thee

that type is one of the new ones, thou knowest.
Thou hast not had a chance to get a good look at
her. She 's shy; phew, how shy she is! and with a
stubborn temper! And such a temper! However,
just that shyness is what pleases me in her. 'T is
a sign of independence. I 'm simply over head
and ears in love with her, my dear fellow!"

Tárkhoff launched into a discussion of his " object," and even read me the beginning of a poem
entitled " My Muse." His affectionate outpour-
ings were not to my taste. I secretly envied him.
I speedily went away from him.

A FEW days later I chanced to pass through one
of the rows in the Gostíny Dvor.[1] It was Satur-
day; a vast throng of purchasers was assembled;
from every quarter, amid the jostling and the
crush, the shopkeepers' cries of invitation rang
out. After having bought what I required, I
was thinking only of how I might most speedily
rid myself of their importunate pursuit—when
suddenly I came to a halt . . . involuntarily; in
a fruit shop I had caught sight of my friend's
acquaintance. Múza, Múza Pávlovna! She was
standing with her side toward me and, apparently, was waiting for something. After some

[1] A great aggregation of shops, dealing in all sorts of wares,
congregated under one roof, like an Oriental bazaar. The passages
on which the shops abut are called " rows." The literal translation
is the " The Guests' Court," guest being the ancient term for a
high-class merchant, especially from foreign parts.—TRANSLATOR.

hesitation I made up my mind to approach and enter into conversation with her. But no sooner had I crossed the threshold of the shop and taken off my cap, than she staggered backward in affright, and turning swiftly to an old man in a frieze cloak, for whom the shopman was weighing out a pound of raisins, she seized him by the arm, as though placing herself under his protection. The latter, in his turn, wheeled round and faced me—and picture to yourself my amazement! Whom did I recognise in him? Púnin!

Yes, it was he; those were his little, swollen eyes, his plump lips, his soft, pendent nose. He had even changed very little during the last seven years; save that he had shrivelled a little.

" Nikándr Vavílitch! " I exclaimed. " Don't you know me? "—Púnin gave a start, opened his mouth, and riveted his eyes on me. . . .

" I have not that honour," he began—and suddenly squeaked out: " The little master from Tróitzkoe! " My grandmother's estate bore the name of Tróitzkoe.[1] " Can it be the Tróitzky little master? "—The pound of raisins fell from his hand.

" Exactly so," I replied; and picking Púnin's purchase from the floor, I exchanged kisses with him.

He panted with delight and emotion; he al-

---

[1] Trinity village. Religious appellations for towns, villages, and streets are very popular in Russia.—TRANSLATOR.

most burst into tears, he took off his cap,—which allowed me to convince myself that the last traces of hair had disappeared from his " egg,"—pulled a handkerchief from the bottom of it, blew his nose, thrust the cap into his bosom in company with the raisins, put it on again, again dropped the raisins. . . . I know not how Múza behaved during all this time; I tried not to look at her. I do not suppose that Púnin's agitation arose from profuse attachment to my person; it was simply that his nature could not tolerate any unexpected shock.—The nervousness of poor folk!

" Come along to our house, to our house, my dear little dove," he stammered at last; " surely you will not disdain to visit our modest little nest? You are a student, I see. . . ."

" Certainly not. On the contrary, I shall be very glad."

" Are you disengaged at present?"

" Entirely so."

" That 's fine! How pleased Paramón Semyónitch will be! He returns home earlier than usual to-day, and the madame lets her off on Saturdays. But stay, pardon me, I am quite daft. Of course, you are not acquainted with our niece?"

I hastened to interject the remark that I had not, as yet, the pleasure . . . .

" That is a self-understood thing! Where could you have met her? Múzotchka. . . . Ob-

serve, my dear sir; this young girl's name is Múza
—and it is not a nickname, but her real name.
. . . . By what fatality! Múzotchka, I present
thee to Mr. . . . Mr. . . . ."

" B***," I prompted him.

" To Mr. B***," he repeated. " Múzotchka!
Give heed! Thou seest before thee the very most
excellent, the very most amiable of youths. Fate
brought me in contact with him when he was still
of a very tender age! I beg that thou wilt love
and favour him!"

I made a low obeisance. Múza, scarlet as a
poppy, darted a sidelong glance at me, and immediately dropped her eyes.

" Ah!" I thought,—" thou art one of those
who do not turn pale in difficult circumstances,
but flush crimson; I must take note of that!"

" Be indulgent to her; this girl of ours is not
a woman of fashion,"—remarked Púnin, and
walked out of the shop into the street; Múza and
I followed him.

THE house in which Púnin lodged was situated
at a considerable distance from the bazaar,
namely, on Garden Street. On the way thither
my former preceptor in the branch of poetry contrived to impart to me not a few details concerning his manner of existence. Since the date of
our parting he and Babúrin had made a large
circuit through Holy Russia, and only lately, a

year and a half previously, had they found a permanent asylum in Moscow. Babúrin had managed to get into the office of a wealthy merchant-manufacturer as secretary-in-chief. "It is not a lucrative little place," remarked Púnin, with a sigh;—"there is a great deal of work, and the pay is small . . . but what is one to do? And God be thanked even for that much! I also am endeavouring to find some copying work, and lessons, only, so far, my efforts have remained unsuccessful. My chirography, as you may remember, is old-fashioned, not agreeable to the present taste; and as for lessons, I am greatly hindered by the lack of decent attire; moreover, I fear that in the matter of instruction—instruction in Russian literature—I am not suited to the present taste either; hence I sit hungry." (Púnin burst out into his hoarse, dull laugh. He preserved his former, somewhat magniloquent turn of speech, and his former habit of rhyming.) "Everybody is seeking after novelties! I suppose you also do not revere your old gods any longer, but prostrate yourself before the new ones?"

"And you, Nikándr Vavílitch,—is it possible that you still revere Kheraskóff?"

Púpin halted and flourished both hands in the air at once.

"In the highest degree, my dear sir! in the hiigh-est de-gree!"

" And you do not read Púshkin? You do not like Púshkin? "

Again Púnin elevated his hands higher than his head.

" Púshkin? Púshkin is a serpent sitting concealed in the green boughs, to whom is given the voice of a nightingale! "

While Púnin and I conversed thus together, picking our way cautiously over the unevenly-laid brick sidewalk of " white-stoned " Moscow,[1] of that same Moscow in which there is not a single stone, and which is not white at all—Múza walked quietly beside us, on the side away from me. When speaking of her I referred to her as " your niece." Púnin fell silent for a while, scratched the back of his head, and communicated to me in a low voice that he had called her by that name . . . . it just happened so; that she was in no way related to him; that she was an orphan who had been picked up and taken charge of by Babúrin in the town of Vorónezh; but that he, Púnin, might call her his daughter, since he loved her as much as though she had been his real daughter. I did not doubt that, although Púnin intentionally lowered his voice, Múza heard perfectly everything he said; and whether it was

[1] The famous phrase in full runs: " White-stoned, golden-domed, Holy Mother Moscow." Russia being a land of wood, not a land of stone, buildings of the latter material are rare. Buildings with double walls having a wide-filled space between them of brick or rubble stuccoed and tinted in gay colours, are generally called " stone."— TRANSLATOR.

from wrath, or timidity, or shame, at all events, shadows and blushes flitted across her face by turns, and it twitched slightly all over: eyelids and brows, and lips, and the narrow nostrils. All this was very charming, amusing, and strange.

BUT at last we reached "the modest little nest." And, in fact, it was very modest, that little nest. It consisted of a small, one-story house, almost grown into the ground, with a sagging roof of boards and four dim little windows in the front façade. The furnishing of the rooms was extremely poor, and not quite clean. Between the windows and on the walls hung about a dozen tiny wooden cages containing larks, canary-birds, goldfinches and chaffinches. "My subjects!" —said Púnin, triumphantly, pointing to them with his finger. Almost before we had managed to enter and look about us, before Púnin had succeeded in despatching Múza for the samovár, Babúrin himself made his appearance. He seemed to me to have aged far more than Púnin, although his walk remained firm and, generally speaking, the expression of his face remained intact; but he had grown thin and bent, and his cheeks were sunken, and grey hairs had made their appearance in his thick black locks, worn in a brush.

He did not recognise me, and displayed no special pleasure when Púnin mentioned my name. He did not smile even with his eyes; he barely inclined his head; he inquired—very carelessly and dryly—whether my grandmother [1] was alive— that was all. As much as to say: " You can't surprise me with your noble visit, and I don't consider it flattering in the least." The republican had remained a republican.

Múza returned; a decrepit old woman bore in behind her a badly-cleaned samovár. Púnin began to bustle about and to entertain me; Babúrin seated himself at the table, propped his head on both hands, and cast a weary glance around him. But he got to talking after tea. He was dissatisfied with his position. " He 's a fist,[2] not a man," —that was the way he expressed himself with regard to his employer; " the people in his employ are in his eyes rubbish, of no account whatsoever; and is it such a long time since he dragged about in a peasant's coat of coarse, undyed wool himself? He 's all cruelty and greediness. Service with him is worse than that under the crown! And all commerce here stands on an inflated basis, and is upheld only by wind! " On hearing such cheerless remarks, Púnin heaved a sigh of compunction, assented, nodding his head now up and down, now from side to side. Múza preserved a stubborn silence. . . . She was, obvi-

[1] Babúrin used the plain word, instead of the polite diminutive " dear," which it is customary to employ in speaking of another person's relatives.—TRANSLATOR.

[2] The appellation applied to usurers and skinflints of the lower classes.—TRANSLATOR.

ously, tormented by the thought: Was I a discreet man or a chatterer? And if I was playing the part of a discreet man, was it not with a purpose? Her black, vivacious, restless eyes kept flashing from beneath her drooping lids. Only once did she glance at me, and that in so searching, penetrating, almost vicious a manner . . . . it fairly made me jump. Babúrin hardly spoke to her at all; but every time he did address her, a surly, not paternal affection was audible in his voice.

Púnin, on the contrary, kept inciting Múza to frolic; but she answered him reluctantly. He called her a snowbird, a snowflake.

"Why do you apply such names to Múza Pávlovna?" I asked.

Púnin burst out laughing.—"Because she is so very cold."

"She is sensible," interposed Babúrin, "as is befitting a young girl."

"We may also call her our housewife,"—exclaimed Púnin.—"Hey? Paramón Semyónitch?"—Babúrin scowled; Múza turned away. —I did not understand that hint at the time.

Thus passed two hours . . . not in a very lively manner, although Púnin endeavoured in every possible way to "entertain the honourable company." Among other things he curled himself up in front of the cage of one of the canaries, opened the door, and commanded: "On the *cum-*

pol! Come, give us a concert!"—The canary immediately fluttered out, perched on the *cumpol,* that is to say, on Púnin's bald head, and turning from side to side and flapping its wings, it began to twitter with all its might. During the whole of the concert Púnin never stirred, and only beat time lightly with his finger, and screwed up his eyes. I could not help roaring with laughter . . . but neither Babúrin nor Múza laughed.

Just before my departure Babúrin surprised me by an unexpected question. He desired to learn from me, as from a man who was studying in the university, what sort of a person Zeno was and what was my opinion of him.

"What Zeno?" I asked, not without surprise.

"Zeno, the ancient sage. Is it possible that you do not know about him?"

I confusedly recalled the name of Zeno as the founder of the school of stoics; but knew absolutely nothing else about him.

"Why, he was a philosopher," I said at last.

"Zeno,"—pursued Babúrin, with pauses between his words,—"was that same wise man who explained that suffering is no evil, for patience conquers all things, while there is but one good in this world, justice; and virtue itself is nothing else than justice."

Púnin reverentially lent an ear.

"That apothegm was communicated to me by one of the residents here who possesses a great many ancient books," went on Babúrin;—" it pleased me greatly. But you do not occupy yourself with that sort of subjects, I perceive."

Babúrin spoke the truth. I did not occupy myself with such subjects—that was a fact. From the time of my entrance into the university I had been quite as good a republican as Babúrin himself. I would have talked with delight of Mirabeau and Robespierre. But why mention Robespierre! . . . over my writing-table hung lithographed portraits of Fouquier-Tinville and Chalier!—But Zeno!! What wind had blown Zeno hither?

On taking leave of me Púnin urgently insisted that I should visit them on the following day, which was Sunday; Babúrin did not invite me at all, and even remarked through his teeth that conversation with common people, with plebeians, could not afford me great satisfaction, and that, probably, my *grandmother* would not like it. . . . At this point I interrupted his speech and gave him to understand that I no longer took orders from my grandmamma.

" But have you entered into possession of the estates? "—inquired Babúrin.

" No, I have not," I replied.

" Well, and consequently . . . ." Babúrin did not finish the phrase which he had begun; but I finished it for him: " Consequently, I am a little boy."

" Farewell," I said aloud, and withdrew.

I had already emerged from the courtyard into the street—when suddenly Múza ran out of the house and, thrusting into my hand a bit of paper, crumpled into a wad, immediately disappeared. I stopped at the first street-lantern and unfolded that paper. It proved to be a note. With difficulty did I decipher the pale lines, which had been scrawled with a pencil. " For God's sake," —Múza wrote to me,—" Come to-morrow after dinner to the Alexander Park near the Kutáfya tower [1] I will wait for you do not refuse me do not make me unhappy I must see you without fail." There were no orthographical errors in this note, but there were no punctuation-marks, either. I returned home in a state of perplexity.

WHEN more than a quarter of an hour before the appointed time, on the following day, I began to approach the Kutáfya tower (it was at the beginning of April, the buds were swelling, the grass was turning green, the sparrows were noisily chirping and wrangling in the bare lilac-bushes), to my no small amazement I beheld a little on one side, not far from the fence, Múza. She had forestalled me. I was about to advance toward her; but she came to meet me.

" Let us go to the Kremlin wall," she whis-

[1] One of the towers in the Kremlin wall, which is encircled on the west by the Alexander Park.—TRANSLATOR.

pered, in a hurried voice, as she skimmed over the ground with downcast eyes,—" for there are people here."

We walked along the path up hill.

" Múza Pávlovna," I was beginning. . . . But she immediately interrupted me.

" Please do not condemn me,"—she said in the same soft, abrupt tone as before. " Do not think any ill of me. I wrote you that letter, and appointed a meeting because . . . . I was afraid. . . . . It seemed to me, yesterday,—you appeared to be laughing in your sleeve all the while.—Listen," she added, with sudden force, stopping short and turning toward me; " listen; if you tell with whom . . . . if you mention the name of the person at whose house we met I will fling myself into the water, I will drown myself, I will lay violent hands on myself!"

At this point, for the first time, she glanced at me with that keen, searching look with which I was already familiar.

" And I believe she actually would do it. . . . I fear she would!" I thought to myself.

" Good heavens, Múza Pávlovna!" I hastily articulated. " How can you have such a bad opinion of me? Do you think I am capable of betraying my friend and of injuring you? And, in conclusion, there is nothing reprehensible in your relations, so far as I am aware. . . . For God's sake, calm yourself!"

Múza heard me out, without stirring from the spot or looking at me again.

" There is one thing more I must tell you," she began, again starting to advance along the path, —"otherwise you may think, 'Why, she is crazy!' I must tell you that that old man wants to marry me!"

" What old man? The bald one? Púnin?"

" No—not that one! The other. . . . Paramón Semyónitch."

" Babúrin?"

" The very same."

" Is it possible? Has he proposed to you?"

" He has."

" But of course you have not accepted him?"

" Yes, I have accepted him . . . . because, at that time I understood nothing about it. Now— it is quite another matter."

I clasped my hands.—" Babúrin—and you! Why, he must be nearly fifty years of age."

" He says that he is forty-three. But that makes no difference. If he were five-and-twenty I would n't marry him. What joy would there be? A whole week will pass without his smiling even once. Paramón Semyónitch is my benefactor, I am greatly indebted to him, he gave me an asylum, he reared me, I should have gone to destruction had it not been for him, I am bound to regard him as a father. . . . But be his wife!

I 'd rather die! I 'd rather go straight into my coffin! "

" Why are you always alluding to death, Múza Pávlovna? . . ."

Again Múza halted.

"Why, do you think life is so fair? I may even say that I fell in love with your friend Vladímir Nikoláitch through grief and sorrow,—and then there 's Paramón Semyónitch with his proposals. . . . . Púnin, although he bores one with his poetry, yet does n't scare one, at all events; he does n't make me read Karamzín [1] of an evening, when my head is ready to tumble off my shoulders with weariness! And what care I for those old men? They call me cold, to boot. Could anybody be hot—with them? If they undertake to force me—I 'll run away. But Paramón Semyónitch is always saying ' liberty! liberty! ' Well, then, I want liberty, too. Otherwise, what does it amount to? I am free to do anything, but I am to be kept in prison? I tell him so myself. But if you betray me, or even give a hint—remember, that 's the last you will ever see of me! "

Múza placed herself across the path.

" That 's the last you will ever see of me! "— she repeated sharply. Even now she did not raise her eyes; she seemed to be aware that she would instantly betray herself—would show

---

[1] Meaning the famous history of Russia by Karamzín.—TRANSLATOR.

what she had in her soul—if any one were to look her straight in the eye. . . . And precisely for that reason she did not raise her eyes except when angry or vexed—and then she riveted them straight on the person with whom she was talking. . . . But her rosy, charming little face breathed forth irrevocable decision.

"Well,"—flashed through my mind,—"Tárkhoff is right. This young girl is a new type."

"You have nothing to fear from me," I articulated at last.

"Really? Even in . . . . See here, you said something about our relations. . . . So even in case . . . ." She stopped short.

"Even in that case you have no occasion for fear, Múza Pávlovna. I am not your judge, and your secret is buried—here." I pointed to my breast.—"Believe me, I know how to appreciate. . . ."

"Have you my letter with you?"—suddenly inquired Múza.

"Yes."

"Where is it?"

"In my pocket."

"Give it to me . . . . be quick, be quick!"

I pulled out the paper I had received on the day before. Múza clutched it with her harsh little hand, stood in front of me a little, as though about to thank me, but suddenly started, glanced behind her, and without even nodding, she briskly descended the slope.

I glanced in the direction whither she had gone. Not far from the tower, enveloped in a Spanish cloak known as an almaviva (almavivas were then very fashionable), I beheld a figure which I instantly recognised as that of Tárkhoff.

"Ah, brother,"—I thought, "thou must have been informed if thou art standing guard over her. . . ." And whistling softly to myself I wended my way homeward.

I HAD only just finished drinking tea the next morning when Púnin called upon me. He entered the room with a decidedly confused mien, began to bow and scrape, to glance about, and to make excuses for his lack of discretion, as he put it. I hastened to reassure him. Sinful man that I was, I imagined that Púnin had come with the intention of borrowing a little money. But he confined himself to asking for a glass of tea with rum, seeing that the samovár was still standing on the table.

"Not without trepidation and sinking of heart have I come to this meeting with you,"—he began, biting off a bit of sugar. I am not afraid of you; but I am in great terror of your respected grandmamma! My attire also renders me unassuming, as I have already informed you."—Púnin passed his finger along the edge of his old coat.—" At home I don't mind it, and on the street 't is no harm either; but when one gets into gilded palaces, one's poverty rises up before him, and he becomes abashed!"—I occupied two small rooms in the entresol and, of course, it never would have entered any one's head to call them palaces, much less gilded palaces; but Púnin was, probably, talking about the whole of my grandmamma's house; but that was not distinguished for its luxury either. He upbraided me for not having called on them the evening before: " Paramón Semyónitch expected you," said he, " although he declared that you would not come on any account. And Múzotchka expected you also."

" What? Múza Pávlovna also?" I asked.

" She also. But what a charming young girl we have turned out to possess, have n't we? Say!"

" Very charming," I assented.

Púnin mopped his bare head with remarkable alacrity.—" A beauty, my dear sir, a pearl or even a brilliant—I 'm telling you the truth." —He bent down to my very ear.—" And of noble blood, also," he whispered to me; " only— you understand—on the left hand; the forbidden fruit was tasted. Well, sir, her parents died, her relatives withdrew and abandoned her to the caprice of Fate! which means despair, death by hunger! But at this point Paramón Semyónitch, the well-known, age-long deliverer, intervened! He took her, clothed her, warmed her, and reared the birdling; and our joy has blossomed forth! I tell you, he 's a man of the rarest merit!''

Púnin threw himself back against the back of the arm-chair, flung up his arms, and, again bending forward, once more began to whisper, but still more mysteriously than before: '' For Paramón Semyónitch himself, you see . . . . Don't you know? He also is of exalted extraction— and also on the left side. They say his father was a reigning Prince of Georgia, from the tribe of King David. . . .[1] How do you understand that? In a few words—but how much said? The blood of King David! What do you think of that? But according to other authorities, the progenitor of Paramón Semyónitch was a certain Indian Shah, Babur White Bone! That 's fine, is n't.it? Hey?''

'' Well,'' I asked, '' and was Babúrin also abandoned to the caprice of Fate?''

Again Púnin mopped his pate.—'' Absolutely! And even with greater cruelty than was our little queen! From his earliest childhood life has been nothing but a struggle! I confess that I have even composed a four-lined portrait of Paramón

[1] The former royal family of Georgia, while not claiming to be Jews, do claim descent from King David.—TRANSLATOR.

Semyónitch in that connection. Wait . . . .
how the dickens does it go? Yes!

" From his swaddling-clothes not sparing th' oppression
      of fierce fates
   To the verge of the abyss did ill Babúrin hale!
   But flame glitters in the fog, gold's rays on the dung-
      heap shine, —
   And lo! with victory's laurel his brows are crowned! "

Púnin recited these lines in a measured, sing-song tone, and with a rotund pronunciation of the *o's,* as is proper in reading verses.

" So there now, that is why he is a republican! "
I exclaimed.

" No, that is not the reason," replied Púnin ingenuously. — " He forgave his father long ago; but he is utterly unable to tolerate injustice; other people's woes disturb him! "

I wanted to turn the conversation upon what I learned from Múza on the day before, namely, upon Babúrin's wooing, — but did not know how to set about it. Púnin himself extricated me from my dilemma.

" Didn't you notice anything? " he asked me suddenly, slily screwing up his little eyes. — " When you were at our house? Anything peculiar? "

" Why, was there anything to notice? " I queried in my turn.

Púnin glanced over his shoulder, as though

desirous of convincing himself that no one was eavesdropping on us.—"Our little beauty, Múzotchka, will soon become a married lady!"

"What?"

"Madame Babúrin," articulated Púnin with intensity, and smiting himself several times on the knees with his palms, he began to wag his head like a porcelain Chinaman.

"It cannot be!" I exclaimed with simulated amazement.

Púnin's head instantly stopped wagging, and his hands ceased their motion.—"And why cannot it be, allow me to inquire?"

"Because Paramón Semyónitch is old enough to be your young lady's father; because such a disparity in age precludes all possibility of love —on the part of the bride."

"Precludes?" Púnin caught me up irritably. "And how about gratitude? And purity of heart? And tenderness of feelings? Precludes! This is the way you ought to argue: Supposing Múza is a very beautiful young girl; but to win the affection of Paramón Semyónitch, to be his consolation, his support—his wife in short! Isn't that the highest bliss even for such a young girl? And she understands that! Do you look, cast an attentive glance! Múzotchka is all reverence, all agitation and rapture in the presence of Paramón Semyónitch."

"Therein precisely lies the trouble, Nikándr

Vavílitch, that, as you say, she is all trepidation. A person is not in trepidation before the one she loves."

"With that I do not agree! Here, take me, for example; it seems as though no one could possibly love Paramón Semyónitch more than I do, yet I . . . I tremble before him."

"But you—are quite another matter."

"Why am I another matter? Why? Why?" interrupted Púnin. I simply did not know him; he had waxed hot and serious, was almost wrathful—and did not talk in rhymes.—"No," he insisted: "I perceive that you have not a penetrating eye! No! You are not a reader of hearts!"

I ceased to contradict him . . . . and in order to give another turn to the conversation, I proposed that we should busy ourselves with reading, in memory of old times.

Púnin was silent for a space.

"From the same authors as of old? From the real ones?" he inquired at last.

"No; from the new authors."

"From the new authors?" repeated Púnin incredulously.

"From Púshkin," I replied. There suddenly occurred to my mind "The Gipsies," to which Tárkhoff had recently alluded. And here also, by the way, a song is sung about an old husband. Púnin fidgeted about a little, but I made him sit down on the divan that he might listen the more conveniently, and began to read Púshkin's poem. Now I came to "old husband, menacing husband"; Púnin listened to the song to the end—and all at once rose abruptly to his feet.

"I can't stand it," he articulated with a profound emotion which surprised even me:—"excuse me; I cannot listen any longer to that writer. He is an immoral lampooner, he is a liar .... he disturbs me. I can't stand it! Permit me to terminate my present visit."

I began to try to persuade Púnin to remain; but he insisted, with a certain stupid and frightened obduracy, in having his own way; he repeated several times that he felt disturbed and wished to refresh himself in the open air—and therewith his lips trembled slightly and his eyes avoided meeting mine—just as though I had insulted him. And so he went away.

A little while later I left the house and betook myself to Tárkhoff.

WITHOUT asking leave of any one, I went straight to his quarters, after the unceremonious habit of students. There was no one in the first room. I called Tárkhoff by name, and, receiving no answer, I was about to go away; but the door of the adjoining room opened, and my friend made his appearance. He looked at me in rather a queer way and shook my hand in silence. I had gone to him with the intention of telling him all I had learned from Púnin; and although I immediately felt that I had made an inopportune call upon Tárkhoff, still, after chatting about irrelevant subjects for a while, I wound up by communicating to him Babúrin's intentions with respect to Múza. This information obviously did not surprise him greatly; he quietly seated himself at the table and, fixing his eyes intently upon me and maintaining silence as before, he imparted to his features an expression . . . . an expression which seemed to say: "Well, what more hast thou to tell? Come, expound thy ideas." I looked more attentively into his face. . . . It seemed to me animated, somewhat derisive, even somewhat impudent. But this did not prevent my "expounding my ideas." On the contrary. "Thou art making a display of swagger," I thought to myself, "so I will not spare thee!" And thereupon, I immediately launched out into a dissertation upon the evil of sudden passions, upon the duty of every man to respect the freedom and individuality of another person, —in a word, I launched out into an exordium of useful and practical advice. As I discoursed in this manner, I paced up and down the room for the sake of greater ease. Tárkhoff did not interrupt me, and did not stir on his chair; he merely twiddled his fingers on his chin.

"I know,"—said I . . . . (what in particular prompted me to speak has never been clear to myself, but the most probable explanation is envy;—but certainly not the interests of morality, as a matter of fact). "I know," said I, "that this is not an easy affair, not a matter of jest; I am convinced that thou lovest Múza, and that Múza loves thee, that this is no momentary whim on thy part. . . But here, let us assume!" (At this point I folded my arms on my breast.) . . . "Let us assume that thou hast satisfied thy passion; but what comes next? Surely, thou wilt not marry her? And in the meantime thou art destroying the happiness of a good, honest man, her benefactor—and—who knows?"—(here my face expressed simultaneously penetration and grief) —" perhaps also her own happiness. . . ."

And so forth, and so forth, and so forth! ! !

My speech lasted about a quarter of an hour. Tárkhoff still remained silent. This silence began to disconcert me. Now and then I glanced at him, not so much for the sake of assuring myself as to the impression which my words were producing as for the purpose of finding out why he did not reply and did not assent, but sat there like a deaf and dumb person. But at last it seemed to me that a change . . . yes, actually, a change, was taking place in his countenance. It was beginning to express uneasiness, agitation, painful agitation . . . . But, strange to say, that animated, radiant, laughing something, which had struck me on my very first glance at Tárkhoff, still did not abandon that agitated, that anguished face!

I had not yet decided whether I ought to congratulate myself on the success of my sermon when Tárkhoff suddenly rose to his feet and, squeezing both my hands, said hurriedly: "Thanks, thanks. Thou art right, of course . . . . although one might say a good deal on the other side. . . . for what, as a matter of fact, is thy lauded Babúrin? An honourable dullard— nothing more! Thou dignifiest him with the name of republican—but he is simply a misanthrope! Ugh! That's what he is!—All his republicanism consists in his never getting on well with anybody."

"Ah! so that is thy opinion! A misanthrope! He does not get on with people! !—But art thou aware," I went on with sudden vehemence,—"art thou aware, my dear Vladímir Nikoláitch, that never to get on well anywhere is the sign, in our day, of a good, a noble nature? Only empty people—bad people—get on well everywhere and reconcile themselves to everything!—Thou sayest that Babúrin is an honourable dullard! ! ! —Well, and is it better, in thy opinion, to be a dishonourable wit?"

"Thou art distorting my words!" exclaimed Tárkhoff.—"I merely meant to explain to thee

in what manner I understand that gentleman.—
Dost thou think that he is such a rare specimen?
Not at all!—I also have met men of the same ilk
in my time.—A man sits with a very pompous
mien, holds his tongue, is obstinate, stares with
wide-open eyes. . . Oho, ho! That signifies that
yonder, inside of him, there is a great deal! But
there isn't anything inside of him, there isn't a
single idea in his head,—there 's nothing but the
sense of his own worth."

"And even that is a respectable thing," I interrupted.—" But allow me to inquire where
thou hast succeeded in studying him so?—Thou
art not acquainted with him, art thou? Or art
thou depicting him . . . . from Múza's words?"

Tárkhoff shrugged his shoulders.—" Múza
and I . . . do not talk about him.—Hearken,"
he added, with an impatient movement of his
whole body—" hearken to me: if Babúrin is such
a noble and honourable nature, how is it that he
does not see that Múza is no mate for him?—One
of two things; either he understands that he is
exerting a sort of violence over her in the name
of gratitude, or something of that sort . . . .
and then what becomes of his honour?—Or he
does not understand this . . . . and then how
can one avoid calling him a dullard?"

I was about to retort—but Tárkhoff seized my
hands and began to speak in a hurried voice.—
" However . . . . of course . . . . I admit that

thou art right, a thousand times right. . . .
Thou art my true friend . . . but now leave me,
please."

I was astonished.—"Leave thee?"

"Yes. Seest thou, I must ponder well over
all thou hast just said to me. . . . I do not
doubt that thou art right . . . . but now leave
me."

"Thou art in such a state of agitation" . . .
I was beginning.

"Agitation? I?"—Tárkhoff burst out laughing, but immediately caught himself up.—"Yes,
of course! How could it be otherwise? Thou
sayest thyself that this is no jesting matter. Yes,
I must think it over . . . alone."—He continued to squeeze my hands.—"Good-bye, my dear
fellow, good-bye!"

"Good-bye," I repeated. "Good-bye, brother!"—As I departed I cast a last glance
at Tárkhoff. He seemed content. With what?
Because I, like a faithful friend and comrade,
had pointed out to him the danger of the path
on which he had set his foot,—or because I was
going away? The most diversified thoughts re-
volved in my head all day long, until evening,—
until the very minute when I entered the house
occupied by Púnin and Babúrin; for I went to
them that same day. I must confess that certain
of Tárkhoff's expressions had landed in my
soul . . . . kept ringing in my ears. . . . And, in

fact, was it possible that he did not see that she was no mate for him?

But how could that be possible! Babúrin, the self-sacrificing Babúrin,—the honourable dullard!

Púnin had told me, during his visit, that I had been expected at their house on the preceding evening. Possibly; but decidedly no one was expecting me that day. . . . I found them all at home, and all were amazed to see me. Babúrin and Púnin were both indisposed; Púnin had a headache and was lying curled up on the stove-bench [1] with his head bound up in a gay-coloured kerchief and the half of a split cucumber applied to each temple. Babúrin was suffering from a suffusion of bile; all yellow, almost dark-brown, with dark circles round his eyes, a furrowed brow, and an unshaven beard, he bore very little resemblance to a bridegroom! I wanted to go away. . . But they would not let me and even regaled me with tea. I passed a very cheerless evening. Múza, it is true, was suffering from no aches. She was even less shy than ordinary, but evidently vexed and vicious. . . . At last she could endure it no longer, and as she handed me a cup of tea she hurriedly whispered: "No matter what you say, or what efforts you make, you

---

[1] Old-fashioned Russian tiled stoves were built with a bench-like projection, on which it was possible to sleep.—TRANSLATOR.

will effect nothing in that quarter. . . . That's so!" I looked at her in amazement, and seizing a favourable moment, I asked her, also in an undertone:—"What is the meaning of your words?"

"This," she replied, and her black eyes flashing viciously from beneath her elevated eyebrows riveted themselves on my face, and immediately were averted; "this—that I heard everything you said there to-day, and I have nothing to say 'thank you' for, but things won't be as you would have them."

"You were there!" involuntarily burst from me. . . .

But at this point Babúrin pricked up his ears and glanced in our direction.—Múza went away from me.

Ten minutes later she again succeeded in approaching me. It seemed to afford her pleasure to say daring and dangerous things to me, and to say them in the presence of her protector, under his surveillance, making of it just so much of a secret as was requisite in order not to arouse his suspicion. It is a well-known fact that walking on the edge, on the very brink of an abyss, is a favourite feminine occupation.

"Yes, I was there," whispered Múza, without changing countenance; only her nostrils quivered slightly and her lips writhed awry.—"Yes, and if Paramón Semyónitch asks me what I am whispering about with you, I shall instantly tell him. What do I care!"

"Do be more cautious," I entreated her:— "really, I believe they are beginning to notice. . . ."

"But I tell you that I am ready to tell everything. Yes, and who is taking notice? One is craning his neck from the stove-bench like a sick gosling, but he can't hear anything; and the other is pondering on philosophy. Don't you be afraid!"—Múza's voice was elevated a little, and her cheeks became slightly suffused with a sort of dull, malicious flush; and it was wonderfully becoming to her, and she had never looked so pretty. As she cleared the table, and put the cups and saucers in their places, she moved swiftly about the room; there was something defiant about her light, easy walk,—as though she were saying: "Judge me as you like, I'll do as I please, and I'm not afraid of you!"

I cannot conceal the fact that Múza appeared enchanting to me on that particular evening. "Yes," I thought to myself, "that ill-natured girl is a new type. . . . She is charming. Those hands are capable of strangling, I'll wager. . . . Well! There's no harm in that!"

"Paramón Semyónitch!" she suddenly exclaimed:—"a republic is the sort of kingdom where every one does what he pleases?"

"A republic is not a kingdom, madame," replied Babúrin, raising his head and with lowering brows:—"it is a . . . . an organisation where everything is founded on law and justice."

"Consequently,"—pursued Múza,—"in a republic no one can force another person?"

"No one can."

"And every one can dispose of himself freely?"

"He can."

"Ah! That's all I wanted to know."

"Why didst thou want to know it?"

"Because; I need it.—I needed to have *you* say that."

"That young lady of ours is eager for knowledge," remarked Púnin from the stove-bench.

When I went out into the anteroom Múza escorted me, not out of politeness, of course, but out of that same malevolence. I asked her as I bade her farewell,—"Is it possible that you love him so strongly?"

"I don't know whether I love him or not," she answered; "only what's fated to happen will happen."

"Look out, don't play with fire . . . . you'll get burned."

"Better get burned than freeze to death. As for you . . . . so much for your advice! And how do you know that he will not marry me? How do you know that I am irrevocably bent on getting married? Well, and if I go to perdition . . . . What business is it of yours?"

She banged the door behind me.

I remember that on my way home it gave me considerable pleasure to think that my friend Vladímir Tárkhoff had got himself into a pretty scrape . . . oï, oï, oï—with the "new type" . . . . Really, one must pay for one's luck somehow!

As to his being in luck I could not, unhappily for myself, cherish any doubt.

THREE days passed. I was sitting in my room before my writing-table, and not so much working as preparing to breakfast . . . . when I heard a rustle, raised my head, and was petrified with amazement. Before me, motionless, terrible, white as chalk, stood a ghost . . . . stood Púnin. Slowly blinking, he stared at me with his little, puckered-up eyes; a wild, hare-like terror was what they expressed, and his arms hung down like whip-lashes.

"Nikándr Vavílitch! What ails you? How did you get here? Has no one seen you? What has happened? Come, speak!"

"She has run away,"—articulated Púnin in a barely audible, hoarse whisper.

"What are you saying?"

"She has run away," he repeated.

"Who?"

"Múza. She went away in the night, and left a note behind her."

"A note?"

"Yes. 'I thank you,' says she, 'but I shall not return. Don't hunt for me.'—We rushed about hither and thither; we interrogated the cook; the cook knew nothing. I cannot speak aloud. Excuse me. My voice has broken."

"Múza Pávlovna has left you!" I exclaimed. "You don't say so! Mr. Babúrin must be in despair. What does he mean to do now?"

"He does not mean to do anything. I wanted to run to the Governor-General; he forbade me; I wanted to make a declaration to the police; he forbade me and even got angry. He says: 'She is free to do as she likes. I don't want to persecute her.' He has even gone off to work in his counting-house, only, of course, he no longer bears human semblance. He loved her an awful lot. . . . Okh, okh, we both loved her greatly."

Here Púnin betrayed, for the first time, that he was not a statue, but a living man; he elevated both fists on high and brought them down on his pate, which shone like ivory.

"The ungrateful creature!" he groaned; "who was it that fed thee, gave thee drink, saved thee, shod thee, reared thee? Who was it that cared for thee, who was it that gave his whole life, his whole soul? . . . . And thou hast forgotten it all! To desert me is, of course, of no account, but Paramón Semyónitch, Paramón . . . ."

I begged him to sit down, to rest. . . .

Púnin shook his head in the negative. . " No, it is not necessary. And I have come to you. . . . I know not why. I am like a crazy man; it gives me the shudders to stay at home alone; where am I to go? I stand in the middle of the room, and shut my eyes and call: ' Múza! Múzotchka!' I shall lose my mind if I go on like that. But no, why do I lie? I know why I came to you. The other day, you know, you read to me that thrice-accursed song . . . . you remember, where the old husband is spoken of? Why did you do that? Did you know anything then . . . . or did you guess?" Púnin darted a glance at me.—" Dear little father, Piótr Petróvitch," he exclaimed, suddenly trembling all over,—" perhaps you know where she is? Dear little father,[1] to whom has she gone?"

I grew confused and involuntarily dropped my eyes. . . .

" Did she tell you in her letter," I began. . . .

" She said that she was going away from us because she had fallen in love with another man. Dear little father, my dear little dove, you surely must know where she is? Save her, let us go to her; we will persuade her. Have mercy, consider

---

[1] A respectfully affectionate mode of address for persons of all ranks, from the Emperor down.—TRANSLATOR.

whom she has killed!"—Púnin suddenly flushed crimson, all his blood flew to his head, he plumped heavily down on his knees.—"Save her, father, let us go to her!"

My man made his appearance on the threshold and stopped short in amazement.

It cost me not a little trouble to get Púnin on his feet again, to explain to him that even if I had any suspicions, still it was impossible to act abruptly, especially two of us together; that thereby we should only ruin the whole business, that I was ready to make an effort, but could not answer for anything. Púnin did not reply to me, but he did not listen to me, and only repeated, from time to time, in his cracked voice:—"Save her and Paramón Semyónitch." At last he fell to weeping.

"Tell me one thing, at least," he entreated; "that . . . . *he* is handsome and young?"

"He is young," I replied.

"He is young," repeated Púnin, daubing the tears all over his cheeks. "And she is young. . . . . That's the root of all the mischief!"

This rhyme [1] occurred accidentally; poor Púnin was in no mood for poetry. I would have given a great deal to hear once more his oratorical speeches, or even his almost noiseless laugh. . . . Alas! those speeches were gone forever;—I never heard his laugh again.

[1] "I oná molodá. . . . Vot vtchyóm vsyá byedá!"—Translator.

I promised to communicate with him as soon as I should learn anything positive. . . . But I did not mention Tárkhoff.—Púnin suddenly collapsed utterly.—"Very good, sir, very good, sir, I thank you, sir," he remarked, with a pitiful grimace, and employed the s,[1] which he had never done before.—"Only, you know, sir, you must not say anything to Paramón Semyónitch, sir . . . or he will wax wroth!—In one word, he has forbidden it! Farewell, sir!"

As he was departing, and had his back turned toward me, Púnin appeared to me so pitiful a creature that I was amazed; he limped on both feet, and squatted at every step. . . .

"'T is a bad business! What is called 'Finis,'" I thought.

ALTHOUGH I had promised Púnin to collect information concerning Múza, yet when I set out for Tárkhoff's that same day, I did not in the least expect to find out anything, for I was firmly persuaded either that I should not find him at home or that he would refuse to receive me. My assumption proved to be erroneous. I found Tárkhoff at home, he received me, and I even found out everything I wished to know; but the information proved to be utterly useless to me. No sooner had I set my foot across his threshold

---

[1] S added to a word is a polite abbreviation of "sir," or "madame."—TRANSLATOR.

than Tárkhoff came to me with a swift, decisive step, and with his eyes beaming, blazing in his face, which had grown handsome and serene, and said firmly and boldly:

"Hearken, brother Pétya! I can guess why thou art come, and what thou art preparing to talk to me about; but I warn thee that if thou dost allude to her by so much as a single word, or to her performance, or to what, according to thy opinion, common sense demands of me, we shall no longer be friends, not even acquaintances, and I shall request thee to treat me like a stranger."

I stared at Tárkhoff: he was all in a quiver; like a tautly-stretched chord, he was all tinkling; he was hardly able to restrain the transports of his surging young blood; strong, joyous happiness had burst its way into his soul and had taken possession of him—and he had taken possession of it.

"Is that thine irrevocable decision?" I articulated sadly.

"Yes, brother Pétya; my irrevocable decision."

"In that case, all that remains for me is to say to thee, 'Good-bye.'"

Tárkhoff slightly contracted his brows. . . . He was feeling so greatly at his ease.

"Good-bye, brother Pétya," he said, in a slightly nasal tone, with a frank smile, merrily displaying all his white teeth.

What was I to do? I left him alone with his "happiness."

When I slammed the door behind me, another door in the room slammed also, and I heard it.

I WAS still heavy at heart, on the following day, when I wended my way to my ill-starred acquaintances. I secretly cherished the hope—such is human weakness!—that I should not find them at home, and again I was mistaken. Both of them were at home. Any one would have been struck by the change which had taken place in them during the last three days. Púnin had grown ghastly white and bloated. What had become of his loquacity? He spoke languidly, feebly, still in the same hoarse voice as before, and had a surprised and bewildered aspect. Babúrin, on the contrary, had shrivelled up and turned black; taciturn in the past, he now barely gave utterance to spasmodic sounds; an expression of stony sternness seemed to have frozen on his features.

I felt that it was impossible to hold my tongue; but what was there to say? I confined myself to whispering to Púnin: "I have found out nothing, and my advice to you is—abandon all hope." Púnin glanced at me with his swollen, red little eyes—the only bit of red that was left in his face—mumbled something unintelligible, and limped away. Babúrin probably divined what Púnin and I were talking about, and opening his tightly-compressed lips, which seemed to be fairly glued together, he articulated in a deliberate voice:

" My dear sir! something unpleasant has happened to us since the date of your last call; our ward, Múza Pávlovna Vinográdoff, finding it no longer convenient to reside with us, has decided to leave us, and has left us her written announcement of the same. As we do not consider ourselves justified in hindering her, we have allowed her to act as she sees fit. We wish her well,"—he added, not without an effort,—" and respectfully request you not to mention that subject, as such remarks are futile and even vexatious."

" So this man, as well as Tárkhoff, prohibits my speaking of Múza," I thought to myself, and I could not but marvel inwardly. Not without cause did he hold Zeno in such high esteem. I would have liked to impart to him some information concerning that sage, but my tongue refused its office, and well for me it was that it did so.

I soon went my way. In taking leave of me, neither Púnin nor Babúrin said to me, " until we meet again! " Both, in one voice said: " Farewell, sir! " Púnin even returned to me a number of the *Telegraph,* which I had brought to him: as much as to say—" I have no further use for this."

A week later I had a strange encounter. Spring had come in early and suddenly; at midday the temperature reached eighteen degrees.[1] Everything was beginning to turn green and spring forth from the mellow, grey earth. I had hired a saddle-horse in the riding-school and was riding out of town, to the Sparrow Hills. On the way I met a light cart drawn by a pair of spirited Vyátka horses, bespattered to the very ears, with plaited tails, and red ribbons in their forelocks and manes. The harness on the horses was sporty, with brass discs and tassels, and they were driven by a dandified young postilion in a blue, sleeveless long coat, a yellow shirt of Persian silk stuff, and a low hat with peacock feathers around the crown.[2]

By his side sat a young girl of the petty burgher or merchant class, in a short jacket of gay-coloured brocade, and with a large blue kerchief on her head, who was fairly shrieking with laughter. The postilion was grinning also. I turned my horse to one side, but was paying no particular attention to the merry pair as they flitted swiftly past, when suddenly the young man shouted at his horses. . . . Why, that was Tárkhoff's voice! I glanced round. . . In fact, it was he; it was indubitably he, arrayed as a postilion, and was not that Múza by his side?

---

[1] Réaumur, equal to 72.5° Fahrenheit.—Translator.

[2] In summer stylish postilions—the drivers of the tróika—usually wear a row of peacock eyes in this manner.—Translator.

But at that moment the Vyátka horses [1] started up, and that was the last I saw of them. I tried to launch my steed at a gallop after them, but it was an old riding-school satellite, with the so-called " generals' gait," with a swing; at a gallop he advanced still more slowly than at a trot.

" Divert yourselves, my dear people! " I growled through my teeth.—I must remark that I had not seen Tárkhoff during the whole course of that week, although I had called on him three times. He was never at home. Neither had I seen Púnin and Babúrin. . . . I had not called on them.

I caught a cold on my ride; although it was very hot, yet a piercing wind was blowing. I became frightfully ill,—and when I was convalescent, grandmamma and I went off to the country—" to graze "—in accordance with the doctor's advice. I did not happen to be in Moscow again; toward autumn I changed to the Petersburg University.

III

(1849)

MORE years passed—not seven, but full twelve, —and I was over two-and-thirty years of age.

[1] The descendants of Lifland (Livonian) cobs sent to the western government of Vyátka by Peter the Great. They are small, round, spirited, and generally of a yellow or bright bay colour.—TRANSLATOR.

My grandmother had long since been dead; I was living in Petersburg, an official in the Ministry of the Interior. I had lost sight of Tárkhoff; he had entered the military service, and was almost constantly in the country districts. He and I had met a couple of times in a friendly, cordial manner; but our conversations did not touch upon the past. At the epoch of our meetings he was already married, so far as my memory serves me. One sultry summer day, cursing both the official duties which detained me in Petersburg, and the oppressive heat, the stench and dust of the city, I was wending my way along Pea Street. A funeral procession barred my way. It consisted in all of one chariot, that is, properly speaking, of a rickety hearse, whereon, rudely tossed about by the jolts of the pavement full of holes, rocked a wretched wooden coffin, half covered with threadbare black cloth. An old, white-headed man was walking alone after the hearse.

I glanced at him. . . . The face was familiar. . . . . He also turned his eyes on me. . . . Great heavens! why, it was Babúrin!

I removed my hat, stepped up to him, mentioned my name—and walked along beside him.

" Whom are you burying? " I asked.

" Nikándr Vavílievitch Púnin," he replied.

I had had a presentiment, I had known beforehand that he would mention that name, and nevertheless my heart quivered within me. It was painful for me, and yet I was glad that accident had afforded me the possibility of paying the last debt to my preceptor. . . .

" May I go with you, Paramón Semyónitch? "

" You may. . . . I am escorting him alone; now there will be two of us."

Our march lasted for more than an hour.[1] My companion moved along without raising his eyes or unsealing his lips. He had become definitively an old man since I had seen him for the last time; furrowed with wrinkles, the bronze hue of his face stood out in sharp contrast to his white hair. The traces of a harsh, toilsome life, of incessant struggles, were revealed in Babúrin's whole being; poverty and want had gnawed him to the bone.

When everything was over, when that which had been Púnin had been hidden forever in the damp . . . . precisely that, the damp earth of the Smolénsk cemetery, Babúrin, after standing for a couple of minutes with bowed, uncovered head before the newly-made mound of sandy clay, turned toward me his exhausted face, which had, as it were, become obdurate, and his dry, sunken eyes, gruffly thanked me and was about to go away; but I detained him.

" Where do you live, Paramón Semyónitch? Permit me to call upon you. I was not in the

---

[1] It is customary for the male relations and friends to walk to the cemetery (or at least a part of the way) behind the coffin. The Emperor Alexander III did this for his old nurse, for example.—TRANSLATOR.

least aware that you were living in Petersburg. We might recall old times, we might talk about our dead friend."

Babúrin did not immediately answer me.

" This is the third year I have been in Petersburg," he said at last;—" my quarters are on the very outskirts of the town. However, if you really wish to visit me, pray come."—He gave me his address.—" Come in the evening; we are always at home in the evening . . . . both of us."

" Both . . . of you? "

" I am married. My wife is not quite well today; that is why she did not escort the corpse. However, one man is enough to fulfil that empty formality, that rite. But who puts any faith in all that? "

I was somewhat surprised by Babúrin's last words, but said nothing, took a drozhky, and offered to drive Babúrin to his home, but he declined.

That same evening I set out to visit him. On the way I thought constantly of Púnin. I recalled how I had met him for the first time, and how enthusiastic and diverting he had been then; then in Moscow, when he had tamed down—especially during our last meeting; and now his account with life was finished altogether. Evidently, life does not jest! Babúrin's quarters were in the Výborg side,[1] in a tiny house which

---

[1] Or ward; the poorest quarter of the town, across the Nevá to the northeast of the main city.—TRANSLATOR.

reminded me of the little Moscow nest; the Petersburg one was even more poverty-stricken, if anything. When I entered his room he was sitting in one corner on a chair, with both hands drooping on his knees; a tallow candle, which needed snuffing, dimly illuminated his white, drooping head. He heard the sound of my foot-steps, turned round and greeted me more cor-dially than I anticipated. A few moments later his wife made her appearance; in her I instantly recognised Múza—and only then did I under-stand why Babúrin had invited me to his house; he had wished to show me that he had attained his object in spite of all.

Múza had changed a great deal—in face, in voice, and in movements; but her eyes had un-dergone the greatest change of all. Formerly, they had been wont to dart about like minnows, those malicious, beautiful eyes; their glance had stung, like a pin. . . . Now they had a straight-forward, calm, intense gaze; the black irises had grown dull. "I am broken, I am docile, I am good-natured," her dull, quiet glance seemed to say. Her perennial, subdued smiles said the same thing. And her clothing was subdued; light-brown with tiny pea-dots. She was the first to approach me, and to inquire whether I recognised her. She evidently was not abashed, and that, not because she had lost her sense of shame or her memory, but simply because vanity had de-serted her. Múza had a great deal to say about the deceased Púnin, and she spoke in an even voice which, also, had grown cold. I learned that of late years he had become a complete invalid, had fallen almost into a state of second childhood, so that he even got bored unless he had his toys; it is true that they assured him that he was sewing them together out of rags for sale . . . . he himself was amused with them. But his passion for poetry did not become extinguished. A few days before his death he was still declaiming from the " Rossiad." On the other hand, he was afraid of Púshkin, as children are afraid of the bugaboo. His attachment to Babúrin had suffered no diminution either; he worshipped him as of yore, and when already in the grip of the gloom and chill of death, he still had lisped with his faltering tongue: " Benefactor! "

I learned also from Múza that soon after the Moscow affair Babúrin had again been obliged to make the rounds of Russia, roaming like a nomad from one private post to another; that in Petersburg he had again been, for a time, in private service, which, however, he had been compelled to leave a few days previously, on account of an unpleasantness with his employer. Babúrin had taken it into his head to stand up for the workmen . . . . Múza's perpetual smile, which accompanied her remarks, evoked melancholy meditations within me; it completed the impression which had been produced upon me by her husband's appearance. It was difficult for them to earn their daily bread—there could be no doubt as to that. He himself took but little part in our conversation; he seemed even more care-worn than embittered. . . . Something was distressing him.

"Paramón Semyónitch, please to come here," said the cook, suddenly presenting herself on the threshold.

"What is it? What's wanted?" he asked in alarm.

"Please to come here," repeated the cook, significantly and insistently. Babúrin buttoned up his coat and left the room.

WHEN Múza and I were left alone, she looked at me with a slightly altered gaze, and said, in a voice, which also had undergone a change, and no longer with a smile:

"I do not know, Piótr Petróvitch, what you think of me now, but I suppose you remember what I used to be like . . . . I was self-confident, merry . . . and ill-tempered. I wanted to live at my ease. And this is what I have to say to you now. When I was abandoned and was as though bereft of my wits, and was only waiting either for God to take me, or until I should summon up the courage to make an end of myself, I again met Paramón Semyónitch, as I had before in Vorónezh—and again he saved me . . . .

I have never heard an unkind word from him, I have not heard a single word of reproach, he has required nothing from me—I was not worth it; but he loved me . . . and I became his wife. What was there for me to do? I had not succeeded in dying;—neither had I succeeded in living as I wished. . . . Where was I to go? And even that was a mercy. That is all there is to it."

She ceased speaking, and turned aside for a moment . . . . the former submissive smile again made its appearance on her lips. " Don't ask me whether I find life easy," I thought I now read in that smile.

The conversation passed to commonplace topics. Múza told me that Púnin had left behind him a cat which he had greatly loved, but that from the moment of his death she had gone to the garret and had sat there meowing constantly, as though she were calling some one. . . . The neighbours had got very much alarmed, and imagined that Púnin's spirit had passed into the cat.

" Paramón Semyónitch is distressed about something," I remarked at last.

" And have you noticed that? "—Múza heaved a sigh.—" It is impossible for him not to be distressed. It is needless for me to tell you that Paramón Semyónitch has remained faithful to his convictions. . . . The present order of things could only strengthen them." (Múza expressed herself in an entirely different manner from what she had done in Moscow; her language had acquired a literary, well-read tinge.) "But I do not know whether I can trust you, and how you will take . . . ."

" Why do you assume that you cannot trust me? "

" Why, you are in the government service, you are an official."

" Well, and what of that? "

" Consequently, you are devoted to the government."

I marvelled inwardly . . . at Múza's youthfulness.—" I will not dilate on my relations to the government, which does not even suspect my existence," said I; " but you may feel at ease. I shall make no bad use of your confidence. I sympathise with your husband's convictions . . . . more than you suppose."

Múza shook her head.

" Yes; that is all true," she began, not without hesitation; " but this is the difficulty: Paramón Semyónitch may soon be forced to put his convictions into action. They cannot remain hidden. There are comrades who cannot now be deserted. . . ."

Múza suddenly became silent, as though she had bitten her tongue. Her last words surprised and rather alarmed me. Probably my face betrayed what I was feeling—and Múza had noticed this.

I have already said that our meeting took place in the year 1849. Many persons still remember what a troublesome and painful time that was, and by what events it was marked in Petersburg. I had been struck by several strange things in Babúrin's behaviour, in his whole manner. A couple of times he had alluded with such keen bitterness and hatred, with such detestation, to the governmental measures, to persons of high station, that I had felt perplexed. . . .

" Well," he had suddenly asked me: " and have you liberated your peasants? "

I had been compelled to admit that I had not.

" But your grandmother is dead, I believe? "

I was compelled to admit that also.

" That's just like you Messrs. Nobles," Babúrin growled through his teeth. . . . " To pluck the chestnuts out of the fire . . . with other people's hands . . . you are fond of that."

In his room, in the most conspicuous place, hung a well-known lithograph which depicted Byelínsky.[1] On the table lay a little volume of the ancient *Polar Star* of Bestúzheff.[2]

Babúrin did not return for a long time after the cook had called him out. Múza cast several

---

[1] Vissarión Grigórievitch Byelínsky (1811–1848), the most famous of Russian critics.—TRANSLATOR.

[2] The *Polar Star* existed from 1823 to 1825. Bestúzheff was the editor.—TRANSLATOR.

uneasy glances at the door through which he had departed. At last she could endure it no longer; she rose, excused herself, and also left the room by the same door. A quarter of an hour later she returned with her husband; their faces expressed anxiety—or at least, so it seemed to me.— But suddenly Babúrin's visage assumed another —a harsh, almost fanatical—expression. . . .

" What will be the end of this? "—he suddenly began in an extremely abrupt, sobbing voice, which was utterly different from his ordinary one, as he rolled his roving, wild eyes around.—" You live on and on, and you hope that things will get better, perchance, that you will be able to breathe more easily,—but, on the contrary, things get worse and constantly worse!—They have crowded us altogether to the wall! In my youth I endured every sort of thing; they even . . . . beat me . . . perhaps . . . . yes!" he added, wheeling violently round on his heels, and, as it were, attacking me:—" before I had attained my majority, I received torture . . . . yes;—I will not mention other injustices. . . . But is it possible that we are destined to return to those former times? —What are they doing now with the young people?—Why, assuredly, in the end that will break down all patience. . . Break it! Yes, just wait a bit!"

I had never seen Babúrin in such a condition. —Múza even turned pale all over. . . . Babúrin suddenly began to clear his throat and dropped down on a bench. Not wishing to embarrass him or Múza by my presence, I decided to go away, and had already bade them good-bye, when, suddenly, that same door into the next room opened, and a head made its appearance. . . . . But not the head of the cook,—the dishevelled, thoroughly frightened head of a young man.

"A calamity, Babúrin, a calamity has happened!" he whispered hastily, but immediately withdrew at the sight of my figure.

Babúrin rushed from the room in pursuit of the young man. I pressed Múza's hand warmly, and retired, with evil forebodings in my heart.

"Come to-morrow," she whispered tremulously.

"I will come without fail," I replied.

On the following day I was still lying in bed when my man handed me a letter from Múza.

"Dear Sir, Piótr Petróvitch!" [she wrote]: "The gendarmes arrested Paramón Semyónitch last night and carried him off to the fortress, or I know not whither; they did not say. They rummaged all our papers, sealed up a great deal, and took it with them. Also books and letters. They say that an enormous number of people have been arrested in town. You can picture to yourself what I am feeling. It is well that Nikándr Vavílitch did not live to see this day! He took himself off in the nick of time. Advise me what I ought to do. I am not afraid for myself—I shall not die of hunger—but the thought of Paramón Semyónitch gives me no peace. Please come to me, if you are not afraid of visiting people in our position.

" Yours very truly,

" Múza Babúrin."

In half an hour I was with Múza. When she saw me, she offered me her hand, and, although she did not say a word, an expression of gratitude flitted across her countenance. She wore the same gown as on the day before; from all the signs, it was evident that she had not gone to bed or slept all night. Her eyes were red, but from lack of sleep, not from tears. She had not wept. She was in no mood for that. She wished to act, she wished to fight against the catastrophe which had overtaken her. The former energetic, self-willed Múza had been resurrected in her. She had no time even for indignation, although she was choking with indignation. How she might aid Babúrin, to whom she ought to have recourse, in order to alleviate his lot—that was what she was thinking of and nothing else. She wished to go instantly . . . . to entreat . . . . to demand. . . . But whither was she to go? What was she to demand? That was what she was desirous of learning from me, that was what she wished to consult with me about.

I began by advising her to be patient. For a time, there was nothing else left for her to do except to wait, and, so far as possible, institute inquiries. To undertake anything decisive now, when the affair was only just beginning, was barely under way, was simply not to be thought of, imprudent. It was foolish to reckon upon success, even if I had possessed a far greater amount of importance and influence. . . But what could I, a petty official, do? She herself had no protection. . . .[1]

It was not easy to explain all this to her. . . . But at last she understood my arguments; she understood, also, that it was not egotistical feeling which was guiding me when I demonstrated to her the futility of all efforts.

" But, tell me, Múza Pávlovna," I began, when at last she seated herself on a chair (up to that moment she had been standing, as though ready to go instantly to the aid of Babúrin), " how did Paramón Semyónitch, at his age, get mixed up in such a scrape? I am convinced that only young men, like the one who came last night to warn you, are implicated in it. . . ."

" Those young men are our friends!"—exclaimed Múza, and her eyes began to flash and dart about as of old. Something powerful, irrepressible seemed to be rising up from the bottom of her soul . . . . and I suddenly recalled the appellation " a new type," which Tárkhoff had applied to her once on a time.—" Age counts for nothing when it is a question of political con-

---

[1] American: " pull."—TRANSLATOR.

victions!" Múza laid special emphasis on these last two words. One might have thought that, with all her grief, she found it not unpleasant to show herself off before me in this new, unexpected light—the light of a cultured woman,—of the mature, worthy spouse of a republican!— "Some old men are younger than some young men,"—she went on,—"more capable of sacrifice. . . . But that is not the question."

"It strikes me, Múza Pávlovna," I remarked, —"that you are exaggerating somewhat. Knowing the character of Paramón Semyónitch as I do I was confident in advance that he would sympathise with every . . . . honourable impulse; but, on the other hand, I have always regarded him as a sensible man. . . . Can it be that he does not understand the utter impossibility, the complete absurdity of conspiracies among us here in Russia? In his position, in his profession . . . ."

"Of course," interposed Múza, with bitterness in her voice, "he is of the burgher class; and in Russia it is permissible only to nobles to enter into conspiracies, like that of the fourteenth of December, for example.[1] . . . I suppose that is what you were about to say."

"In that case, why do you complain?" came

[1] In 1825, at the accession to the throne of Nicholas I. The conspirators—the "Decembrists"—were transported "for life" to Siberia. Later on they were pardoned and permitted to return to Russia; but some of them were homesick for Siberia and preferred to remain there, as the granddaughter of one of the conspirators told me.—TRANSLATOR.

near breaking from my tongue . . . but I restrained myself.—"Do you assume that the results of the fourteenth of December are of a character to encourage others?" I said aloud.

Múza frowned.—"There's no use in discussing this with thee," I read on her downcast face.

"Is Paramón Semyónitch greatly compromised?" I brought myself to say, at last. Múza made no reply. . . . A hungry, wild meowing resounded from the garret.

Múza shuddered.—"Akh, it is well that Nikándr Vavílitch did not behold all this!" she moaned, almost in despair.—"He did not behold his benefactor, our benefactor, probably the best and most honourable man in all the world, forcibly seized by night,—he did not see how they treated the venerable old man, how they addressed him as 'thou' . . . . how they threatened him—and with what they threatened him!
. . . . merely because he is of the burgher class! That officer, a young man, also, must belong to the category of those conscienceless, soulless people, such as I in my lifetime . . . ."

Múza's voice broke. She was trembling all over, like a leaf.

Her long-repressed indignation had burst forth at last; old memories set in vibration, brought to the surface by her general spiritual agitation, began to surge up. . . But I convinced myself thoroughly, at that moment, that the

" new type " had remained the same passionate, impulsive nature as of old. . . . . Only Múza was not carried away by the same things as in her younger years. That which, on my first visit, I had taken for resignation, for submission, and what really had been such—that quiet, dull gaze, that cold voice, that evenness and simplicity— all that had meaning only in relation to the past, the irrevocable. . . .

But now the present was beginning to speak.

I tried to soothe Múza, I tried to transfer our conversation to some more practical territory. Several measures, which could not be deferred, must be taken; we must find out where Babúrin really was; and then he and Múza must be provided with the means of subsistence. All this presented no small difficulties; it was necessary to hunt up, not money, directly, but work which, as every one knows, is a far more complicated problem. . . .

I left Múza with a whole swarm of calculations in my head.

I soon learned that Babúrin was confined in the fortress.[1] . . . .

The trial process began . . . . and dragged its slow length along. I saw Múza several times every week. She also had several interviews with

[1] The famous fortress of St. Peter and St. Paul, directly across the Nevá from the Winter Palace, which contains within its enclosure the mint, and the cathedral in which all the Emperors, beginning with Peter the Great, are buried.—TRANSLATOR.

her husband. But at the very moment when this whole sad affair came to a crisis, I was not in Petersburg. Unforeseen business had compelled me to go to the south of Russia. During my absence I learned that Babúrin had been acquitted by the court; it turned out that his entire fault had consisted solely in the fact that the young men had occasionally assembled at his house, because he was a man not fitted to arouse suspicion—and he had been present at these conferences; but he was exiled by administrative process, for colonisation, to one of the western governments of Siberia. Múza went with him.

" . . . Paramón Semyónitch did not desire it," she wrote to me; " because, according to his ideas, no one has a right to sacrifice himself for another man—nor for a cause; but I answered him that there was no sacrifice about it. When I told him in Moscow that I would be his wife, I thought to myself: ' forever and unalterably!' And thus unalterably it must stand until the end of my days. . . ."

IV

(1861)

TWELVE years more elapsed. . . . Every one in Russia knows and will forever remember what took place between 1849 and 1861. In my personal life, also, many changes took place, upon

which, however, it is not worth while to dilate.
New interests, new cares presented themselves in
it. . . . The Babúrin pair first retreated to the
background, then vanished completely. Nevertheless, I continued to correspond with Múza—
very rarely, it is true; sometimes more than a
year elapsed without any news whatever of her
and her husband. I learned that soon after 1855
he had been permitted to return to Russia; but
that he himself had preferred to remain in the
small Siberian town, where Fate had cast him, and
where he, apparently, had woven himself a nest,
had found an asylum, a circle of activity. . . .

And lo! toward the end of March, 1861, I received the following letter from Múza:

" I have not written to you for so long, most respected
P. P., that I do not know whether you are alive or not;
but if you are alive, then may you not have forgotten
our existence? But never mind; I cannot refrain from
writing to you to-day. Hitherto everything has been
going on as of old with us; Paramón Semyónitch and I
have been busy with our schools, which are gradually
making progress; over and above that Paramón Semyónitch has been busying himself with reading and correspondence, and with his customary disputations with the
Old Ritualists, ecclesiastical persons and exiled Poles;
his health has been tolerably good . . . . So has mine.
But now the manifesto of February 19 reached us yesterday![1] We had been expecting it for a long time,

---

[1] Emancipating the serfs.—TRANSLATOR.

for a long time rumours had been in circulation about
what was going on in Petersburg . . . . but still I cannot describe to you what this was like! You know my
husband well; bad fortune has not changed him in the
least; on the contrary, he has become stronger and more
energetic than ever. (I cannot conceal the fact that
Múza wrote *yenergetic*.)[1] He has an iron strength of
will, but this time he could not control himself! His
hands trembled when he read it; then he embraced me
thrice, and exchanged the triple kiss with me, tried to say
something,—but no! He could not! And he wound up
by melting into tears, which was a very remarkable thing
to see, and suddenly shouted out: 'Hurrah! Hurrah!
O God, preserve the Tzar!'[2]—Yes, Piótr Petróvitch,
those were his very words! Then he added: 'Lord, now
lettest thou thy servant depart in peace.'[3] . . . And
again: 'This is the first step; it must be followed by
others'; and just as he was, without a cap, he ran to communicate this great piece of news to our friends. The
weather was extremely cold, and a violent snow-storm was
beginning; I tried to hold him back, but he would not
heed me. And when he came home he was all powdered
with snow, his hair, his face, and his beard—he has a beard
that descends on his chest now—and even the tears on his
cheeks were congealed! But he was very lively and merry
and ordered me to open a bottle of Don champagne, and
in company with our friends, whom he had brought back
with him, he drank to the health of the Tzar and of Russia, and of all Russian freemen; and raising his glass and

---

[1] She used the wrong sort of *e*.—TRANSLATOR.

[2] The national hymn begins with these five words.—TRANSLATOR.

[3] Only two words are necessary to indicate this canticle in Russian.
—TRANSLATOR.

lowering his eyes to the ground, he said: 'Nikándr Va-vílitch, dost thou hear? There are no more slaves in Russia! Rejoice even in thy grave, old comrade!' And he said a great deal more of the same sort, such as, 'My expectations have been realised!' He said also, that now it was no longer possible to turn back; that this was, in its way, a pledge or promise. . . . I cannot recall all, but it is a long time since I have seen him so happy. And so I decided to write to you, in order that you might know how we rejoiced and exulted in the distant Siberian wilds, and that you might rejoice with us. . . . "

I received this letter about the end of March; and in the beginning of May another arrived, still from Múza.—She informed me that her husband, Paramón Semyónitch Babúrin, had died on the twelfth of April from inflammation of the lungs, at the age of sixty-seven. She added that she intended to remain there, where his body reposed, and continue the work which had been bequeathed to her by him, since that had been Paramón Semyónitch's last will—and she knew no other law.

I have not heard anything about Múza since.

ON THE EVE:

A ROMANCE

(1859)

ON THE EVE:
A ROMANCE

I

IN the shade of a lofty linden-tree, on the bank of the Moscow River, not far from Kúntzovo, two young men were lying on the grass, on one of the very hottest summer days of the year 1853. One, three-and-twenty years of age, judging from his appearance, of lofty stature, swarthy of visage, with a pointed and somewhat crooked nose, a high forehead, and a repressed smile on his broad lips, was lying on his back, and thoughtfully gazing into the distance, with his small, grey eyes screwed up; the other was lying on his chest, with his curly, fair-haired head propped on both hands, and was also gazing at something in the distance. He was three years older than his comrade, but seemed much younger: his moustache was barely sprouting, and a light down curled on his chin. There was something childishly pretty, something alluringly elegant, in the small features of his fresh, round face, in his sweet, brown eyes, his handsome, full lips, and small, white hands. Everything about him exhaled the happy gaiety of health, breathed forth youth—the unconcern, self-confidence, self-indulgence, and charm of youth. He rolled his eyes about, and smiled, and put his head on one side as small boys do when they know that people like to look at them. He wore an ample white coat, in the nature of a blouse; a blue kerchief encircled his slender neck, a crumpled straw hat lay upon the grass beside him.

In comparison with him, his companion appeared to be an old man, and no one would have thought, to look at his angular form, that he was enjoying himself, that he was at his ease. He was lying in an awkward posture; his large head, broad above and pointed below, was uncouthly set upon his long neck; uncouthness was expressed by every movement of his arms, of his body, clothed in a tight-fitting, short black coat, of his long legs, with elevated knees, resembling the hind legs of a grasshopper. Nevertheless, it was impossible not to recognise the fact that he was a well-bred man; the stamp of " goodbreeding " was perceptible all over his ungainly person, and his countenance, which was homely and even somewhat ridiculous, expressed a habit of thought and kindliness. His name was Andréi Petróvitch Berséneff; his comrade, the fair-haired young man, was named Shúbin, Pável Yakóvlitch.

" Why dost thou not lie on thy breast, as I am

doing?" began Shúbin. "It's much better so. Especially when you stick your feet in the air, and click your heels together—this way. The grass is just under your nose: it's tiresome to gaze at the landscape—watch some fat little beetle crawl up a blade of grass, or an ant bustling about. Really it's much nicer. But thou hast assumed a sort of pseudo-classical pose, precisely like a ballet-dancer when she leans her elbows on a cardboard cliff. Remember, that thou hast now a perfect right to rest. It's no joke to have graduated third in the class! Take your rest, sir; cease to strain yourself; stretch out your limbs!"

Shúbin enunciated the whole of this speech through his nose, half-languidly, half-jestingly (spoiled children talk in that manner to the friends of the family, who bring them sugarplums), and, without waiting for an answer, he went on:

"What surprises me most of all, in the ants, beetles, and other worthy insects, is their wonderful seriousness; they run to and fro with countenances as grave as though their lives were of some importance! Why, good gracious, man, the lord of creation, the most exalted of beings, may be looking at them, but they care nothing for him; perhaps, even, a gnat may alight upon the nose of the lord of creation, and begin to utilise him as food. This is insulting. But, on the other hand, in what respect is their life inferior to ours?

And why should n't they put on airs of importance if we permit ourselves to be pompous? Come now, philosopher, solve this riddle for me! Why dost thou maintain silence? Hey? "

" What . . . " ejaculated Berséneff, coming to himself with a start.

" What! " repeated Shúbin. " Thy friend expounds profound thoughts to thee, and thou dost not listen to him."

" I was admiring the view. Look, how hotly yonder fields are blazing in the sunlight! " (Berséneff lisped a little.)

" A good bit of color that,"—replied Shúbin. —" In a word, it is nature! "

Berséneff shook his head. " Thou shouldst be more enthusiastic over all this than I am. It 's in thy line: thou art an artist."

" No, sir; it 's not in my line,"—retorted Shúbin, and pushed his hat back upon the nape of his neck.—" I 'm a butcher, sir; my business is flesh, modelling flesh, shoulders, feet, hands, but here there are no contours, there is no finish, it melts off in all directions. . . Go, seize it if you can! "

" Why, precisely therein lies its beauty,"—remarked Berséneff. " By the way, hast thou finished thy bas-relief? "

" Which one? "

" The child with the goat."

" Damn it! damn it! damn it! "—exclaimed

6

Shúbin, in a drawl.—" I 've been looking at the real thing, at the old masters, at the antique, and I 've smashed my miserable stuff. Thou pointest out nature to me, and sayest: ' Therein lies beauty.' Of course, there is beauty in everything, there 's beauty even in thy nose, but one can't run after every bit of beauty. The ancients—why, even they did n't run after it; it descended of itself into their works, God knows whence, perhaps from heaven. The whole world belonged to them; we cannot expand ourselves so widely; our arms are too short. We fling out a bait at one tiny point, and then we watch for results. If there 's a bite, bravo! if there is no bite . . . . ."

Shúbin thrust out his tongue.

" Stop, stop,"—responded Berséneff. " That is a paradox. If thou art not in sympathy with beauty, if thou dost not love it wherever thou encounterest it, it will not give itself to thee in thine art. If a fine view, if fine music, have nothing to say to thy soul,—I mean, if thou art not in sympathy with them . . . ."

" Ekh, get out, thou sympathiser! "—retorted Shúbin hastily, and broke into a laugh at his own newly-coined word, but Berséneff became pensive.—" No, my dear fellow,"—resumed Shúbin, " thou philosopher-sage, third in thy class at the Moscow University, 't is a terrible thing to argue with thee, especially for me, a student who

7

did not finish his course; but just let me tell thee something: with the exception of my art, I love beauty only in women . . . . in young girls, and that only since quite recently. . . . "

He rolled over on his back, and clasped his hands under his head.

A few moments passed in silence. The still-ness of the sultry midday weighed heavily upon the radiant and slumbering earth.

" By the way, speaking of women,"—began Shúbin again.—" Why does n't somebody take Stákhoff in hand? Hast thou seen him in Moscow? "

" No."

" The old fellow has gone quite out of his mind. He sits for whole days together at the house of his Augustína Christiánovna,—he is hor-ribly bored, but there he sits. They gaze at each other, so stupidly. . . . It 's repulsive even to look at. Just think of it! With what a family God has blessed that man: but no, give him his Augustína Christiánovna! I don't know of any-thing more hideous than her duck-like physiog-nomy! The other day, I modelled a caricature of her, in Dantesque style. It turned out quite well. I 'll show it to thee."

" And the bust of Eléna Pávlovna,"—inquired Berséneff,—" is that progressing? "

" No, my dear fellow, it is not progressing. That face is enough to drive one to desperation.

You look, and the lines are pure, severe, regular; apparently, there is no difficulty about catching the likeness. Nothing of the sort. . . . It won't yield itself, any more than a treasure will drop into your hands. Hast thou noticed how she listens? Not a single feature moves, only the expression of her glance changes incessantly,—and that alters the whole face. What is a sculptor to do, and a bad sculptor into the bargain? She's a wonderful being . . . . a strange being,"—he added, after a brief pause.

" She is a wonderful girl,"—Berséneff repeated after him.

" And the daughter of Nikolái Artémievitch Stákhoff! After that, just talk about blood, about race! And the amusing thing is, that she really is his daughter, she resembles him, and resembles her mother, Anna Vasílievna. I respect Anna Vasílievna with all my heart,—she is my benefactress: but she's a hen, all the same. Where did Eléna get that soul of hers? Who kindled that fire? There's another riddle for thee, philosopher!"

But the " philosopher," as before, made no reply. In general, Berséneff did not sin through loquacity, and, when he spoke, expressed himself awkwardly, hesitated, gesticulated unnecessarily: but on this occasion a special sort of stillness had descended upon his spirit, a stillness akin to weariness and sadness. He had recently settled in the country, after a long and difficult task which had occupied him for several hours every day. Inactivity, the softness and purity of the air, the consciousness of having attained his object, the whimsical and careless conversation with his friend, the suddenly-evoked image of a beloved being, all these varied but, at the same time, in some way similar impressions were merged together within him into one general feeling, which soothed, agitated him, and enfeebled him. . . . . . He was a very nervous young man. It was cool and quiet beneath the linden-tree; the flies and bees which fluttered about in its shadow seemed to hum in a more subdued manner; the clean, fine grass, of emerald hue, with no golden gleams, did not wave; the tall blades stood motionless as though enchanted; the tiny clusters of yellow blossoms on the lower branches of the linden hung like dead things. Their sweet perfume penetrated into the very depths of the breast with every breath, but the breast inhaled it willingly. Far away, beyond the river, as far as the horizon, everything was glittering and blazing; from time to time a little breeze swept past, and broke and increased the scintillation; a radiant vapour quivered over the earth. No birds were to be heard: they do not sing in the hours of sultry heat; but the grasshoppers were shrilling everywhere, and it was pleasant to listen to that hot sound of life, as one sat in the shade, at ease: it inclined to slumber, and evoked dreaminess.

"Hast thou observed,"—began Berséneff suddenly, aiding his speech with gesticulations of his arms,—"what a strange feeling Nature arouses in us? Everything about her is so full, so clear, I mean to say, so satisfying in itself, and we understand this, and admire it, and, at the same time, she always—at least in my own case—causes a certain uneasiness, a certain agitation, even sadness. What is the meaning of this? Are we more powerfully conscious in her presence, face to face with her, of all our own incompleteness, our lack of clearness, or is that satisfaction wherewith she contents herself not enough for us, while the other—I mean the one which she does not possess—is necessary for us?"

"H'm,"—replied Shúbin,—"I'll tell thee, Andréi Petróvitch, whence all this arises. Thou hast described the sensations of the solitary man, who does not live, but merely looks on, and swoons in ecstasy. What's the good of looking on? Live thyself, and thou wilt be a fine, dashing fellow. Knock at the door of Nature as thou wilt, she will not respond with a single comprehensible word, because she is dumb. She will ring and grieve, like the chord of a lyre, but thou must not expect any song from her. A living soul—and a woman's soul in particular—will respond. Therefore, my noble friend, I counsel thee to provide thyself with a friend of the heart, and all thy melancholy sensations will immediately vanish. That's what we 'need,' as thou art wont to say. Seest thou, that agitation, that sadness, is simply a sort of hunger. Give the stomach the right sort of food, and everything will reduce itself to order at once. Take thy place in space, be a body, my dear fellow. And, after all, what is Nature, and what's the good of her? Just listen: Love . . . what a mighty, burning word! Nature . . . what a cold, scholastic expression! And then " (Shúbin began to chant): " ' Long life to Márya Petróvna!' or no," he added, " not to Márya Petróvna, but that makes no difference! *Vous me comprenez.*"

Berséneff half sat up, and propped his chin on his clasped hands.—" Why this raillery,"—he said, without looking at his companion,—" why this jeering? Yes, thou art right: Love is a great word, a great feeling. . . . But of what sort of love art thou speaking? "

Shúbin also half sat up.—" Of what love? Of whatever sort you please, if only it be present. I will confess to thee that, in my opinion, there is no such thing as different sorts of love. . . . If thou hast loved . . . . "

" I have, with all my heart,"—interjected Berséneff.

" Well, yes, that is a matter of course: the soul is not an apple: it cannot be divided. If thou hast been in love, thou art in the right. And I had no intention to jeer. I have such tenderness in my heart now, it is so softened . . . . I merely wished to explain why nature, according to thee, has that effect upon us. Because she rouses in us the necessity for love, and is not able to satisfy it. She impels us gently to other, living embraces, but we do not understand her, and we expect something from her herself. Akh, Andréi, Andréi, it is beautiful. This sun, this sky, everything, everything around us, is very beautiful, but thou art sad; but if, at this moment, thou heldest in thy hand the hand of a beloved woman, if that hand and the whole woman were thine, if thou wert even gazing with her eyes, feeling not with thine own solitary feeling, but with her feeling,—Nature would not inspire thee with sadness, Andréi, and thou wouldst not begin to notice her beauty: she herself would rejoice and sing, she would join in thy hymn, because thou wouldst then have endowed her, the dumb, with a tongue! "

Shúbin sprang to his feet, and strode back and forth a couple of times, but Berséneff bowed his head, and a slight flush suffused his face.

" I do not entirely agree with thee,"—he began:—" Nature is not always hinting at . . at . . . . . . love to us." (He could not utter the word " love " at once.) " She also menaces us: she reminds us of . . . terrible . . . yes, of unattainable mysteries. Is not she bound to engulf us, is not she incessantly devouring us? In her are both life and death; and in her death speaks as loudly as life."

" And in love there is both life and death,"— interposed Shúbin.

" And moreover,"—went on Berséneff,— " when I, for example, stand in springtime, in the forest, in a green copse, when I fancy I hear the sounds of Oberon's horn " (Berséneff was a little shamefaced when he had uttered these words)—" is that—"

" It is a thirst for love, a thirst for happiness, nothing else! "—exclaimed Shúbin. "I, too, know those sounds, I know that languor and anticipation which invade the soul beneath the shadows of the forest, in its bosom; or, in the evening, in the open fields, when the sun is setting and the vapour is rising from the river behind the bushes. But from the forest and from the river, and from the earth, and from the sky, from every little cloud, from every blade of grass, I expect, I demand happiness, in everything I feel its approach, I hear its summons. ' My god is a bright and merry god! ' That is the way I once began a poem; confess: it was a magnificent first line, but I could n't possibly match it with a second. Happiness! happiness! until life is over, so long as all our members are in our power, so long as we are going not down hill but up hill! Devil take it! "

—continued Shúbin, with sudden fervour—" we are young, we are not monsters, we are not stupid: let us conquer happiness for ourselves! "

He shook his curls, and glanced upward in a self-confident, almost challenging manner at the sky. Berséneff looked at him.

" Is there really nothing higher than happiness? "—he said softly.

" What, for example? "—inquired Shúbin, and paused.

" Why, here, for example, thou and I, as thou sayest, are young; we are good fellows, let us assume; each of us wishes happiness for himself. . . . . But is that word ' happiness ' the sort of word which would have united us, would have kindled us to flame, would have made us offer each other our hands? Is it not an egotistical, a distintegrating word, I mean to say? "

" And dost thou know any words which do unite? "

" Yes,—and there are not a few of them; and thou knowest them also."

" You don't say so? What words are they? "

" Why, take art, for instance,—since thou art an artist,—fatherland, science, liberty, justice."

" And love? "—asked Shúbin.

" Love, also, is a word which unites; but not that love for which thou art now thirsting: not love as enjoyment, but love as sacrifice."

Shúbin frowned.

" That 's all right for the Germans; I want to love for myself; I want to be number one."

" Number one,"—repeated Berséneff.—" But it strikes me that the whole significance of life consists in placing one's self as number two."

" If everybody were to act as thou counsellest,"—remarked Shúbin, with a lugubrious grimace,—" nobody on earth would eat pineapples: everybody would leave them for some one else."

" As a matter of fact, pineapples are not indispensable; however, have no apprehensions: there will always be people to be found who would like to take the bread out of other people's mouths."

The two friends remained silent for a while.

" I met Insároff again the other day,"—began Berséneff:—" I invited him to call on me; I am very anxious to introduce him to thee . . . . and to the Stákhoffs."

" What Insároff is that? Akh, yes, that Servian or Bulgarian, of whom thou hast spoken to me? Is n't it he who has put all those philosophical thoughts into thy head? "

" Perhaps so."

" Is he a remarkable individual? "

" Yes."

" Clever, gifted? "

" Clever? . . . Gifted? I don't know, I don't think so."

"No? What is there remarkable about him?"

"Thou wilt see. But now, I think it is time to be going, Anna Vasílievna is expecting us, I fancy. What time is it?"

"Two o'clock. Come along. How stifling it is! This conversation has set all my blood aflame. And there was a moment when thou, also . . . I 'm not an artist for nothing: I have taken note of everything. Confess, a woman occupies thy mind? . . ."

Shúbin tried to peer into Berséneff's face, but the latter turned away, and emerged from beneath the shade of the linden. Shúbin followed him, treading with graceful swagger on his tiny feet. Berséneff moved clumsily, raised his shoulders high as he walked, thrust forward his neck: but, notwithstanding this, he appeared a better-bred man than Shúbin, more of a gentleman, we should have said, had not that word become so trite among us.

II

THE young men descended to the Moscow River, and strolled along its banks. The water exhaled coolness, and the soft plash of the little waves caressed the ear.

"I should like to take another bath,"—remarked Shúbin,—"but I'm afraid of being late. Look at the river: it is fairly beckoning to us. The ancient Greeks would have recognised it as a nymph. But we are not Greeks, O nymph!— we are thick-skinned Scythians."

"We have water-nymphs also," remarked Berséneff.

"Get out with your water-nymphs! What use have I, a sculptor, for those offspring of a confused, cold fancy, those images born in the reek of a peasant's hut, in the gloom of winter nights? I must have light, space. . . When, my God, shall I go to Italy? When . . . ."

"That is, thou intendest to say, to Little Russia?"

"Shame upon thee, Andréi Petróvitch, to reproach me for a thoughtless bit of stupidity, of which, even without that, I have bitterly repented. Well, yes, I behaved like a fool: Anna Vasílievna, that kindest of women, did give me money for a trip to Italy, but I betook myself to the Topknots,[1] to eat dough-balls, and . . . ."

" Don't finish thy remark, please,"—interrupted Berséneff.

" Nevertheless, I will say that that money was not spent in vain. I beheld there such types, especially feminine types. . . Of course, I know: outside of Italy there is no salvation!"

" Thou wilt go to Italy,"—remarked Berséneff, without turning toward him—" and thou wilt accomplish nothing. Thou wilt merely flap thy wings, but thou wilt not soar. We know you!"

" But Stavásser soared. . . And he is not the only one. And if I don't soar—it will signify that I am an aquatic penguin, without wings. I 'm stifling here, I want to go to Italy,"—went on Shúbin,—" there is sun, there is beauty there. . ."

A young girl, in a broad-brimmed straw hat, with a rose-coloured parasol over her shoulder, made her appearance, at that moment, in the path along which the two friends were walking.

" But what do I behold? Beauty is coming to meet us even here! The greeting of a humble artist to the enchanting Zóya!"—suddenly exclaimed Shúbin, with a theatrical flourish of his hat.

[1] The scornful Great Russian name for the Little Russian.—TRANSLATOR.

The young girl to whom this exclamation was addressed shook her finger at him, and allowing the two friends to approach her, she said, in a ringing voice, with the merest suggestion of a lisp:

" Why don't you come to dinner, gentlemen? The table is set."

" What do I hear? " said Shúbin, clasping his hands.—" Is it possible that you, charming Zóya, have brought yourself to come in search of us, in this heat? Is that how I am to construe the meaning of your speech? Tell me, can it be? Or no, do not utter that word: repentance will kill me on the spot."

" Akh, do stop, Pável Yakóvlevitch,"—returned the young girl, not without vexation:— " why do you never speak seriously to me? I shall get angry,"—she added, with a coquettish shrug of the shoulders and a pout.

" You will not be angry with me, my ideal Zóya Nikítishna: you will not wish to plunge me into the abyss of wild despair. But I do not know how to talk seriously, because I am not a serious man."

The girl shrugged her shoulders, and turned to Berséneff.

" He is always like that: he treats me like a child; and I am already over eighteen years old. I 'm grown up."

" O heavens! "—moaned Shúbin, and rolled up his eyes; but Berséneff laughed noiselessly.

The girl stamped her little foot.

" Pável Yakóvlevitch! I shall get angry! Hé-lène started to come with me,"—she went on,— " but stopped behind in the garden. The heat frightened her, but I 'm not afraid of heat. Let us go."

She set out along the path, lightly swaying her slender figure at every step, and tossing back from her face, with her pretty little hand covered with a black mitt, the long, soft locks of her hair.

The friends followed her (Shúbin now silently pressed his hands to his heart, again he raised them above his head), and, a few moments later, they found themselves in front of one of the numerous suburban villas which surround Kúntzovo. A small wooden house, with a partial second storey, painted pink, stood amid a garden, and peeped forth from among the verdure of the trees in a naïve sort of way. Zóya was the first to open the wicket-gate, run into the garden, and cry out: " I have brought the wanderers! " A young girl, with a pale and expressive face, rose from a bench beside the path, and on the threshold of the house a lady in a lilac-silk gown made her appearance, and, raising an embroidered batiste handkerchief above her head to protect it from the sun, she smiled languidly and indolently.

III

ANNA VASÍLIEVNA STÁKHOFF, born Shúbin, had been left a full orphan at seven years of age, and heiress to a fairly large property. She had relatives who were very wealthy, and relatives who were very poor; the poor ones on her father's side, the wealthy ones on her mother's: Senator Bólgin, the Princess Tchikurásoff. Prince Ardalión Tchikurásoff, who was appointed as her guardian, placed her in the best boarding-school in Moscow, and when she left school took her into his own house. He lived in handsome style, and gave balls in the winter. Anna Vasílievna's future husband, Nikolái Artémievitch Stákhoff, won her at one of these balls, where she wore " a charming pink gown, with a head-dress of tiny roses." She preserved that head-dress. . . . Nikolái Artémievitch Stákhoff, the son of a retired captain who had been wounded in the year 1812, and had received a lucrative post in Petersburg, had entered the military school at the age of sixteen, and graduated into the Guards. He was handsome, well built, and was considered about the best cavalier at evening parties of the middle class, which he chiefly frequented: he did not have access to fashionable society. Two dreams had occupied him from his youth up: to become an Imperial aide-de-camp and to make an advantageous marriage; he speedily renounced the first dream, but clung all the more tenaciously to the second. As a result of this, he went to Moscow every winter. Nikolái Artémievitch spoke French very respectably, and had the reputation of being a philosopher, because he did not indulge in carouses. While he was still only an ensign, he had been fond of arguing obstinately on the question, for example, as to whether it is possible for a man, in the course of his whole life, to traverse the entire globe, and whether it is possible for him to know what goes on at the bottom of the sea—and he always maintained the opinion that it is not possible.

Nikolái Artémievitch had passed his twenty-fifth birthday when he " hooked " Anna Vasílievna; he resigned his commission, and retired to the country to engage in farming. Rural existence soon palled on him, and the estate was on a quit-rent basis;[1] he settled in Moscow, in his wife's house. In his youth, he had never played at card-games, but now he became passionately fond of loto, and when that was prohibited, of whist. He was bored to death at home; he entered into relations with a widow of German extraction,

[1] That is, the serfs paid an annual sum for the privilege of being released from agricultural labours for the master, and of earning their living in the towns, at any trade wherein they were skilled.—TRANSLATOR.

and spent almost all his time at her house. In the summer of '53 he did not remove to Kúntzovo; he remained in Moscow, ostensibly with the object of taking a course of mineral waters; in reality, he did not wish to part from his widow. He did not talk much with her, however, but mostly argued as to whether the weather could be predicted, and so forth. Once, some one called him " a *frondeur*"; this appellation pleased him greatly. " Yes," he thought, drawing down the corners of his lips in a self-satisfied way, and swaying to and fro, " I am not easily satisfied; you can't cheat me." Nikolái Artémievitch's critical faculty consisted in this—that, for instance, when he heard the word "nerves," he would say: " And what are nerves? " or some one would allude in his presence to the triumphs of astronomy, and he would say: " And do you believe in astronomy? " But when he wished overwhelmingly to dumfound his antagonist, he said: " All that is mere phrases." It must be confessed that such retorts appeared (and still appear) to many persons irrefutable; but Nikolái Artémievitch had not even a suspicion that Augustína Christiánovna, in her letters to her cousin, called him *" Mein Pinselchen."* [1]

Nikolái Artémievitch's wife, Anna Vasílievna, was a small, thin woman, with delicate features, inclined to emotion and melancholy. At board-

[1] My simpleton.

ing-school she had busied herself with music, and had read romances, then she had cast aside all this; she had begun to take pleasure in dress, and this taste had persisted; she had undertaken the education of her daughter, but had weakened, and given her over to the hands of a governess; and it ended in her doing nothing whatever, except grieving and indulging in gentle agitation. The birth of Eléna Nikoláevna had shattered her health, and she was not able to have any more children; Nikolái Artémievitch was in the habit of alluding to this circumstance, by way of justifying his acquaintance with Augustína Christiánovna. Her husband's infidelity greatly embittered Anna Vasílievna; what particularly wounded her was that, one day, by a trick, he presented his German with a pair of grey horses from her (Anna Vasílievna's) stud. She never reproached him to his face, but she complained of him, on the sly, to every one in the house in turn, even to her daughter. Anna Vasílievna was not fond of society; it pleased her to have a visitor sit with her, and narrate something; when left alone, she immediately fell ill. She had a very loving and tender heart: life speedily ground her between the millstones.

Pável Yakólevitch Shúbin was her grand-nephew. His father was in the government service in Moscow. His brothers had entered the cadet corps; he was the youngest, his mother's darling, of delicate constitution: he remained at home. He had been destined for the university, and had passed his examinations with difficulty. From his earliest years, he had begun to display an inclination for sculpture: ponderous Senator Bólgin one day saw a statuette of himself at his aunt's (the lad was sixteen years old at that time), and declared that he intended to protect the youthful talent. The sudden death of Shúbin's father came near changing the young man's whole future. The senator, the patron of talent, presented him with a plaster bust of Homer— and that was all; but Anna Vasílievna aided him with money, and in a lame sort of fashion, at the age of nineteen, he entered the medical course of the university. Pável felt no predilection for medicine, but, according to the distribution of the students which existed at that period, it was impossible for him to enter any other course; moreover, he hoped to study anatomy. But he did not study anatomy; he did not pass into the second year, and without waiting for the examinations, he left the university, to devote himself wholly to his vocation. He toiled zealously, but by fits and starts; he roamed about the environs of Moscow; he modelled and drew the portraits of peasant maidens; he entered into relations with various persons, young and old, of high and low degree, —with Italian model-makers and Russian artists; he would not listen to the suggestion of the

Academy, and recognised no professor. He possessed decided talent: he began to be known in Moscow. His mother, a Parisian by birth, taught him French, bustled and worried about him day and night, was proud of him, and when she died of consumption, at an early age, she entreated Anna Vasílievna to take charge of him. He was then in his twenty-first year. Anna Vasílievna complied with her last wish: he occupied a small chamber in a wing of the house.

IV

" Come, let us go to dinner,"—said the mistress of the house, in a mournful voice, and all betook themselves to the dining-room.—" Sit next to me, Zoé,"—said Anna Vasílievna; " and do thou, Hélène, entertain our guest; and please, Paul, do not play pranks and do not tease Zoé. I have a headache to-day."

Again Shúbin rolled his eyes heavenward; Zoé replied to him by a half-smile. This Zoé, or, to speak more accurately, Zóya Nikítishna Müller, was a pretty, little, slightly cross-eyed Russian German, with a little nose cleft at the tip, and tiny red lips, fair-haired and plump. She sang Russian romances far from badly, played neatly on the piano divers pieces, sometimes merry, sometimes sentimental; she dressed with taste, but in a childish way, somehow, and too spotlessly. Anna Vasílievna had taken her as a companion for her daughter, but kept her almost uninterruptedly by her own side. Eléna made no complaint on this score: she positively did not know what to say to Zóya when she chanced to be left alone with her.

The dinner lasted rather a long time; Berséneff chatted with Eléna about university life, about his intentions and hopes. Shúbin listened, and maintained silence, eating with exaggerated avidity, and from time to time casting comical mournful glances at Zóya, who responded to him with the same phlegmatic smile as before. After dinner, Eléna went into the garden with Berséneff and Shúbin; Zóya gazed after them, and slightly shrugging her shoulders, seated herself at the piano. Anna Vasílievna began to say: "Why don't you go for a walk also?" but without waiting for an answer, she added: "Play me something sad. . . ."

"*La dernière pensée de Weber?*" asked Zóya.

"Akh, yes, Weber,"—said Anna Vasílievna, dropping into an arm-chair, and a tear sprang to her eyelashes.

Meanwhile, Eléna had led the friends to an arbour of lilacs, with a small wooden table in the centre, and benches all round it. Shúbin cast a glance around, gave several little skips, and saying in a whisper, "Wait!" ran off to his own room, brought a lump of clay, and began to model a figure of Zóya, shaking his head, muttering, and laughing the while.

"At your old tricks again,"—remarked Eléna, with a glance at his work, and turned to Berséneff, with whom she pursued the conversation which had been begun at dinner.

"My old tricks!"—repeated Shúbin.—"The

subject is downright inexhaustible! To-day, in particular, she drove me beyond patience."

" Why so? " inquired Eléna.—" One would think that you were talking about some malicious, disagreeable old hag. A pretty, young girl . . . ."

" Of course,"—interrupted Shúbin,—" she is pretty, very pretty; I am convinced that any passer-by, on glancing at her, is inevitably bound to think: ' There's a girl with whom it would be pleasant to . . . dance a polka;' I am also convinced that she knows this, and that it is agreeable to her.—Why those bashful grimaces, that modesty? Come, you know very well what I mean to say," he added through his teeth.— " However, you are otherwise occupied at present."

And, smashing Zóya's figure, Shúbin set hastily, and as though vexed, to moulding and kneading his clay.

" And so, you would like to be a professor? " —Eléna asked Berséneff.

" Yes," replied the latter, crushing his red hands between his knees. " That is my cherished dream. Of course, I am very well aware of everything which I lack to become worthy of so lofty . . . . I mean to say that I am too inadequately prepared, but I hope to receive permission to go abroad; I shall remain there three or four years, if necessary, and then . . . . ."

He paused, dropped his eyes, then suddenly raised them and, with an awkward smile, smoothed back his hair. When Berséneff talked with a woman, his speech became still more deliberate, and he lisped still more decidedly.

" You wish to be a professor of history? "—inquired Eléna.

" Yes, or of philosophy,"—he added, lowering his voice,—" if that should prove to be possible."

" He is already devilish strong in philosophy,"—remarked Shúbin, making deep lines with his finger-nail in the clay,—" so why should he go abroad? "

" And shall you be perfectly satisfied with your position? "—asked Elena, resting her elbow on the table, and looking him straight in the face.

" Perfectly, Eléna Nikoláevna, perfectly. What profession can be better? Upon my word, to follow in the footsteps of Timoféi Nikoláevitch. . . . . The mere thought of such a career fills me with joy and agitation,—yes, ... with agitation, which . . . . which springs from the consciousness of my own small powers. My deceased father gave me his blessing on that matter. . . . . I shall never forget his last words."

" Did your father die last winter? "

" Yes, Eléna Nikoláevna, in February."

" They say,"—pursued Eléna,—" that he left a remarkable work in manuscript: is that true? "

31

" Yes, he did. He was a wonderful man. You would have loved him, Eléna Nikoláevna."

" I am convinced of that. And what are the contents of that work?"

" It is somewhat difficult to convey to you the cóntents of the work in a few words, Eléna Nikoláevna. My father was a learned man, a Schellingist: he employed terms which are not always lucid. . . ."

" Andréi Petróvitch,"—Eléna interrupted him, —" pardon my ignorance; but what does a Schellingist mean?"

Berséneff smiled slightly.

" A Schellingist signifies, a follower of Schelling, the German philosopher; and Schelling's doctrine consisted in . . . . ."

" Andréi Petróvitch!"—suddenly exclaimed Shúbin:—" for God's sake! Thou dost not intend to deliver a lecture on Schelling to Eléna Nikoláevna? Spare her!"

" It is not a lecture at all," muttered Berséneff, and flushed crimson,—" I wanted . . . ."

" And why not a lecture?"—interposed Eléna; " you and I are greatly in need of a lecture, Pável Yakóvlevitch."

Shúbin fixed his eyes on her, and suddenly burst out laughing.

" What are you laughing at?"—she asked coldly and almost sharply.

Shúbin stopped short.

ON THE EVE

" Come now, don't get angry,"—he said, after a pause.—" I beg your pardon. But really, what possesses you,—good gracious!—now, in such weather, under these trees, to discuss philosophy? Let us talk, rather, about nightingales, about roses, about youthful eyes and smiles."

" Yes, and about French romances, and woman's fripperies," went on Eléna.

" And about fripperies, if you like," retorted Shúbin, " if they are pretty."

" Very well. But what if we do not care to talk about fripperies? You call yourself a free artist, why do you infringe upon the freedom of others? And permit me to ask you, if that 's your way of thinking, why you attack Zóya? It is particularly convenient to discuss fripperies and roses with her."

Shúbin suddenly flared up, and half rose from the bench.—" Ah, you don't say so? " he began, in a nervous voice.—" I understand your hint; you are sending me off to her, Eléna Nikoláevna. In other words, I am intruding here."

" I had no thought of sending you away from here."

" You mean to say,"—went on Shúbin testily, —" that I am not worthy of any other society, that I am a mate for her, that I am as empty and silly and shallow as that sickly-sweet little German? Is n't that so, madam? "

Eléna contracted her brows.—" You have not

33

always expressed yourself about her in that manner, Pável Yakóvlevitch," she remarked.

" Ah! reproach! reproach, now! " cried Shúbin.
—" Well, yes, I do not conceal the fact, there was a moment—precisely that, one moment—when those fresh, commonplace little cheeks . . . . But if I wished to pay you back with reproach, and remind you . . . . Good-bye, madam," he suddenly added,—" I am on the point of talking at random."

And dealing a blow upon the clay, which he had moulded into the shape of a head, he rushed out of the arbour and went off to his own room.

" A child,"—remarked Eléna, gazing after him.

" An artist," said Berséneff, with a gentle smile.—" All artists are like that. One must pardon them their caprices. That is their prerogative."

" Yes," returned Eléna,—" but, so far, Pável has not established that prerogative for himself. What has he accomplished up to the present time? Give me your arm, and let us walk in the avenue. He disturbed us. We were talking about your father's writings."

Berséneff gave Eléna his arm, and went into the garden with her; but the conversation which had been begun, having been broken off too soon, was not renewed. Berséneff again began to set forth his views on the vocation of professor, on his future career. He moved quietly by Eléna's side, stepped awkwardly, supported her arm clumsily, now and then jostled her with his shoulder, and never once looked at her; but his speech flowed lightly, if not quite freely, he expressed himself simply and pertinently, and in his eyes, which roved slowly over the boles of the trees, over the sand of the path, over the grass, there beamed the quiet emotion of noble feelings, and in his tranquil voice there was audible the joy of a man who is conscious that he is successfully expressing himself to another person who is dear to him. Eléna listened attentively to him, and, half turned toward him, never removed her eyes from his face, which had paled slightly,—from his eyes, which were friendly and gentle, although they avoided an encounter with her eyes. Her soul unclosed, and something tender, just, good, was poured into her heart, or sprang up within it.

V

Shúbin did not leave his room until nightfall. It was already perfectly dark; the moon, not yet at the full, hung high in the heaven, the Milky Way gleamed white, and the stars had begun to stud the sky, when Berséneff, having taken his leave of Anna Vasílievna, Eléna, and Zóya, went to his friend's door. He found it locked, and tapped.

"Who's there?" rang out Shúbin's voice.

"I,"—replied Berséneff.

"What dost thou want?"

"Let me in, Pável; have done with thy caprices; art not thou ashamed of thyself?"

"I'm not capricious; I'm asleep, and beholding Zóya in my dreams."

"Stop that, please. Thou art not a child. Let me in. I must have a talk with thee."

"Hast not thou talked enough already with Eléna?"

"Have done, have done with that; let me in!"

Shúbin replied by a feigned snore; Berséneff shrugged his shoulders, and went home.

The night was warm, and, somehow, peculiarly quiet, as though everything round about were listening and watching; and Berséneff, enveloped by the motionless mist, involuntarily came to a halt, and began also to listen and watch. A faint murmur, like the rustle of a woman's gown, arose from time to time in the crests of the trees near by, and excited in Berséneff a sweet and painful sensation—a sensation of semi-alarm. Little shivers coursed down his cheeks, his eyes were chilled with quick-springing tears; he would have liked to walk absolutely without noise, to hide himself, to steal along stealthily. A keen little breeze attacked him on the flank: he shivered slightly, and stood stock-still; a sleepy beetle tumbled from a bough and landed on the path with a clatter: Berséneff emitted a soft " Ah! " and again came to a halt. But he began to think of Eléna, and all these transient sensations instantly vanished; only the vivifying impression of the nocturnal freshness, and the nocturnal stroll, and the image of the young girl absorbed his whole soul. Berséneff walked on with drooping head, and called to mind her words, her questions. It seemed to him that he heard the tread of rapid footsteps behind him. He listened intently: some one was running, some one was pursuing him; the panting breath was audible, and all at once, out of the black circle of shadow cast by a huge tree, Shúbin popped up in front of him, with no hat upon his dishevelled hair, and ghastly pale in the moonlight.

" I am glad thou hast taken this path," he articulated with difficulty; " I should not have slept all night if I had not overtaken thee. Give me thine arm. Thou art on thy way home, I suppose? "

" Yes."

" I will accompany thee."

" But how wilt thou go without thy hat? "

" Never mind about that. I have taken off my neckcloth also. It is warm now."

The friends advanced a few paces.

" I was very foolish to-day, was n't I? " asked Shúbin suddenly.

" To speak frankly, yes. I could not understand thee. I have never seen thee like that. And what was it that angered thee, pray? A few trifles! "

" H'm! " muttered Shúbin.—" What a way thou hast of expressing thyself!—but I am in no mood for trifles. Seest thou," he added,—" I am bound to inform thee, that I . . . . that . . . . Think of me what thou wilt . . . . I . . . . well, here goes! I am in love with Eléna! "

" Thou art in love with Eléna! "—repeated Berséneff, and stopped short.

" Yes," went on Shúbin, with forced carelessness.—" Does that surprise thee? I will tell thee more. Until this evening I was able to hope that, in course of time, she would come to love me. . . . But to-day I have become convinced

38

that I have nothing to hope for,—she has fallen in love with some one else."

" With some one else? With whom, then? "

" With whom? With thee! " cried Shúbin, and slapped Berséneff on the shoulder.

" With me! "

" With thee,"—repeated Shúbin.

Berséneff fell back a pace, and stood stock-still. Shúbin gazed keenly at him.

" And does that surprise thee? Thou art a modest youth. But she does love thee. . . . Thou mayest rest at ease on that score."

" What nonsense thou art chattering! " ejaculated Berséneff, at last, with vexation.

" No, it is n't nonsense. But why are we standing here? Let 's go on. It 's easier when we are walking. I have known her for a long time, and I know her well. I cannot be mistaken. Thou art after her own heart. There was a time when she liked me: but, in the first place, I am too frivolous a young man for her, while thou art a serious being, thou art a morally and physically clean individual, thou . . . . Stay, I am not through. . . Thou art a conscientious enthusiast, a genuine representative of those priests of science, of which,—no, not of which,—of *whom,* —of whom the middle-class Russian gentry are so justly proud. And, in the second place, the other day, Eléna caught me kissing Zóya's arms! "

" Zóya's? "

" Yes, Zóya's. What wouldst thou have me do? She has such fine shoulders."

" Shoulders? "

" Why, yes, shoulders—arms—is n't it all the same? Eléna caught me in the midst of these familiar occupations after dinner, while before dinner I had been objurgating Zóya in her presence. Eléna, unfortunately, does not understand how perfectly natural such contradictions are. Then *thou* didst turn up: thou art a believer . . . what the deuce is it that thou believest in? . . . thou art eloquent, thou blushest, thou growest confused, thou grievest over Schiller, over Schelling (and she is always hunting up distinguished persons), and so thou hast carried off the victory, while unhappy I endeavour to jest . . . and . . . nevertheless . . ."

Shúbin suddenly burst into tears, stepped aside, sat down on the ground, and clutched himself by the hair.

Berséneff went up to him.

" Pável,"—he began,—" what childishness is this? Good gracious! What is the matter with thee to-day? God knows what nonsense thou hast taken into thy head. And thou art weeping! Really, it seems to me that thou art pretending."

Shúbin raised his head. The tears glistened on his cheeks in the moonlight, but his face was smiling.

" Andréi Petróvitch,"—he said,—" thou may-

est think of me what thou wilt. I am even ready
to admit that I have a fit of hysterics at the present moment; but God is my witness that I am in
love with Eléna, and that Eléna loves thee. However, I promised to escort thee home, and I will
keep my word."

He rose.

"What a night! silvery, dark, young! How
fine it is now for those who are in love! How
delightful they find it not to sleep! Shalt thou
sleep, Andréi Petróvitch?"

Berséneff made no reply, and accelerated his
gait.

"Why art thou in such a hurry?"—went on
Shúbin.—"Trust my words, such a night will
never be repeated in thy life. But Schelling awaits
thee at home. He has done thee a service to-day,
't is true; but do not hasten, nevertheless. Sing,
if thou knowest how,—sing still more loudly; if
thou dost not know how—take off thy hat, throw
back thy head, and smile at the stars. They are
all gazing at thee—at thee alone: the stars do
nothing else but gaze at people who are in love,—
that is why they are so charming. Thou art in
love, art thou not, Andréi Petróvitch? . . . Thou
dost not answer me. . . . Why dost thou not
answer?"—began Shúbin again.—"Oh, if thou
feelest thyself happy, hold thy peace, hold thy
peace! I chatter, because I am an unlucky wretch,
I am not beloved; I am a juggler, an artist, a

buffoon; but what wordless raptures would not I quaff in these nocturnal streams of light, beneath these stars, beneath these brilliants, if I knew that I were loved? . . . . Berséneff, art thou happy?"

Berséneff remained silent, as before, and strode swiftly along the level road. Ahead, among the trees, the lights of the hamlet in which he lived began to twinkle; it consisted of half a score, in all, of small villas. At its very beginning, on the right of the road, beneath two wide-spreading birch-trees, was a tiny shop; all its windows were already closed, but a broad streak of light fell in fan-shape from the open door, upon the trampled grass, and surged upward upon the trees, sharply illuminating the whitish under side of their dense foliage. A young girl, a lady's maid, to all appearance, was standing in the shop, with her back to the road, and bargaining with the shopkeeper: from beneath the red kerchief, which she had thrown over her head, and held fast under her chin with her bare hand, her plump cheek and slender neck were just visible. The young men stepped into the band of light, Shúbin glanced at the interior of the shop, halted, and, exclaimed: "Ánnushka!" The young girl turned briskly round. A pretty, rather broad, but rosy face, with merry brown eyes and black brows, was revealed.—"Ánnushka!"—repeated Shúbin. The girl looked at him, took fright, grew abashed—and without finishing her purchase, descended the steps, slipped hastily past, and with hardly a glance behind her walked down the road to the left. The shopkeeper, a corpulent man and indifferent to everything in the world, like all suburban shopkeepers, grunted and yawned after her, while Shúbin turned to Berséneff with the words: " That . . that . . thou seest . . . . I am acquainted with a family here . . . thou must not think. . . ." and without finishing his speech, he ran after the retreating girl.

" Wipe away thy tears, at least,"—shouted Berséneff after him, and could not refrain from laughing. But when he reached home, the expression of his face was not merry; he was no longer laughing. Not for one moment did he believe what Shúbin had said to him, but the words he had uttered had sunk deep into his soul. " Pável was making a fool of me,"—he thought . . . " but when she does fall in love . . . whom will she love? "

A piano stood in Berséneff's room, small and not new, but with a soft and agreeable, although not quite pure tone. Berséneff sat down at it, and began to strike chords. Like all Russian nobles, he had studied music in his childhood, and, like almost all Russian nobles, he played very badly; but he was passionately fond of music. Properly speaking, what he loved in it was not the art, nor the forms wherewith it expresses itself (symphonies and sonatas, even operas, made him low-spirited), but its poetry: he loved those sweet and troubled, aimless and all-embracing emotions which are evoked in the soul by blending and the shifting successions of sounds. For more than an hour he did not leave the piano, repeating the same chords over and over many times, awkwardly seeking new ones, pausing and allowing the sounds to die away on diminished sevenths. His heart ached within him, and his eyes were more than once suffused with tears. He was not ashamed of them; he was shedding them in the dark. " Pável is right," he thought; " I have a presentiment that he is right: this evening will not be repeated." At last he rose, lighted a candle, donned his dressing-gown, took from its shelf the second volume of Raumer's " History of the Hohenstaufens,"—and heaving a sigh or two, began to read diligently.

VI

In the meantime, Eléna had returned to her own
chamber, seated herself in front of the open window, and leaned her head on her hand. It had
become her habit to spend a quarter of an hour
every evening at the window of her chamber.
During that time, she held converse with herself,
rendered herself an account of the day that was
past. She had recently celebrated her twentieth
birthday. She was tall of stature, had a pale and
dark-skinned face, large grey eyes under arched
brows, surrounded with tiny freckles, a perfectly
regular brow and nose, a tightly compressed
mouth, and a decidedly pointed chin. The braids
of her dark-chestnut hair hung low on her slender
neck. In the whole of her being, in the expression of her face, which was attentive and somewhat timid, in her mutable glance, in her smile,
which seemed strained, in her soft and uneven
voice, there was something nervous, electrical,
something impulsive and precipitate,—in a word,
something which could not please every one, which
even repelled some people. Her hands were narrow, rosy, with long fingers; her feet also were
narrow; she walked rapidly, almost impetuously,

with her body slightly bent forward. She had grown up very strangely; at first she had worshipped her father, then she had become passionately attached to her mother, and had cooled toward both of them, especially toward her father. Of late, she had treated her mother like an ailing grandmother; and her father, who had been proud of her, as long as she had possessed the reputation of being a remarkable child, began to be afraid of her when she grew up, and said of her, that she was some sort of an enthusiastic republican, God knows whom she took after! Weakness agitated her, stupidity angered her, a lie she never forgave " unto ages of ages ";[1] her demands made no concessions to anything whatever, her very prayers were often mingled with reproach. A person had but to lose her respect, —and she promptly pronounced judgment, often too promptly,—and he forthwith ceased to exist for her. All impressions took deep root in her soul: she did not take life easily.

The governess to whom Anna Vasílievna had entrusted the task of finishing her daughter's education,—an education, we may remark in parenthesis, which had never even been begun by the bored young lady—was a Russian, the daughter of a ruined bribe-taker, graduate of a Government Institute, a very sentimental, ami-

---

[1] The equivalent, in the Eastern Church, of "for ever and ever."—TRANSLATOR.

able, and deceitful creature; she was forever falling in love, and ended by marrying, in her fiftieth year (when Eléna had already passed her seventeenth birthday), some officer or other who immediately abandoned her. This governess had been very fond of literature, and was herself in the habit of scribbling bad verses; she imbued Eléna with a taste for reading, but reading alone did not satisfy the girl; from her childhood up, she had thirsted for activity, for active good: the poor, the hungry, the sick, interested her, disturbed, tortured her; she saw them in her dreams, she questioned all her acquaintances about them; she bestowed alms carefully, with an involuntary air of gravity, almost with emotion. All oppressed animals,—gaunt watch-dogs, kittens condemned to death, sparrows which had tumbled out of the nest, even insects and reptiles found a protector and defender in Eléna; she tended them herself, she did not despise them. Her mother did not interfere with her; on the other hand, her father was very much incensed with his daughter for her vulgar coddling, as he called it, and declared that one could not take a step in the house without treading on a dog or a cat. " Lénotchka,"—he would shout at her, " come hither, make haste, a spider is sucking a fly, release the unhappy victim! " And Lénotchka, all in a flutter would run to him, release the fly, and separate its legs which were stuck together. " Come, now,

let it bite thee, if thou art so kind," remarked her
father ironically; but she paid no heed to him.
At the age of ten, Eléna made acquaintance with
a poor little girl, Kátya, and was in the habit of
going in secret to meet her in the garden. She
carried her dainties, made her presents of ker-
chiefs, and ten-kopék coins—Kátya accepted no
toys. She sat down beside her on the dry earth,
in the thicket, behind a clump of nettles; with a
sensation of joyous humility she ate her black
bread, listened to her stories. Kátya had an aunt,
an ill-tempered old woman, who frequently beat
her; Kátya hated her, and was always talking
about running away from her aunt, and of how
she would live entirely free from all restraint.
With secret reverence and terror, Eléna listened
to these new, unfamiliar words, stared attentively
at Kátya, and at such times everything about her
—her black, quick eyes, almost like those of a wild
beast, her sunburned arms, her dull little voice,
even her tattered clothing—seemed to Eléna to
be something peculiar, almost holy. Eléna would
return home, and for a long time thereafter think
about the poor, about God's will; she thought of
how she would cut herself a staff from a nut-
tree, throw a beggar's wallet over her shoulder,
and run off with Kátya; how she would roam
about the highways in a wreath of corn-flowers:
she had once seen Kátya with such a wreath. If
one of her relatives entered the room at that

moment, she became shy, and looked queer. One day, she ran through the rain to her rendezvous with Kátya, and splashed her frock; her father caught sight of her and called her a slut, a little peasant. She flushed crimson all over, and had a terrible and wonderful sensation at her heart. Kátya often hummed some half-barbarous, soldiers' ditty; Eléna learned the song from her . . . . Anna Vasílievna overheard her, and flew into a rage.

"Where hast thou picked up that abomination?"—she asked her daughter. Eléna merely stared at her mother, and said not a word: she felt that she would sooner allow herself to be rent in pieces than to betray her secret, and again she had a sweet and terrified feeling in her heart. However, her acquaintance with Kátya did not last long: the poor little girl fell ill of a fever, and died a few days later.

Eléna grieved greatly, and it was long before she could get to sleep at night after she heard of Kátya's death. The last words of the little beggar child rang incessantly in her ears, and it seemed to her that they were calling her. . . .

But the years followed years; swiftly and inaudibly, like the waters beneath the snows, Eléna's youth flowed past in outward idleness, in inward strife and unrest. She had no friends: she did not become intimate with a single one of the young girls who visited the Stákhoffs' house.

Parental authority never weighed heavily upon Eléna, and at the age of sixteen she became almost entirely independent; she lived her own life, but a lonely life. Her soul burned and expired alone, she beat her wings like a bird in a cage, but there was no cage: no one checked her, no one restrained her, yet she was restless and pined. Sometimes she did not understand herself, she was even afraid of herself. Everything around her seemed to her either senseless or incomprehensible. "How can one live without love? but there is no one to love!" she thought, and fear fell upon her at that thought, at those sensations. At eighteen, she came near dying of a malignant fever. Shaken to the very foundations, her whole organism, strong and healthy by nature, was unable, for a long time, to recover itself; the last traces of illness disappeared, at last, but Eléna Nikoláevna's father still talked, not without wrath, about her nerves. Sometimes she took it into her head that she wanted something which no one, in the whole of Russia, wishes, thinks of. Then she calmed down, even laughed at herself, spent day after day in careless unconcern; but suddenly something powerful, nameless, which she was not able to control, fairly seethed up within her, and demanded to burst its way out. The tempest passed over, the weary wings, which had not soared, drooped; but these fits left their mark upon her. Try as she would not to betray what was taking place within her, the sadness of her agitated soul was revealed in her very external composure, and her relatives often had a right to shrug their shoulders, to marvel, and to fail to comprehend her " peculiarities."

On the day upon which our story began, Eléna did not leave her window until long after her accustomed time. She thought a great deal about Berséneff, about her conversation with him. She liked him; she had faith in the warmth of his feelings, in the purity of his intentions. Never before had he talked with her as on that evening. She recalled the expression of his bold eyes, of his smile—and smiled herself, and fell into reverie, but it was no longer about him. She set to gazing out into " the night " through the open window. For a long time she gazed at the dark, low-hanging heaven; then she rose, with a gesture tossed the hair back from her face, and, without herself knowing why, she stretched out, toward that heaven, her bare, cold arms; then she dropped them, knelt down before her bed, pressed her face to her pillow, and in spite of all her efforts not to yield to the feeling which was sweeping in upon her, she fell to weeping with strange, amazed, but burning tears.

VII

On the following day, at twelve o'clock, Bersé-neff set out for Moscow with a cabman who was returning thither. He had to get some money from the post-office to purchase certain books, and he wished, incidentally, to see Insároff and have a conference with him. The idea had occurred to Berséneff, during his last chat with Shúbin, to invite Insároff to visit him at the villa. But he did not speedily find him: he had removed from his former lodgings to other quarters, which were awkward to reach. They were situated in the rear courtyard of a hideous stone house, built in the Petersburg style, between Arbát Square and Povarskáya Street. In vain did Berséneff wander from one dirty entrance to another, in vain did he call out now to the yard-porter, now to " somebody." Even in Petersburg the yard-porters endeavour to avoid the gaze of visitors, and much more so in Moscow: no one answered Berséneff's shouts: only a curious tailor, in nothing but his waistcoat, and with a skein of grey thread on his shoulder, silently thrust through the hinged pane of a window high up his dull and unshaven face. with black, bruised eyes, and a black, hornless goat, which had climbed upon a dung-heap turned round, bleated pitifully, and began to chew its cud more briskly than before. A woman in an old sleeved cloak and patched shoes took pity, at last, upon Berséneff, and pointed out to him Insároff's lodgings. Berséneff found him at home. He had hired a chamber from the very tailor who had gazed so indifferently from the hinged pane at the embarrassment of the straying man,—a large, almost perfectly bare chamber, with dark-green walls, three square windows, a tiny bed in one corner, a leather-covered couch in another, and a huge cage suspended close to the ceiling; in this cage a nightingale had once lived. Insároff advanced to meet Berséneff as soon as the latter crossed the threshold, but did not exclaim, " Ah, is that you! " or, " Akh, my God! what brings you here? " He did not even say, " Good-morning," but simply shook him by the hand, and led him to the only chair in the room.

" Sit down,"—he said, and seated himself on the edge of the table.

" Things are still in disorder with me, as you see,"—added Insároff, pointing at a pile of papers and books on the floor; " I have not yet installed myself properly. I have not had time as yet."

Insároff spoke Russian with perfect correctness, pronouncing each word strongly and clearly; but his guttural, though agreeable voice had a certain ring which was not Russian. Insároff's foreign extraction (he was a Bulgarian by birth) was still more plainly apparent in his personal appearance: he was a young man five-and-twenty years of age, thin and wiry, with a hollow chest and angular arms; he had sharp features, a nose with a hump, bluish-black straight hair, a small forehead, small deep-set eyes with an intent gaze, and thick eyebrows; when he smiled, very handsome white teeth made their appearance for an instant from beneath thick, harsh, too clearly outlined lips. He was dressed in an old but neat frock-coat, buttoned to the chin.

" Why have you removed from your former lodging? "—Berséneff asked him.

" This one is cheaper; it is nearer the university."

" But it is vacation-time now . . . And what possesses you to live in town during the summer? You ought to have hired a villa, if you had made up your mind to move."

Insároff made no reply to this remark, and offered Berséneff a pipe, with the words: " Excuse me, I have no cigarettes or cigars."

Berséneff lighted the pipe.

" Now I," he went on,—" have hired a little house near Kúntzovo. It is very cheap, and very convenient. So that there is even an extra room up-stairs."

Again Insároff made no reply.

Berséneff stretched himself.

" I have even been thinking,"—he began again, emitting the smoke in a thin stream,—" that if, for example, I were to find any one . . . you, for example,—that is what I was thinking . . . . who would like . . . . who would consent to install himself up-stairs in my house . . . . how nice it would be! What do you think of it, Dmítry Nikanóritch? "

Insároff turned his small eyes on him.— " Are you proposing that I should live with you in your villa? "

" Yes; I have an extra chamber up-stairs."

" I am very much obliged to you, Andréi Petróvitch; but I do not think that my means will permit me to do it."

" What do you mean by that? "

" They will not permit me to live in a villa. I cannot afford two sets of lodgings."

" Why, but I . . . " Berséneff began, then paused.—" You would not be at any extra expense,"—he went on.—" Your present lodgings could be retained for you, let us assume; on the other hand, everything is very cheap there; we might even arrange, for example, to dine together."

Insároff maintained silence, Berséneff felt awkward.

" At all events, come and visit me sometime,"—

he began, after waiting a while.—" A couple of steps from me lives a family with whom I am very anxious to make you acquainted. If you only knew, Insároff, what a splendid young girl there is there! One of my most intimate friends lives there also, a man of great talent; I am convinced that you will take to him." (A Russian loves to stand treat—if with nothing else, then with his acquaintances.)—" Really, now, do come. But, better still, come and live with us,—really you ought. We might work together, read . . . you know, I am busying myself with history and philosophy. You are interested in all that. I have a great many books."

Insároff rose and paced the room.—" Allow me to inquire,"—he asked at last,—" how much you pay for your villa? "

" One hundred rubles."

" And how many rooms has it? "

" Five."

" Consequently, by computation, one room would cost twenty rubles? "

" Yes. . . But, good gracious! I don't need it at all. It is simply standing empty."

" Possibly; but listen,"—added Insároff with a decided but, at the same time, ingenuous movement of the head:—" I can accept your proposition only in case you will consent to take the money from me according to the computation. I am able to give twenty rubles, the more so as, according to your words, I shall be effecting an economy on everything else there."

" Of course; but, really, I am ashamed to do it."

" It cannot be done otherwise, Andréi Petró-vitch."

" Well, as you like; only, what an obstinate fellow you are! "

Again Insároff said nothing.

The young men came to an agreement as to the day on which Insároff was to move. They called the landlord, but first he sent his daughter, a a little girl seven years of age, with a huge, mot-ley-hued kerchief on her head; she listened with attention, almost in affright, to everything In-sároff said to her, and silently went away; after her, her mother, who was near her confinement, made her appearance, also with a kerchief on her head, only it was tiny. Insároff explained to her that he was going to move to a country villa near Kúntzovo, but retained the lodging, and en-trusted all his things to her; the tailor's wife also seemed to take fright, and retired. Finally, the master of the house came; at first, he seemed to understand all about it, and only remarked thoughtfully: " Near Kúntzovo? " but then sud-denly flung open the door, and shouted, " Are the lodgings to be kept for you, pray? " Insároff soothed him. " Because, I must know," repeated the tailor gruffly, and disappeared.

Berséneff went his way, very much pleased with the success of his proposition. Insároff escorted him to the door, with an amiable courtesy which is not much in use in Russia; and when he was left alone, he carefully removed his coat, and busied himself with putting his papers in order.

VIII

On the evening of that same day, Anna Vasílievna was sitting in her drawing-room, and preparing to weep. Besides herself, there were in
the room her husband and a certain Uvár Ivráno-
vitch Stákhoff, Nicolái Artémievitch's great-
uncle, a cornet on the retired list, aged sixty, a
man obese to the point of being unable to move,
with small, sleepy, yellow eyes, and thick, colourless lips in a bloated yellow face. Ever since his
retirement from the army, he had lived uninterruptedly in Moscow on the interest from a small
capital which had been bequeathed to him by his
wife, a member of the merchant class. He did
nothing, and it is hardly probable that he thought;
but if he did think, he kept his thoughts to himself. Only once in the course of his life had he
become excited and displayed activity, namely:
when he read in the newspapers about a new instrument at the London International Exposition: a "controbombardon," and wanted to im-
port that instrument, and even inquired where
he was to send the money, and through what
office. Uvár Ivánovitch wore a capacious sack-
coat, snuff-brown in hue, and a white necker-

chief, ate much and often, and only in embarrassing circumstances,—that is to say, on every occasion when it behooved him to express any opinion,—did he wiggle the fingers of his right hand convulsively in the air, beginning first with the thumb and running to the little finger, then beginning with the little finger and ending with the thumb, with difficulty articulating: " It ought . . . somehow, you know . . ."

Uvár Ivánovitch was seated in an arm-chair by the window and breathing hard, Nikolái Artémievitch was pacing up and down the room with great strides, with his hands thrust into his pockets: his face expressed displeasure.

He came to a halt, at last, and shook his head. —" Yes,"—he began,—" in our day, young people were brought up differently. Young people did not permit themselves to be lacking in respect for their elders." (He pronounced the *man*[1] through his nose, in French fashion.) " But now, all I can do is to look on and marvel. Perhaps *I* am not right, and they are; but I was not a born dolt. What do you think about it, Uvár Ivánovitch? "

Uvár Ivánovitch merely stared at him, and twiddled his fingers.

" There is Eléna Nikoláevna, for instance,"—pursued Nikolái Artémievitch—" I don't understand Eléna Nikoláevna, really I don't. I 'm not

---

[1] *Mankírovat*, to be lacking in respect.—Translator.

sufficiently lofty for her. Her heart is so capacious that it embraces all nature, down to the very tiniest cockroach or frog,—in a word, everything, with the exception of her father. Well, very good; I know it, and I don't meddle. For it is a question of nerves, and learning, and soaring heavenward, and all that is not in our line. But Mr. Shúbin . . . let us assume that he is an artist, a wonderful, remarkable artist, I do not dispute that; but for him to be lacking in respect toward his elder, toward a man to whom, nevertheless, he may be said to owe a great deal,—that is what I, I must confess, *dans mon gros bon sens,* cannot allow. I am not exacting by nature, no, but there is a limit to all things."

Anna Vasílievna rang the bell in an agitated manner. A page entered.

" Why does not Pável Yakóvlevitch come? " she said. " Why cannot I get him to come? "

Nikolái Artémievitch shrugged his shoulders. —" But why, for goodness sake, do you want to summon him? I am not demanding it in the least, I do not even desire it.

" Why do you ask the reason, Nikolái Artémievitch? He has disturbed you; perhaps he has interfered with your course of treatment. I want to call him to account. I want to know in what way he has angered you."

" I tell you again that I do not demand it.

And what possesses you . . . *devant les domestiques* . . . .''

Anna Vasílievna blushed slightly.—'' There is no need of your saying that, Nikolái Artémievitch. I never . . . *devant* . . . . *les domestiques* . . . Go away, Fédiushka, and see that thou bringest Pável Yakóvlevitch hither immediately.''

The page left the room.

'' But that is not in the least necessary,''— muttered Nikolái Artémievitch between his teeth, and again he began to stride up and down the room. '' I had not that in view at all, when I started the subject.''

'' Mercy me! Paul ought to apologise to you.''

'' Good heavens! What do I want of his apologies? And what are apologies? Mere phrases.''

'' What do you mean by not wanting him to apologise? He must be brought to his senses.''

'' Bring him to his senses yourself. He will listen to you more readily than to me. But I make no charges against him.''

'' Really, Nikolái Artémievitch, you have been out of humour ever since your arrival to-day. I have even seen you growing thin before my very eyes. I 'm afraid your course of treatment is not helping you.''

'' My course of treatment is indispensable to me,''—remarked Nikolái Artémievitch; ''my liver is out of order.''

At that moment, Shúbin entered. He seemed weary. A slight, almost mocking smile played about his lips.

"You sent for me, Anna Vasílievna?"—he said.

"Yes, of course I sent for thee. Good heavens! Paul, this is terrible. I am very much displeased with thee. How canst thou be lacking in respect to Nikolái Artémievitch?"

"Has Nikolái Artémievitch been complaining to you about me?"—asked Shúbin, and glanced at Stákhoff, with the same mocking smile on his lips. The latter turned away and dropped his eyes.

"Yes, he has. I do not know how thou art to blame toward him, but thou must apologise instantly, because his health is very much shaken at present; and, in short, we are all bound, in our youth, to respect our benefactors."

"Ekh, is that logic?" thought Shúbin, and turned to Stákhoff.—"I am ready to apologise to you, Nikolái Artémievitch," he said with a courteous half-bow, "if I really have offended you in any way."

"I did n't in the least . . . mean it that way," —returned Nikolái Artémievitch, as before avoiding Shúbin's eyes.—"However, I willingly pardon you, because, you know, I am not an exacting man."

"Oh, there is not the slightest doubt about

that!"—said Shúbin. "But permit me to inquire whether Anna Vasílievna is acquainted with the precise nature of my offence?"

"No, I know nothing,"—remarked Anna Vasílievna, and stretched out her neck.

"Oh, gracious heavens!"—exclaimed Nikolái Artémievitch hastily:—"how many times already have I begged and entreated, how many times have I said how repugnant to me are all these explanations and scenes! When a man comes home once in an age, he wants to rest,—I tell you, in the domestic circle, *intérieur,* he wants to be a family man;—but there are scenes, unpleasantnesses. There's not a minute's peace. One is forced to go to the club . . or somewhere . . against his will. The man is alive, he has a physical side, it has its demands, but here . . . ."

And without completing the phrase he had begun, Nikolái Artémievitch swiftly quitted the room and banged the door. Anna Vasílievna gazed after him.—"To the club?"—she whispered bitterly:—"You are not going to the club, giddypate! There is no one at the club to whom you can give horses from my stud-farm—and grey ones, at that! My favourite colour. Yes, yes, a light-minded man!"—she added, raising her voice:—"You are not going to the club. As for thee, Paul,"—she continued, as she rose,— "art not thou ashamed of thyself? Thou art not a child, I think. There now, I have a headache coming on. Where is Zóya, dost thou know?"

"I think she is up-stairs, in her own room. That sagacious little fox always hides herself in her own den in such weather as this."

"Come now, please, please stop that!"— Anna Vasílievna fumbled about her.

"Hast thou seen my wine-glass of grated horse-radish? Paul, please do not anger me in future."

"Why should I anger you, Aunty? Let me kiss your hand. And I saw your horse-radish on a little table in the boudoir."

"Dárya is forever forgetting it somewhere or other,"—said Anna Vasílievna, and went away, rustling her silk gown.

Shúbin started to follow her, but paused on hearing behind him the deliberate voice of Uvár Ivánovitch.

"Thou didst not get . . . . what thou hast deserved . . . . puppy,"—said the retired cornet, with stops and pauses.

Shúbin stepped up to him.—"And for what ought I to have been punished, laudable Uvár Ivánovitch?"

"For what? Thou art young, therefore respect. Yes."

"Whom?"

"Whom? Thou knowest well whom. Grin away."

Shúbin folded his arms on his chest.

"Akh, you representative of primitive, universal principle,"—he exclaimed,—" you black-earth force, you foundation of the social edifice!"

Uvár Ivánovitch wiggled his fingers.— " Enough, my good fellow; don't try my patience."

" Here you have a nobleman who is not young, apparently,"—went on Shúbin,—" yet how much happy, childish faith still lies smouldering within him! Revere him! But do you know, you elemental man, why Nikolái Artémievitch is wroth with me? You see, I spent the whole morning, to-day, with him, at his German woman's; you see, we sang a trio to-day, ' Leave me not '; you just ought to have heard it. That would affect you, I think. We sang, my dear sir, we sang— well, and I got bored; I saw that things were not as they should be; there was a lot of tenderness. I began to tease them both. It turned out finely. First she got angry with me; then with him; then he got furious with her, and told her that he was happy nowhere but at home, and that he had a paradise there; and I said to her: ' Ach! ' German fashion; he went away, and I remained; he came hither,—to paradise, that is to say,—but paradise nauseates him. So he took to growling. Well, sir, and who is to blame now, in your opinion?"

" Thou, of course,"—replied Uvár Ivánovitch.

Shúbin stared at him.—" May I make so bold as to ask you, respected knight-errant,"—he began, in an obsequious voice:—" whether it is your pleasure to utter those enigmatic words in consequence of some combination of your thinking faculties, or under the inspiration of the momentary necessity to produce that vibration known as sound? "

" Don't tempt me,"—groaned Uvár Ivánovitch. . . .

Shúbin laughed, and ran out of the room.— " Hey, there,"—shouted Uvár Ivánovitch, a quarter of an hour later:—" I say . . . . . a glass of whiskey."

The page brought the whiskey and a little solid refreshment on a tray. Uvár Ivánovitch softly took the wine-glass from the tray, and stared at it long and intently, as though he did not quite understand what sort of thing he had in his hand. Then he looked at the page and asked if his name were not Váska. Then he assumed a pained expression, took a bite, and dived into his pocket for his handkerchief. But the page had long since carried off the tray and the carafe to their place, and had eaten the remains of the herring, and had already succeeded in falling asleep, leaning up against his master's overcoat, while Uvár Ivánovitch was still holding his handkerchief in front of his face with outspread fingers, and staring now out of the window, now at the floor and walls, with the same fixed attention.

SHÚBIN returned to his own chamber in the wing and was about to open a book. Nikolái Artémie-vitch's valet cautiously entered the room and handed him a small, three-cornered note, the seal of which bore a large coat-of-arms.—" I hope," ran this note, " that you, as an honourable man, will not permit yourself to hint, by so much as a single word, at a certain note of hand which was discussed this morning. You know my relations and my principles, the insignificance of the sum itself, and other circumstances,—in short, there are family secrets which must be respected, and family peace is such a sacred thing, that only *êtres sans cœurs,* among whom I have no reason to reckon you, repudiate them! (Return this note.) N. S."

Shúbin scrawled below it, with a pencil: " Don't worry, I don't pick people's pockets of their handkerchiefs yet "; returned the note to the valet, and again took up his book. But it soon slipped from his hands. He gazed at the crimson sky, at two sturdy young pine-trees, which stood apart from the other trees, and thought: " Pine-trees are blue by daylight, but how magnificently green they are in the evening," and betook himself to the garden, in the secret hope of meeting Eléna there. He was not disappointed. Ahead of him, on the path between the shrubs, her gown was fluttering. He overtook her, and as he came alongside, he said:

"Don't glance in my direction, I am not worthy of it."

She cast a fleeting glance at him, gave an evanescent smile, and pursued her way toward the depths of the garden. Shúbin followed her.

"I request that you will not look at me,"— he began—"yet I address you: a manifest contradiction! But that makes no difference: it 's not the first time I 've done it. I just remembered that I had not yet asked your pardon, in proper form, for my stupid sally of yesterday. You are not angry with me, Eléna Nikoláevna?"

She paused, and did not answer him at once— not because she was angry, but her thoughts were far away.

"No,"—she said at last,—"I am not in the least angry."

Shúbin bit his lip.

"What an anxious . . . and what an indifferent face!" he murmured.—"Eléna Nikoláevna," —he went on, raising his voice:—"permit me to narrate to you a little anecdote. I had a friend; this friend also had a friend, who first behaved himself as an honest man should, and then took to drink. So, early one morning, my friend meets him on the street (and please to observe that they had ceased to know each other) — meets him, and perceives that he is drunk. My friend took and turned away from him. But the other man stepped up, and says: ' I would n't have been angry if you had not bowed, but why do you turn away? Perhaps I do this from grief. Peace to my ashes!'"

Shúbin relapsed into silence.

" Is that all? "—asks Eléna.

" Yes."

" I do not understand you. What are you hinting at? You just told me not to look in your direction."

" Yes, but now I have told you how bad it is to turn away."

" But did I . . . " Eléna was beginning.

" But did n't you? "

Eléna flushed faintly, and offered Shúbin her hand. He pressed it firmly.

" You seem to have caught me in ill-feeling," —said Eléna,—" but your suspicion is unjust. I never even thought of avoiding you."

" Let us admit that, let us admit it. But confess that at this moment you have in your head a thousand thoughts, not one of which you will confide to me. Well? am not I speaking the truth? "

" Perhaps so. "

" But why is it? Why? "

" My thoughts are not clear to myself,"—said Eléna.

" That is precisely the reason why you should confide them to another person,"—interposed Shúbin. " But I will tell you what the matter is. You have a bad opinion of me."

" I? "

" Yes, you. You imagine that everything about me is half-spurious, because I am an artist; that I not only am not capable of any business whatever,—as to that, you are, in all probability, quite right,—but even of any genuine, profound feeling; that I cannot even weep sincerely, that I am a chatterbox and a scandal-monger,—all because I am an artist. After that, are n't we unfortunate, God-slain people? You, for example, whom I am ready to worship, do not believe in my repentance."

" Yes, Pável Yakóvlevitch, I do believe in your repentance, I believe in your tears. But it seems to me, that your very repentance amuses you, and so do your tears."

Shúbin shuddered.

" Well, as the doctors express it, I seem to be an incurable case, *casus incurabilis*. All that is left for me to do, is to bow my head and submit. But in the meantime, O Lord, can it be true, can it be that I am forever fretting over myself, when such a soul is living by my side? And to know, that one will never penetrate into that soul, will never find out, why it grieves, why it rejoices, what is fermenting within it, what it craves, whither it is going. . . . Tell me,"—he said, after a brief pause:—" would you never, for any consideration, under any circumstances whatever, fall in love with an artist?"

Eléna looked him straight in the eye.

" I think not, Pável Yakóvlevitch; no."

" Which remains to be demonstrated,"—remarked Shúbin, with comical dejection.—" After this, I assume that it would be more decent for me not to interfere with your solitary stroll. A professor would have asked you: ' But on the foundation of what data have you said no? ' But I am not a professor, I am a child, according to your view; so remember, do not turn away from children. Farewell. Peace to my ashes!"

Eléna was on the point of detaining him, but changed her mind and said:—" Farewell."

Shúbin quitted the yard. At a short distance from the Stákhoffs' villa Berséneff met him. He was walking with brisk strides, with bowed head, and his hat pushed back on his nape.

" Andréi Petróvitch!"—shouted Shúbin.

The latter came to a halt.

" Go along, go along,"—continued Shúbin:— " I did it thoughtlessly, I will not detain thee,— and wend thy way straight to the garden; thou wilt find Eléna there.—She is expecting thee, I think . . . . she is expecting some one, at any

rate. . . . Dost thou understand the force of the
words ' she is expecting '? And knowest thou,
brother, one remarkable circumstance? Imagine, here I have been living in the same house with
her for two years. I am in love with her, and yet
it was only just now, a moment ago, that I have
—not precisely understood but—seen her. I
have seen her, and thrown apart my hands in despair. Don't look at me, please, with that falsely
sarcastic grin, which is not very becoming to thy
sedate features. Well, yes, I understand, thou
wouldst remind me of Ánnushka. What of that?
I don't deny it. Ánnushkas are mates for such
fellows as I. So, long live the Ánnushkas, and the
Zóyas, and even the very Augustína Christiá-
novnas! Go along to Eléna, now, while I go off
to . . . . to Ánnushka, art thou thinking? No,
brother, brother, worse; to Prince Tchikurásoff.
He 's a Mæcenas of Kazán Tatar origin, after the
style of Bólgin. Seest thou this note of invitation, these letters: R. S. V. P.? Even in the
country I have no peace. *Addio!* "

Berséneff listened to Shúbin's tirade to the
end, in silence and as though somewhat ashamed
on his account, then he entered the yard of the
Stákhoff villa. And Shúbin really did go to
Prince Tchikurásoff, to whom he uttered, with
the most amiable mien, the most pointed imperti-
nences. The Mæcenas of Kazán Tatar origin
shouted with laughter, the Mæcenas's guests

laughed also, and no one was merry, and when they parted all were in a rage. Thus do two slightly-acquainted gentlemen, when they meet on the Névsky, suddenly display their teeth in a grin at each other, mawkishly wrinkle up their eyes, noses, and cheeks, and then immediately, as soon as they have passed each other, assume their former indifferent or morose, chiefly apoplectic expression.

X

ELÉNA received Berséneff in a friendly manner, not in the garden, but in the drawing-room, and immediately, almost impatiently, renewed their conversation of the previous evening. She was alone: Nikolái Artémievitch had quietly slipped off somewhere, Anna Vasílievna was lying down up-stairs with a wet bandage on her head. Zóya was sitting beside her, with her skirt primly arranged, and her hands folded on her knees; Uvár Ivánovitch was reposing in the mezzanine on a broad, comfortable divan, which had received the nickname of " the doze-compeller." Again Berséneff alluded to his father: he held his memory sacred. Let us say a few words about him.

The owner of eighty-two souls,[1] whom he emancipated before his death, an *illuminatus,* a former student at Göttingen, the author of a manuscript work, " The Presentations or Prefigurings of the Soul in the World,"—a work wherein Schellingism, Swedenborgianism, and republicanism were intermingled in the most original manner—Berséneff's father brought him to Moscow while he was still a small lad, immediately after the death of his mother, and himself

[1] Male serfs.—TRANSLATOR.

undertook his education. He prepared himself for every lesson, and toiled with remarkable conscientiousness and with utter lack of success: he was a dreamer, a book-worm, a mystic, he talked with a stutter, in a dull voice, expressed himself obscurely and in an involved way, chiefly in comparisons, and was abashed even in the presence of his son, whom he passionately loved. It is not surprising that the son was merely staggered by his lessons, and did not advance a hair's breadth. The old man (he was about fifty years of age, having married very late in life) divined, at last, that things were not going as they should, and placed his Andriúsha in a boarding-school. Andriúsha began to learn, but did not escape from parental oversight: the father visited him incessantly, boring the head of the school to death with his exhortations and conversations; the inspectors also were bored by the unbidden visitor: he was constantly bringing them what they called most amazing books on education. Even the scholars felt uncomfortable at the sight of the old man's tanned and pock-marked face, his gaunt figure, constantly clad in a spike-tailed grey dress-coat. The school-boys never suspected that this surly gentleman, who never smiled, with his stork-like gait and long nose, heartily sympathised and grieved with every one of them, almost the same as he did with his own son. One day he took it into his head to harangue them on the subject of

Washington: " Youthful nurslings! " he began,
but at the first sounds of his queer voice the
youthful nurslings dispersed. The honest graduate of Göttingen did not live on roses: he was
constantly crushed by the course of history, by
all sorts of problems and considerations. When
young Berséneff entered the university, he accompanied him to the lectures; but his health had
already begun to fail. The events of the year
'48 shattered it to the very foundation (he was
forced to make his book all over), and he died
in the winter of the year 1853, before his son
graduated from the university, but not until he
had congratulated him in advance on having obtained his degree, and consecrated him to the service of science. " I transfer the torch to thee,"—
he said to him, two hours before his death,—" I
have held it as long as I could, do not thou let
go of the torch until the end."

Berséneff talked for a long time to Eléna about
his father. The awkwardness which he had felt
in her presence vanished, and he·did not lisp as
badly as before. The conversation turned on
the university.

" Tell me,"—Eléna asked him,—" were there
any remarkable individuals among your comrades? "

Again Berséneff recalled Shúbin.

" No, Eléna Nikoláevna, to tell you the truth,
there was not a single individual of mark among

us. Yes, and why should there be! There was such a time at the Moscow University, they say! Only, not now. Now it is a school, not a university. I have had a hard time with my comrades," he added, dropping his head.

"A hard time? . . . . ." whispered Eléna.

"However,"—went on Berséneff,—"I must correct myself: I know one student—he is not in my course, it is true—who really is a remarkable man."

"What is his name?"—asked Eléna with vivacity.

"Insároff, Dmítry Nikanórovitch. He is a Bulgarian."

"Not a Russian?"

"No, not a Russian."

"But why is he living in Moscow?"

"He has come hither to study. And do you know, with what object he is studying? He has a certain idea: the liberation of his native land. And his lot is unusual. His father was a fairly well-to-do merchant, a native of Tirnóvo. Tirnóvo is now a small town, but in olden times it used to be the capital of Bulgaria, when Bulgaria was still an independent kingdom. He traded in Sofía, he had relations with Russia; his sister, Insároff's own aunt, still lives in Kíeff, married to a former teacher of history in a gymnasium there. In 1835, that is to say, about eighteen years ago, a frightful crime was perpetrated: Insároff's mother suddenly disappeared, without leaving a trace: a week later, she was found with her throat cut."

Eléna shuddered. Berséneff paused.

" Go on, go on," she said.

"Rumours were in circulation that she had been abducted and murdered by a Turkish Aga; her husband, Insároff's father, discovered the truth and wanted to avenge himself, but he only wounded the Aga with his dagger. . . He was shot."

" Shot? Without a trial? "

" Yes. Insároff at that time was in his eighth year. He was left on the hands of the neighbours. His sister learned of the fate of her brother's family, and wanted to have her nephew with her. He was taken to Odessa, and thence to Kíeff. In Kíeff he lived for twelve years. That is why he speaks Russian so well."

" Does he speak Russian? "

" As well as you and I do. When he was twenty years of age (that was in the beginning of 1848), he wanted to return to his native land. He went to Sofía and Tirnóvo, and traversed the whole of Bulgaria, in its length and breadth, spent two years there, and learned his native language again. The Turkish government persecuted him, and probably, during those two years, he was subjected to great perils; I once saw on his neck a broad scar, which must have been the vestige of a wound; but he does not like to talk about it. He is a taciturn fellow, also, in his way. I have tried to make him tell me all about it,— but in vain. He replies in general phrases. He is frightfully stubborn. In the year 1850 he returned again to Russia, to Moscow, with the intention of perfecting his culture, of getting better acquainted with the Russians. Later on, when he graduates from the university . . . . . ."

" And what then? " interrupted Eléna.

" Whatever God sends. It is difficult to conjecture in advance."

For a long time Eléna did not remove her eyes from Berséneff.

" You have interested me greatly with your story," she said.—" What is he like personally, that friend of yours,—what did you say his name is? . . . Insároff? "

" How can I tell you? He is not bad-looking, according to my taste. But you shall see him for yourself."

" How so? "

" I shall bring him hither to your house. He is coming to our hamlet the day after to-morrow, and is to live in the same lodgings with me."

" Really? But will he care to come to us? "

" I should say so! He will be very glad to come."

" He is not proud."

" He?—He? Not in the least. That is to say,

he is proud, if you like to call it that, but not in
the sense in which you mean. For instance, he
will not borrow money from any one!"

" And is he poor? "

" Yes, he is not rich. When he went to Bulgaria, he got together a few crumbs, which had
remained intact of his father's property, and his
aunt aids him; but all that is a mere trifle."

" He must have a great deal of character,"—
remarked Eléna.

" Yes. He is a man of iron. And, at the same
time, as you will see, there is something childlike,
sincere about him, with all his concentration, and
even secretiveness. In truth, his sincerity is not
our trashy sincerity, the sincerity of people who
have absolutely nothing to conceal. . . . . But
I will bring him to you,—just wait."

" And he is not shy? "—Eléna put another
question.

" No, he is not shy. Only self-conceited people are shy."

" And are you conceited? "

Berséneff became confused, and flung his
hands apart.

" You arouse my curiosity,"—continued Eléna.
—" But come, tell me, did not he avenge himself
on that Turkish Aga? "

Berséneff smiled.

" People avenge themselves only in romances,
Eléna Nikoláevna; and, moreover, in the twelve

years which had elapsed, the Aga might have died."

" But has Mr. Insároff told you nothing about it? "

" Nothing."

" Why did he go to Sofía? "

" His father had lived there."

Eléna became thoughtful.

" To free his fatherland! "—she said.—" Those are awkward words even to utter, they are so great. . . . ."

At that moment, Anna Vasílievna entered the room, and the conversation came to an end.

Strange sensations agitated Berséneff when he returned home that evening. He did not repent of his intention to make Eléna acquainted with Insároff: he regarded as very natural the profound impression which his recitals about the young Bulgarian had produced. . . . Had not he himself endeavoured to strengthen that impression! But a secret and gloomy feeling stealthily made its nest in his heart; he was depressed with a sadness which was not pleasant. This sadness did not, however, prevent his taking up the " History of the Hohenstaufens," and beginning to read it, at the very same page where he had left off on the previous evening.

XI

Two days later, Insároff, in accordance with his promise, presented himself to Berséneff with his luggage. He had no servant, but he put his room in order without any assistance, placed the furniture, wiped up the dust, and swept the floor. He fidgeted for a particularly long time over the writing-table, which absolutely refused to fit the wall-space designated for it; but Insároff, with the taciturn persistence peculiar to him, had his way. Having got settled, he asked Berséneff to take from him ten rubles in advance, and arming himself with a stout staff, he set off to inspect the environs of his new residence. He returned, three hours later, and in reply to Berséneff's invitation to share his meal, he said that he would not refuse to dine with him that day, but he had already made an arrangement with the landlady, and thenceforth he would get his food from her.

" Good gracious! "—retorted Berséneff: " You will be badly fed: that woman does not know the first thing about cooking. Why are not you willing to dine with me? We could have shared the expense."

" My means do not permit me to dine as you do,"—replied Insároff, with a calm smile.

There was something about that smile which did not admit of insistence: Berséneff did not add a word. After dinner, he proposed to Insároff that he should take him to the Stákhoffs; but the latter replied that he intended to devote the entire evening to writing to his Bulgarian correspondents, and therefore begged him to defer the visit to the Stákhoffs until another day. Berséneff was already acquainted with the inflexibility of Insároff's will, but only now, when he found himself under the same roof with him, was he definitively able to convince himself of the fact that Insároff never changed any of his decisions, just as he never put off the fulfilment of a promise he had once given. This more than German punctiliousness seemed, at first, brutal, and even slightly ridiculous, to Berséneff, a radically Russian man; but he speedily became accustomed to it, and ended by thinking it, if not worthy of respect, at least extremely convenient.

On the day after his removal, Insároff rose at four o'clock in the morning, explored nearly the whole of Kúntzovo, bathed in the river, drank a glass of cold milk, and set to work; and he had not a little work on hand: he was studying Russian history, and law, and political economy, and was translating Bulgarian ballads and chronicles, collecting materials concerning the Eastern Question, compiling a Russian grammar for the Bulgarians, and a Bulgarian grammar for the Russians. Berséneff dropped into his room, and talked to him about Feuerbach. Insároff listened to him attentively, and replied rarely, but practically; from his replies it was obvious that he was trying to make up his mind whether it was necessary for him to occupy his mind with Feuerbach, or whether he could dispense with him. Berséneff then turned the conversation on his work, and asked Insároff to show him some of it. Insároff read to him his translation of two or three Bulgarian ballads, and expressed a desire to know his opinion. Berséneff thought the translation accurate, but not sufficiently vivacious. Insároff took his remark under consideration. From the ballads, Berséneff passed to the contemporary situation of Bulgaria, and here, for the first time, he observed what Insároff underwent at the mere mention of his native land: it was not that his face flushed hotly, or that his voice was raised—no! but his whole being seemed to gather strength and strain onward, the outlines of his lips became more clearly and more pitilessly defined, and in the depths of his eyes some sort of a dull, unquenchable fire kindled. Insároff was not fond of dilating upon his own trip to his native land, but about Bulgaria in general he talked willingly with every one; he talked, without haste, about the Turks, about their oppressions, about the woes and calamities of his fellow-countrymen, about their hopes; the concentrated deliberation of a sole and long-existing passion was audible in his every word.

" I 'm afraid that Turkish Aga paid his debt to him for the death of his mother and father," —Berséneff was thinking in the meantime.

Before Insároff had ceased speaking, the door opened, and Shúbin made his appearance on the threshold.

He entered the room in a rather too free-and-easy, good-natured way; Berséneff, who knew him well, immediately comprehended that something had stirred him up.

" I will introduce myself without ceremony," —he began, with a bright and frank expression of countenance:—" my name is Shúbin; I am a friend of this young man here." (He pointed at Berséneff.) " You are Mr. Insároff, I think, are you not? "

" I am Insároff."

" Then give me your hand, and let us make acquaintance. I do not know whether Berséneff has talked to you about me, but he has talked to me about you. You have taken up your abode here? Capital! Don't be angry with me for staring intently at you. I am a sculptor by profession, and I foresee that before long I shall ask your permission to model your head."

" My head is at your service,"—said Insároff.

" What are we doing to-day, hey? "—said Shú-bin, suddenly seating himself on a low stool, with both arms propped upon his widely-parted knees.—" Andréi Petróvitch, has Your Well-born any plan for the present day? The weather is glorious; it is so redolent of hay and dry strawberries . . . . that it is as though one were drinking herb tea. We ought to get up some sort of jollification. Let's show the new resident of Kúntzovo all its numerous beauties. (" He is stirred up," Berséneff continued to think to himself.) " Come, why art thou silent, my friend Horatio? Open thy wise lips. Shall we get up some sort of an affair, or not? "

" I don't know,"—remarked Berséneff:—" that's as Insároff says. I think he is preparing to work."

Shúbin wheeled round on his stool.

" Do you want to work? "—he asked, somewhat through his nose.

" No,"—replied Insároff;—" I can devote to-day to a stroll."

" Ah! "—ejaculated Shúbin.—" Well, that's fine. Come along, my friend Andréi Petróvitch, cover your wise head with a hat, and let us walk straight ahead, whithersoever our eyes gaze. Our eyes are young—they see far. I know of a very bad little eating-house, where they will give us a

very nasty little dinner; and we shall be very
jolly. Come along."

Half an hour later, all three of them were
strolling along the shore of the Moscow River.
It appeared that Insároff had a decidedly queer,
long-eared cap, over which Shúbin went into not
entirely natural ecstasies. Insároff strode along
at a leisurely pace, gazed about him, breathed the
air, talked and smiled composedly: but he had
consecrated that day to pleasure, and was enjoying himself to the full.

" That 's the way good little boys walk on Sundays," whispered Shúbin in Berséneff's ear.
Shúbin himself cut up all sorts of capers, ran
on ahead, assumed the poses of famous statues,
turned somersaults on the grass; Insároff's composure did not exactly irritate him, but it made
him play antics. " What makes thee grimace so,
Frenchman!" Berséneff remarked to him a
couple of times. " Yes, I am a Frenchman,—
half a Frenchman,"—Shúbin retorted; " but do
thou keep the mean between jest and seriousness,
as a certain waiter used to say to me." The young
men turned away from the river, and walked
along a deep, narrow gully, between two walls of
tall, golden rye; a bluish shadow fell upon them
from one of these walls; the radiant sun seemed
to glide across the crests of the ears; the larks
were singing, the quails were calling; everywhere

about the grass grew green; a warm breeze fluttered and raised its blades, and rocked the heads of the flowers. After prolonged ramblings, rests, and chat—(Shúbin even tried to play at leap-frog with a toothless, wretched passing peasant, who laughed incessantly, whatever the gentlemen did to him)—the young men arrived at the " very bad little " eating-house. The servant almost upset each one of them, and actually did feed them with a very nasty dinner, with some sort of wine from beyond the Balkans, all which, however, did not prevent their heartily enjoying themselves, as Shúbin had predicted that they would; he himself was the most noisily merry— and the least merry of them all. He drank the health of the incomprehensible but great Venélin, the health of the Bulgarian King Krum, Khrum, or Khrom, who lived about the time of Adam.

" In the ninth century,"—Insároff corrected him.

" In the ninth century? "—exclaimed Shúbin. —" Oh, what bliss! "

Berséneff remarked that, in the midst of all his antics, sallies, and jests, Shúbin seemed to be constantly examining Insároff,—kept sounding him, as it were,—and was the prey of inward agitation,—while Insároff remained calm and clear as before.

At last they returned home, changed their clothes, and, in order not to spoil the programme which they had adopted in the morning, they decided to betake themselves that same evening to the Stákhoffs. Shúbin ran on ahead to give notice of their coming.

XII

" THE *Hero* Insároff will deign to come hither in a moment! " he exclaimed triumphantly, as he entered the drawing-room of the Stákhoffs, where, at that moment, there was no one but Eléna and Zóya.

" *Wer?* "—asked Zóya in German. When taken by surprise, she always expressed herself in her native tongue. Eléna drew herself up. Shúbin glanced at her with a playful smile on his lips. She was vexed, but said nothing.

" You have heard,"—he repeated:—" Mr. Insároff is coming hither."

" I have heard,"—she replied,—" and I have heard what you called him. I am amazed at you, I really am. Mr. Insároff has not yet set his foot here, and you already consider it necessary to make wry faces."

Shúbin suddenly relaxed.

" You are right, you are always right, Eléna Nikoláevna:—but I did n't mean it, God is my witness that I did not. We have been strolling together all day, and he is an excellent man, I assure you."

" I did not ask you about that,"—said Eléna, rising from her seat.

" Is Mr. Insároff young? "—inquired Zóya.

" He is one hundred and forty-four years old," answered Shúbin, with vexation.

The page announced the arrival of the two friends. Berséneff introduced Insároff. Eléna asked them to be seated, and sat down herself, but Zóya went away up-stairs: Anna Vasílievna must be informed. A conversation began,—rather insignificant, like all first conversations. Shúbin kept silent watch from a corner, but there was nothing to watch. In Eléna he observed the traces of repressed vexation with himself, Shúbin,—and that was all. He glanced at Berséneff and at Insároff, and, as a sculptor, he compared their faces. Neither of them was handsome, he thought: the Bulgarian had a face full of character, a sculpturesque face; it was well illuminated now; the Great Russian demands rather painting: he has no lines, but he has physiognomy. But, probably, one might fall in love with the latter as well as with the former. She was not in love yet, but she would fall in love with Berséneff, he decided in his own mind.—Anna Vasílievna made her appearance in the drawing-room, and the conversation took a turn completely of the summer-villa order,—precisely that, the villa order, not the country order. It was a very varied conversation in the matter of the abundance of the subjects discussed; but brief, tiresome pauses broke it off every three minutes. In one of these pauses, Anna Vasílievna turned to Zóya. Shúbin understood her mute hint, and made a wry face, but Zóya seated herself at the piano and played and sang all her little pieces. Uvár Ivánovitch showed himself for a moment in the doorway, but wiggled his fingers and retreated. Then tea was served, and the whole party went into the garden. . . It had grown dark out of doors, and the guests went away.

Insároff had really made less of an impression on Eléna than she herself had expected; or, to speak more accurately, his straightforwardness and unconstrainedness had pleased her,—and his face had pleased her. But Insároff's whole being, composedly firm, and simple in an everyday way, somehow did not accord with the image which she had formed in her own mind from Berséneff's accounts. Eléna, without herself suspecting it, had expected something " more fatal." But, thought she, he said very little to-day; I myself am to blame: I did not question him, I will wait until the next time . . . . but his eyes are expressive, honest eyes. She felt that she did not wish to bow down before him and give him a friendly hand, and she was surprised: not thus had she pictured to herself people, like Insároff, who were " heroes." This last word reminded her of Shúbin, and she flushed up and waxed indignant, as she lay in her bed.

" How do you like your new acquaintances? "
Berséneff asked Insároff on their way home.

" I like them very much,"—replied Insároff,
—" especially the daughter. She must be a
splendid girl. She gets agitated, but in her case
it must be a good agitation."

" We must go to them as often as we can,"—
remarked Berséneff.

" Yes, we must,"—said Insároff—and said
nothing more the whole way home. He immediately locked himself up in his room, but his candle burned until long after midnight.

Before Berséneff had succeeded in reading a
page of Raumer, a handful of fine gravel was
flung and rattled against the panes of his window. He involuntarily started, opened the window, and espied Shúbin, pale as a sheet.

" What a turbulent fellow thou art! thou
night-moth! " began Berséneff.

" Hush! " Shúbin interrupted him:—" I have
come to thee by stealth, as Max did to Agatha.
It is imperatively necessary that I should say a
few words to thee in private."

" Then come into the room."

" No, that is unnecessary,"—replied Shúbin,
leaning his elbows on the window-sill:—" it 's
jollier this way, more like Spain. In the first
place, I congratulate thee; thy stocks have gone
up. Thy vaunted, remarkable man has been
a dead failure. I can vouch for that. And,

in order to demonstrate to thee my disinterestedness, listen: here's a formal inventory of Mr. Insároff: Talents, none; poetry, has n't any; capacity for work, an immense amount; memory, a
great deal; mind, neither varied nor profound,
but healthy and lively, aridity and power, and
even a gift of language, when the subject is his
—between ourselves be it said—most deadly
tiresome Bulgaria. What? thou wilt say, I am
unjust? One more remark: thou wilt never be
on terms of calling him *thou,* and no one ever has
called him *thou;* I, as an artist, am repulsive to
him, a fact of which I am proud. He's dry, dry,
and he can grind all of you to powder. He is
bound up with his land—not like our empty ves-
sels, who fawn on the people; as much as to say:
'Flow into us, thou living water!' On the other
hand, his problem is easier, more readily understood: all it amounts to is, to turn out the Turks,
and a great matter that is! But all these qualities, thank God, do not please women. There's
no fascination, *charme;* nothing of that which
thou and I possess."

"Why dost thou implicate me in this?"—muttered Berséneff.—"And thou art not right as
to the rest: thou art not in the least repulsive to
him, and he is on the footing of *thou* with his
fellow-countrymen, ... that I know."

"That is another matter! For them he is a
hero; but I must say that my conception of

heroes is different: a hero ought not to know how to talk—a hero bellows like a bull; on the other hand, when he moves his horns the walls tumble down. And he himself ought not to know why he moves, yet he does move. However, perhaps heroes of another calibre are required in our times."

" Why does Insároff occupy thy mind so much? "—inquired Berséneff.—" Is it possible that thou hast run hither merely for the purpose of describing his character to me? "

" I came hither,"—began Shúbin,—" because I was very sad at home."

" Not really! Dost not thou wish to weep again? "

" Laugh away! I came hither because I am ready to bite my own elbows, because despair is gnawing me—vexation, jealousy . . . . ."

" Jealousy!—of whom? "

" Of thee, of him, of everybody. I am tormented by the thought that if I had understood her earlier, if I had set about the business intelligently . . . . But what 's the use of talking! It will end in my constantly laughing, fooling, playing antics, as she says, and then I shall take and strangle myself."

" Well, as for strangling thyself, thou wilt not,"—remarked Berséneff.

" On such a night, of course not; but only let us live until the autumn. On such a night as this people die also, but it is from happiness. Akh, happiness! Every shadow stretched out athwart the road from the trees seems to be whispering, now: 'I know where happiness is. . . . Wilt thou have me tell thee?' I would invite thee to a stroll, but thou art now under the influence of prose. Sleep, and mayest thou dream of mathematical figures! But my soul is bursting. You, gentlemen, behold a man laugh, and that signifies, according to you, that he is at ease; you can prove to him that he is contradicting himself, which means that he is not suffering. . . Begone with you!"

Shúbin swiftly withdrew from the window. "Ánnushka!" Berséneff felt like shouting after him, but he restrained himself; in fact, Shúbin looked unlike his natural self. A couple of minutes later, Berséneff even fancied that he heard sobs; he rose, and opened the window; everything was quiet, only somewhere, in the distance, some one—probably a passing peasant—struck up "The Mozdok Steppe."

XIII

In the course of the first two weeks after Insároff's removal to the neighbourhood of Kúntzovo, he did not visit the Stákhoffs more than four or five times; Berséneff went to them every other day. Eléna was always glad to see him, a lively and interesting conversation always arose between him and her, but, nevertheless, he frequently returned home with a melancholy countenance. Shúbin scarcely showed himself; he busied himself with his art, with feverish activity: he either sat behind locked doors in his chamber and rushed thence in his blouse, all smeared with clay, or spent days in Moscow, where he had a studio, whither came to him models and Italian model-makers, his friends and teachers. Eléna never once talked with Insároff as she would have liked to talk; in his absence, she prepared herself to question him about many things, but when he came she felt ashamed of her preparations. Insároff's very composure daunted her: it seemed to her that she had no right to make him express his opinions, and she resolved to wait; withal she felt that with every visit of his, however insignificant were the words which were exchanged between them, he attracted her more and more: but she had not happened to be left alone with him,—and in order to get close to a person it is necessary to have at least one private conversation with him. She talked a great deal about him to Berséneff. Berséneff understood that Eléna's imagination had been struck by Insároff, and rejoiced that his friend had not proved a failure, as Shúbin had asserted; he narrated to her, with fervour, everything he knew about him, down to the very smallest details (we frequently, when we wish to please a person ourselves, extol our friends in conversation with him, almost never suspecting, moreover, that by that very fact we extol ourselves), and only now and then, when Eléna's pale cheeks flushed slightly, and her eyes began to beam and open widely, did that noxious sadness, which he had already experienced, grip his heart.

One day Berséneff went to the Stákhoffs at eleven in the morning, an unusual hour for him. Eléna came to the drawing-room to receive him.

" Just imagine,"—he began with a forced smile:—" our Insároff has disappeared."

" Disappeared? " said Eléna.

" Yes, disappeared. Day before yesterday, in the evening, he went off somewhere, and since then there has been no sign of him."

" Did not he tell you where he was going? "

" No."

Eléna sank down on a chair.

" Probably he went to Moscow,"—she remarked, striving to appear indifferent, and, at the same time, surprised that she was striving to appear indifferent.

" I do not think so,"—returned Berséneff.— " He did not go away alone."

" With whom, then? "

" Two men, who must have been fellow-countrymen of his, came to him the day before yesterday."

" Bulgarians? Why do you think that? "

" Because, so far as I was able to overhear them, they were talking with him in a language which was unknown to me, yet was Slavonic. . . . . Now you, Eléna Nikoláevna, have always thought that there was very little that was mysterious about Insároff: what could be more mysterious than this visit? Imagine: they entered his room—and began to shout and quarrel, and so savagely, so viciously. . . And he shouted also."

" He also? "

" He also. He shouted at them. They seemed to be complaining of each other. And if you could but have seen those visitors! Swarthy, dull faces, with broad cheek-bones and aquiline noses, each of them over forty years of age, badly dressed, dusty, sweaty, with the aspect of artisans—neither artisans nor gentlemen. . . God knows what sort of men."

" And he went away with them? "

" Yes. He fed them, and went off with them. My landlady said that, between the two, they devoured a huge pot of buckwheat groats. She says they vied with each other in gulping it down, just like wolves."

Eléna gave a faint laugh.

" You will see,"—she said:—" all this will turn out in some very prosaic manner."

" God grant it! Only, you are wrong to use that word. There is nothing prosaic about In-sároff, although Shúbin declares . . . ."

"Shúbin!"—interrupted Eléna, and shrugged her shoulders.—" But admit that those two gen-tlemen who gulped down the groats . . . . ."

" Themistocles also ate on the eve of the bat-tle of Salamis,"—remarked Berséneff, with a smile.

" Exactly so: but, on the other hand, the bat-tle took place on the following day."

" But you must let me know when he returns," —added Eléna, and tried to change the conver-sation,—but the conversation languished. Zóya made her appearance, and began to walk about the room on tiptoe, thereby giving it to be under-stood that Anna Vasílievna had not yet waked up.

Berséneff took his departure.

On that same day, in the evening, a note was brought from him to Eléna. " He has returned," —he wrote to her:—" sunburned, and dusty to the very eyebrows; but why and whither he went, I do not know; cannot you find out? "

" ' Cannot you find out! ' "—whispered Eléna. —" Does he talk with me? "

XIV

ABOUT two o'clock on the following day, Eléna was standing in the garden, in front of a small kennel, where she was rearing two watch-dog pups. (The gardener had found them abandoned under the hedge, and had brought them to his young mistress, concerning whom the laundresses had told him that she had compassion on all wild beasts and animals.) She glanced into the kennel, convinced herself that the puppies were alive and well and that they had been littered down with fresh straw, turned around, and almost shrieked aloud: directly in front of her, alone, Insároff was walking up the alley.

"Good morning,"—he said, approaching her, and removing his cap. She noticed that he had, in fact, grown very sunburned during the last three days.—"I wanted to come hither with Andréi Petróvitch, but he lingered for some reason or other; so I set out without him. There was no one at your house,—everybody is asleep or out walking,—so I came hither."

"You seem to be apologising,"—replied Eléna.—"That is entirely unnecessary. We are all very glad to see you. . . . Let us sit down on that bench yonder, in the shade."

She seated herself. Insároff sat down beside her.

" You have not been at home of late, I believe? "—she began.

" No,"—he replied: " I went away. . . . Did Andréi Petróvitch tell you? "

Insároff glanced at her, smiled, and began to play with his cap. When he smiled, he winked his eyes swiftly and thrust out his lips, which imparted to him a very good-natured aspect.

" Andréi Petróvitch, probably, told you also that I had gone off with some . . . horrible people,"—he went on, continuing to smile.

Eléna was somewhat disconcerted, but immediately felt that it was necessary always to speak the truth to Insároff.

" Yes," she said, with decision.

" What did you think of me? "—he suddenly asked her.

Eléna raised her eyes to his.

" I thought,"—she said . . . . " I thought that you always know what you are doing, and that you are not capable of doing anything bad."

" Well, I thank you for that. See here, Eléna Nikoláevna,"—he began, moving closer to her, in a confidential sort of way:—" there is only a small family of us here; among us there are people who are not highly educated; but all

104

are firmly devoted to the general cause. Unhappily, quarrels cannot be avoided, and all know me, trust me; so they called on me to arbitrate in a quarrel. I went."

" Was it far from here? "

" I went more than sixty versts, to the Troitzky suburb.[1] There, at the monastery, there are also some of our people. At all events, I did not have my trouble for nothing: I arranged the matter."

" And did you find it difficult? "

" Yes. One persisted in being stubborn. He would not give up the money."

" What? Was the quarrel about money? "

" Yes; and not a large amount, either. But what did you suppose it was? "

" And for such a trifle you travelled sixty versts—you wasted three days? "

" It is not a trifle, Eléna Nikoláevna, when one's fellow-countrymen are concerned. To refuse in such a case, would be a sin. Here, I perceive that you do not refuse your aid even to puppies, and for that I laud you. And as for my having wasted time, that is of no consequence. I will make it up later on. Our time does not belong to us."

" To whom, then? "

" To every one who needs us. I have told you

[1] The Trinity—Sergyéi Monastery, forty miles from Moscow.—TRANSLATOR.

all this without circumlocution, because I value your opinion. I can imagine how Andréi Petróvitch amazed you!"

"You value my opinion,"—said Eléna in a low tone:—"why?"

Again Insároff smiled.

"Because you are a nice young lady, not an aristocrat . . . that 's all."

A brief silence ensued.

"Dmítry Nikanórovitch,"—said Eléna: "do you know that this is the first time you have been so frank with me?"

"How so? It strikes me, that I have always told you everything I thought."

"No; this is the first time, and I am very glad of it,—and I, also, wish to be frank with you. May I?"

Insároff laughed and said:

"You may."

"I warn you, that I am very curious."

"Never mind, speak on."

"Andréi Petróvitch has told me a great deal about your life, about your youth. I know one circumstance, one frightful circumstance. . . . I know that, afterward, you went home to your fatherland. . . . Do not answer me, for God's sake, if my question appears to you to be indiscreet,—but one thought tortures me. . . . Tell me, did you meet that man . . . . ."

Eléna's breath failed her. Her daring both

mortified and terrified her. Insároff gazed intently at her, narrowing his eyes slightly, and touching his chin with his fingers.

" Eléna Nikoláevna,"—he began, at last, and his voice was softer than usual, which almost frightened Eléna:—" I understand what man you just referred to. No, I did not meet him, and God be thanked for that! I did not seek him. I did not seek him because I did not consider that I had a right to kill him,—I would have killed him quite calmly,—but it was not a case for private vengeance, when it is a question of national, general vengeance . . . . or no, that is not the proper word . . . when it is a question of the emancipation of a nation. The one would have interfered with the other. In its own good time, that will not escape, either. . . . . That will not escape, either,"—he repeated—and shook his head.

Eléna cast a sidelong glance at him.

" You love your native land greatly? " she articulated timidly.

" That is not settled, as yet,"—he replied.— " You see, when some one of us shall die for her, then it may be said that he loved her."

" So that, if you should be deprived of the possibility of returning to Bulgaria,"—went on Eléna:—" you would be very unhappy in Russia? "

Insároff dropped his eyes.

" It seems to me that I should not survive that,"—he said.

" Tell me,"—began Eléna again:—" is the Bulgarian language difficult to learn? "

" Not at all. A Russian ought to be ashamed not to know Bulgarian. A Russian ought to know all the Slavonic dialects. Would you like to have me bring you some Bulgarian books? You will see how easy it is. What ballads we have! As good as the Servian. And, stay, I will translate one of them for you. . . . Do you know anything at all about our history? "

" No, I know nothing,"—replied Eléna.

" Wait, I will bring you a book. You will see the principal facts, at least, in it. Now listen to the ballad. . . However, I had better bring you a written translation. I am convinced that you will like us. If you only knew what a blessed land is ours! Yet they trample it under foot, they torture it,"—he added, with an involuntary gesture of his hands, and his face darkened:— " they have taken from us everything, everything: our churches, our rights, our lands; the accursed Turks drive us like a flock, they cut our throats. . . . ."

" Dmítry Nikanórovitch! " exclaimed Eléna. He paused.

" Forgive me. I cannot speak of it with indifference. You just asked me, whether I loved my native land? What else on earth can one love? What alone is unchangeable, what is above all suspicion, what else is it impossible not to believe in, except God? And when that fatherland needs thee . . . . Observe: the humblest peasant in Bulgaria and I,—we desire one and the same thing. We have but one aim, all of us. You must understand what confidence and strength that gives!"

Insároff paused for a moment, and again began to talk about Bulgaria. Eléna listened to him with devouring, profound, and melancholy attention. When he had finished, she asked him once more:

" So, you would not remain in Russia, on any terms?" . . .

And when he went away, she gazed long after him. He had become for her a different man that day. The man to whom she bade farewell was not the same man whom she had greeted two hours before.

From that day forth, he began to come more and more frequently, and Berséneff came more and more rarely. Between the two friends a strange something had established itself of which both were plainly conscious, but which they could not name, and were afraid to explain. A month passed in this manner.

XV

Anna Vasílievna was fond of staying at home,
as the reader is already aware: but sometimes,
quite unexpectedly, she manifested an unconquerable desire for something out of the ordinary, some wonderful *partie de plaisir;* and the
more difficult was this *partie de plaisir,* the more
preparations and preliminary arrangements did
it require, the more excited did Anna Vasílievna
become, the more agreeable was it to her. If that
mood descended upon her in the winter, she ordered that two or three adjoining boxes should
be engaged, assembled all her acquaintances, and
went to the theatre, or even to a masquerade; in
the summer, she went somewhere out of town,
the farther the better. On the following day,
she complained of headache, groaned, and did
not get out of her bed, and a couple of months
afterward, the thirst for the " out of the ordinary " was again kindled within her. So it happened now. Some one referred, in her presence,
to the beauties of Tzarítzyno,[1] and Anna Vasí-

[1] A village twelve miles from Moscow, with an unfinished palace,
begun by Katherine II., and a park. To reach it from Kúntzovo, six
miles from town), involves traversing the whole breadth of Moscow.
—Translator.

lievna suddenly announced that she intended to go to Tzarítzyno on the next day but one. The house was in an uproar; a special messenger sped to Moscow for Nikolái Artémievitch; with him also hastened the butler to purchase wine, pasties, and all sorts of edibles; Shúbin was commanded to engage a calash and postilion (the carriage alone was insufficient), and to arrange for relays of horses; the page ran twice to Berséneff and Insároff, and carried them two notes of invitation, written first in Russian, then in French, by Zóya; Anna Vasílievna busied herself with the travelling toilets of the young ladies. In the meantime, the *partie de plaisir* came near being upset: Nikolái Artémievitch arrived from Moscow in a sour and ill-disposed, rebellious frame of mind (he was still in the sulks at Augustína Christiánovna); and on learning what was on hand, he announced, with decision, that he would not go;—that to rush from Kúntzovo to Moscow, and from Moscow to Tzarítzyno, and from Tzarítzyno to Moscow, and from Moscow back to Kúntzovo, was folly; and, in short, he added, " Let it first be proved to me, that any one spot on the earth's surface can be any jollier than any other spot, then I will go." Of course, no one could prove this to him, and Anna Vasílievna, in the absence of any sedate cavalier, was on the point of renouncing her *partie de plaisir,* when she remembered Uvár

Ivánovitch, and in her distress she sent to his room for him, saying: "A drowning man clutches at a straw." They waked him up; he went down-stairs, listened in silence to Anna Vasílievna's proposal, twiddled his fingers, and, to the general surprise, consented. Anna Vasílievna kissed him on the cheek, and called him a darling; Nikolái Artémievitch smiled scornfully, and said, " *Quelle bourde!* " (he was fond, on occasion, of using "chic " French words) ; and, on the following morning, at seven o'clock, the carriage and the calash, loaded to the brim, rolled out of the yard of the Stákhoffs' villa. In the carriage sat the ladies, the maid, and Berséneff; Insároff installed himself on the box; and in the calash were Uvár Ivánovitch and Shúbin. Uvár Ivánovitch himself, by a movement of his fingers, had summoned Shúbin to him; he knew that the latter would tease him the whole way, but between the " black earth force " and the young artist there existed a certain strange bond and a bickering frankness. On this occasion, however, Shúbin left his fat friend in peace: he was taciturn, abstracted, and gentle.

The sun already stood high in the cloudless azure when the carriages drove up to the ruins of the castle of Tzarítzyno, gloomy and forbidding even at noon-day. The whole company alighted on the grass, and immediately moved on to the park. In front walked Eléna and

Zóya with Insároff; behind them, with an expression of complete bliss on her face, trod Anna Vasílievna, arm in arm with Uvár Ivánovitch. He panted and waddled, his new straw hat sawed his forehead, and his feet burned in his boots, but he was enjoying himself. Shúbin and Berséneff closed the procession. " We will be in the reserves, my dear fellow, like certain veterans," Shúbin whispered to Berséneff. " Bulgaria is there now," he added, indicating Eléna with a movement of his brows.

The weather was glorious. Everything round about was blooming, humming and singing; in the distance gleamed the water of the ponds; a light, festive feeling took possession of the soul.—" Akh, how nice! akh, how nice! "— Anna Vasílievna kept incessantly repeating; Uvár Ivánovitch nodded his head approvingly, and once he even remarked: " What 's the use of talking! " Eléna exchanged words with Insároff from time to time; Zóya held the broad brim of her hat with two fingers, thrust her tiny feet, clad in light-grey boots with blunt toes, coquettishly from beneath her rose-coloured barège gown, and peered now to one side, now behind her. " Oho! " suddenly exclaimed Shúbin, in a low tone: " Zóya Nikítishna is looking back, I do believe. I 'll go to her. Eléna Nikoláevna despises me now, but she respects thee, Andréi Petróvitch, which amounts to the same thing.

I 'll go; I 've been sulking long enough. But I advise thee, my friend, to botanise: in thy position, that is the best thing thou canst devise; and it is useful from a scientific point of view also. Good-bye!" Shúbin hastened to Zóya, crooked his arm, saying, *"Ihre Hand, Madame,"* took her arm, and marched on ahead with her. Eléna halted, summoned Berséneff, and took his arm, but continued to chat with Insároff. She asked him, what were the words in his language for lily of the valley, ash, oak, linden . . . . ("Bulgaria!" thought poor Andréi Petróvitch.)

All at once, a shriek rang out in front; all raised their heads. Shúbin's cigar-case flew into a bush, flung by the hand of Zóya. "Wait, I 'll pay you off for that!" he exclaimed, dived into the bush, found his cigar-case, and was about to return to Zóya; but no sooner had he approached her, than again his cigar-case flew across the path! Five times this performance was repeated, he laughing and menacing all the while; but Zóya only smiled quietly, and writhed like a kitten. At last he grasped her fingers, and squeezed them so that she squealed and for a long time afterward blew on her hand, pretending to be angry, while he hummed something in her ear.

"Rogues, the young folks," remarked Anna Vasílievna merrily to Uvár Ivánovitch.

The latter twiddled his fingers.

" What a girl Zóya Nikítishna is! "—Berséneff said to Eléna.

" And Shúbin? "—she replied.

Meanwhile, the whole party had reached the arbour, known by the name of the Pretty Arbour, and halted to admire the view of the Tzarítzyno ponds. They stretched out, one beyond the other, for several versts; the dense forest lay dark beyond them. The grass which covered the entire slope of the hill to the principal pond imparted to the water itself a remarkably-brilliant emerald hue. Nowhere, even on the shore, was there a wave swelling or foam gleaming white; not even a ripple flitted over the even surface. It seemed as though a mass of chilled glass had spread itself out in a huge font, and the sky had descended to its bottom, and the undulating trees were gazing immovably at themselves in its transparent bosom. All admired the view long and in silence; even Shúbin subsided, even Zóya grew pensive. At last, all were unanimously seized with a desire to go upon the water. Shúbin, Insároff, and Berséneff ran a race with one another on the grass. They hunted up a big, gaily-painted boat, found a couple of oarsmen, and called the ladies. The ladies descended to them; Uvár Ivánovitch cautiously went down after them. While he was entering the boat, and seating himself, there was a great deal of laugh-

ter. " Look out, master! Don't drown us! "
remarked one of the rowers, a snub-nosed young
fellow, in a sprigged calico shirt.—" Come, come,
you windbags! " said Uvár Ivánovitch. The
boat pushed off. The young men tried to take
the oars, but only one of them—Insároff—knew
how to row. Shúbin suggested that they sing
in chorus some Russian song, and himself started
up: " Adown dear Mother Volga . . . ." Berséneff, Zóya, and even Anna Vasílievna joined
in (Insároff did not know how to sing) ; but a
discord ensued in the third verse, the singers
got into confusion and Berséneff alone tried to
continue in his bass voice: " Naught in her waves
can be seen,"—but he, also, speedily became
disconcerted. The rowers exchanged winks, and
grinned in silence.—" Well? "—Shúbin turned
to them,—" evidently, the ladies and gentlemen
cannot sing? "—The young fellow in the
sprigged calico shirt merely shook his head.—
" Just wait then, Snub-nose,"—retorted Shúbin.
" We 'll show you. Zóya Nikítishna, sing us
' Le Lac,' by Niedermeyer. Don't row, you! "
—The wet oars were elevated in the air, like
wings, and there remained motionless, sonor-
ously trickling drops; the boat floated on a little
further, and came to a standstill, barely circling
on the water, like a swan. Zóya affected airs.
"Allons!" said Anna Vasílievna caressingly.
. . . . Zóya flung aside her hat, and began to

116

sing: *" O lac, l'année à peine a fini sa car-rière . . . ."*

Her small but clear little voice fairly hurtled across the mirror-like surface of the pond; far away, in the forest, every word was re-echoed; it seemed as though some one there were singing also, in a voice which was distinct and mysterious, but not human or of this world. When Zóya had finished, a thunderous bravo rang out from one of the arbours on the shore, and from it rushed forth several red-faced Germans, who had come to Tzarítzyno to have a carouse. Several of them were coatless, minus cravats, and even minus waistcoats, and they roared, " Bis! " so violently, that Anna Vasílievna gave orders to row to the other end of the pond as quickly as possible. But, before the boat reached the shore, Uvár Ivánovitch had managed to astonish his acquaintances again: observing that, at one spot of the forest, the echo repeated every sound with particular distinctness, he suddenly began to call like a quail. At first all started, but immediately they experienced genuine pleasure, the more so as Uvár Ivánovitch gave the call with great fidelity and lifelikeness. This encouraged him, and he tried to mew like a cat; but his mewing did not turn out so successful; he called once more like a quail, looked at them all, and relapsed into silence. Shúbin rushed to kiss him: he repulsed him. At that moment the boat made its landing, and the whole party got out on the shore. In the meanwhile, the coachman, aided by the footman and the maid, had brought the baskets from the carriage, and prepared the dinner on the grass, beneath the aged linden-trees. All seated themselves around the out-spread table-cloth, and began on the pasties and other viands. All had an excellent appetite, and Anna Vasílievna kept constantly offering things to her guests, and urging them to eat more, as-serting that this was very healthful in the open air; she addressed such remarks even to Uvár Ivánovitch.—" Be easy! " he bellowed at her, with his mouth crammed full. " The Lord has given such a splendid day! " she kept incessantly repeating. It was impossible to stop her: she seemed to have grown twenty years younger. " Yes, yes," she said; " I was very comely, in my time, also; they would n't have rejected me from the first ten, as to looks."—Shúbin joined Zóya, and kept constantly pouring wine for her; she refused, he urged her, and it ended in his drinking a glass himself, then urging her to drink again; he also assured her that he wanted to lay his head on her knees: she would not, on any terms, permit him " so great a familiarity." Eléna seemed more serious than all the rest, but in her heart there was a wondrous calm, such as she had not experienced for a long time. She felt herself infinitely amiable, and constantly

wished to have by her side not only Insároff but
also Berséneff. . . . . Andréi Petróvitch dimly
apprehended what this meant, and sighed by
stealth.

The hours flew past; evening drew on. Anna
Vasílievna suddenly started up in affright.—
" Akh, good heavens, how late it is! "—she said.
" We have had a good time, but all good things
must come to an end." She began to fidget, and
all began to fidget about, rose to their feet, and
walked in the direction of the castle, where the
equipages were. As they passed the ponds, all
halted to admire Tzarítzyno for the last time.
Everywhere flamed the brilliant hues which precede evening: the sky was crimson, the foliage
gleamed with flitting sparks, agitated by the
rising breeze; the distant waters flowed on,
touched with gold; the reddish towers and arbours, scattered here and there about the park,
stood out sharply against the dark green.
" Farewell, Tzarítzyno, we shall not forget our
trip of to-day! " said Anna Vasílievna. . . .
But at that moment, as though in confirmation
of her last words, a strange event occurred, which
really was not so easily forgotten.

Namely: Anna Vasílievna had not finished
wafting her farewell greeting to Tzarítzyno,
when suddenly, a few paces from her, behind a
tall bush of lilacs, there rang out discordant exclamations, laughter and shouts—and a whole

horde of dishevelled men, the very same admirers of singing who had so vigorously applauded Zóya, poured out on the path. The admirers of singing appeared to be very drunk. They halted at sight of the ladies; but one of them, of huge stature, with a bull neck, and inflamed eyes like a bull's, separated himself from his companions, and, bowing clumsily and reeling as he walked, approached Anna Vasílievna, who was petrified with fright.

"*Bon jour, madame,*"—he said, in a mighty voice,—"how is your health?"

Anna Vasílievna staggered backward.

"And why,"—pursued the giant, in bad Russian,—"were not you willing to sing *bis* when our company shouted, 'bis,' and 'bravo'?"

"Yes, yes, why?"—rang out in the ranks of the company.

Insároff was on the point of stepping forward, but Shúbin stopped him, and himself went to Anna Vasílievna's rescue.

"Allow me,"—he began,—"respected stranger, to express to you the unfeigned amazement into which you have thrown us all by your behaviour. So far as I can judge, you belong to the Saxon branch of the Caucasian race; consequently, we are bound to assume in you a knowledge of the social decencies, and yet you are addressing a lady to whom you have not been introduced. At any other time, believe me, I would be particularly glad to make closer acquaintance with you; for I observe in you such a phenomenal development of muscles,—biceps, triceps, and deltoidæus,—that, as a sculptor, I would regard it as a genuine pleasure to have you for a nude model; but, on the present occasion, leave us in peace."

The " respected stranger " listened to the whole of Shúbin's speech, scornfully twisted his head on one side, and stuck his arms akimbo.

" I understands nodings vat you say to me," he said at last.—" You dinks, perhaps, dat I am a master shoemaker or vatchmaker? Eh! I am officer, I am official, yes."

" I have no doubt of that,"—began Shúbin . . . .

" And dis is vat I says,"—went on the stranger, brushing him off the path like a branch with his powerful hand,—" I says: vy did n't you sing *bis* when we shouted, ' Bis '? And now I am going avay, immediately, dis very minute, only, dis is vat is necessary, dat dis fräulein, not dis madam, dat is not necessary, but dis vun, or dis vun " (he pointed at Eléna and Zóya), " should give me *einen Kuss,* as we say in German, a kees, yes; vat of dat? it is noding."

" Nothing, it is nothing," rang out again in the ranks of the company.—" *Ih! der Stakra-menter!* " said one German, who was already roisterously drunk, choking with laughter.

Zóya clutched at Insároff's arm, but he tore himself free from her, and placed himself directly in front of the insolent giant.

"Please go away,"—he said to him in a low but sharp voice.

The German laughed ponderously.—"Vat you mean by avay? I like dat! Can't I valk here also? Vat you mean by avay? Vy avay?"

"Because you have dared to disturb a lady," —said Insároff, and suddenly paled,—"because you are drunk."

"Vat? I am drunk? Do you hear? *Hören Sie das, Herr Provisor?* I 'm an officer, and he dares . . . Now I shall demand *Satisfaction! Einen Kuss will ich!*"

"If you take another step,"—began Insároff . . . . .

"Vell? And vat den?"

"I will throw you into the water."

"Into de vater? *Herr Je!* Is dat all? Come, let 's see, it 's very curious, how you 'll throw me into de vater. . . ."

The officer raised his arms, and started forward, but suddenly something remarkable happened: he gave a groan, his whole huge body swayed, rose from the ground, his legs kicked in the air, and before the ladies had time to shriek, before any one could understand how the thing was done, the *officer,* with his whole mass, splashed heavily in the pond, and immediately disappeared beneath the swirling water.

" Akh! " screamed the ladies in unison.

" *Mein Gott!* " was audible from the other side.

A minute elapsed . . . and the round head, all plastered with damp hair, made its appearance above the water; it emitted bubbles, that head; two arms gesticulated convulsively at its very lips. . . .

" He will drown, save him, save him! " Anna Vasílievna shrieked to Insároff, who was standing on the shore, his legs planted far apart, and panting.

" He 'll swim out," he said, with scornful and pitiless indifference.—" Let us go,"—he added, offering Anna Vasílievna his arm,—" come along, Uvár Ivánovitch, Eléna Nikoláevna."

" A . . . a . . . . o . . . . o . . ." at that moment resounded the yell of the unlucky German, who had contrived to grasp the shore reeds.

All moved on after Insároff, and all were obliged to pass that same " *companie.*" But, deprived of their head, the roisterers had quieted down, and did not utter a word; one only, the bravest of them all, muttered, as he shook his head: " Well, but this . . . this, God knows, what . . . after this "; and another even pulled off his hat. Insároff seemed to them very for-

midable, and with good cause: something malevolent, something dangerous had come forth in his
face. The Germans rushed to fish their comrade
out, and the latter, as soon as he found himself
on dry land, began tearfully to curse and shout
after those " Russian bandits," that he would
complain, that he would go to Count von Kieze-
ritz himself. . . .

But the " Russian bandits " paid no attention
to his shouts, and made all haste to the castle. All maintained silence while they walked
through the park, only Anna Vasílievna sighed
slightly. But at last they approached their carriages, halted, and an irrepressible, interminable
shout of laughter arose from them, as with the
heaven-dwellers of Homer. First Shúbin burst
out shrilly, like a crazy person; after him Berséneff rattled away like a shower of peas; then
Zóya scattered fine pearls of laughter; Anna
Vasílievna, also, suddenly went into such parox-
ysms of mirth, that Eléna could not refrain from
smiling; even Insároff, at last, could not resist.
But louder and longer than all the rest, shouted
Uvár Ivánovitch; he roared until he had a stitch
in the side, until he sneezed, until he strangled.
He would quiet down a little, and say through
his tears: " I . . . think . . . that that knocked
him out . . . . but . . . he . . . . splash, ker-
flop! " . . . And with the last, convulsively ex-
pelled word, a fresh outburst of laughter shook

his whole frame. Zóya spurred him on still more.
" I see his legs in the air," said she. . . .

" Yes, yes," chimed in Uvár Ivánovitch,—" his
legs, his legs . . . and then! and he went spla-ash
ker-flop!"

" Yes, and how did he manage it, for the German was twice as big as he?" asked Zóya.

" I 'll tell you,"—replied Uvár Ivánovitch,
wiping his eyes,—" I saw him seize the man by
his belt with one hand, thrust under his leg, and
then, slap-dash! I hear: ' What 's this?' . . .
but he went splash, ker-flop!"

The equipages had been on their way for a
long time, the castle of Tzarítzyno had long vanished from sight, and still Uvár Ivánovitch could
not calm down. Shúbin, who was again driving
with him in the calash, became ashamed of him
at last.

And Insároff felt conscience-stricken. He
sat in the carriage opposite Eléna (Berséneff
had placed himself on the box) and preserved
silence: she, also, was silent. He thought that
she was condemning him; but she was not condemning him. She had been very greatly
frightened at the first moment; then she had been
struck by the expression of his face; after that,
she had been engaged in meditation. It was
not quite clear to her what she was meditating
about. The feeling which she had experienced
during the course of the day had disappeared;

she was conscious of this; but it had been re-
placed by something else which, as yet, she did
not comprehend. The *partie de plaisir* had
lasted too long: the evening had imperceptibly
merged into night. The carriage rolled swiftly
onward, past ripe fields, where the air was suffocating and fragrant and redolent of grain,
again past broad meadows, and their sudden
coolness beat upon the face in a light wave. The
sky seemed to be smoking at the edges. At last
the moon floated up, dull and red. Anna Vasílievna was dozing; Zóya was hanging out of the
window, and gazing at the road. At last it occurred to Eléna that she had not spoken to Insároff for more than an hour. She turned to
him with a trivial question: he immediately answered her joyously. Certain indefinite sounds
began to be wafted through the air: Moscow was
hastening to meet them. Ahead of them twin-
kled tiny points of light; their number kept
constantly increasing; at last, the stones of the
pavement rang beneath their wheels. Anna Vasílievna waked up; all in the carriage began to talk,
although not one of them was able to hear what
the conversation was about, so loudly did the
pavement resound beneath the two carriages and
the thirty-two hoofs of the horses. Long and
wearisome did the transit from Moscow to Kúntzovo appear; everybody was asleep or silent,
with heads nestled in various corners; Eléna

alone did not close her eyes: she never removed them from Insároff's dark figure. Melancholy had descended upon Shúbin: the breeze blew in his eyes, and irritated him; he muffled himself in the collar of his cloak, and all but wept. Uvár Ivánovitch was snoring blissfully, swaying to right and left. At last the equipages came to a halt. Two footmen carried Anna Vasílievna from the carriage; she was completely done up, and announced to her fellow-travellers, as she took leave of them, that she was barely alive; they began to thank her, but she merely repeated: " Barely alive." Eléna shook Insároff's hand for the first time; and sat for a long time, without undressing, at her window; while Shúbin seized the opportunity to whisper to Berséneff as the latter departed:

" Well, and why is n't he a hero?—he pitches drunken Germans into the water! "

" But thou didst not do even that,"—retorted Berséneff, and went home with Insároff.

The dawn was already invading the sky when the two friends regained their lodgings. The sun had not yet risen, but the chill had already set in, the grey dew covered the grass, and the first larks were carolling on high in the half-twilight aërial abyss, whence, like a solitary eye, gazed one huge, last star.

XVI

SHORTLY after Eléna had made Insároff's acquaintance, she had (for the fifth or sixth time) begun a diary. Here are excerpts from that diary:

" *June* . . . . Andréi Petróvitch brings me books, but I cannot read them. I am ashamed to confess this to him; I do not wish to return the books, to lie, to say that I have read them. It seems to me that that would grieve him. He notices everything in me. Apparently, he is very much attached to me. He is a very nice man, is Andréi Petróvitch.

" . . . . What is it that I want? Why is my heart so heavy, so languid? Why do I gaze with envy at the birds which flit past? I believe that I would like to fly with them, fly—whither I know not, only far away from here. And is not that desire sinful? Here I have a mother, a father, a family. Do not I love them? No! I do not love them as I would like to love them. It is terrible for me to speak this out, but it is the truth. Perhaps I am a great sinner; perhaps that is the reason why I am so sad, why I have no peace. Some hand or other lies heavy on me, is crushing me. It is as though I were in prison, and as though the walls were on the point of falling upon me. Why do not other people feel this? Whom shall I love, if I am cold to my own people? Evidently, papa is right: he accuses me of loving only dogs and cats. I must think this over. I pray but little; I must pray. . . . But it seems to me that I could love!

" . . . . I am still timid with Mr. Insároff. I do not know why; I am not so very young, I think, and he is so simple and kind. He sometimes wears a very serious face. It must be that he has no time for us. I feel it, and I am ashamed, as it were, to rob him of his time. Andréi Petróvitch—is another matter. I am ready to chat with him all day long. But he keeps talking to me about Insároff. And what terrible details! I saw him in my dreams last night, with a dagger in his hand. And he seemed to say to me: ' I will kill thee, and kill myself.' What nonsense!

" . . . . Oh, if some one would only say to me: ' Here, this is what thou shouldst do! ' To be good—that is not enough; to do good . . . yes; that is the principal thing in life. But how shall I do good? Oh, if I could only control myself! I do not know why I think so often of Mr. Insároff. When he comes, and sits, and listens attentively, but makes no effort himself, no fuss, I gaze at him, and find it agreeable—nothing more; but when he goes away, I keep recalling his words, and I am vexed with myself, and I even grow excited . . . I know not why. (He speaks French badly, and is not ashamed of it—I like that.) However, I always do think a great deal about new people. In chatting with him, I suddenly recalled our butler Vasíly, who dragged a helpless old man from a burning cottage, and came near perishing himself. Papa called him a fine fellow, mamma gave him five rubles, but I wanted to bow down at his feet.

He had a simple, even a stupid face, and he became a drunkard afterward.

" . . . . To-day I gave a copper coin to a poor woman, and she said to me : ' Why art thou so sad ? ' And I did not even suspect that I had a sad aspect. I think it arises from the fact that I am alone, always alone, with all my good and all my bad. I have no one to whom I can give my hand. The one who approaches me is not the one I want, and the one I would like . . . . passes me by.

" . . . . I do not know what is the matter with me to-day ; my head is in a snarl, I am ready to fall on my knees and beg and pray for mercy. I do not know who is doing it, or how it is being done, but it seems as though I were being murdered, and I shriek inwardly and rebel : I weep, and cannot hold my peace. . . . My God ! My God ! quell thou these transports in me ! Thou alone canst do this, all else is powerless : neither my insignificant alms, nor occupations, nothing, nothing, nothing can help me. I would like to go off somewhere as a servant, truly : I should feel more at ease.

" What is the use of youth, why do I live, why have I a soul, to what end is all this ?

" . . . . Insároff, Mr. Insároff—I really do not know how to write—continues to occupy my thoughts. I would like to know what he has in his soul. Apparently, he is so frank, so accessible, yet nothing is visible to me. Sometimes he looks at me with eyes which seem to be scrutinising . . . or is that only my fancy ? Paul is constantly teasing me—I am angry with Paul. What does he want ? He is in love with me . . . but I do not want his love. He is in love with Zóya also. I am unjust to him; he told me yesterday, that I did not know how to be unjust half-way . . . that is true. It is very wrong.

" Akh, I feel that unhappiness is necessary to a man, or poverty, or illness, otherwise he grows arrogant at once.

" . . . . Why did Andréi Petróvitch tell me to-day about those two Bulgarians? It seemed as though he told me that with a purpose. What is Mr. Insároff to me? I am angry with Andréi Petróvitch.

" . . . . I take up my pen and do not know how to begin. How unexpectedly he talked with me in the garden to-day! How affectionate and confidential he was! How quickly this has come about! It is as though we were old, old friends, and had only just recognised each other. How could I have failed to understand him hitherto! How near he is to me now! And this is the astonishing part of it: I have become much calmer now. I find it ridiculous: yesterday I was angry with Andréi Petróvitch,—at him,—I even called him *Mr. Insároff;* but to-day . . . Here, at last, is an upright man; here is some one on whom I can rely. This man does not lie: he is the first man I have met who does not lie: all the rest lie, lie continually. Andréi Petróvitch, dear and kind, why do I insult you? No! Andréi Petróvitch is more learned than he, perhaps, perhaps he is even cleverer. . . But, I do not know, he is such a small man beside him. When he speaks of his fatherland, he grows, and grows, and his face becomes handsome, and his voice is like steel, and it seems as though there were not a man in the world before whom he would lower his eyes. And he not only talks—he acts, and will act. I shall question him. . . . How suddenly he turned to me, and smiled at me! . . .

Only brothers smile in that way. Akh, how content I am! When he came to us for the first time, I did not, in the least, think that he would become a close friend so soon! And now it even pleases me that I remained indifferent that first time. Indifferent! Can it be that I am not indifferent now? . . .

" . . . . . It is a long time since I felt such inward peace. It is so still within me, so still. And there is nothing to record. I see him often, that is all. What else is there to record?

" . . . . Paul has shut himself in his room, Andréi Petróvitch has taken to coming more rarely . . . . Poor fellow! it seems to me that he . . . however, that is impossible. I love to talk with Andréi Petróvitch: never a word about himself, always something practical, useful. With Shúbin the case is different. Shúbin is as gorgeously arrayed as a butterfly, and admires his array: butterflies do not do that. However, both Shúbin and Andréi Petróvitch . . . I know what I want to say.

" . . . . *He* finds it agreeable to come to our house, I see that. But why? What has he found in me? Really, our tastes are similar: neither of us is fond of poetry: neither of us knows anything about art. But how much better he is than I am! He is calm, I am in perpetual agitation; he has a road, a goal—but as for me, whither am I going? where is my nest? He is calm, but all his thoughts are far away. The time will come when he will leave us forever, and go away to his own land, yonder, beyond the sea. What of that? God grant he may! Nevertheless, I shall be glad that I have known him while he was here.

ON THE EVE

" Why is not he a Russian? No, he cannot be a Russian.

" And mamma likes him. She says: ' He is a modest man.' Kind mamma! She does not understand him. Paul holds his peace: he has divined that his hints are displeasing to me, but he is jealous of him. Wicked boy! And by what right? Have I ever . . . . .

" All this is nonsense! Why does this keep coming into my head?

" . . . . But it is really strange that so far, up to the age of twenty, I have never been in love with any one. It seems to me that D. (I shall call him D., I like that name: Dmítry) is so clear in soul because he has given himself wholly to his cause, to his dream. What is there for him to be agitated about? He who has consecrated himself wholly . . . wholly . . . . wholly . . . . has little grief, he no longer is responsible for anything. It is not *I* who will; *it* wills. By the way, he and I both love the same flowers. I plucked a rose to-day. One petal fell, he picked it up. . . . . I gave him the whole rose.

" . . . . D. comes often to us. Yesterday he sat here the whole evening. He wants to teach me Bulgarian. I felt at ease with him, as though at home. Better than at home.

" . . . . The days fly. . . . . I am both happy and, for some reason, apprehensive, and I feel like thanking God, and the tears are not far off. O warm, bright days!

" . . . . I still feel light of heart, as of yore, and only rarely a little sad. I am happy. *Am* I happy?

" . . . . It will be long before I shall forget the

133

jaunt of yesterday. What strange, novel, terrible impressions! When he suddenly seized that giant and hurled him, like a small ball, into the water, I was not frightened . . . . but he frightened me. And afterward—what an ominous, almost cruel face! How he said: ' He 'll swim out ! ' It upset me completely. It must be that I have not understood him. And then, when every one was laughing, when I laughed, how pained I felt for him! He was ashamed, I felt that,—he was ashamed before me. He told me that, later on, in the carriage, in the darkness, when I tried to scrutinise him, and was afraid of him. Yes, one cannot jest with him, and he does know how to defend himself. But why that viciousness, why those quivering lips, that venom in the eyes? Or, perhaps it could not be otherwise. Is it impossible to be a man, a champion, and remain gentle and soft? Life is a harsh matter, he said to me not long ago. I repeated this remark to Andréi Petróvitch; he did not agree with D. Which of them is right? And how that day began! How happy I was to walk by his side, even in silence. . . . But I am glad that it happened. Evidently, it was as it should be.

" . . . . Again uneasiness. . . . . I am not quite well.

" . . . . All these last days I have not recorded anything in this note-book, because I did not wish to write. I felt that, whatever I might write, it would not be what was in my soul. . . . And what is in my soul? I have had a long interview with him, which has revealed to me many things. He told me about his plans (by the way, I know now why he has that wound on the neck. . . My God! when I think that he was already condemned

to death, that he barely escaped, that he was wounded
. . . . .). He foresees a war, and rejoices at it. And,
nevertheless, I have never seen D. so sad. What can
he . . . . he! . . . . be sad about? Papa returned
from the town, found us together, and gave us rather a
strange look. Andréi Petróvitch came: I notice that he
has grown very thin and pale. He reproached me for,
as he said, treating Shúbin too coldly and carelessly.
But I had quite forgotten Paul. When I see him, I will
try to repair my fault. But I am not in the mood for
him now . . . . nor for any one in the world. Andréi
Petróvitch talked to me with a sort of compassion. What
is the meaning of all this? Why is all around me and
within me dark? It seems to me, that around me and
within me something enigmatic is in progress, that the
answer must be sought . . . .

" . . . . I did not sleep last night; my head aches.
Why should I write? He went away so soon to-day,
and I wanted to talk to him. . . . . He seems to shun
me. Yes, he does shun me.

" . . . . The answer is found, a light has dawned
upon me! O God! have pity on me. . . . I am in love!"

XVII

On the day when Eléna inscribed this last, fateful word in her diary, Insároff sat in Berséneff's room, and Berséneff stood before him with an expression of amazement on his face. Insároff had just announced to him his intention to remove to Moscow on the following day.

"Good gracious!"—exclaimed Berséneff:—"the very finest part of the season is beginning. What will you do in Moscow? What a sudden decision! Or have you received some news?"

"I have received no news," returned Insároff—"but, according to my views, it is impossible for me to remain here."

"But how is it possible . . . . ."

"Andréi Petróvitch,"—said Insároff,—"be so good as not to insist, I entreat you. It pains me to part with you, but it cannot be helped."

Berséneff stared fixedly at him.

"I know,"—he said at last,—"you are not to be convinced. And so, the matter is settled?"

"Completely settled,"—replied Insároff, rising and withdrawing.

Berséneff strode about the room, seized his hat, and betook himself to the Stákhoffs.

" You have something to impart to me,"—
Eléna said to him, as soon as they were left alone
together.

" Yes; how did you guess? "

" No matter. Tell me, what is it? "

Berséneff communicated to her Insároff's resolve.

Eléna turned pale.

" What does it mean? "—she articulated with
difficulty.

" You know,"—said Berséneff,—" that Dmítry Nikanórovitch does not like to give an account of his actions. But I think . . . . Let
us sit down, Eléna Nikoláevna; you do not seem
to be quite well . . . . I think I can guess the
real cause of this sudden departure."

" What—what is the cause? " repeated Eléna,
clasping Berséneff's hand tightly, without herself being aware of it, in her hands, which had
grown cold.

" Well, you see,"—began Berséneff with a
melancholy smile—" how shall I explain it to you?
I must revert to last spring, to the time when I became more intimately acquainted with Insároff.
I then met him at the house of a relation; this relation had a daughter, a very pretty young girl.
It seemed to me that Insároff was not indifferent to her and I said so to him. He laughed, and
answered me that I was mistaken, that his heart
had not suffered, but that he would go away at

once, if anything of that sort should happen with him, as he did not wish—those were his very words—to betray his cause and his duty for the satisfaction of his personal feelings. ' I am a Bulgarian,' he said, ' and I want no Russian love.' "

" Well . . . and do you . . . . now . . . ." whispered Eléna, involuntarily turning away her head, like a person who is expecting a blow, but still not releasing Berséneff's hand from her grasp.

" I think "—he said, and lowered his voice—" I think that that has now happened which I then erroneously assumed."

" That is to say . . . you think . . . . do not torture me! "—broke out Eléna suddenly.

" I think,"—hastily went on Berséneff,—" that Insároff has now fallen in love with a Russian maiden, and, in accordance with his vow, he is resolved to flee."

Eléna gripped his hand still more tightly, and bent her head still lower, as though desirous of hiding from the sight of an outsider the flush of shame which overspread her whole face and neck with sudden flame.

" Andréi Petróvitch, you are as kind as an angel,"—she said,—" but, surely, he will come to bid us farewell? "

" Yes, I assume that he will certainly come, because he does not wish to go . . . ."

" Tell him, tell him . . . ."

But here the poor girl broke down: tears streamed from her eyes, and she rushed from the room.

" So that is how she loves him," thought Berséneff, as he slowly wended his way homeward. " I did not expect that; I did not expect that it was already so strong. I am kind, she says,"— he continued his meditations . . . . " Who shall say by virtue of what feelings and motives I have communicated all this to Eléna? But not out of kindness, not out of kindness. Is it that accursed desire to convince myself whether the dagger is still sticking in the wound? I must be content—they love each other, and I have helped them. . . . ' The future mediator between science and the Russian public,' Shúbin calls me; evidently it is written in my destiny that I shall be a mediator. But what if I have made a mistake? No, I have not. . . ."

It was bitter for Andréi Petróvitch, and Raumer never entered his head.

On the following day, at two o'clock, Insároff presented himself at the Stákhoff's. As though expressly at that hour, in Anna Vasílievna's drawing-room sat a neighbour, the wife of the arch-priest, who was a very kind and respectable woman, but had had a trifling unpleasantness with the police, because she had taken it into her head, at the very hottest part of the day, to bathe in a pond near a road along which the family of some influential general or other was wont to drive. The presence of an outsider was, at first, even agreeable to Eléna, from whose face every drop of blood had fled as soon as she heard Insároff's tread; but her heart died within her at the thought that he might take leave without having spoken with her in private. He also appeared embarrassed, and avoided her gaze. "Is it possible that he will take leave at once?" thought Eléna. In fact, Insároff was on the point of addressing Anna Vasílievna, when Eléna rose, and hastily called him aside to the window. The arch-priest's wife was surprised, and tried to turn round; but she was so tightly laced that her corset squeaked at every movement she made. She remained motionless.

"Listen,"—said Eléna hurriedly,—"I know why you are come; Andréi Petróvitch has told me of your intention; but I beg you, I entreat you, not to bid us farewell to-day, but to come hither to-morrow at an earlier hour—about eleven o'clock. I must say a couple of words to you."

Insároff inclined his head in silence.

"I shall not detain you. . . . Do you promise me?"

Again Insároff bowed, but said nothing.

"Come here, Lénotchka,"—said Anna Vasílievna,—" see here: what a splendid reticule the mátushka [1] has!"

" I embroidered it myself," said the arch-priest's wife.

Eléna quitted the window.

Insároff did not remain more than a quarter of an hour at the Stákhoffs'. Eléna watched him covertly. He fidgeted about on his seat as usual, did not know where to fix his eyes, and went away in a strange, abrupt manner, just as though he had vanished.

The day passed slowly for Eléna; still more slowly did the long, long night drag out its course. Eléna, at times, sat on her bed, clasping her knees with her arms, and with her head resting on them; again she walked to the window, pressed her burning brow to the cold glass, and thought, thought, thought, until she was exhausted, the same thoughts, over and over again. Her heart had not precisely turned to stone, nor yet had it vanished from her breast; she did not feel it, but the veins in her head throbbed violently, and her hair burned her, and her lips were parched. " He will come . . . he did not bid mamma good-bye . . . he will not deceive . . . . . Can it be that An-dréi Petróvitch spoke the truth? It cannot be.

---

[1] *Mátushka*—dear little mother—is the characteristic Russian form of address for women of all classes; but it is particularly applied to the wives of ecclesiastics. *Bátiushka*—dear little father—is used, generally and specifically, in the same way.—TRANSLATOR.

. . . . He did not promise in words to come. . . Can it be that I have parted from him forever? " . . . . Such thoughts as these never quitted her . . . precisely that, never quitted her: they did not come, they did not return,—they surged to and fro incessantly within her, like a fog. —" He loves me! " suddenly flared up through all her being, and she stared intently into the gloom; a mysterious smile, unseen by any one, parted her lips . . . . . but she instantly shook her head, laid the clenched fingers of her hand against her nape, and again, like a fog, the former thoughts surged within her. Just before dawn, she undressed herself, and went to bed, but could not sleep. The first fiery rays of the sun beat into her room. . . . " Oh, if he does love me! "—she suddenly exclaimed, and, unabashed by the light which illuminated her, she stretched out her arms in an embrace. . . .

She rose, dressed herself, went down-stairs. No one was awake in the house as yet. She went into the garden; but in the garden it was so still, and green, and cool, the birds chirped so confidingly, the flowers gazed forth so gaily, that she felt uncomfortable.—" Oh! "—she thought, " if it is true, there is not a single blade of grass which is happier than I,—but is it true? " She returned to her chamber, and, for the sake of killing time, began to change her gown. But everything slipped and fell from her hands, and she was still sitting, half-clad, in front of her dressing-glass when she was summoned to drink tea. She went down-stairs; her mother observed her pallor, but said merely: " How interesting thou art to-day! " and, sweeping a glance over her, she added: "That gown is very becoming to thee; thou shouldst always put it on when thou hast a mind to please any one." Eléna made no reply, and seated herself in a corner. In the meanwhile, the clock struck nine; two hours still remained before eleven. Eléna took up a book, then tried to sew, then took to her book again; then she made a vow to herself that she would walk the length of one avenue one hundred times, and did it; then for a long time she watched Anna Vasílievna laying out her game of patience . . . . and glanced at the clock: it was not yet ten. Shúbin came into the drawing-room. She tried to talk to him, and begged him to excuse her, without knowing why she did so. . . . Her every word did not so much cost her an effort as it evoked in her a sort of surprise. Shúbin bent down to her. She expected a jeer, raised her eyes, and beheld before her a sorrowful and friendly face. . . She smiled at that face. Shúbin also smiled at her in silence, and quietly left the room. She wanted to detain him, but did not immediately recall his name. At last the clock struck eleven. She began to wait, wait, wait, and listen. She could no longer do anything: she had ceased even to think. Her heart came to life, and began to beat more and more loudly, and, strange to say! the time seemed to fly more swiftly. A quarter of an hour elapsed, half an hour passed, several minutes more passed, as it seemed to Eléna; and suddenly she started: the clock did not strike twelve, it struck one.— "He will not come, he is going away without saying good-bye. . . ." This thought, together with the blood, rushed to her head. She felt that she was choking, that she was on the point of sobbing. . . . She ran to her room, and fell face down on her clasped hands on the bed.

For half an hour she lay motionless; tears streamed between her fingers on the pillow. Suddenly she sat up: something strange had taken place in her; her face underwent a change, her wet eyes dried of their own accord and beamed, her eyebrows drew together, her lips compressed themselves. Another half-hour passed. For the last time, Eléna bent her ear to hear whether a familiar voice would be wafted to her. She rose, put on her hat and gloves, threw a mantilla over her shoulders, and slipping unseen out of the house, she walked briskly along the road which led to Berséneff's lodging.

XVIII

Eléna walked along with drooping head and eyes fixed unswervingly in front of her. She feared nothing, she considered nothing; she wanted to see Insároff once more. She walked on, without noticing that the sun had long since disappeared, veiled in heavy, dark clouds, that the wind was roaring in gusts among the trees and whirling her gown about, that the dust had risen suddenly, and was sweeping in a column along the road. . . . Large raindrops began to patter, she did not notice them; but the rain came faster and faster, with constantly increasing violence, the lightning flashed, the thunder pealed. Eléna halted, and glanced about her. . . . Fortunately for her, not far from the spot where the thunderstorm had overtaken her, there was an ancient, abandoned chapel, over a ruined well. She ran to it, and entered beneath the low shed. The rain poured down in torrents; the whole sky was obscured. With mute despair Eléna stared at the fine network of swiftly falling drops. Her last hope of seeing Insároff had vanished. A poor old beggar-woman entered the little chapel, shook herself, said with an obeisance, " Out of the rain, dear little mother," and, grunting and groaning, seated herself on a projection beside the well. Eléna put her hand in her pocket: the old woman observed the gesture, and her face, wrinkled and yellow, but once beautiful, lighted up. " Thank thee, my benefactor, my dear," she began. There was no purse in Eléna's pocket, but the old woman still held her hand outstretched. . . .

" I have no money, granny,"—said Eléna,— " but here, take this, it will be of some use."

She gave her her handkerchief.

" O-okh, my beauty,"—said the beggar-woman, " of what use to me is thy little kerchief? None, unless to give to my granddaughter when she marries. May the Lord reward thee for thy kindness! "

A clap of thunder pealed out.

" O Lord Jesus Christ," muttered the beggar, and crossed herself thrice.—" But I think I 've seen thee before,"—she added, after a pause. " Hast not thou given me Christ's alms? "

Eléna cast a glance at the old woman, and recognised her.

" Yes, granny,"—she replied.—" Didst not thou ask me why I was so sad? "

" Just so, my dear, just so. That 's how I knew thee. And thou seemest to be living in affliction now also. Here, thy little handkerchief is damp—with tears, of course. Okh, you young girls, you all have one grief, one great woe! "

"What grief, granny?"

"What grief? Ekh, my good young lady, thou canst not dissemble with me, an old woman. For I have been young myself, my dear, I too have passed through those trials. Yes. And here 's what I will say to thee, for thy kindness: if a good man, not a giddy fellow, has fallen to thy lot, do thou cling to him—cling tighter than death. If it is to be, it will be; if it is not to be, evidently such is the will of God. Yes. Why art thou surprised at me? I 'm that same fortune-teller. If thou wishest, I will carry away all thy woe with thy handkerchief! I 'll carry it away, and that 's the end of it. Seest thou, the rain is slackening; do thou wait a bit yet, but I will go on. It won't be the first time I 've been drenched by it. Now remember, my dear little dove: there was a grief, the grief has flowed away, there is not a trace of it. Lord, have mercy!"

The beggar rose from the projection, emerged from the chapel, and went her way. Eléna stared after her in amazement. "What does it mean?" she whispered involuntarily.

The rain descended in a steadily decreasing network, the sun flashed forth for a moment. Eléna was already preparing to abandon her refuge. All at once, half a score of paces from the chapel, she beheld Insároff. Wrapped in his cloak, he was walking along the selfsame road by which Eléna had come; he appeared to be hastening homeward.

She braced herself with her hand on the decrepit railing of the little porch, and tried to call him, but her voice failed her. . . . Insároff was already passing on without raising his head. . . . .

"Dmítry Nikanórovitch!"—she said at last. Insároff came to an abrupt halt, and glanced around. . . . . At the first moment he did not recognise Eléna, but he immediately advanced toward her.—"You! you here!" he exclaimed.

She drew back, in silence, into the chapel. Insároff followed Eléna.

"You here?"—he repeated.

Still she said nothing, and merely gazed at him with a sort of long, soft glance. He dropped his eyes.

"You have come from our house?"—she asked him.

"No . . . not from your house."

"No?"—repeated Eléna, and tried to smile. —"Is that the way you keep your promises? I have been expecting you all the morning."

"I made no promise yesterday, if you remember, Eléna Nikoláevna."

Again Eléna smiled faintly, and passed her hand across her face. Both face and hand were very pale.—"Evidently, you meant to go away without saying good-bye to us?"

"Yes,"—said Insároff, surlily and dully.

" What? After our acquaintance, after those conversations, after everything. . . . Consequently, if I had not met you here by chance " (Eléna's voice began to tremble, and she paused for a moment) . . . " you would have gone away, and would not have pressed my hand for the last time, and you would not have regretted it? "

Insároff turned away.—" Eléna Nikoláevna, please do not talk like that. Even without that, I am not in a cheerful mood. Believe me, my decision has cost me a great effort. If you knew . . . . ."

" I do not wish to know,"—Eléna interrupted him, in affright,—" why you are going. . . . Evidently, it is necessary. Evidently, we must part. You would not grieve your friends without cause. But do friends part in this way? For you and I are friends, are we not? "

" No,"—said Insároff.

" What? . . ." said Eléna. Her cheeks became suffused with a faint flush.

" That is precisely the reason why I am going away,—that we are not friends. Do not force me to say that which I do not wish to say,—which I will not say."

" You were frank with me in former days," articulated Eléna, with a tinge of reproach.

" I could be frank then,—I had nothing to hide; but now . . . ."

" But now? "—asked Eléna.

" But now . . . . But now I must depart. Farewell."

If, at that moment, Insároff had raised his eyes to Eléna, he would have perceived that her face was growing brighter and brighter, in proportion as he himself grew more frowning and lowering; but he stared persistently at the floor.

" Well, good-bye, Dmítry Nikanórovitch,"— she began.—" But, at least, since we have already met, give me your hand now."

Insároff started to extend his hand.—" No, I cannot do that, either,"—he said, and again turned away.

" You cannot? "

" I cannot. Farewell." And he went toward the exit from the chapel.

" Wait a little longer,"—said Eléna.—" You seem to be afraid of me. But I am braver than you are,"—she added with a sudden slight shiver coursing all over her body.—" I can tell you . . . would you like to have me? . . . . why you have found me here? Do you know where I was going? "

Insároff looked at Eléna in amazement.

" I was going to you."

" To me? "

Eléna covered her face.—" You have wanted to make me say that I love you,"—she whispered: —" there now . . . . I have said it."

" Eléna! "—cried Insároff.

She removed her hands, cast a glance at him, and threw herself on his breast.

He held her in a close embrace, and remained silent. There was no need for him to tell her that he loved her. Eléna could understand, from his mere exclamation, from the instantaneous transfiguration of the whole man, from the way in which the bosom to which she clung so confidingly rose and fell, from the way in which the tips of his fingers caressed her hair, that she was beloved. He maintained silence, and she required no words. " He is here, he loves . . . . What more is needed? " The silence of bliss, the silence of a tranquil harbour, of a goal attained, that heavenly silence which imparts even to death itself both meaning and beauty, filled her whole being with its divine flood. She wished for nothing, because she possessed everything.—" Oh, my brother, my friend, my dear! "—whispered her lips, and she herself did not know whose heart it was, his or hers, which beat so sweetly and melted in her breast.

And he stood motionless, he held in his strong embrace this young life which had surrendered itself to him, he felt on his breast this new, infinitely precious burden: a feeling of emotion, a feeling of inexpressible gratitude, shattered his firm soul to dust, and tears, which he had never yet shed, welled up to his eyes. . . . .

But she did not weep; she merely kept reiterating: " Oh, my friend,—oh, my brother! "

" So thou wilt follow me everywhere? "—he said to her, a quarter of an hour later, still holding her, as before, in his embrace, and supporting her.

" Everywhere, to the end of the world. Where thou art, there I shall be."

" And thou art not deceiving thyself, thou knowest that thy parents will never consent to our marriage? "

" I am not deceiving myself; I know it."

" Thou knowest that I am poor, almost a beggar? "

" Yes."

" That I am not a Russian, that it is not decreed that I shall dwell in Russia, that thou wilt be compelled to break all thy ties with thy fatherland, with thy kin? "

" I know, I know."

" Thou knowest, also, that I have consecrated myself to a difficult cause, an ungrateful cause, that I . . . that we shall be forced to undergo not only dangers, but even privations,—humiliation, perchance? "

" I know, I know everything . . . . I love thee! "

" That thou wilt be obliged to abandon all thy habits,—that yonder, alone, among strangers, thou mayest be compelled, perhaps, to toil . . . . "

She laid her hand on his lips.—"I love thee, my darling."

He began passionately to kiss her slender, rosy hand. Eléna did not remove it from his lips, and with a sort of childlike joy, with laughing curiosity, she looked on while he covered now the hand, now its fingers, with kisses. . . .

All at once she flushed scarlet, and hid her face on his breast.

He raised her head caressingly, and gazed intently into her eyes.—"Long live my wife, before men and before God!" he said to her.

XIX

An hour later, Eléna, with her hat on one arm, her mantilla on the other, entered the drawing-room of the villa. Her hair was slightly out of curl, a tiny pink spot was visible on each cheek, the smile refused to depart from her lips, her eyes, blinking and half-shut, also smiled. She could hardly walk from fatigue, but this fatigue was agreeable to her, and everything pleased her. Everything seemed to her fair and caressing. Uvár Ivánovitch was sitting near the window; she went up to him, laid her hand on his shoulder, stretched herself a little, and laughed in an involuntary sort of way.

" What is it? " he asked, in surprise.

She did not know what to say. She wanted to kiss Uvár Ivánovitch.

" Splash, ker-flop! " she said at last.

But Uvár Ivánovitch did not move an eyelash, and kept on staring in astonishment at Eléna. She dropped her hat and mantilla on him.

" My dear Uvár Ivánovitch,"—she said,—" I am sleepy, I am tired,"—and again she began to laugh, and dropped into an arm-chair beside him.

" H'm,"—shouted Uvár Ivánovitch, and began to twiddle his fingers.

And Eléna looked around her, and thought:
—" I must soon part from all this . . . and it
is strange: I have no fear, no doubt, no pity. . . .
No, I am sorry for mamma! " Then again the
chapel rose up before her, again her voice rang
out, she felt his arms around her, her heart was
glad, but stirred feebly: the languor of happiness lay upon it. She recalled the old beggar-
woman. " She really did carry away all my
woe,"—she thought. " Oh, how happy I am!
how undeserved it is! how sudden!" If she had let
go of herself in the slightest degree, she would
have shed sweet, interminable tears. She restrained them only by laughing. Whatever attitude she assumed, it seemed to her that there
could be none better, more easy: it was as though
she were being rocked to sleep. All her movements were slow and soft; what had become of
her precipitation, her angularity? Zóya entered:
Eléna decided that she had never beheld a more
charming little face; Anna Vasílievna entered:
Eléna felt a prick of compunction, but with
what tenderness did she embrace her kind mother,
and kiss her on the brow, near the hair, which was
already beginning to turn grey! Then she betook
herself to her own room: how everything smiled
at her there! With what a sensation of shamefaced triumph and submission did she seat herself on her bed, where, three hours before, she had
spent such bitter moments! " And, of course, I

knew even then that he loved me," she thought, —" yes, and before that . . . Aï, no! no! that is a sin. ' Thou art my wife . . .' " she whispered, covering her face with her hands, and flung herself on her knees.

Toward evening she became more pensive. Sadness took possession of her at the thought that she would not soon see Insároff again. He could not remain with Berséneff without arousing suspicion, so this is what he and Eléna had decided upon: Insároff was to return to Moscow, and come to visit them a couple of times before the autumn; she, on her side, had promised to write him letters, and, if possible, appoint a meeting somewhere in the neighbourhood of Kúntzovo. At tea-time she descended to the drawing-room, and found there all her own household, and Shúbin, who looked keenly at her as soon as she made her appearance; she wanted to chat with him, in a friendly way, but, as of old, was afraid of his penetration, was afraid of herself. It struck her that not for nothing had he left her in peace for more than two weeks. Berséneff soon arrived, and transmitted to Anna Vasílievna Insároff's greeting, together with his apologies for having returned to Moscow, without having presented his respects to her. The name Insároff was uttered, for the first time that day, in Eléna's presence; she felt that she blushed; she understood, at the same time, that it was proper for her to express her regret at the departure of so good an acquaintance: but she could not force herself to dissimulate, and continued to sit motionless and silent, while Anna Vasílievna moaned and grieved. Eléna tried to keep near Berséneff: she was not afraid of him, although he knew a part of her secret; she sought refuge under his wing from Shúbin, who continued to stare at her—not sneeringly, but attentively. Berséneff, also, was overcome by surprise in the course of the evening: he had expected to see Eléna more melancholy. Happily for her, a dispute about art arose between him and Shúbin—she moved away, and listened to their voices as though athwart a dream. Gradually, not only they, but the whole room, everything which surrounded her, began to seem to her like a dream—everything: the samovár on the table, and Uvár Ivánovitch's short waistcoat, and Zóya's smooth finger-nails, and the portrait in oils on the wall of Grand Duke Konstantín Pávlovitch, everything retreated, everything became shrouded in a mist, everything ceased to exist. Only, she felt sorry for them all. " What do they live for? " she thought.

" Art thou sleepy, Lénotchka? "—her mother asked her. She did not hear her mother's question.

" A half-just suggestion, dost thou say? " . . . These words, sharply uttered by Shúbin, suddenly aroused Eléna's attention. "Good gracious,"—he went on,—"that is what taste itself consists of. A half-just suggestion evokes despondency,—that is not according to Christianity; man is indifferent to the unjust,—that is stupid,—but he feels vexation and impatience at the half-just. For instance, if I were to say that Eléna Nikoláevna is in love with one of us, what sort of a suggestion would that be, eh?"

"Akh, Monsieur Paul,"—said Eléna, "I would like to show you my vexation, but really I cannot. I am very tired."

"Why dost not thou go to bed?"—said Anna Vasílievna, who always dozed in the evening herself, and therefore liked to send others to bed. —"Bid me good-night, and go under God's protection,—Andréi Petróvitch will excuse thee."

Eléna kissed her mother, bowed to all, and left the room. Shúbin escorted her to the door.— "Eléna Nikoláevna," — he whispered to her on the way: "You trample upon Monsieur Paul, you walk pitilessly over him, but Monsieur Paul blesses you, and your little feet, and the shoes on your little feet, and the soles of your shoes."

Eléna shrugged her shoulders, unwillingly offered him her hand—not the one which Insároff had kissed—and, on reaching her room, she undressed at once, went to bed, and fell asleep. Her slumber was profound, tranquil . . . . . such as not even children have; only a convalescent child, whose mother is sitting beside his cradle, gazing at him and listening to his breathing, sleeps in that way.

XX

" Come to my room for a minute,"—said Shúbin to Berséneff, as soon as he had bidden Anna
Vasílievna good-night:—" I have something to
show thee."

Berséneff went to his room in the wing. He
was surprised at the multitude of studies, statu-
ettes, and busts, enveloped in damp cloths, and
set about in all corners of the room.

" I see that thou art at work in earnest,"—he
remarked to Shúbin.

" A fellow must do something,"—replied the
latter.—" If one thing does n't succeed, another
must be tried. However, I, like a Corsican, occupy myself more with the vendetta than with
pure art. *Treme Bisanzia!*"

" I do not understand thee,"—said Berséneff.

" Just wait. See here, please to inspect, my
dear friend and benefactor, my vengeance number one."

Shúbin removed the wrappings from one
figure, and Berséneff beheld a capital bust of Insároff, with an excellent resemblance to the original. Shúbin had seized the features faithfully,
to the very smallest detail, and had imparted

to him a magnificent expression: honourable, noble, and bold.

Berséneff went into raptures.

" Why, this is simply splendid! "—he cried.— " I congratulate thee. It is fit for the exhibition! Why dost thou call this a magnificent product of revenge? "

" Why, sir, because I intend to present this magnificent product, as you are pleased to express it, to Eléna Nikoláevna, on her name-day. Do you understand this allegory? We are not blind, we see what goes on around us, but we are gentlemen, my dear sir, and we take our revenge in a gentlemanly way."

" And here,"—added Shúbin, unveiling another figure,—" since the artist, according to the newest code of æsthetics, enjoys the enviable right of incarnating in his own person all sorts of turpitudes, elevating them to a pearl of creation, so we, in elevating this pearl, number two, have avenged ourselves not at all after a gentlemanly fashion, but simply *en canaille*."

He cleverly pulled away the sheet, and there presented itself to the eyes of Berséneff a statuette, in Dantesque taste, of that same Insároff. Anything more malicious and witty it would have been impossible to imagine. The young Bulgarian was represented as a ram rearing on its hind legs and inclining its horns to butt. Stupid dignity, passion, stubbornness, awkwardness, limitedness, were fairly stamped upon the physiognomy of " the spouse of thin-legged sheep," and, at the same time, the likeness was so striking, so indubitable, that Berséneff could not help roaring with laughter.

" Well? Is it amusing?"—said Shúbin:— " hast recognised the hero? Dost thou advise me to send that to the exhibition also? This, my dear fellow, I shall present to myself on my own name-day. . . . . Your High-Born, permit me to cut a caper!"

And Shúbin gave three leaps, hitting himself behind with the soles of his shoes.

Berséneff picked up the sheet from the floor, and threw it over the statuette.

" Okh, thou art magnanimous," began Shúbin. —" Who the deuce is it, in history, who is considered particularly magnanimous? Well, never mind! But now,"—he went on, solemnly and sadly unwrapping a third, rather large mass of clay,—" thou shalt behold something which shall prove to thee the meekness and perspicacity of thy friend. Thou shalt convince thyself, once more, how a true artist feels the need and the benefit of boxing his own ears. Behold!"

The sheet fluttered in the air, and Berséneff beheld two heads, placed side by side and close together, as though they had grown fast. . . . . He did not immediately comprehend the point; but, on looking more closely, he recognised in one of them Ánnushka, and in the other Shúbin himself. They were, however, caricatures rather than portraits. Annushka was represented as a handsome, plump girl with a low brow, eyes swimming in fat, and a saucily upturned nose. Her large lips smiled brazenly; her whole face expressed sensuality, heedlessness, and audacity not devoid of good-nature. Shúbin had depicted himself as a gaunt, lean reveller, with sunken cheeks, feebly dangling wisps of thin hair, a senseless expression in his dim eyes, and a nose sharpened like that of a corpse.

Berséneff turned away in disgust.

" A pretty couple, is n't it, brother? "—said Shúbin.—" Wilt not thou condescend to write an appropriate inscription? I have devised inscriptions for the first two pieces. Under the bust will stand: ' A Hero who intends to save his Fatherland!'—Under the statuette: ' Sausage-makers, beware!' And under this piece—what thinkest thou of this?—' The future of the artist Pável Yakóvleff Shúbin.' .... Is that good? "

" Stop,"—returned Berséneff.—" Was it worth while to waste time on such ....." he could not immediately hit upon a fitting word.

" An odious thing, didst thou mean to say? No, brother, pardon me, if anything is to go to the exhibition, it should be this group."

" An odious thing, that 's precisely what it is," —repeated Berséneff.—" And why this non-sense? Thou hast not in thee those pledges for such a development wherewith, unhappily, our artists are so abundantly gifted. Thou hast simply calumniated thyself."

" Dost thou think so? "—said Shúbin gloomily. —" If they do not exist in me, and if I get inoculated with them, . . . a certain person will be responsible for it. Art thou aware,"—he added, with a tragic frown,—" that I have already tried to drink? "

" Art thou lying? "

" I have tried—by God! I have,"—returned Shúbin, and suddenly grinned and beamed,— " and it tastes bad, brother, it gets into your throat, and your head is like a drum afterward. Even the great Lushtchíkin—Kharlámpy Lushtchíkin, the greatest funnel in Moscow, and, according to others, the ' Great-Russian Funnel '— declared that I should never come to anything. The bottle is nothing to me, according to his words."

Berséneff tried to deal a blow at the group, but Shúbin withheld him.—" Enough, brother, don't strike; it 's good as a lesson, as a scarecrow."

Berséneff began to laugh.

" In that case, all right, I 'll spare thy scarecrow,"—said he—" and long live eternal, pure art! "

" Yes, long may it live! "—chimed in Shúbin. —" With it good is better, and bad is no calamity! "

The friends shook hands warmly, and parted.

XXI

Eléna's first sensation, on awaking, was joyful terror. " Is it possible? Is it possible? " she asked herself, and her heart swooned with happiness. Memories surged in upon her . . . . she was submerged by them. Then again, that same blissful, enraptured silence overshadowed her. But in the course of the morning, Eléna was gradually invaded by uneasiness, and during the days which followed she felt weary and bored. She knew now what she wanted, it is true, but that made it none the easier for her. That never-to-be-forgotten meeting had wrenched her forever out of the old rut: she no longer stood in it, she was far away, and yet everything around her went on in its customary routine, everything took its course, as though nothing were changed; the former life moved on as before; as formerly, Eléna's sympathy and co-operation were counted upon. She tried to begin a letter to Insároff, but even that did not succeed: the words came out on the paper, not exactly dead, but false. She ended her diary: underneath the last line she drew a large dash. That was the past, and with all her thoughts, with all her being, she had gone on into the future. She was ill at ease. To sit with her mother, who suspected nothing, to listen to her, to answer her—to talk with her—seemed to Eléna a sort of crime; she was conscious of the presence in herself of something false; she grew agitated, although she had nothing to blush for; more than once there arose in her soul an almost unconquerable desire to reveal everything, without reserve, no matter what might happen afterward. "Why," she thought, "did not Dmítry carry me off then, from the chapel, whithersoever he wished? Did not he tell me that I am his wife in the sight of God? Why am I here?" She suddenly began to avoid every one, even Uvár Ivánovitch, who was more amazed and wiggled his fingers more than ever. Nothing around her seemed to her either pleasing, or nice, or even a dream; like a nightmare it oppressed her breast with an immovable, dead burden: it seemed to be reproaching her, and raging at her, and wanting to have nothing to do with her. . . . "Thou art ours, nevertheless," it seemed to say. Even her poor nurslings, the persecuted birds and beasts, gazed at her—at least, so it seemed to her—distrustfully and in hostile wise. She became remorseful and ashamed of her feelings. "But this is my home, all the same," she thought; "my family, my native land. . ."—"No, it is no longer thy native land, it is not thy family,"—another voice kept asserting. Terror took pos-

session of her, and she was vexed at her pusilla-
nimity. The mischief was only beginning, and
she had already lost patience. . . Was that what
she had promised?

She did not speedily regain control of herself.
But one week passed, then another. . . . Eléna
had recovered her composure somewhat, and had
grown used to her new position. She wrote two
little notes to Insároff, and carried them herself
to the post-office: not on any account—both because of bashfulness and from pride—could she
have made up her mind to confide in her maid.
She had already begun to expect him. . . But in
his stead, one fine morning, Nikolái Artémievitch made his appearance.

XXII

No one in the household had ever yet beheld retired Ensign of the Guards Stákhoff so sour and,
at the same time, so self-confident and pompous
as on that day. He came into the drawing-room
in overcoat and hat,—came in slowly, planting his
legs wide apart, and clicking his heels; he walked
up to the mirror, and gazed long at himself, shaking his head and biting his lips with calm severity.
Anna Vasílievna greeted him with outward excitement and inward joy (she never greeted him
otherwise); he did not even take off his hat, did
not even bid her good-morning, and silently permitted Eléna to kiss his chamois-leather glove.
Anna Vasílievna began to question him about his
course of treatment—he made her no reply; Uvár
Ivánovitch made his appearance,—he glanced at
him and said: " Ba! " As a rule, he treated Uvár
Ivánovitch coldly and condescendingly, although
he recognised in him " traces of the genuine Stákhoff blood." It is a well-known fact that almost
all Russian noble families are convinced of the
existence of exclusive race characteristics, peculiar to them alone: more than once it has been our
lot to hear discussions " among our own people "
concerning " Podsaláskinsky " noses, and " Pe-

repryéevsky " napes. Zóya came in, and made a curtsey before Nikolái Artémievitch. He grunted, threw himself into an arm-chair, ordered coffee, and only then did he take off his hat. The coffee was brought to him; he drank a cupful and, gazing at each person present in turn, articulated through his teeth: " *Sortez, s'il vous plait,*" and turning to his wife, he added: " *Et vous, madame, restez, je vous prie.*"

All left the room, with the exception of Anna Vasílievna. Her head was trembling with excitement. The solemnity of Nikolái Artémievitch's mien impressed her. She expected something unusual.

" What is it? " she cried, as soon as the door was shut.

Nikolái Artémievitch cast an indifferent glance at Anna Vasílievna.

" Nothing in particular. What do you mean by putting on the aspect of some sort of a victim? " he began, quite unnecessarily pulling down the corners of his mouth at every word.— " I only wanted to warn you that you will have a new guest at dinner to-day."

" Who is it? "

" Kurnatóvsky, Egór Andréevitch. You do not know him. Chief secretary in the Senate."

" Is he to dine with us to-day? "

" Yes."

" And it was merely for the purpose of saying

this to me that you have made every one leave the room?"

Again Nikолái Artémievitch cast a glance at Anna Vasílievna,—this time an ironical glance.

"Does that surprise you? Wait a bit, before you are surprised."

He relapsed into silence. Anna Vasílievna also preserved silence for a while.

"I should like . . . ." she began . . . .

"I know that you have always regarded me as an 'immoral' man,"—began Nikолái Artémievitch suddenly.

"I!" murmured Anna Vasílievna, in amazement.

"And perhaps you are right. I do not wish to deny that, as a matter of fact, I have sometimes given you just cause for dissatisfaction" ("The grey horses!" flashed through Anna Vasílievna's head),—"although you must confess, yourself, that with the well-known state of your constitution . . . ."

"But I am not blaming you in the least, Nikолái Artémievitch."

"*C'est possible.* At any rate, I have no intention of justifying myself to-day. Time will justify me. But I consider it my duty to assure you that I know my obligations, and am capable also of looking out . . . . for the interests of . . . . the family which has been confided to my care."

"What does all this mean?" thought Anna Vasílievna. (She could not know that, on the previous evening, in the English Club, in one corner of the divan-room, a dispute had arisen as to the lack of capacity on the part of Russians to make speeches. "Which of us knows how to talk? Just name some one?" one of the disputants had exclaimed.—"Why, here 's Stákhoff, for instance,"—the other had replied, and had pointed to Nikolái Artémievitch, who was standing near by, and who almost squeaked aloud with satisfaction.)

"For example,"—pursued Nikolái Artémievitch,—"there 's my daughter Eléna. Don't you think that it is time for her to walk with firm tread in the pathway . . . to marry, I mean to say. All these philosophisings and philanthropies are good enough in their way, but only to a certain degree, only to a certain age. It is time for her to come out of the clouds, to emerge from the society of divers artists, scholars, and some Montenegrins or other, and do as everybody else does."

"How am I to understand your words?" asked Anna Vasílievna.

"Here now, be so good as to listen to me,"—replied Nikolái Artémievitch, pulling down his lips as before.—"I will tell you plainly, without circumlocution: I have made acquaintance with—I have become intimate with—this young man, Mr. Kurnatóvsky, in the hope of having him for my son-in-law. I venture to think that, when you have seen him, you will not accuse me of partiality or of precipitancy of judgment." (Nikolái Artémievitch admired his own eloquence as he talked.) "He is excellently educated, a lawyer, with fine manners, thirty-three years of age, chief secretary, collegiate councillor, and wears the order of St. Stanislaus on his neck. You will, I hope, do me the justice to admit that I am not one of those *pères de comédie* who rave over rank alone; but you yourself have told me that Eléna Nikoláevna likes active, resolute men: Egór Andréevitch is the most active man in his profession; now, on the other hand, my daughter has a weakness for magnanimous deeds: so you must know that Egór Andréevitch, just as soon as he attained the possibility—you understand me, the possibility—of existing comfortably on his salary, immediately refused, in the interests of his brothers, to make use of the annual allowance assigned to him by his father."

"And who is his father?" asked Anna Vasílievna.

"His father? His father is also a famous man in his way, of the highest integrity, *un vrai stoique,* a retired major, I believe, and manager of all the estates of the Counts B . . . ."

"Ah!" said Anna Vasílievna.

" Ah! well: what does ' Ah! ' mean? " Nikolái Artémievitch caught her up.—" Do you mean to say that you are infected with prejudices? "

" Why, I did not say anything,"—began Anna Vasílievna.

" Yes, you did; you said: ' Ah! ' . . . At any rate, I have considered it necessary to forewarn you of my way of thinking, and I venture to opine . . . . I venture to hope that Mr. Kurnatóvsky will be received à bras ouverts. He 's no obscure Montenegrin."

" Of course; only, I must summon Vánka, the cook, and order him to add a course."

" You understand that I do not enter into that,"—said Nikolái Artémievitch, rising and putting on his hat, and whistling as he went (he had heard some one say that it is proper to whistle only in one's own house in the country and in the military-riding-school), he strode off for a stroll in the garden. Shúbin peeped at him from the little window of his wing, and silently thrust out his tongue at him.

At ten minutes to four, a posting-carriage drove up to the door of the Stákhoffs' villa, and a man still young, of comely aspect, simply and elegantly attired, alighted from it and ordered that his arrival be announced. He was Egór Andréevitch Kurnatóvsky.

This, among other things, was what Eléna wrote to Insároff on the following day:

" Congratulate me, dear Dmítry, I have a suitor. He dined with us last night; papa made his acquaintance at the English Club, I believe, and invited him. Of course, he did not come as a suitor yesterday. But kind mamma, to whom papa had confided his hopes, whispered in my ear what sort of a visitor he was. His name is Egór Andréevitch Kurnatóvsky; he serves as chief secretary in the Senate. I will first describe to thee his personal appearance. He is short of stature, not so tall as thou art, well built; his features are regular, his hair is closely cut, he wears large side-whiskers. His eyes are small (like thine), brown, alert; his lips flat, broad; in his eyes and on his lips is a perpetual smile, a sort of official smile, as though it were his duty. His manner is very simple, he speaks distinctly, and everything about him is distinct: he walks, laughs, eats, as though he were doing business. ' How she has studied him! ' thou art thinking, perchance, at this moment. Yes; in order that I might describe him to thee. And then, how can one help studying one's suitor. There is something iron about him . . . and something dull and empty at the same time—and honourable; they say that he really is very honourable. At table, he sat next to me, and op- posite sat Shúbin. At first the conversation turned on certain commercial enterprises: they say he is versed in such things, and came near throwing up his position in order to take charge of a large factory. He made a mistake in not doing it! Then Shúbin began to talk about the theatre; Mr. Kurnatóvsky declared—and, I must admit, without any false modesty—that he understood nothing about art. That reminded me of thee . . . but I thought: ' No, after all, Dmítry and I fail to understand art in another way.' This man seemed to be trying to say: ' I do not understand it, and it is unnecessary, but it is permitted in a well-ordered realm.' Toward Petersburg, and the *comme il faut*, however, he is rather indifferent: he once even called himself a proletarian. ' I 'm a common labourer,' he said. I thought: ' If Dmítry had said that, it would not have pleased me, but let this man have his say! let him brag!' He was very courteous toward me; but it seemed to me, all the while, as though a very, very condescending superior official were talking to me. When he wishes to praise any one, he says that So-and-so *has principles*,—that is his favourite expression. He must be self-confident, industrious, capable of self-sacrifice (thou seest: I am impartial), that is to say, in the matter of sacrificing his advantages, but he is a great despot. It would be a calamity to fall into his power! After dinner, they talked about bribes . . . .

" ' I can understand,' said he, ' that, in many cases, the man who takes a bribe is not to blame: he could not act otherwise. But, nevertheless, if he is caught he must be crushed.'

" I exclaimed:—' Crush an innocent man!'

" ' Yes, for the sake of the principle.'

" ' Which one?' inquired Shúbin. Kurnatóvsky was not exactly disconcerted, nor yet precisely astonished, and said: ' There 's no use in explaining it.'

" Papa, who appears to worship him, chimed in, and said that, of course, it was useless, and, to my vexation, that conversation came to an end. In the evening, Berséneff came, and got into a frightful wrangle with him. Never before have I beheld our kind Andréi Petróvitch in such a state of excitement. Mr. Kurnatóvsky did not in the least deny the benefits of science, universities, and so forth . . . yet I understood Andréi Petróvitch's wrath. He looks on all that as a sort of gymnastics. Shúbin approached me after dinner, and said: ' This man, and a certain other ' (he can never utter your name) ' are both practical persons, but behold, what a difference! There is the genuine, living ideal, furnished by life; while here there is not even the sense of duty, but simply official honesty and activity without underpinning.'— Shúbin is clever, and I remembered his words for thee; but, in my opinion, what is there in common between you? Thou *believest*, and the other man does not, because it is *impossible to believe in one's self alone.*

" It was late when he went away, but mamma contrived to inform me that he was pleased with me, that papa was in raptures . . . . I wonder if he has not already said of me that I ' have principles '? And I came near answering mamma, that I was very sorry, but that I already had a husband. Why is it that papa dislikes thee so much? Mamma might have managed, somehow or other . . . .

" Oh, my dear one! I have described this gentleman to thee so circumstantially in order to stifle my anguish. I cannot live without thee,—I see thee, hear thee constantly . . . . I await thee, only not in our house, as thou hast wished,—imagine, how painful and awkward it would be for us!—but, thou knowest, where I wrote thee, in that grove . . . Oh, my darling! How I love thee! "

XXIII

THREE weeks after Kurnatóvsky's first visit,
Anna Vasílievna, to the great joy of Eléna, removed to Moscow, to her great wooden house
near the Pretchístenka,—a house with columns,
white lyres and wreaths over every window, a
second partial storey, servants' quarters, a front
garden, and a huge, verdant courtyard with a
well in the yard and dog-kennels beside the well.
Anna Vasílievna had never returned from her
country villa so early, but that year there was
an epidemic of influenza when the first frosts of
autumn set in; Nikolái Artémievitch, on his side,
having finished his course of treatment, had begun to yearn for his wife; moreover, Augustína
Christiánovna had gone away to visit her cousin
in Revel: some foreign family or other had
arrived in Moscow, and was exhibiting plastic
poses, *des poses plastiques,* the description
of which, in the *Moscow News,* had greatly
excited the curiosity of Anna Vasílievna. In
short, further sojourn in the villa was incon-
venient, and even, as Nikolái Artémievitch
phrased it, incompatible with the execution of his

"previous plans." The last two weeks seemed very long to Eléna. Kurnatóvsky came a couple of times, on Sundays: on other days he was occupied. He came specifically for Eléna, but talked more with Zóya, who liked him very much. *"Das ist ein Mann!"* she thought to herself, as she gazed at his swarthy, manly countenance, and listened to his self-confident, condescending speeches. In her opinion, no one had such a wonderfully fine voice, no one understood so well how to utter: " I had the hon-n-nour! " or, " I am very glad." Insároff did not come to the Stákhoffs, but Eléna saw him once, by stealth, in the little grove, close to the Moscow River, where she had appointed the meeting. They barely managed to exchange a few words with each other. Shúbin returned to Moscow in company with Anna Vasílievna; Berséneff, a few days later.

Insároff was sitting in his chamber, and for the third time re-reading letters which had been brought to him from Bulgaria by private hand: they were afraid to send them by the post. He was greatly startled by them. Events were developing swiftly in the East: the occupation of the principality by the Russian army had agitated all minds; a thunder-storm was brewing, the breath of war, close at hand, inevitable, was already perceptible. The conflagration was increasing round about, and no one could foresee how far it would reach, where it would stop;

ancient griefs, long-cherished hopes—everything was beginning to stir. Insároff's heart beat violently: and *his* hopes also had been realized. "But is it not too early? is it not futile?" he thought, as he clenched his hands. "We are not ready yet.—But so be it! I must go."

There was a faint rattling outside the door, it opened swiftly—and Eléna entered the room.

Insároff began to tremble all over, rushed to her, fell on his knees before her, embraced her waist, and pressed his head close to it.

"Thou didst not expect me?"—she said, panting for breath. (She had run swiftly up-stairs.) "My darling! my darling!—So this is where thou livest? I found thee quickly. The daughter of thy landlady showed me the way. We came to town day before yesterday. I wanted to write to thee, but thought it would be better to come myself. I have come to thee for a quarter of an hour. Rise, lock the door."

He rose, hurriedly locked the door, returned to her, and took her hands. He could not speak, he was suffocating with joy. She gazed into his eyes with a smile . . . . . There was so much happiness in them . . . . She was abashed.

"Wait,"—she said affectionately, drawing her hands away from him.

She untied the ribbons of her hat, flung it aside, dropped the mantilla from her shoulders, smoothed her hair, and seated herself on the small, ancient divan. Insároff did not stir, and gazed at her as though enchanted.

" Sit down,"—said she, without raising her eyes to his, and pointing to a place by her side.

Insároff seated himself, only not on the divan, but on the floor at her feet.

" Here, take off my gloves,"—she said, in a wavering voice. She was beginning to feel alarmed.

He set to work first to unbutton, then to draw off one glove, pulled it half-way off, and glued his lips hungrily to the slender, delicate wrist which shone white beneath it.

Eléna trembled, and tried to push him away with the other hand,—he began to kiss the other hand. Eléna drew it toward her, he threw back his head, she looked into his face, bent forward— and their lips melted together . . . .

A moment passed . . . . She tore herself away, rose, whispered, " No, no," and walked swiftly to the writing-table.

" I am the mistress of the house, here, so thou must have no secrets from me,"—she said, endeavouring to appear at her ease, and standing with her back toward him.—" What a lot of papers! What letters are these? "

Insároff frowned. — " These letters? " — he said, rising from the floor.—" Thou mayest read them."

Eléna turned them over in her hand.—"There

are so many of them, and they are written in such fine script, and I must go away directly . . . . I care nothing for them! They are not from my rival? . . . Why, they are not in Russian,"—she added, as she looked over the thin sheets.

Insároff approached her, and touched her waist. She suddenly turned toward him, smiled brightly at him, and leaned on his shoulder.

" These letters are from Bulgaria, Eléna: my friends write me, they summon me."

" Now? Thither? "

" Yes . . . . now. There is still time, it is still possible to pass through."

Suddenly she flung both arms about his neck. —" Thou wilt take me with thee, wilt thou not? "

He pressed her to his heart.—" O, my dear girl, O my heroine, how hast thou uttered that word! But would not it be a sin, would not it be madness on my part, for me, a homeless, solitary man, to carry thee away with me? . . . And to what a place, moreover! "

She put her hand on his mouth.—" Hush-sh! . . . or I shall get angry, and never come to see thee again. Is not everything settled, is not everything finished between us? Am not I thy wife? Does a wife part from her husband? "

" Wives do not go to war,"—he said, with a half-melancholy smile.

" Yes, when they can stay behind. But can I remain here? "

"Eléna, thou art an angel! . . . But reflect, perhaps I shall be forced to leave Moscow . . . . within a fortnight. I can no longer think of university lectures or of completing my work."

"What of that?" interrupted Eléna.—"Thou must go away soon? Why, if thou wishest it, I will remain with thee now, this very moment, forever with thee, and I will not return home,—wilt thou have it so? Let us set off at once, shall we? "

Insároff clasped her in his arms with redoubled power.—"May God punish me," he cried,—"if I am doing an evil deed! From this day forth, we are united forever! "

"Am I to remain? "—asked Eléna.

"No, my pure girl; no, my treasure. To-day thou art to return home, but hold thyself in readiness. This is an affair which cannot be executed at once; it must be well thought out. Money is needed, a passport . . . . . "

"I have money,"—interrupted Eléna: "eighty rubles."

"Well, that is not much,"—remarked Insároff:—"but everything is useful."

"But I can get more, I can borrow, I can ask mamma . . . . No, I will not ask her . . . . But I can sell my watch . . . . I have earrings, two bracelets, . . . lace."

"It is not a question of money, Eléna; the passport, thy passport, what are we to do about that? "

" Yes, what are we to do about that? But is a passport indispensably necessary? "

" Yes."

Eléna burst out laughing.—" What an idea has occurred to me! I remember, when I was still a little girl, ... a chambermaid left us. She was caught and forgiven; she lived a long time with us; . . . yet every one called her ' Tatyána the Runaway.' I did not think, then, that perhaps I should be a runaway also, like her."

" Art not thou ashamed of thyself, Eléna! "

" Why? Of course, it is better to go with a passport. But if that is impossible . . ."

" We will arrange all that hereafter, hereafter. Wait,"—said Insároff.—"Only give me a chance to look about me, to think it over. We will discuss it all together, in proper fashion. And I have money."

Eléna pushed back with her hand the hair which had fallen over his brow.—" Oh, Dmítry! won't it be jolly to go away together? "

" Yes,"—said Insároff: " and yonder, whither we are going . . . ."

" Well? "—interposed Eléna: " will it not be jolly to die together? but no, why should we die? we shall live, we are young. How old art thou? Twenty-six? "

" Yes."

" And I am twenty. We have a great deal of time ahead of us. Ah! didst thou intend to run away from me? Thou didst not want Russian love, thou Bulgarian! Let us see now, how thou wilt get rid of me! But what would have happened to us, if I had not come to thee?"

"Eléna, thou knowest what made me go away."

"I know: thou hadst fallen in love, and wert frightened. But is it possible that thou didst not suspect that thou wert beloved?"

"I swear by my honour, Eléna, I did not."

She gave him a swift and unexpected kiss.— "That's why I love thee. And now, good-bye."

"Canst not thou remain longer?" asked Insároff.

"No, my darling. Dost thou think that it was easy for me to get away alone? The quarter of an hour is long past."—She put on her mantilla and hat.—"And do thou come to us to-morrow evening. No, the day after to-morrow. It will be constrained, tiresome, but there is no help for it: at least, we shall see each other. Good-bye. Let me go."—He embraced her for the last time. —"Aï! look, thou hast broken my chain. Oh, how awkward! Well, never mind. So much the better. I will pass along the Smiths' Bridge, and leave it to be repaired. If I am asked, I shall say that I have been to the Smiths' Bridge."[1] —She grasped the door-handle.—"By the way, I forgot to tell thee: Monsieur Kurnatóvsky will, in all probability, propose to me in a few days.

[1] The fashionable shopping thoroughfare in Moscow.—TRANSLATOR.

But I shall do . . . this . . . to him."—She placed the thumb of her left hand to the tip of her nose, and flourished the rest of her fingers in the air.—" Good-bye. Until we meet again. Now I know the way . . . . But do not waste time. . . . ."

Eléna opened the door a little way, listened, turned toward Insároff, nodded her head, and flew out of the room.

For a minute, Insároff stood in front of the closed door, and listened also. The door below, opening on the courtyard, slammed. He went to the divan, sat down, and covered his eyes with his hand. Nothing of the sort had ever happened with him before.—" How have I deserved this love? "—he thought.—" Is it not a dream? "

But a faint odour of mignonette which Eléna had left behind her in his poor, dark, little room reminded him of her visit. In company with it, there seemed to linger still in the air the accents of a youthful voice, the sound of light young footsteps, and the warmth and freshness of a young, virgin body.

XXIV

INSÁROFF decided to wait for more decisive news, and began to make preparations for departure. It was a very difficult matter. So far as he himself was concerned, no obstacles awaited him: all he had to do was to ask for his passport,—but what was he to do about Eléna? It was not possible to obtain a passport for her in a legal manner. Marry her in secret, and then present himself with her before her parents? . . . " Then they would let us go,"—he thought. " But what if they did not? We shall go, all the same. But if they enter complaint . . . if . . . No, it will be better to obtain a passport, in some way."

He made up his mind to take counsel (of course, without mentioning any names) with one of his acquaintances, a retired—or, rather, a discharged—procurator, an experienced, clever old fellow in the line of secret affairs. This respected man did not live near by: Insároff jogged along slowly, for a whole hour, in a wretched cab, to him, and did not find him at home, to boot; and on the way back, he got drenched to the marrow, thanks to a heavy shower which suddenly came up. On the following morning, Insároff, in spite of a decidedly violent headache, again wended his way to the retired procurator. The ex-procurator listened to him attentively, taking snuff out of a snuff-box adorned with the picture of a full-busted nymph; and casting sidelong glances at his visitor with his cunning little eyes, which also were snuff-coloured,—listened, and demanded " more circumstantiality in the exposition of the facts"; and observing that Insároff entered unwillingly into details (he had come to him much against his will), he confined himself to the advice to arm himself, first of all, with " cash," and asked him to call again,"when," he added, inhaling snuff over his open snuff-box, " your confidence shall have increased, and your distrust shall have decreased " (he pronounced his o's broadly.[1] " But a passport," he went on, as though to himself, " is a work of—man's hands; you are travelling, for instance: who knows whether you are Márya Bredíkhin, or Karolina Vogelmayer? " A feeling of disgust stirred in Insároff, but he thanked the procurator, and promised to return in a few days.

That evening he went to the Stákhoffs. Anna Vasílievna received him caressingly, reproached him for having completely forgotten them, and, thinking him pale, inquired about his health;

[1] A peculiarity of the clergy, and of those who have received their education in ecclesiastical seminaries, which are open also to those who do not intend to enter the priesthood, for a general education. The Old Church Slavonic, used in the services of the Church, requires that pronunciation. The o is also pronounced thus in certain districts.—TRANSLATOR.

Nikolái Artémievitch did not speak a word to him, but merely looked at him with a pensively-careless curiosity; Shúbin treated him coldly, but Eléna amazed him. She was expecting him; she had put on the gown which she had worn on the day of their first meeting in the chapel; but she greeted him with so much composure, she was so amiable and unconcernedly gay, that, to look at her, no one would have thought that the fate of that young girl was already settled, and that the mere secret consciousness of happy love imparted animation to her features, lightness and charm to all her movements. She poured tea, in company with Zóya, jested, chattered; she knew that Shúbin would watch her, that Insároff would be incapable of donning a mask, would be incapable of feigning indifference, and she had armed herself in advance. She was not mistaken: Shúbin never took his eyes from her, and Insároff was extremely taciturn and gloomy throughout the evening. Eléna felt so happy, that she took it into her head to tease him.

" Well, how goes it? "—she suddenly asked him:—" is your plan progressing? "

Insároff was disconcerted.

" What plan? "—he said.

" Why, have you forgotten? "—she replied, laughing in his face: he alone could understand the meaning of that happy laugh:—" your selections from Bulgarian authors for Russians? "

" *Quelle bourde!* " muttered Nikolái Artémie-vitch, through his teeth.

Zóya seated herself at the piano. Eléna shrugged her shoulders almost imperceptibly, and indicated the door to Insároff with her eyes, as though sending him home. Then she touched the table twice with her finger, making a pause between, and looked at him. He understood that she was appointing a meeting two days hence, and she smiled swiftly when she perceived that he understood her. Insároff rose, and began to take leave: he felt ill. Kurnatóvsky made his appearance. Nikolái Artémievitch sprang to his feet, raised his right hand above his head, and softly lowered it into the palm of the chief secretary. Insároff tarried a few moments longer, in order to have a look at his rival. Eléna nodded her head stealthily, slyly; the master of the house did not consider it necessary to introduce them to each other; and Insároff went away, after having exchanged a final glance with Eléna. Shúbin pondered and pondered—and argued vehemently with Kurnatóvsky over a juridical question which he knew nothing about.

Insároff did not sleep all night, and in the morning felt ill; but he occupied himself with reducing his papers to order, and with writing letters, but his head was heavy and confused, somehow. By dinner-time he was in a fever: he could eat nothing. The fever augmented rapidly toward evening; an aching pain made its appearance in all his limbs, and he had a torturing headache. Insároff lay down on the same little divan where Eléna had so recently sat; he thought, " I am rightly punished. Why did I betake myself to that old scoundrel? " and tried to get to sleep . . . . . But the malady held him in its grasp. His veins began to throb with fearful violence, his blood blazed with sultry heat, his thoughts circled round and round like birds. He became unconscious. Like a man who has been crushed, he lay prone, and, suddenly, it seemed to him that some one was softly laughing and whispering over him. With an effort he opened his eyes; the light of the candle, which needed snuffing, cut them like a knife . . . . What was this? The old procurator was standing before him in a dressing-gown of figured Oriental stuff, with a bandana handkerchief, as he had seen him on the preceding day . . . . " Karolina Vogelmayer," uttered the toothless mouth. As Insároff gazed, the old man broadened out, swelled, grew, and now he was no longer a man but a tree . . . . Insároff must climb up its branches. He got caught, fell breast downward on a sharp stone, and Karolina Vogelmayer squatted on her heels, in the shape of a female peddler, and lisped: " Patties, patties, patties,"—and then blood flowed, and swords gleamed intolerably . . . . " Eléna! "—and everything vanished in a crimson chaos.

XXV

" Some one has come to you, I don't know what he is,—a locksmith, or something of that sort, seemingly," said his servant to Berséneff, on the following evening:—the man was distinguished for his stern treatment of his master, and for a sceptical turn of mind,—" he wants to see you."

" Call him in,"—said Berséneff.

The " locksmith " entered. Berséneff recognised in him the tailor, the landlord of the lodgings where Insároff lived.

" What dost thou want? " he asked him.

" I have come to your grace,"—began the tailor, slowly shifting from foot to foot, and at times flourishing his right hand, with the last three fingers done up in a bandage.—" Our lodger, whoever he is, is very ill."

" Insároff? "

" Exactly so,—our lodger. I don't know, but yesterday he was on his feet from early morning; in the evening, he only asked for a drink, and my housewife carried water to him; but in the night he began to be delirious, we could hear it through the partition; and this morning he could not speak, and he lies there like a log, and such a fever as he has! 'My God!' I thought, 'who can tell?—the first thing you know, he will die; and I shall have to give notice at the police-station. For he is alone.' And my housewife she says to me: 'Go,' says she, 'to that person, from whom our man hired quarters out of town: perhaps he will tell thee what to do, or will come himself.' So I 've come to your grace, because we cannot, that is . . . ."

Berséneff snatched up his cap, thrust a ruble into the tailor's hand, and immediately drove with him in hot haste to Insároff's lodgings.

He found him lying on the divan unconscious, fully dressed. His face was terribly distorted. Berséneff immediately ordered the landlord and landlady to undress him and carry him to his bed, while he himself flew for a doctor and brought him. The doctor prescribed leeches, Spanish flies, and calomel simultaneously, and ordered him to be bled.

" Is he dangerously ill? " asked Berséneff.

" Yes, very,"—replied the doctor.—" The most violent sort of inflammation of the lungs exists; pneumonia is fully developed, the brain may be implicated also, but the patient is young. His very strength is directed against himself now. I was sent for rather late in the day; however, we will do everything which science demands.

The doctor was still young himself, and believed in science.

Berséneff remained for the night. The landlord and landlady turned out to be kindly and even active folk, as soon as a man was found who took it upon him to tell them what ought to be done. A doctor's assistant made his appearance, and the medical tortures began.

Toward morning, Insaroff recovered consciousness for a few minutes, recognised Berséneff, inquired, " I am ill, apparently? " gazed about him with the dull eyes and languid surprise of a person who is seriously ill, and relapsed into unconsciousness. Berséneff went home, changed his clothing, gathered up some books, and returned to Insároff's lodgings. He had decided to settle down there, for the present, at least. He fenced off the bed with screens, and arranged a little nook for himself near the divan. The day passed neither cheerfully nor quickly. Berséneff absented himself for the purpose of dining. Evening came. He lighted a candle with a shade, and began to read. Everything was quiet round about. In the landlord's quarters, on the other side of the partition, there was audible now a suppressed whispering, now a yawn, now a sigh . . . . One of the family sneezed, and was reproved in a whisper: behind the screens resounded the heavy and uneven breathing, occasionally broken by a brief groan, and an anxious tossing of the head upon the pillow . . . . Strange thoughts descended upon Berséneff. He was in the chamber of a man whose life hung on a thread, of a man who, as he knew, loved Eléna . . . . He recalled the night when Shúbin had run after him and declared to him that she loved him—Berséneff! And now . . . . " What am I to do now? " he asked himself. " Shall I inform Eléna of his illness? Shall I wait? This news is sadder than that which I once imparted to her: 't is strange how fate persists in placing me as a third person between them! " He decided that it was better to wait. His glance fell upon the table, covered with heaps of papers . . . . "Will he carry out his ideas? " thought Berséneff. " Can it be possible that all will vanish? " And he felt sorry for the young life which was being extinguished, and he vowed to himself that he would save it . . . .

It was a bad night. The sick man raved a great deal. Several times Berséneff rose from his little couch, approached the bed on tiptoe, and listened sadly to his mutterings. Once only did Insároff enunciate, with sudden distinctness: " I will not, I will not, thou must not . . ." Berséneff started [1] and looked at Insároff: his face, anguished and ghastly at that moment, was immovable, and his hands lay helpless . . . . " I will not," he repeated, almost inaudibly.

The doctor came early in the morning, shook his head, and prescribed new remedies.—" The

---

[1] In the Russian, it is plain that the " thou " refers to a woman. —TRANSLATOR.

crisis is still remote,"—he said, as he put on his hat.

" And after the crisis? "—asked Berséneff.

" After the crisis? There are two issues: *aut Cæsar, aut nihil.*"

The doctor departed. Berséneff took a few turns in the street: he needed fresh air. He returned, and took up a book. He had finished Raumer long ago: he was now studying Grote.

All at once, the door opened gently, and the head of the landlady's little daughter, covered, as usual, with a heavy kerchief, was thrust into the room.

" Here,"—she said in a low voice, " is the young lady who gave me the ten kopéks that time. . . . ."

The head of the landlady's little daughter disappeared, and in its place Eléna made her appearance.

Berséneff sprang to his feet, as though he had been scalded; but Eléna did not move, did not cry out. . . . She seemed to have comprehended everything in an instant. A strange pallor overspread her face, she approached the screens, glanced behind them, clasped her hands, and stood rooted to the spot. Another moment, and she would have flung herself on Insároff, but Berséneff restrained her:—" What are you doing? "—he said in an agitated whisper.— " You might kill him! "

She reeled. He led her to the little divan, and seated her.

She looked into his face, then measured him with a glance, then fixed her eyes on the floor.

" Is he dying? "—she asked so coldly and calmly that Berséneff was frightened.

" For God's sake, Eléna Nikoláevna,"—he began, " why do you ask that? He is ill, it is true, —and quite dangerously . . . . But we will save him; I will answer for that."

" He is unconscious? "—she asked, in the same manner as before.

" Yes, he is insensible now . . . . That is always the case at the beginning of these illnesses; but that signifies nothing,—nothing, I assure you. Drink this water."

She raised her eyes to his, and he understood that she had not heard his replies.

" If he dies,"—she said, still in the same voice, —" I shall die also."

At that moment Insároff moaned faintly; she shuddered, clasped her head, then began to untie her hat-strings.

" What are you doing? " Berséneff asked her.

She made no reply.

" What are you doing? "—he repeated.

" I shall stay here."

" What . . . . for long? "

" I don't know, perhaps all day, all night, for-ever. . . I don't know."

" For God's sake, Eléna Nikoláevna, come to
your senses. Of course I could not, in the least,
expect to see you here; but, nevertheless, . . . I
assume that you have come hither for a short time.
Remember, they may miss you at home . . . . ."

" And what of that? "

" They will search for you . . . . they will
find you . . . ."

" And what of that? "

" Eléna Nikoláevna! You see . . . he cannot defend you now."

She dropped her head, as though meditating,
raised her handkerchief to her lips, and convulsive
sobs suddenly burst forth from her breast with
shattering force. . . . She flung herself face
down on the couch and tried to stifle them, but
her whole body heaved and throbbed like a bird
which has just been caught.

" Eléna Nikoláevna . . . . for God's sake
. . . ." Berséneff kept repeating over her.

" Ah? What is it? "—rang out Insároff's
voice.

Eléna straightened up, Berséneff stood stock-
still on the spot . . . . After a pause, he approached the bed. Insároff's head was lying, as
before, helplessly on the pillow: his eyes were
closed.

" Is he delirious? "—whispered Eléna.

" Apparently," replied Berséneff; " but that
is nothing; it is always so, especially if . . . ."

" When did he fall ill? "—interrupted Eléna.

" Day before yesterday; I have been here since yesterday. Rely upon me, Eléna Nikoláevna. I will not leave him; all means shall be employed. If necessary, we will call a consultation of doctors."

"" He will die without me,"—she exclaimed, wringing her hands.

" I give you my word to send you news every day about the progress of his malady; and if actual danger should arise . . . ."

" Swear to me that you will send for me instantly, whatever may be the time, by day or night; write a note straight to me . . . . I care for nothing now. Do you hear? do you promise to do this? "

" I promise, in the sight of God."

" Swear it."

" I swear."

She suddenly seized his hand, and before he could draw it away she pressed it to her lips.

" Eléna Nikoláevna . . what are you doing? " he whispered.

" No . . . no . . . it is not necessary . . . ." muttered Insároff incoherently, and sighed heavily.

Eléna approached the screens, clenched her handkerchief in her teeth, and gazed long, long at the sick man. Dumb tears streamed down her cheeks.

" Eléna Nikoláevna,"—said Berséneff to her,
—" he may come to himself and recognise you;
God knows whether that will be well. Besides,
I am expecting the doctor at any minute . . . ."

Eléna took her hat from the divan, put it on,
and paused. Her eyes roved sadly over the room.
She seemed to be recalling . . . .

" I cannot go,"—she whispered at last.

Berséneff pressed her hand.—" Collect your
forces,"—he said,—" calm yourself; you are leaving him in my care. I will go to see you this
very evening."

Eléna glanced at him and said:—" Oh, my
kind friend!" burst out sobbing, and rushed out
of the room.

Berséneff leaned against the door. A sad and
bitter feeling, not devoid of a certain strange
pleasure, oppressed his heart. "My kind friend!"
he thought, and shrugged his shoulders.

" Who is there?"—rang out Insároff's voice.

Berséneff went to him.—" I am here, Dmítry
Nikanórovitch. What do you want? How do
you feel?"

" Only you?" asked the sick man.

" Only I."

" And she?"

" What she?" said Berséneff, almost in affright.

Insároff remained silent.—" Mignonette,"—
he whispered, and his eyes closed again.

XXVI

For eight whole days Insároff hung between life
and death. The doctor came incessantly, feeling
an interest still, as a young man, in a difficult
patient. Shúbin heard of Insároff's dangerous
condition, and visited him; his fellow-countrymen—the Bulgarians—made their appearance;
among them, Berséneff recognised the two strange
figures who had aroused his amazement by their
visit to the villa; all expressed their sincere sympathy, and several offered to take Berséneff's
place at the bedside of the sick man; but he did not
consent, remembering the promise he had made to
Eléna. He saw her every day, and communicated to her by stealth—sometimes in words,
sometimes in a tiny note—all the details of the
malady's course. With what heartfelt appre-
hension did she await him! How she listened to
him, and questioned him! She herself longed
constantly to go to Insároff; but Berséneff entreated her not to do so: Insároff was rarely alone.
On the first day, when she learned of his illness,
she nearly fell ill herself; as soon as she got home
she locked herself up in her room, but she was
called to dinner, and she presented herself in

the dining-room with such a face that Anna Vasílievna was frightened, and insisted upon putting her to bed. However, Eléna succeeded in controlling herself. "If he dies," she kept reiterating, "I shall die also." This thought soothed her, and gave her strength to appear indifferent. Moreover, no one disturbed her: Anna Vasílievna busied herself with her influenza; Shúbin worked with exasperation; Zóya resigned herself to melancholy, and made preparations for perusing "Werther"; Nikolái Artémievitch was greatly displeased by the frequent visits of the "scholar," the more so as his "views" with regard to Kurnatóvsky made but slow progress: the practical chief secretary was perplexed and was waiting. Eléna did not even thank Berséneff: there are services for which it is painful and mortifying to give thanks. Only once, on her fourth meeting with him (Insároff had passed a very bad night, and the doctor had hinted at a consultation),—only at that meeting did she remind him of his oath. "Well, in that case let us go," he said to her. She rose, and started to dress herself. "No,"—he said; "let us wait until to-morrow."—Toward evening, Insároff was a little easier.

Eight days did this trial last. Eléna seemed calm, but could eat nothing, did not sleep at night. A dull pain existed in all her limbs; a sort of dry, burning mist seemed to fill her head. "Our young lady is melting away like a candle," her maid remarked concerning her.

At last, on the ninth day, the crisis came. Eléna was sitting in the drawing-room beside Anna Vasílievna, and, without knowing what she was about, was reading to her the *Moscow News*. Berséneff entered. Eléna cast a glance at him (how swift and timid and piercing and startled was the first glance which she cast at him every time!), and immediately divined that he had brought good news. He smiled and gave her a slight nod: she rose to greet him.

" He has come to himself, he is saved; in a week he will be entirely well,"—he whispered to her.

Eléna put out her hand, as though warding off a blow, and said nothing; but her lips quivered and a crimson flush overspread her whole face. Berséneff entered into conversation with Anna Vasílievna, and Eléna went away to her own room, fell on her knees, and began to pray, to thank God . . . . Light, bright tears streamed from her eyes. She suddenly became conscious of an extreme lassitude, laid her head on her pillow, whispered, " Poor Andréi Petróvitch! " and instantly fell asleep with moist eyelashes and cheeks. It was long since she had slept and had not wept.

XXVII

BERSÉNEFF's words were realised only in part: the danger was past, but Insároff's strength returned slowly, and the doctor talked about a profound and general shock to his whole organism. Nevertheless, the sick man left his bed and began to walk about the room. Berséneff removed to his own lodgings; but he dropped in every day to see his friend, who was still weak, and every day, as before, he informed Eléna as to the condition of his health. Insároff did not dare to write to her, and alluded to her only indirectly in his conversations with Berséneff; while Berséneff, with feigned indifference, told him about his visits to the Stákhoffs, endeavouring, however, to give him to understand that Eléna had been greatly grieved, and that now she had recovered her composure. Neither did Eléna write to Insároff; she had something else in her head.

One day, when Berséneff had just informed her, with a joyful countenance, that the doctor had already given Insároff permission to eat a cutlet, and that now, probably, he would soon be out, she became pensive and dropped her eyes . . .

" Guess what I want to say to you,"—she said. Berséneff was disconcerted. He understood her.

" Probably,"—he replied, averting his eyes:—
" you want to tell me that you wish to see him."

Eléna blushed, and in a barely audible tone
articulated: " Yes."

" Well, what then? I think you will find it
very easy."—(" Fie! " he thought,—" what a
hateful feeling is in my heart! ")

" You mean to say that I have done it already . . . . " said Eléna.—" But I am afraid
. . . . . now, you say, he is rarely alone."

" That is not a difficult matter to remedy,"—
returned Berséneff, still without looking at her.—
" Of course I cannot forewarn him; but give me
a note. Who can prevent your writing to him
. . . to so good a friend, in whom you take an
interest? There is nothing reprehensible in that.
. . . Appoint . . . that is to say, write to him
when you will come."

" I am ashamed,"—whispered Eléna.

" Give me the note, I will carry it."

" That is not necessary; but I wanted to ask
you . . . . do not be angry with me, Andréi Petróvitch . . . . not to go to him to-morrow! "

Berséneff bit his lip.

" Ah! Yes, I understand; very good, very
good."—And adding two or three words more, he
hastily departed.

" So much the better, so much the better,"—
he thought, as he hurried homeward. " I have not
learned anything new, but so much the better.

What 's the use of clinging to the rim of another person's nest? I repent of nothing, I have done what my conscience bade me, but now it is enough. Let them go their way! Not without cause was my father wont to say to me: 'You and I, my dear fellow, are not sybarites, we are not aristocrats, we are not the spoiled darlings of fate and of nature, we are not even martyrs,—we are toilers, toilers, and again toilers. Don thy leathern apron, toiler, and take thyself to thy work-bench, in thy dark workshop! But let the sun shine on others! Our dull life has a pride and a happiness of its own also!' "

On the following morning, Insároff received by the city post a brief note: " Expect me," wrote Eléna, and he gave orders that all callers should be refused.

XXVIII

As soon as Insároff read Eléna's note, he immediately began to put his room to rights, asked his
landlady to carry away the phials of medicine,
took off his dressing-gown, and put on his coat.
His head reeled with weakness and joy, and his
heart beat violently. His legs gave way beneath
him: he dropped on the divan, and began to look
at his watch. " It is now a quarter to twelve,"—
he said to himself:—" she cannot possibly get
here before twelve; I will think of something else
for a quarter of an hour, or I cannot bear it. She
cannot possibly come before twelve . . . . ."

The door opened, and with the light rustle of a
silken gown, all pale and fresh, young and happy,
Eléna entered, and fell upon his breast with a
faint cry of joy.

" Thou art alive, thou art mine,"—she kept
repeating, as she embraced and caressed his head.
He was on the point of swooning; he panted with
this proximity, these touches, this happiness.

She sat down beside him, nestled up to him,
and began to look at him with that laughing,
caressing, and tender glance which beams only in
the loving eyes of women.

Her face suddenly became overcast.

" How thin thou hast grown, my poor Dmí-try,"—she said, passing her hand over his neck,—" what a beard thou hast! "

" And thou, too, hast grown thin, my poor Eléna,"—he replied, catching her fingers with his lips.

She shook back her curls merrily.

" That is nothing. Thou shalt see how we will recover! The storm has passed over, as on the day when we met in the chapel; it has rushed up and passed away."

He replied to her only by a smile.

" Akh, what days, Dmítry, what cruel days! How can people survive those they love! I knew beforehand, every time, what Andréi Petróvitch was going to tell me, I really did: my life sank and rose together with thine. Good morning, my Dmítry! "

He did not know what to say to her. He wanted to throw himself at her feet.

" I have also observed,"—she went on, tossing back his hair—" I have been making a great many observations during this time, in my leisure—when a person is very, very unhappy, with what stupid attention he watches everything which goes on around him! Really, I sometimes stared at a fly, and all the while, what cold and terror there was in my own soul! But all that is over, it is over, is it not? Everything is bright in future, is it not?

" Thou art the future for me,"—replied Insá-roff,—" it is bright for me."

" And for me too! But dost thou remember, when I was with thee then, the last time . . . . no, not the last time,"—she repeated, with an involuntary shudder,—" but when we talked together, I alluded to death, I know not why; I did not then suspect that it was standing guard over us. But thou art well now, art thou not? "

" I am much better, I am almost well."

" Thou art well, thou didst not die. Oh, how happy I am! "

A brief silence ensued.

" Eléna? "—Insároff said interrogatively.

" What, my dear one? "

" Tell me, has it not occurred to you that this illness was sent to us as a chastisement? "

Eléna looked seriously at him.

" That thought has occurred to me, Dmítry. But I thought: Why should I be chastised? What duty have I violated, against what have I sinned? Perhaps my conscience is not like that of others, but it was silent; or, perhaps, I am to blame toward thee?—I hinder thee, I hold thee back . . . ."

" Thou art not holding me back, Eléna; we will go together."

" Yes, Dmítry, we will go together, I will follow thee . . . . That is my duty. I love thee . . . . I know no other duty."

" Oh, Eléna! "—said Insároff:—" what invincible chains does thy word lay upon me! "

" Why talk about chains? "—she interposed. —" We are free people. Yes,"—she went on, gazing thoughtfully at the floor, while with one hand she continued to stroke his hair as before,— " I have gone through a great deal of late, of which I had never the least conception! If any one had predicted to me that I, a well-born, well-bred young lady, would leave the house alone, under divers fictitious pretexts, and go whither besides,—to a young man's lodgings!—how enraged I should have been! And all that has come to pass, and I do not feel the slightest indignation. God is my witness that I do not! " she added, and turned toward Insároff.

He gazed at her with such an expression of adoration, that she gently lowered her hand from his hair to his eyes.

" Dmítry! "—she began again,—" of course thou dost not know, but I saw thee yonder, on that dreadful bed,—I saw thee in the claws of death, unconscious . . . . "

" Thou sawest me? "

" Yes."

He remained silent.—" And was Berséneff here? "

She nodded her head.

Insároff bent toward her.—" Oh, Eléna! " he whispered:—" I dare not look at thee."

" Why? Andréi Petróvitch is so kind! I was
not ashamed before him. And what have I to be
ashamed of? I am ready to tell all the world that
I am thine . . . . . And I trust Andréi Petróvitch like a brother."

" He saved me! "—cried Insároff.—" He is the
noblest, the best of men! "

" Yes . . . . . And knowest thou, that I am
indebted to him for everything? Knowest thou,
that he was the first to tell me that thou lovedst
me? And if I could reveal all . . . . . Yes, he
is a most noble man."

Insároff looked intently at Eléna.—" He is in
love with thee, is he not? "

Eléna dropped her eyes.—" He did love me,"
she said, in a low voice.

Insároff clasped her hand closely.—" Oh, you
Russians,"—he said,—" you have hearts of gold!
And he—he nursed me, he did not sleep at night
. . . . And thou—thou, my angel . . . . No re-
proach, no wavering . . . . and all this for me,
for me! . . . ."

" Yes, yes, all for thee, because thou art beloved. Akh, Dmítry! How strange it is! I think
I have already spoken to thee about it,—but never
mind, it is pleasant to me to repeat it, and it will
be pleasant for thee to hear it,—when I beheld
thee for the first time . . . ."

" Why are there tears in thine eyes? "—Insároff interrupted her.

" Tears? In my eyes? "—She wiped her eyes with her handkerchief.—" Oh, the stupid! He does not yet know that people weep for happiness. As I was going to say: When I beheld thee for the first time, I perceived nothing particular in thee, truly. I remember, at first I liked Shúbin much better, although I never loved him; and as for Andréi Petróvitch,—oh! there was a moment when I thought: Can he be the man? But thou— I felt nothing; on the other hand . . . afterward . . . . afterward . . . . thou didst fairly seize my heart with both hands! "

" Spare me! "—said Insároff. He tried to rise, but immediately sank back on the divan.

" What ails thee? " asked Eléna anxiously.

" Nothing. . . . I am still a little weak . . . . This happiness is beyond my strength."

" Then sit quietly. Do not dare to stir, do not get excited,"—she added, shaking her finger at him.—" And why have you taken off your dressing-gown? It is too early for you to put on foppish airs! Sit still, and I will tell you stories. Listen, and be silent. After your illness, it is injurious for you to talk much."

She began to tell him about Shúbin, about Kurnatóvsky, about what she had been doing for the last fortnight,—that, according to the newspapers, war was inevitable, and consequently, as soon as he should be entirely well, he must find means for departure without wasting a moment's time. . . . She said all this, as she sat by his side, leaning against his shoulder. . . .

He listened to her,—listened, now paling, now flushing . . . . Several times he attempted to stop her, and then he suddenly drew himself up.

" Eléna,"—he said to her, with a strange, harsh sort of voice,—" leave me, go away."

" What,"—she said, with surprise.—" Dost thou feel ill? "—she added quickly.

" No . . . I am all right . . . . but, leave me, please."

" I do not understand thee. Thou art driving me away? . . . What is it thou art doing? "— she said suddenly: he had bent down from the divan almost to the floor, and was pressing his lips to her feet.—" Don't do that, Dmítry . . . . Dmítry . . . ."

He raised himself up, part way.

" Then leave me! Seest thou, Eléna, when I fell ill I did not at once lose consciousness, I knew I was on the verge of destruction; even in my fever, even in my delirium, I was dimly conscious that death was advancing toward me, that I had bidden farewell to life, to thee, to everything, I was parting with hope . . . . and all at once, that revival, that light in the darkness, thou . . . . . thou wert by my side, in my room, ... thy head, thy breath. . . . . This is beyond my strength! I feel that I love thee passionately, I hear thee calling thyself mine, I can answer for nothing. . . . Go away!"

"Dmítry . . . ." whispered Eléna, and hid her head on his shoulder. Only now did she understand him.

"Eléna,"—he went on,—" I love thee, thou knowest it; I am ready to give my life for thee . . . but why hast thou come to me now, when I am weak, when I am not in control of myself, when all my blood is aflame? . . . Thou art mine, thou sayest . . . . thou lovest me . . . . "

"Dmítry,"—she repeated, all flushed, and pressing herself still more closely to him.

" Eléna, have pity on me—go away! I feel I may die—I cannot endure these attacks . . . . my whole soul longs for thee . . . reflect, death has almost parted us . . . and now thou art here, in my arms . . . . Eléna . . . . "

She trembled all over. . . " Then take me," she whispered, almost inaudibly.

XXIX

Nikolái Artémievitch was striding to and fro in his study, with frowning brows. Shúbin was sitting by the window, and, with one leg thrown over the other, was calmly smoking a cigar.

"Please stop pacing from corner to corner," he said, knocking the ashes from his cigar. "I am still waiting to hear what you have to say, I am watching you—and my neck is tired. Moreover, there is something forced, melodramatic, about your stride."

"You want to do nothing but jest,"—replied Nikolái Artémievitch. "You will not enter into my position, you will not understand that I have become accustomed to that woman, that I am attached to her—in short, that her absence must torture me. Here it is almost December, winter is at the end of our noses. . . . What can she be doing in Revel?"

"She must be knitting stockings . . . for herself; for herself—not for you."

"Laugh away, laugh away; but let me tell you, that I do not know such another woman. Such honesty, such disinterestedness . . . ."

"Has she put in that note for collection?" inquired Shúbin.

" Such disinterestedness,"—repeated Nikolái Artémievitch, raising his voice,—" is wonderful. They tell me that there are a million other women in the world; but I say: Show me that million; show me that million, I say: *ces femmes, qu'on me les montre!* And she does not write, —that is what is deadly!"

" You are as eloquent as Insároff,"—remarked Shúbin:—" but do you know what I would advise you to do?"

" When?"

" When Augustína Christiánovna returns . . . you understand me?"

" Well, yes; what then?"

" When you see her . . . . Do you follow the development of my idea?"

" Well, yes, yes."

" Try to beat her: what will be the result?"

Nikolái Artémievitch turned away in wrath.

" I thought he really would give me some practical advice. But what can one expect from him! An artist, a man devoid of principles . . . ."

" Devoid of principles! Why, they say that your favourite, Mr. Kurnatóvsky, a man with principles, cleaned a hundred rubles out of you yesterday. That is not delicate, you must admit."

" What of it? We were playing a commercial game. Of course, I might have expected

215

. . . But people are so incapable of appreciating him in this house . . . ."

" That he thought: ' Here goes! ' " put in Shúbin:—" ' Whether he is to be my father-in-law or not, is a matter which is still hidden in the urn of fate, but a hundred rubles are good for a man who does not take bribes.' "

" Father-in-law! What the devil do you mean by being a father-in-law?—*Vous rêvez, mon cher.* Of course, any other girl would have been delighted with such a suitor. Judge for yourself: he 's a dashing, clever man, he has made his own way in the world, he has toiled hard for a livelihood in two governments . . . ."

" In the Government of * * * *, he led the Governor by the nose,"—remarked Shúbin.

" Very likely. Evidently, that was as it should be. He 's practical, energetic . . . ."

" And plays cards well,"—remarked Shúbin again.

" Well, yes, he does play cards well. But Eléna Nikoláevna . . . . Can she understand? I want to know where is the man who will undertake to understand what she wants? Sometimes she is merry, again she is bored; suddenly, she grows so thin that one does not wish to look at her, and then, all of a sudden, she recovers, and all this without any visible cause . . . . ."

A homely footman entered with a cup of coffee, a cream-jug, and rusks on a tray.

" The father is pleased with the suitor,"—went

on Nikолái Artémievitch, waving a rusk,—" but what does the daughter care about that? That was all right in former, patriarchal times, but now we have changed all that. *Nous avons changé tout ça.* Now a young lady talks with whomsoever she pleases; she goes about Moscow without à lackey, without a maid, as in Paris; and all that is accepted. The other day I asked: ' Where is Eléna Nikoláevna?' I am told, ' She has been pleased to go out.' Whither? No one knows. Is that—proper? "

" Do take your cup, and dismiss the man,"—said Shúbin.—" You yourself say that one should not talk *devant les domestiques,"*—he added in an undertone.

The footman cast a sidelong glance at Shúbin, but Nikolái Artémievitch took his cup, poured himself some cream, and clutched up half a score of rusks.

" What I meant to say," he began, as soon as the servant had left the room,—" is that I am of no account in this house. That 's all. Because, in our day, every one judges by the exterior: one man is empty and stupid, but has a pompous mien,—and he is respected; while another, perhaps, is possessed of talents which might . . . . might be of great service, but owing to his modesty . . . . ."

" Are you a statesman, Nikolínka? " inquired Shúbin, in a very subtle voice.

" Have done with your clownish pranks! " exclaimed Nikolái Artémievitch angrily. You forget yourself! Here's a fresh proof for you that I count for nothing in this house, nothing!"

"Anna Vasílievna persecutes you, poor fellow!" said Shúbin, stretching himself. "Ekh, Nikolái Artémievitch, you and I ought to be ashamed of ourselves! You had better prepare some little gift for Anna Vasílievna. Her birthday comes shortly, and you know how she prizes the smallest token of attention on your part."

"Yes, yes," replied Nikolái Artémievitch hastily:—"I am very much obliged to you for reminding me of it. Of course, of course; without fail. And here, I have a trifle; a little clasp, which I purchased a few days ago at Rosenstrauch's; only, I don't know whether it is suitable?"

"I suppose you bought it for the other one, the resident of Revel?"

"That is ... I ... yes ... I thought ...."

"Well, in that case, it certainly is suitable."

Shúbin rose from his chair.

"Where shall we spend the evening, Pável Yakóvlevitch, hey?" Nikolái Artémievitch asked him, looking him amiably in the eye.

"Why, I suppose you are going to the club."

"After the club .... after the club."

Again Shúbin stretched himself.

"No, Nikolái Artémievitch, I must work to-morrow. Some other time."—And he left the room.

Nikolái Artémievitch frowned, paced up and down the room a couple of times, took from a bureau a small velvet case with the " little clasp," and for a long time gazed at it and 'rubbed it up with his silk handkerchief. Then he sat down in front of the mirror, and began carefully to brush his thick black hair, pompously inclining his head now to the right, now to the left, thrusting his tongue into his cheek, and never taking his eyes from his parting. Some one coughed behind him: he glanced round, and beheld the footman who had brought the coffee.

" Why hast thou come? " he asked him.

" Nikolái Artémievitch! " said the lackey, not without considerable solemnity—" you are our master! "

" I know it: what next? "

" Nikolái Artémievitch, please do not be angry with me; only, as I have been in your grace's service since my youth, it is my duty, out of slavish zeal, to inform you . . . . . "

" Well, what is it? "

The lackey shifted from foot to foot.

" You were pleased to say just now,"—he began,—" that you did not know where Eléna Nikoláevna is pleased to go. I have become acquainted with it."

" What lies art thou telling, fool? "

" I can't help it: only three days ago I saw her entering a certain house."

" Where? what? what house? "

" In the * * * alley, near Povarskáya Street. Not far from here. And I asked the yard-porter. ' What lodgers have you? ' says I."

Nikolái Artémievitch began to stamp his feet.

" Hold thy tongue, rascal! How darest thou? . . . Eléna Nikoláevna, in her kindness of heart, is visiting the poor, and thou . . . . Begone, fool! "

The frightened lackey started for the door with a rush.

" Stop! " shouted Nikolái Artémievitch. " What did the yard-porter say? "

" Why, no . . . . thing,—he said nothing. ' A stu . . . student,' says he."

" Hold thy tongue, rascal! Listen, scoundrel: if thou darest to speak of this to any one, even in thy sleep . . . ."

" Have mercy, sir! . . . ."

" Silence! if thou so much as utterest a sound . . . . if any one . . . . if I hear . . . . thou shalt not find refuge from me even under the earth! Dost hear? Take thyself off! "

The lackey vanished.

" O Lord my God! What is the meaning of this? " thought Nikolái Artémievitch, when he found himself alone:—" what was it that blockhead told me? Hey? But I must find out what house it is, and who lives there. I must go myself. A pretty pass things have come to, upon my word! . . . . *Un laquais! .Quelle humiliation!*"

And repeating aloud, "*Un laquais!*" Nikolái Artémievitch locked up the clasp in his bureau, and betook himself to Anna Vasílievna. He found her in bed, with her cheek in a bandage. But the sight of her sufferings merely irritated him, and he speedily reduced her to tears.

XXX

IN the meantime, the storm which had been brewing in the East broke. Turkey declared war on Russia; the date set for the evacuation of the principalities had already passed; the day of the uprising of Sinope was not far distant. The last letters received by Insároff summoned him importunately to his native land. His health was not yet restored: he coughed, felt weak, and had light attacks of fever, but he hardly remained in the house at all. His soul was on fire; he no longer thought of his illness. He was incessantly going about Moscow; he met various persons by stealth; many a time he wrote all night long; he disappeared for days together; he announced to his landlord that he was going away soon, and presented him, in advance, with his simple furniture. Eléna, on her side, was also making preparations to depart. One stormy evening, she was sitting in her own chamber, and as she hemmed a handkerchief she involuntarily listened with sadness to the howling of the wind. Her maid entered, and told her that her papa was in her mamma's bedroom, and requested her to go thither . . . . " Your mamma is crying,"

—she whispered after the departing Eléna,— " and your papa is in a rage . . . ."

Eléna shrugged her shoulders slightly, and entered Anna Vasílievna's bedroom. Nikolái Artémievitch's good-natured wife was half-reclining in a lounging-chair and sniffing at a handkerchief scented with eau de Cologne; he himself was standing by the fireplace, with his coat buttoned up to the throat, in a tall, stiff neckcloth, and with stiffly-starched cuffs, and dimly suggested by his carriage some parliamentary orator. With an oratorical wave of his hand, he motioned his daughter to a chair, and when she, not understanding his gesture, looked inquiringly at him, he said with dignity, but without turning his head: " I beg that you will be seated." (Nikolái Artémievitch addressed his wife as *you* always and his daughter on extraordinary occasions.)

Eléna sat down.

Anna Vasílievna blew her nose tearfully. Nikolái Artémievitch thrust his right hand into the breast of his coat.

" I have summoned you, Eléna Nikoláevna," —he began, after a prolonged silence, " for the purpose of having an explanation with you—or, I had better say, for the purpose of demanding an explanation from you. I am displeased with you,—or, no: that is putting it too mildly; your conduct afflicts, shocks me—me and your mother

. . . . your mother, whom you see here before you."

Nikolái Artémievitch set in action only the bass notes of his voice. Eléna gazed at him in silence, then at Anna Vasílievna, and turned pale.

" There was a time,"—began Nikolái Artémievitch again,—" when daughters did not permit themselves to look down upon their parents,—when the parental authority made the disobedient tremble. That time is past, unfortunately,—so, at least, many persons think: but, believe me, there still exist laws which do not permit . . . . do not permit . . . . in short, laws still exist. I beg that you will direct your attention to this point: laws exist."

" But, papa,"—Eléna was beginning.

" I request that you will not interrupt me. Let us return, in thought, to the past. Anna Vasílievna and I have performed our duty. Anna Vasílievna and I have spared nothing on your education: neither expense nor solicitude. What profit you have drawn from all this solicitude, from all this expenditure—is another question; but I had a right to think . . . Anna Vasílievna and I had a right to think that you would, at least, sacredly preserve those principles of morality which . . . . which we have . . . . which, as our only daughter . . . . *que nous vous avons inculqués*—which we have inculcated in you. We had the right to think that no new ' ideas ' would touch that, so to speak, stipulated inviolability. And what is the result? I am not now referring to the frivolity inherent in your sex, in your age . . . . but who could have expected that you would so far forget yourself . . . . ."

" Papa,"—said Eléna,—" I know what you want to say. . . . ."

" No, thou dost not know what I want to say!"—shouted Nikolái Artémievitch in a falsetto voice, suddenly abandoning the majesty of his parliamentary demeanour, and his suave dignity of speech, and his bass tones:—" Thou dost not know, audacious chit! . . . ."

" For God's sake, *Nicolas*," lisped Anna Vasílievna,—" *vous me faites mourir*."

" Don't tell me that—*que je vous fais mourir*, Anna Vasílievna! you have not the slightest idea what you are about to hear! Prepare yourself for the worst, I warn you!"

Anna Vasílievna was fairly dumfounded.

" No,"—went on Nikolái Artémievitch, turning to Eléna:—" thou dost not know what I want to say to thee!"

" I am to blame before you . . ." she began.

" Hey, at last, then?"

" I am to blame before you,"—went on Eléna, —" in that I did not, long ago confess . . . . ."

" But dost thou know," Nikolái Artémievitch

interrupted her,—" that I can annihilate thee with a single word? "

Eléna raised her eyes to his.

" Yes, madam, with a single word! You need n't look like that! " (He folded his arms on his chest.) " Permit me to ask you, Are you acquainted with a certain house in * * * alley, near Povarskáya Street? Have you visited that house? " (He stamped his foot.) " Answer me, wretched girl, and do not try to deceive me! People, people, lackeys, madam, *de vils laquais,* have seen you going in there to your . . . . . "

Eléna flushed all over, and her eyes began to sparkle.

" I have no occasion to deceive you," she said; " yes, I have visited that house."

" Very fine! you hear, you hear, Anna Vasílievna. And, probably, you know who lives there? "

" Yes, I know: my husband."

Nikolái Artémievitch stared.

" Thy . . . . . "

" My husband,"—repeated Eléna.—" I am married to Dmítry Nikanórovitch Insároff."

" Thou? . . . Married! . . . " Anna Vasílievna articulated with difficulty.

" Yes, mamma. . . . Forgive me! We were married secretly, a fortnight ago."

Anna Vasílievna fell back in her chair; Nikolái Artémievitch retreated a couple of paces.

" Married! To that trumpery fellow, that Montenegrin! The daughter of Nikolái Stákhoff, a member of the ancient hereditary nobility, married to a tramp, to a man of no caste! Without the parental blessing! And dost thou think that I will leave matters thus? that I shall not make complaint? that I shall permit thee . . . that thou . . . . that . . . . I 'll send thee to a convent, and him to the galleys, to the penitentiary battalion! Anna Vasílievna, be so good as to tell her at once that you will deprive her of her inheritance! "

" Nikolái Artémievitch, for God's sake! " moaned Anna Vasílievna.

" And when, in what way, did this take place? Who performed the marriage ceremony for you? Where? My God! What will all our acquaintances, what will everybody say now! And thou, shameless hypocrite, couldst dwell under the parental roof-tree after such a deed! Hast thou not feared a thunderbolt from heaven? "

" Papa,"—said Eléna (she was trembling all over, from head to foot, but her voice was firm), —" you are at liberty to do what you like with me, but you accuse me without cause of shamelessness and hypocrisy. I did not wish . . . . to grieve you any sooner than was necessary; but I would have told you everything, myself, perforce, in a few days, because my husband and I are going away from here next week."

"Going away? Whither?"

" To his native land,—to Bulgaria."

" To the Turks!" cried Anna Vasílievna, and fell in a swoon.

Eléna darted to her mother.

" Away!" roared Nikolái Artémievitch, and seized his daughter by the arm:—" Begone, unworthy one!"

But, at that moment, the bedroom door opened, and a pale head, with glittering eyes, made its appearance; it was the head of Shúbin.

" Nikolái Artémievitch!" he shouted at the top of his voice:—" Augustína Christiánovna has arrived, and summons you to her!"

Nikolái Artémievitch wheeled round in a towering rage, shook his fist at Shúbin, stood still for a moment, then swiftly left the room.

Eléna fell at her mother's feet, and embraced her knees.

UVÁR IVÁNOVITCH was lying on his bed. A shirt devoid of collar, with a big stud, encircled his fat neck, and fell in broad, loose folds on his almost feminine breast, leaving a large cypress-wood cross and an amulet disclosed to view. A light quilt covered his vast limbs. A candle burned dimly on the night-stand, beside a jug of home-brewed beer, and at Uvár Ivánovitch's feet, on the bed, sat the dejected Shúbin.

" Yes,"—he was saying thoughtfully,—" she

is married, and preparing to depart. Your nice little nephew kicked up a row, and roared so that everybody in the house could hear him; he locked himself into the bedroom, for the sake of privacy, but not only the lackeys and the maids,—the very coachmen could hear him! Now he is tearing and flinging about, he almost came to blows with me, and he is rushing around nursing his parental malediction, like a bear his sore head; but there 's no force in him. Anna Vasílievna is overwhelmed, but she is far more grieved over her daughter's departure than over her marriage."

Uvár Ivánovitch wiggled his fingers.

" A mother,"—said he:—" well . . . you know . . . ."

" Your nice little nephew,"—pursued Shúbin, " threatens to complain to the Metropolitan, to the Governor-General, to the Minister, but it will end in her departure. Who finds it a cheerful matter to ruin his only daughter! He 'll crow for a while, and then lower his tail."

" They have . . . no right," remarked Uvár Ivánovitch, and took a drink from the jug.

" Exactly, exactly. And what a thunder-cloud of condemnation, of rumors, of gossip, will arise in Moscow! She was not afraid of them . . . . However, she is above them. She is going away—and whither! it is terrible even to think of it! To what a distance, to what a God-forsaken place! What awaits her there?

I behold her, as it were, leaving a posting-station by night, in a snow-storm, with the temperature thirty degrees below zero. She is parting with her native land, with her family; but I understand her. Whom is she leaving behind her here? Whom has she seen? Kurnatóvskys, and Berséneffs, and the like of us; and they are the best of the lot. Why regret it? One thing is bad; they say that her husband—the devil knows, my tongue can hardly get around that word—they say that Insároff spits blood; that is bad. I saw him the other day; his face was such that one might model Brutus straight from it . . . . . Do you know who Brutus was, Uvár Ivánovitch?"

"Why should n't I know? A man."

"Precisely: 'he was a man.' Yes, a magnificent face, but unhealthy, very unhealthy."

"For fighting . . . it makes no difference," said Uvár Ivánovitch.

"For fighting, it makes no difference, exactly so; you are pleased to express yourself with perfect justice to-day; but for living, it does make a difference. And I suppose he and she wish to live together."

"It 's the way of young people," replied Uvár Ivánovitch.

"Yes, it 's a young, splendid, fearless way. Death, life, struggle, fall, triumph, love, freedom, fatherland . . . . Good, good. God grant it to every one! That 's quite another thing from sitting in a marsh up to your neck, and trying to assume an air of not caring, when, as a matter of fact, in reality you do care. But there— the strings are stretched taut; ring out, so that all the world may hear, or break!"

Shúbin dropped his head on his breast.

"Yes," he went on after a long silence,—"Insároff is worthy of her. But what nonsense! No one is worthy of her. Insároff . . . . Insároff . . . . Why this false submission? Well, let us admit that he is young, he will stand up for himself, although, so far, he has done just the same as the rest of us sinners, and it can't be possible, can it, that we are such complete trash? Come now, take me, for instance,—am I trash, Uvár Ivánovitch? Has God denied me every good quality? Has He bestowed on me no abilities, no talents whatever? Who knows, perhaps the name of Pável Shúbin will become a glorious name in the course of time? Here, a copper coin is lying on your table. Who knows, perhaps, some time or other, a century hence, that coin may become part of a statue of Pável Shúbin, erected in his honour by a grateful posterity?"

Uvár Ivánovitch propped himself on his elbow, and riveted his eyes on the artist, who had talked himself into a fever-heat.

"'T is a long cry,"—he said, at last, twiddling

his fingers, as usual: " it is a question of other people; but thou . . . seest thou? . . . talkest about thyself."

" O great philosopher of the Russian land! " exclaimed Shúbin.—" Every word of yours is pure gold, and not to me, but to you, should the statue be erected, and I shall set about it myself. Here now, just as you are lying at the present moment, in this pose,—as to which one cannot say whether it contains most of laziness or of strength—just so will I cast you. You have staggered me with your just reproof for my egotism and my self-conceit! Yes! yes! there 's no use in talking about one's self; there 's no use in bragging. There is no one, as yet, among us; there are no men, look where you will. All are either small fry, or squabblers, petty Hamlets, cannibals, either underground gloom and thicket, or bullies, empty triflers, and drumsticks! And there 's still another sort of men for you: they have studied themselves with disgraceful minuteness; they are incessantly feeling the pulse of their every sensation, and reporting to themselves. ' Here,' say they, ' is what I feel; this is what I think.' A useful, practical occupation! No, if we had any able men, that young girl, that sensitive soul, would not be leaving us, would not have slipped from us, like a fish into the water! What does it mean, Uvár

Ivánovitch? When is our time coming? When shall we bring forth men in our land?"

" Give us time,"—replied Uvár Ivánovitch,— " they will come."

" They will come? O thou soil! thou black-earth force! thou hast said: ' They will come?' Behold, I shall put thy words on record. But why do you extinguish your candle?"

" I 'm sleepy,—good-bye."

XXXI

Shúbin spoke the truth. The unexpected news
of Eléna's marriage had almost killed Anna
Vasílievna. She took to her bed. Nikolái Artémievitch required of her, that she should not
admit her daughter within her sight; he seemed
to rejoice at the opportunity to display himself
in his complete importance as master of the
house, in all the powers of the head of the family: he blustered and thundered uninterruptedly
at the servants, constantly adding: " I 'll show
you who I am, I 'll let you know—just wait!"
As long as he remained in the house, Anna Vasílievna did not see Eléna, and contented herself
with the presence of Zóya, who waited upon her
with great assiduity, and meanwhile thought
to herself: " *Diesen Insároff vorziehen—und
wem?* " But no sooner did Nikolái Artémievitch absent himself (and this happened with
tolerable frequency: Augustína Christiánovna
really had returned), than Eléna presented herself before her mother,—and the latter gazed at
her long, silently, with tears in her eyes. This
mute reproach pierced Eléna's heart more
deeply than any other; she did not feel repen-

tance then, but profound, infinite compunction, akin to repentance.

"Mamma, dear mamma!"—she kept repeating, as she kissed her hands: "what could I do? I am not to blame, I fell in love with him, I could not act otherwise. Blame fate: it brought me into connection with a man whom papa does not like, who will take me away from you."

"Okh!" Anna Vasílievna interrupted her: —"do not remind me of that. When I remember where it is that thou wishest to go, my heart fairly sinks in my breast!"

"Dear mamma," replied Eléna,—"console thyself at least with this, that things might be still worse: I might have died."

"But, as it is, I have no hope of ever seeing thee again. Either thou wilt end thy life yonder, somewhere, in a wigwam" (Anna Vasílievna pictured Bulgaria to herself as something in the nature of the Siberian marshy fens), "or I shall not survive the separation . . . . ."

"Do not say that, my kind mamma; we shall see each other again, God willing. But there are towns in Bulgaria, just like those here."

"Towns, indeed! War is in progress there now; now, I think, wherever one may go, they are firing cannon . . . . Art thou preparing to start soon?"

"Yes . . . if only papa . . . . He means

to lodge a complaint, he threatens to separate us."

Anna Vasílievna raised her eyes to heaven.

"No, Lénotchka, he will not lodge a complaint. I myself would not have consented, on any terms whatsoever, to this marriage, I would sooner have died; but what is done cannot be undone, and I will not allow my daughter to be disgraced."

Several days passed thus. At last Anna Vasílievna plucked up her courage, and one evening she shut herself up alone with her husband in her bedroom. Everybody in the house became silent, and lent an ear. At first, nothing was audible; then Nikolái Artémievitch's voice began to boom out, then a wrangle ensued, shouts arose, the listeners even thought that they heard groans. . . . . Shúbin, in company with Zóya and the maids, was already on the point of going to the rescue, but the uproar in the bedroom began gradually to diminish, lapsed into conversation, and ceased. Only from time to time did faint sobs resound—then these came to an end. The key rattled, the squeak of a bureau being opened resounded. . . . The door opened, and Nikolái Artémievitch made his appearance. He stared morosely at all whom he encountered, and betook himself to his club; but Anna Vasílievna summoned Eléna to her, embraced her warmly, and, shedding bitter tears, said:

" Everything is settled, he will not make a scandal, and nothing now hinders thee from going away . . . . from abandoning us."

" Will you permit Dmítry to come and thank you,"—Eléna asked her mother, as soon as the latter had regained a little composure.

" Wait, my darling; I cannot see the man who is separating us yet. There is plenty of time before your departure."

" Before our departure," repeated Eléna sadly.

Nikolái Artémievitch had consented " not to make a scandal "; but Anna Vasílievna did not tell her daughter what a price he had set upon his consent. She did not tell her that she had promised to pay all his debts, and had given him in hand one thousand rubles. Over and above this, he had informed Anna Vasílievna, with decision, that he did not wish to meet Insároff, whom he continued to call a Montenegrin; and when he arrived at his club, he began, without the slightest necessity for it, to talk with his partner, a retired general, about Eléna's marriage. " Have you heard," said he, with feigned carelessness,—" that my daughter, owing to her great erudition, has married some sort of student? " The general looked at him through his spectacles, muttered, " H'm! " and asked him what was his play.

XXXII

BUT the day of departure was drawing near. November was already past; the last days of grace had expired. Insároff had long ago completed all his preparations, and was burning with the desire to tear himself away from Moscow as speedily as possible. And the doctor urged him to haste. " You require a warm climate," he said to him; " you will not recover your health here." Eléna was overcome with impatience also; Insároff's pallor, his thinness, troubled her. She often gazed with involuntary alarm at his altered features. Her position in her father's house had become intolerable. Her mother wailed over her, as over a corpse, while her father treated her with scornful coldness: the approaching parting secretly tortured him also, but he regarded it as his duty, the duty of an injured father, to conceal his feelings, his weakness. At last, Anna Vasílievna expressed a wish to see Insároff. He was brought to her quietly, by the back door. When he entered her room, she was unable, for a long time, to speak to him, she could not even bring herself to look at him;

he sat down beside her arm-chair, and with calm respect awaited her first word. Eléna sat there also, holding her mother's hand in hers. At last, Anna Vasílievna raised her eyes, said, " God is your judge, Dmítry Nikanórovitch . . . " and stopped short: the reproaches died on her lips.

" Why, you are ill,"—she cried:—" Eléna, he is ill! "

" I have been ill, Anna Vasílievna," replied Insároff,—" and I have not quite recovered my health yet; but I hope that my native air will set me eventually on my feet."

" Yes . . . Bulgaria," stammered Anna Vasílievna, and thought: " My God, a Bulgarian, a dying man, a voice as hollow as though it came from a cask, eyes sunk in his head; a regular skeleton, his coat hangs on him as though it were made for some one else; yellow as camomile—and she is his wife, she loves him . . . . why, this is a dream! . . ." But she immediately recovered herself.—" Dmítry Nikanórovitch,"—she said:—" is it indispensably —indispensably necessary that you should go? "

" Yes, Anna Vasílievna."

Anna Vasílievna looked at him.

" Okh, Dmítry Nikanórovitch, God grant that you may never experience what I am now experiencing! . . . But you will promise me to take good care of her, to love her . . . . You shall never suffer want as long as I am living! "

Tears choked her voice. She opened her arms, and Eléna and Insároff fell on her breast.

The fatal day arrived at last. It was arranged that Eléna should say good-bye to her parents at home, and should set out on the journey from Insároff's lodgings. The departure was appointed for twelve o'clock. A quarter of an hour before that time, Berséneff arrived. He had supposed that he would find at Insároff's lodgings his fellow-countrymen who would wish to see him off; but they had all already gone on ahead; the two mysterious persons with whom the reader is already acquainted (they had served as witnesses at Insároff's wedding) had also departed. The tailor greeted " the kind gentleman " with a bow; he had been drinking heavily, it must have been from grief, or, possibly, from joy that he was to get the furniture; his wife speedily led him away. Everything was already in order in the room; a trunk, corded with a rope, stood on the floor. Berséneff fell into thought: many memories passed through his soul.

It was long after twelve o'clock, and the postilion had already brought the horses to the door, but " the young pair " still did not make their appearance. At last, hurried footsteps became audible on the stairs, and Eléna entered, accompanied by Insároff and Shúbin. Eléna's eyes were red: she had left her mother lying in a swoon; their parting had been extremely painful. It was more than a week since Eléna had seen Berséneff: of late, he had gone seldom to the Stákhoffs. She had not expected to meet him, exclaimed, " You! thanks!" and threw herself on his neck; Insároff also embraced him. A harrowing silence ensued. What could those three persons say, what were those three hearts feeling? Shúbin comprehended the imperative necessity of putting an end to this anguish by a living sound, a word.

" Our trio has assembled together once more," —he said—" for the last time! Let us submit to the decree of fate, let us bear in mind the good times that are past, and enter upon the new life with God's blessing! ' God bless you on your distant road,'" he struck up, and stopped. He suddenly felt ashamed and awkward. It is a sin to sing where a corpse is lying; and, at that moment, in that room, that past died to which he had alluded, the past of the people who were assembled there. It died for the regeneration of a new life, let us assume; . . . but, nevertheless, it died.

" Well, Eléna," began Insároff, addressing his wife,—" everything is ready, I think. Everything is paid for, packed. Nothing remains to be done, except to carry out this trunk. Landlord!"

The landlord entered the room, accompanied by his wife and daughter. He listened, reeling slightly as he did so, to Insároff's order, threw the trunk on his shoulders, and ran swiftly down the stairs, clattering his boots as he went.

"Now, according to the Russian custom, we must sit down," remarked Insároff.

They all seated themselves: Berséneff placed himself on the little old couch; Eléna sat down beside him; the landlady and her little daughter squatted down on the threshold. All became silent; all were smiling in a constrained way, and no one knew why he was smiling; each one wanted to say something by way of good-bye, and each one (with the exception, of course, of the landlady and her daughter: they merely stared with all their might)—each felt that at such moments it is permissible to say nothing but commonplaces, that any significant, or witty, or even cordial word would be, somehow, out of place, would almost have a false ring. Insároff was the first to rise to his feet and begin to cross himself . . . . "Farewell, our dear little room!" he exclaimed.

Kisses resounded, the loud but cold kisses of parting, good wishes for the journey half uttered, promises to write, the last, half-stifled words of farewell . . . .

Eléna, all bathed in tears, had already taken her seat in the travelling-sledge; Insároff was carefully tucking the lap-robe around her feet; Shúbin, Berséneff, the landlord, his wife, his little daughter with the inevitable kerchief on her head, the yard-porter, a strange artisan in a striped kaftan—were all standing on the front steps, when, suddenly, into the courtyard dashed an elegant sledge, drawn by a high-stepping trotter, and from the sledge, shaking the snow from the collar of his coat, sprang out Nikolái Artémievitch.

"I have found you still here, thank God!" he exclaimed, and hurried to the travelling-sledge.—"Here, Eléna, is our last parental blessing for thee,"—he said, bending down under the hood, and pulling from the pocket of his coat a small holy picture, sewn into a velvet bag, he put it round her neck. She burst out sobbing, and began to kiss his hands, and in the meantime his coachman drew out from the front part of the sledge a bottle of champagne and three glasses.

"Come!" said Nikolái Artémievitch,—but his own tears were fairly trickling down on the beaver collar of his coat,—"we must give you a send-off . . . and wish . . . ." he began to pour out the champagne; his hands shook, the foam rose over the rim and dripped on the snow. He took one glass, and gave the other two to Eléna and Insároff, who had already taken his place by her side.—"God grant you . . . " began Nikolái Artémievitch, and could not finish his sentence—and drank off his wine; they also drank theirs.—" Now it is your turn, gentlemen," he said, addressing Shúbin and Berséneff, —but at that moment the postilion started his horses. Nikolái Artémievitch ran along by the side of the sledge. " See that thou writest to us,"—he said in a broken voice. Eléna thrust out her head, said, " Good-bye, papa, Andréi Petróvitch, Pável Yakóvlevitch; good-bye, all; good-bye, Russia!" and threw herself back. The postilion flourished his whip and whistled; the travelling-sledge turned to the right after it had passed the gate, its runners squeaking as it did so, and vanished.

XXXIII

It was a brilliant April day. Along the broad lagoon which separates Venice from the narrow strip of alluvial sea-sand called the Lido, a sharp-beaked gondola was skimming along, rocking in cadence at every surge which fell on the gondolier's long oar. Beneath its low roof, on soft leather cushions, sat Eléna and Insároff.

Eléna's features had not altered much since the day of her departure from Moscow; but their expression had become different: it was more thoughtful and stern, and her eyes looked forth more boldly. Her whole body had blossomed out, and her hair seemed to lie in more splendid and luxuriant masses along her white brow and her rosy cheeks. Only in her lips, when she was not smiling, there was expressed, by a barely perceptible fold, the presence of a secret, ever-present anxiety. The expression of Insároff's face, on the other hand, had remained the same as of yore, but his features had undergone a cruel change. He had grown haggard and old, he had grown pale and bent; he coughed almost incessantly, with a short, dry cough; and his sunken eyes shone with a strange glare.

On the road from Russia, Insároff had lain
ill for nearly two months at Vienna, and only at
the end of March had he arrived with his wife
at Venice: thence he hoped to make his way
through Zara to Servia and Bulgaria; all other
roads were closed to him. War was already raging on the Danube,—England and France had
declared war on Russia,—all the Slavonic lands
were seething and preparing to rise in revolt.

The gondola landed on the inner edge of the
Lido. Eléna and Insároff wended their way
along the narrow sandy path, planted with con-
sumptive little trees (they are planted every
year, and every year they die), to the outer edge
of the Lido, to the sea.

They strolled along the shore. The Adriatic
rolled before them its dull-blue waves; they
were foaming, hissing, running up on the shore,
and flowing back, leaving behind them on the
sand tiny shells and fragments of seaweed.

" What a melancholy place! " remarked
Eléna. " I 'm afraid it is too cold for thee, but
I can guess why thou hast wished to come
hither."

" Cold! " returned Insároff, with a swift but
bitter laugh. " A pretty soldier I shall be, if I
am to fear the cold. And I have come hither . . .
I will tell thee why. I gaze at this sea, and it
seems to me that from here my native land is
nearer. It lies yonder, thou knowest,"—he

added, stretching out his hand toward the East.
—" And the wind is blowing from that direction."

" Is not this wind bringing in the vessel which thou art expecting? " said Eléna:—" yonder is a sail gleaming white,—can that be it? "

Insároff gazed out on the distant sea, in the direction indicated by Eléna.

" Renditch promised that he would arrange everything for us in the course of a week," he remarked. " I think we can rely upon him . . . . Hast thou heard, Eléna? " he added, with sudden animation:—" they say that the poor Dalmatian fishermen have contributed their lead sinkers— thou knowest, those weights which make the net fall to the bottom—for bullets! They had no money, and their only means of livelihood is their fishing; but they joyfully surrendered their last resource, and now they are starving. What a race! "

" *Aufgepasst!* " shouted an arrogant voice behind them. The dull trampling of horses' hoofs resounded, and an Austrian officer, in a short grey tunic and a green military cap, galloped past them . . . . They barely managed to get out of the way.

Insároff stared gloomily after him.

" He is not to blame,"—said Eléna,—" thou knowest, they have no other place here where they can ride."

"He is not to blame,"—returned Insároff,—
"but he has set my blood to boiling with his shout,
his moustache, his cap, with his whole appearance.
Let us go back."

"Yes, let us go back, Dmítry. Besides, it
really is windy here. Thou didst not take care
of thyself after thy Moscow illness, and didst
pay for it in Vienna. Thou must be more care-
ful now."

Insároff made no reply, but the same bitter
sneer as before flitted across his lips.

"Let us have a row on the Canal Grande,
shall we not?"—went on Eléna. "For during
all the time we have been here, we have never yet
had a good look at Venice. And let us go to
the theatre this evening: I have two tickets for
a box. We will devote this day to each other,
we will forget politics, war, everything, we will
know only one thing: that we are living, breathing, thinking together, that we are united forever . . . . . Shall we?"

"Thou wishest it, Eléna,"—replied Insároff,
—"consequently, I wish it also."

"I knew it,"—remarked Eléna, with a smile.
—"Come along, come along."

They returned to the gondola, seated themselves in it, and ordered the man to row them, in
a leisurely way, along the Canal Grande.

Any one who has not seen Venice in April
can hardly be said to be acquainted with all the

indescribable charms of that enchanted city. The mildness and softness of spring become Venice, as the brilliant summer sun becomes magnificent Genoa, as the gold and purple of autumn become the grand old city,—Rome. Like the spring, the beauty of Venice touches and arouses the desire: it pains and torments the inexperienced heart, like the promise of a non-enigmatic but mysterious happiness near at hand. Everything in it is bright, comprehensible, and everything is enwrapped in a dreamy haze of a sort of love-stricken silence: everything in it holds its peace, and everything breathes a welcome; everything in it is feminine, beginning with its very name: not for nothing has to it alone been given the title of " The Beautiful." The huge masses of the palaces and churches stand light and splendid, like the beautiful dream of a young god; there is something fabulous, something enchantingly strange in the green-grey gleam and the silken play of hues of the dumb water in the canals, in the noiseless flight of the gondolas, in the absence of harsh city sounds, of coarse pounding, rattling, and uproar. " Venice is dying, Venice is deserted," its inhabitants say to you; but perchance all she needs is this very last charm, the charm of fading in the very bloom and triumph of her beauty. He who has not seen her, does not know her: neither Canaletto nor

Guardi—not to mention the more modern artists—is capable of reproducing that silvery tenderness of the air, that fleeting and near-lying distance, that wonderful combination of the most elegant outlines and melting beauties. It is useless for the man who has ended his career, who has been broken by life, to visit Venice: it will be bitter to him, like the memory of unfulfilled dreams of his earliest days; but it will be sweet for him in whom the forces are still seething, who feels himself fortunate; let him bring his happiness beneath her enchanted sky, and no matter how radiant it may be, she will gild it still more with her never-fading aureole. The gondola in which sat Insároff and Eléna floated softly past the Riva dei Schiavoni, the Palace of the Doges, the Piazzetta, and entered the Canal Grande. On both sides stretched marble palaces; they appeared to be gliding softly past, hardly affording the glance an opportunity to embrace and comprehend their beauties. Eléna felt profoundly happy; in the azure of her heaven one dark cloud had hung—and it had departed: Insároff was much better that day. They went as far as the sharp arch of the Rialto, and turned back. Eléna was afraid of the cold in the churches, for Insároff; but she remembered the Accademia delle Belle Arti, and ordered the gondolier to proceed thither. They had soon made the round of all the halls

of that small museum. Being neither connois-
seurs nor dilettanti, they did not pause before
every picture, they did not force themselves: a
sort of brilliant cheerfulness had unexpectedly
taken possession of them. Everything suddenly
seemed to them very amusing. (Children are
familiar with that feeling.) To the great scandal of three English visitors, Eléna laughed
aloud, until tears came, over Tintoretto's " Saint
Mark" leaping down from heaven into the water,
like a frog, to the rescue of a tortured slave; on
his side, Insároff went into ecstasies over the
back and calves of the energetic man in the
green mantle who stands in the foreground of
Titian's " Ascension," and raises his hand after
the Madonna; on the other hand, that same Madonna, a beautiful robust woman calmly and
majestically ascending to the bosom of God the
Father, impressed both Insároff and Eléna;
they liked also the severe and holy picture of the
old man Cima da Conegliano. On emerging
from the academy, they once more glanced
round at the Englishmen, with long, rabbit's
teeth and drooping side-whiskers, who were
walking behind them,—and broke out laughing;
they caught sight of their gondolier with his bob-
tailed jacket and short trousers,—and laughed;
they saw a huckstress with a little knot of grey
hair on the crown of her head,—and laughed
harder than ever; at last, they looked one an-

other in the face,—and roared with laughter; and as soon as they had taken their seats in the gondola, they clasped each other's hands very, very tight. They reached the hotel, ran to their room, and ordered dinner to be served. Their merriment did not desert them even at table. They helped each other to food, they drank to the health of their Moscow friends, they clapped their hands at the cameriere for the savoury dish of fish, and kept demanding of him live *frutti di mare;* the cameriere shrugged his shoulders and bowed, but when he left the room he shook his head, and even whispered with a sigh: " *Poveretti!* " (" Poor things! ") After dinner they went to the theatre.

At the theatre one of Verdi's operas was being played, a decidedly commonplace affair, to tell the truth, but one which had already managed to make the round of all the stages in Europe, and is well known to us Russians—" Traviata." The season in Venice was over, and none of the singers rose above the level of mediocrity; each one shrieked with all his might. The part of *Violetta* was sung by a petty artist who had no reputation, and, judging by the coldness of the audience toward her, she was not a favourite, although not devoid of talent. She was a young, not very pretty, black - eyed girl, with a voice which was not quite even and already cracked. Her costume was motley and bad to the point of absurdity: a red net covered her hair, her gown of faded blue satin compressed her bosom, thick undressed kid gloves reached to her sharp elbows; and how was she, the daughter of some Bergamo shepherd, to know how the demi-mondaines of Paris dress! And she did not know how to carry herself on the stage; but there was a great deal of truth and artless simplicity in her acting, and she sang with that peculiar passion of expression and rhythm of which Italians alone are capable. Eléna and Insároff sat alone in a dark box, close to the stage; the frolicsome mood which had come over them in the Accademia delle Belle Arti had not yet passed off. When the father of the unhappy young man who had fallen into the toils of the temptress made his appearance on the stage, in a greenish-grey dress-suit and a rumpled white wig, opened his mouth askew, and, seized in advance with stage-fright, emitted a mournful bass tremolo, both of them came near bursting with laughter . . . . . But *Violetta's* acting affected them.

" They hardly applaud that poor girl at all," said Eléna,—" but I prefer her a thousand times over to any self-confident, second-rate celebrity, who would put on airs, and writhe, and strive after effect. Apparently, this one does not take it as a jest herself; see, she does not perceive the audience."

Insároff leaned on the edge of the box, and gazed intently at *Violetta.*

" Yes,"—he muttered,—" she is not jesting: she reeks of death."

Eléna held her peace.

The third act began. The curtain rose . . . . . Eléna shuddered at sight of the bed, of the curtains hung about it, of the medicine-bottles, of the shaded lamp . . . She recalled the recent past . . . . " And the future? And the present? " flashed through her mind. As though expressly in reply to the simulated cough of the singer, Insároff's dull, unfeigned cough rang out in the box . . . . . Eléna shot a stealthy glance at him, and immediately imparted to her features a tranquil, composed expression. Insároff understood her, and he himself began to smile, and almost to hum an accompaniment to the singing.

But he soon stopped. *Violetta's* acting grew better and better, more and more free. She rejected everything irrelevant, everything that was not necessary, and *found herself*: rare and loftiest happiness of the artist! She suddenly crossed the line which it is impossible to define, but on the farther side of which dwells beauty. The audience was startled, amazed. The homely girl with the cracked voice was beginning to get them into her hands, to take possession of them. And the singer's voice no longer sounded cracked: it had warmed up and grown strong. *Alfredo* made his appearance; *Violetta's* joyful cry almost aroused that storm whose name is *fanatismo,* and in the presence of which all our Northern howls are as nothing . . . . A moment more—and the audience subsided. The duet began, the best number in the opera, in which the composer has succeeded in expressing all the regrets of madly wasted youth, the last struggle of desperate and impotent love. Carried away, swept on by the breath of general sympathy, with tears of artistic joy and of genuine suffering in her eyes, the songstress surrendered herself to the flood which had raised her on its crest, her face became transfigured, and in the presence of suddenly approaching death, with an outburst of entreaty which reached to heaven, the words were wrung from her: "*Lascia mi vivere . . . morir si giovane!*" ("Let me live . . . to die so young!"), and the whole theatre pealed with the applause of frenzied clapping and rapturous shouts.

Eléna had turned cold all over. She began gently to seek with her hand the hand of Insároff, found it, and clasped it tightly. He returned her pressure; but she did not look at him, neither did he look at her. This pressure did not resemble the one with which, a few hours earlier, they had greeted each other in the gondola.

They rowed to their hotel along the Canal Grande again. Night had already set in,—the bright, soft night. The same palaces stretched forth to meet them, but they seemed different. Those of them which were illuminated by the moon shone golden white, and in that very whiteness the details of the decorations and the outlines of windows and balconies seemed to disappear; they stood out more distinctly on the buildings flooded with the light mist of the level shadow. The gondolas, with their tiny red lights, seemed to glide along more inaudibly and swiftly than ever; mysteriously gleamed their steel beaks, mysteriously did the oars rise and fall on the troubled ripples like tiny silver fishes; here and there, the gondoliers uttered brief, not loud cries (they never sing nowadays); almost no other sounds were audible. The hotel where Insároff and Eléna were living was on the Riva dei Schiavoni; before reaching it, they left the gondola, and walked several times around the Square of San Marco beneath the arcade, where, in front of the tiny cafés, a multitude of holiday-makers was thronging. There is something peculiarly agreeable about walking alone, with a beloved being, in a strange city, among strangers: everything seems most beautiful and significant, one wishes everybody good, and peace, and the same happiness wherewith one is one's self filled. But Eléna could no longer give herself up without anxiety to the consciousness of her happiness: her heart, shaken by recent impressions, could not recover its composure; and Insároff, as they passed the Palace of the Doges, pointed, in silence, to the mouths of the Austrian cannon, peeping out from beneath the low-browed arches, and pulled his hat down over his eyes. Besides, he felt fatigued,—and, bestowing a last glance on the Church of San Marco, on its domes, where, beneath the rays of the moon spots of phosphorescent light were kindled on the bluish leads, they slowly wended their way homeward.

The windows of their little chamber looked out on the broad lagoon which extends from the Riva dei Schiavoni to the Giudecca. Almost directly opposite their hotel rose the sharp-pointed tower of San Giorgio; on the right, high in the air, glittered the golden globe of the Dogana; and decked out like bride stood the most beautiful of churches, the Redentore of Palladius; on the left the masts and yards of ships, the smoke-stacks of steamers, were outlined in black; here and there, like a huge wing, hung a half-reefed sail, the pennants barely stirring. Insároff seated himself at the window, but Eléna did not permit him to enjoy the view for long; fever suddenly made its appearance, and a sort of devouring weakness seized upon him. She put him to bed, and waiting until he fell asleep, she softly returned to the window. Oh, how still and caressing was the night, what dovelike gentleness did the azure air breathe forth, how ought every suffering, every sorrow, to hold its peace and lapse into slumber beneath these holy innocent rays! "Oh, my God!" thought Eléna,—"why does death exist, why is there parting, illness, tears? or why this beauty, this delightful feeling of hope, why the soothing consciousnss of a sure refuge, of deathless protection? What means this smiling, benevolent heaven, this happy, resting earth? Can it be that this is only in us, and that outside of us is eternal cold and silence? Can it be that we are alone . . . . alone . . . . while yonder, everywhere, in all those impenetrable abysses and depths,—everything, everything is alien to us? Why then this yearning for and delight in prayer?" ("*Morir si giovane!*" resounded in her soul.) . . . . "Can it be, that it is impossible to implore, to bring back happiness? . . . O God! can it be, that it is impossible to believe in a miracle?" She bowed her head on her clasped hands. "Is it ended?" she whispered. "Can it be that it is at an end! I have been happy, not minutes, not hours, not whole days—no, whole weeks in succession. And by what right?" Her happiness frightened her. "And what if it cannot be?" she thought. "What if this is not to be had without paying for it? For it has been heaven . . . . and we mortals, poor, sinful mortals . . . . *Morir si giovane!* . . . O, dark spectre, begone! not for me alone is his life necessary!

" But what if this is—a punishment? "—she thought again; " what if we must now pay the full price for our fault? My conscience held its peace, it is silent now, but is that any proof of innocence? O God, can we have been so very wicked? Can it be that Thou, who hast created this night, this sky, wilt chastise us for having loved? And if it be so, if he be guilty, if I am guilty,"—she added, in an involuntary outburst,—" then grant, O God, that he may die, that we may both die, at least an honourable, a glorious death—yonder, in the fields of his fatherland, but not here, not in this obscure room!

" And how about the grief of my poor, lonely mother? " she asked herself, and became confused, and found no reply to her own question. Eléna did not know that the happiness of every mortal is founded on the unhappiness of another, that even his advantage and comfort demand— as a stature demands a pedestal—the disadvantage and discomfort of others.

" Renditch! " muttered Insároff in his sleep.

Eléna went to him on tiptoe, bent over him, and wiped the perspiration from his brow. He tossed about a little on his pillow, and quieted down.

She returned to the window, and again meditations engrossed her. She began to persuade herself, and assure herself that there was no cause for alarm. She even felt ashamed of her weakness. " Can there be any danger? Is not he better? " she whispered. " Why, if we had not been to the theatre to-night, all this would never have entered my mind." At that moment she espied, high above the water, a white sea-gull; some fisherman had, probably, frightened it, and it was soaring silently, with uneven flight, as though looking out for a place where it could alight. " There now, if it flies hither," thought Eléna, " it will be a good sign." . . . . The sea-gull circled slowly in one spot, folded its wings, and, as though it had been shot, fell, with a pitiful cry, somewhere far away, on a dark ship. Eléna shuddered, and then felt ashamed for having shuddered. And, without undressing, she lay down on the bed beside Insároff, who was breathing fast and heavily.

XXXIV

INSÁROFF awoke late, with a dull pain in his head, with a feeling, as he expressed it, of horrible weakness all over his body. Nevertheless, he rose.

" Renditch has not come? " was his first question.

" Not yet," replied Eléna, and gave him the last number of the *Osservatore Triestino,* in which a great deal was said about the war, about the Slavonic lands, about the principalities. Insároff began to read; she busied herself with preparing coffee for him . . . . Some one knocked at the door.

" Renditch," thought both of them, but the person who had knocked said in Russian: " May I come in? " Eléna and Insároff exchanged a glance of astonishment, and, without waiting for their answer, there entered the room a foppishly-attired man with a small, pointed face and bold little eyes. He was beaming all over, as though he had just won a huge sum of money or had heard a pleasing piece of news.

Insároff half-rose from his chair.

"You do not recognise me,"—began the stranger, advancing to him in a free and easy manner, and bowing amiably to Eléna.—"Lupoyároff, you remember? We met in Moscow, at the E . . . s."

"Yes, at the E . . . s," said Insároff.

"Of course, of course! I beg that you will present me to your wife. Madame, I have always cherished a profound respect for Dmítry Vasílievitch . . . . "—(he corrected himself): "Nikanór Vasílievitch,—and am very happy that, at last, I have the honour of making your acquaintance. Just imagine," he went on, turning to Insároff—"I learned only last night that you were here. I, also, am stopping in this hotel. What a city this Venice is—poetry itself, and that's all there is to it! There's one frightful thing about it: these cursed Austrians at every step!—I can't abide the Austrians! By the way, have you heard that a decisive battle has taken place on the Danube: three hundred Turkish officers have been killed, Silistria has been captured, Servia has already declared herself independent,—you, as a patriot, ought to be in raptures, ought n't you? The Slavonic blood in me is fairly boiling! But I would advise you to be extremely cautious; I am convinced that you are being watched. The spying here is awful! yesterday a suspicious sort of man approached me and asked: 'Are you a Russian?'

I told him I was a Dane. . . . But you must be
ill, my dearest Nikanór Vasílievitch. You
ought to take a course of treatment; madame,
you ought to doctor your husband . . . . Yesterday, I was running about the palaces and churches
like a madman—you have been in the Palace of
the Doges, of course? What wealth everywhere!
Especially that great hall, and the Place of Ma-
rino Faliero; there it stands: *decapitati pro
criminibus.* I have been in the famous prisons:
that 's where my soul was troubled—I have always been fond—as perhaps you will remember—of occupying myself with social problems,
and have rebelled against the aristocracy—that 's
where I would have taken the defenders of the
aristocracy: to those prisons; justly did Byron
say: ' I stood in Venice, on the Bridge of Sighs ';
however, he was an aristocrat too. I always was
for progress. The young generation is all for
progress. But how about the Anglo-French?
Let us see whether they will accomplish much:
Bustrapá and Palmerston. Palmerston has become Prime Minister, you know. No,—whatever
you may say, a Russian usurer is no joke. That
Bustrapá is a frightful scoundrel! I 'll give
you Victor Hugo's ' Les Châtiments ' if you
would like it—it 's wonderful! ' *L'Avenir le
gendarme de Dieu* ' is rather boldly put—but
it 's strong, strong. Prince Vyázemsky also said
well: ' Europe keeps reiterating: Bash-Kadyk

Lar,[1] never taking its eyes from Sinope! ' I love poetry. I also have Prud'hon's last book, I have everything. I don't know how you feel about it, but I am glad of the war,—if only they don't order me home, for I am planning to go from here to Florence—to Rome: it 's impossible to go to France—so I am thinking of going to Spain —the women are wonderful there, they say, only there 's a lot of poverty and insects. I would take a flying trip to California,—we Russians can do everything without an effort,—only, I promised an editor that I would study in detail the question of commerce in the Mediterranean. It is not an interesting subject, you will say, it is a special subject, but we need—we need specialists, we have philosophised enough, and now we must have practice, practice. . . . But you are very ill, Nikanór Vasílievitch, perhaps I am tiring you; but never mind, I will stay a little longer . . . . . ."

And Lupoyároff continued to chatter on in the same strain for a good while longer, and when he went away he promised to come again.

Exhausted by the unexpected visit, Insároff lay down on the couch.—"There,"—he said, with a glance at Eléna,—"there 's our young generation for you! Some of them put on airs

---

[1] Near this settlement in the Government of Kars, in November, 1853, a force of ten thousand Russian troops won a brilliant victory over a force of thirty-six thousand Turks. Sinope was the scene of another victory in the same year.—Translator.

of dignity and show off, but in their souls they are just such empty whistlers as that gentleman."

Eléna made no reply to her husband: at that moment, she was much more disquieted over Insároff's feebleness than by the condition of the rising generation in Russia. . . . She seated herself by his side, and took up her work. He closed his eyes, and lay motionless, all pale and gaunt. Eléna glanced at his sharply outlined profile, at his drawn hands, and a sudden terror gripped her heart.

" Dmítry . . . ." she began.

He started.—" Well, has Renditch come? "

" Not yet . . . . but thou hast fever, thou really art not quite well, shall not I send for a doctor? What thinkest thou? "

" That gabbler has alarmed thee. It is not necessary. I will rest a little, and it will all pass off. After dinner, we will go out again . . . . somewhere."

Two hours passed. . . . Insároff still lay on the couch, but could not get to sleep, although he did not open his eyes. Eléna did not leave him: she dropped her work on her knees, and did not stir.

" Why dost not thou go to sleep? " she asked him at last.

" Why, here, wait."—He took her hand, and laid it under his head.—" There, that 's . . . .

good. Wake me immediately, when Renditch comes. If he says that the vessel is ready, we will set out immediately. . . . Everything must be packed."

" It will not take long to pack," replied Eléna.

" But that man babbled about a battle, about Servia,"—said Insároff, a little while later.— " He must have invented the whole of it. But we must go, we must. We must lose no time. . . . Be ready."

He fell asleep, and everything became silent in the room.

Eléna leaned her head against the back of her chair, and gazed for a long time out of the window. The weather had changed for the worse; the wind had risen. Large, white clouds were sweeping swiftly athwart the sky, a slender mast was swaying in the distance, a long pennant with a red cross rose and fell incessantly, rose and fell again. The pendulum of the ancient clock beat heavily, with a sort of mournful, hissing sound. Eléna closed her eyes. She had slept badly all night; gradually she sank into a doze.

She dreamed a strange dream. It seems to her that she is floating in a boat on the Tzarítzyn pond, with some people whom she does not know. They maintain silence, and sit motionless; no one is rowing; the boat moves along of its own volition. Eléna does not feel afraid, but she finds it dull; she wants to discover who the people are, and why she is with them. She gazes, the pond widens out, the banks disappear —it is no longer a pond, but a troubled sea: vast, azure, silent waves rock the boat majestically; something rumbling and menacing rises from the bottom; her unknown fellow-travellers suddenly jump up, shout, flourish their arms . . . . . Eléna recognises their faces: her father is one of them. But some sort of a white whirlwind sweeps over the waves . . . . everything reels, grows confused . . . . .

Eléna surveys her surroundings; as before, everything round about is white. But it is snow, snow, a boundless expanse of snow. And she is no longer in a boat, she is driving in a travelling-sledge, as she did out of Moscow; she is not alone: by her side sits a tiny being, wrapped up in an old sleeved cloak. Eléna scrutinises it closely: it is Kátya, her poor little friend. Eléna grows frightened. " Is n't she dead? " she thinks.

" Kátya, whither are thou and I going? "

Kátya makes no reply, and wraps herself still more closely in her miserable little cloak. Eléna feels cold also; she gazes along the road: the town is visible far away, athwart a veil of snow-dust,—the lofty white towers with their silver domes . . . . " Kátya, Kátya, is this Moscow? " " No," thinks Eléna, " it is the Solovétzk Monastery:[1] there are a great many tiny, cramped cells there, as in a beehive; it is stifling, crowded there,—Dmítry is imprisoned there. I must set him free" . . . . All at once, a gray, yawning abyss opens in front of her. The travelling-sledge falls, Kátya laughs. "Eléna, Eléna!" a voice from the chasm makes itself heard.

"Eléna!" rang distinctly in her ears. She raised her head quickly, turned round, and was stupefied: Insároff, white as snow—the snow of her dream—had half-raised himself from the couch, and was gazing at her with brilliant, dreadful eyes. His hair lay dishevelled on his brow, his lips were open in a strange fashion. Horror, mingled with a sort of painful emotion, was expressed on his suddenly altered face.

"Eléna!"—he articulated;—"I am dying."

With a shriek she fell upon her knees, and pressed herself to his breast.

"All is over!"—repeated Insároff:—"I am dying! . . . Farewell, my poor child! Farewell, my own darling!" . . .

And he fell back at full length on the couch.

Eléna flew out of the room and began to call for help; the cameriere ran for the doctor. Eléna leaned over Insároff.

At that moment, on the threshold of the door, a broad-shouldered, sun-burned man made his

[1] In the White Sea.—TRANSLATOR.

appearance, clad in a thick frieze coat and a low-crowned oil-skin hat. He halted in perplexity.

" Renditch! "—exclaimed Eléna—" it is you! Look, for God's sake, he is in a swoon! What ails him? O God! O God! He was out of doors yesterday, he has just been talking to me . . . ."

Renditch said nothing, and merely moved aside. Past him slipped briskly a tiny figure in a wig and spectacles: he was a doctor who lived in the hotel. He went up to Insároff.

" Signora,"—he said, a few moments later,— " the stranger is dead—*il signore forestiere e morto*—from an aneurism, coupled with a malady of the lungs."

XXXV

On the following day, Renditch was standing
at the window of that same room; in front of
him, enveloped in a shawl, sat Eléna. In the
adjoining room, Insároff was lying in his coffin.
Eléna's face was both terrified and inanimate;
two wrinkles had made their appearance on her
forehead, between her eyebrows: they imparted
a strained expression to her immovable eyes.
On the window-sill lay an open letter from Anna
Vasílievna. She invited her daughter to come
to Moscow, if only for a month, complained of
her loneliness, of Nikolái Artémievitch, sent her
regards to Insároff, inquired about his health,
and begged him to let his wife come.

Renditch was a Dalmatian, a sailor, with
whom Insároff had become acquainted during
his journey to his native land, and whom he had
hunted up in Venice. He was a surly, rough,
old man, and devoted to the Slavonic cause. He
despised the Turks, and hated the Austrians.

"How long are you going to remain in
Venice?" Eléna asked him in Italian. And her
voice was as lifeless as her face.

"One day, in order to take on freight, and not

to arouse suspicion, and then I go straight to
Zara. I shall not gladden my fellow-countrymen. They have been waiting for him this long
while; their hopes were set on him."

" Their hopes were set on him,"—repeated
Eléna mechanically.

" When shall you bury him?" asked Renditch.

Eléna did not reply at once.—" To-morrow."

" To-morrow? I will remain: I wish to cast
a handful of earth into his grave. And I must
help you. But it would be better to lay him in
Slavonic earth."

Eléna glanced at Renditch.

" Captain,"—she said,—" take me with him,
and carry us to the other side of the sea, far
away from here. Can it be done?"

Renditch reflected.—" It can, only it will be
bothersome. We shall have trouble with the
cursed authorities here. But, assuming that we
can arrange all that, and that we bury him yonder; how am I to get you back here?"

" You need not bring me back."

" What? Where will you stay?"

" I will find a place for myself; only take us—
take me."

Renditch scratched the back of his head.—
" As you like, but this is all very bothersome. I
will go and find out: and do you await me here,
a couple of hours hence."

He left the room. Eléna passed into the adjoining chamber, leaned against the wall, and stood there a long time, as though she had been turned to stone. Then she sank on her knees, but could not pray. In her soul there was no repining; she did not dare to ask God why He had not spared, why He had not shown compassion, had not saved; why He had chastised from on high the fault, if fault there had been. Each of us is guilty through the mere fact that he lives, and there is no thinker so great, there is no benefactor of mankind who, by virtue of the benefits he has conferred, can rely upon the right to live . . . . But Eléna could not pray: she was turned to stone.

That same night, a broad boat rowed away from the hotel where the Insároffs had resided. In the boat sat Eléna and Renditch, and a long box stood there covered with a black cloth.

They sailed for about an hour, and finally reached a small, two-masted vessel which was riding at anchor at the very mouth of the harbor. Eléna and Renditch boarded the vessel; the sailors carried the box on board. About midnight a storm arose, but by early morning the ship had passed the Lido. In the course of the day the storm raged with frightful violence, and the experienced sailors in the offices of " Lloyd's " shook their heads, and expected nothing good. The Adriatic Sea, between Venice, Trieste, and the Dalmatian shore, is extremely dangerous.

Three weeks after Eléna's departure from Venice, Anna Vasílievna received in Moscow the following letter:

"My dear parents, I am bidding you farewell forever. You will never see me more. Dmítry died yesterday. All is at an end for me. To-day I am setting out for Zara with his body. I shall bury him, and what will become of me, I do not know! But I have no longer any fatherland except D's fatherland. An insurrection is in preparation there, they are making ready for war; I shall go as a sister of mercy: I shall nurse the sick, the wounded. I do not know what will become of me, but even after Dmítry's death I shall remain faithful to his memory, to his life's work. I have learned Bulgarian and Servian. Probably I shall not survive all this—so much the better. I have been brought to the verge of the abyss, and must fall in. Not in vain did Fate unite us: perhaps I killed him, who knows; now it is his turn to draw me after him. I sought happiness—and perchance I shall find death. Evidently, so it had to be; evidently, there was a fault . . . . But death palliates and reconciles all things,— does it not? Forgive me for all the sorrow I have caused you: it was against my will. But why should I return to Russia? What is there to do in Russia?

"Accept my last kisses and blessings, and do not condemn me." E.

ABOUT five years have passed since then, and no further news has arrived of Eléna. All letters and inquiries have been fruitless: in vain did Nikolái Artémievitch himself, after the conclusion of peace, travel to Venice—to Zara; in Venice he learned what is already known to the reader, but in Zara no one could give him any decisive information concerning Renditch and the vessel which he had hired. Obscure rumours were in circulation, to the effect that, several years previously, the sea, after a violent storm, had cast up on the shore a coffin in which had been found the corpse of a man . . . . According to other, more trustworthy information, the coffin in question had not been cast up by the sea at all, but had been brought and interred close to the shore by a foreign lady who had come from Venice; some persons added that that lady had afterward been seen in Herzegovina with the army which was then assembling; they even described her attire, black from head to foot. At any rate, all trace of Eléna has vanished forever and irretrievably, and no one knows whether she is still alive, whether she is hiding herself somewhere, or whether the little game of life has already come to an end, whether the slight fermentation is ended, and death's turn has come. It sometimes happens that a man, on awaking, will ask himself, with involuntary terror:—" Can it be that I am already thirty . . . forty . . . . fifty years of age? How has life passed so swiftly? How has death approached so near?" Death is like a fisherman who has caught a fish in his net, and leaves it there for a while in the water: the fish still swims, but the net is about it, and the fisherman will haul it in— when he sees fit.

WHAT has become of the other personages of our story?

Anna Vasílievna is still alive; she has aged greatly since the blow which overtook her; she grumbles less, but grieves much more. Nikolái Artémievitch also has grown old and gray, and has parted from Augustína Christiánovna. . . . He now curses everything foreign. His house-keeper, a handsome woman, a Russian, thirty years of age, goes about in silken gowns, and wears gold finger-rings and earrings. Kurna-tóvsky, like a man with a temperament, and in his quality of an energetic dark-complexioned person, an admirer of fair-haired women, has married Zóya; he keeps her in strict subjection, and she has even ceased to think in German. Berséneff is in Heidelberg: he was sent abroad at the expense of the Government; he has vis-ited Berlin and Paris, and is not wasting his time; he will turn out a clever philosopher. The learned public has taken notice of his articles " Concerning certain Peculiarities of the Old

Germanic Law, in the Matter of Judicial Punish-ments" and "Concerning the Significance of the Town Principle in the Question of Civili-sation"; only it is a pity that both articles should be written in rather a heavy style and mottled with foreign words. Shúbin is in Rome; he has consecrated himself wholly to his art, and is regarded as one of the most remarkable and promising of the young sculptors. Strict tour-ists think that he has not sufficiently studied the ancients, that he has not "style," and reckon him as belonging to the French school; he has multitudes of orders from the English and the Americans. One of his bacchantes created a great sensation recently; the Russian Count Bóboshkin, the well-known plutocrat, was on the point of purchasing it for one thousand scudi, but preferred to give three thousand to another sculptor, a Frenchman *pur sang,* for a group representing "A young Peasant-girl dy-ing of love on the breast of the Genius of Spring." Shúbin now and then corresponds with Uvár Ivánovitch, who alone has not changed in the least or in any way. "Do you remember," he wrote to him, lately, "what you said to me on the night when poor Eléna's mar-riage became known, when I was sitting on your bed and chatting with you? Do you remember, how I asked you then whether there would be men among us, and you answered me: 'There will.' O black - earth force! And now, here, from this place, from my 'most beautiful distance,' once more I ask you:—Well, how now, Uvár Ivánovitch, will there be any?"

Uvár Ivánovitch wiggled his fingers, and riveted his enigmatic gaze on the distance.